The Sex Is Out
of This World

CRITICAL EXPLORATIONS IN SCIENCE FICTION AND FANTASY
(a series edited by Donald E. Palumbo and C.W. Sullivan III)

1 *Worlds Apart? Dualism and Transgression in Contemporary Female Dystopias* (Dunja M. Mohr, 2005)

2 *Tolkien and Shakespeare: Essays on Shared Themes and Language* (ed. Janet Brennan Croft, 2007)

3 *Culture, Identities and Technology in the* Star Wars *Films: Essays on the Two Trilogies* (ed. Carl Silvio, Tony M. Vinci, 2007)

4 *The Influence of* Star Trek *on Television, Film and Culture* (ed. Lincoln Geraghty, 2008)

5 *Hugo Gernsback and the Century of Science Fiction* (Gary Westfahl, 2007)

6 *One Earth, One People: The Mythopoeic Fantasy Series of Ursula K. Le Guin, Lloyd Alexander, Madeleine L'Engle and Orson Scott Card* (Marek Oziewicz, 2008)

7 *The Evolution of Tolkien's Mythology: A Study of the History of Middle-earth* (Elizabeth A. Whittingham, 2008)

8 *H. Beam Piper: A Biography* (John F. Carr, 2008)

9 *Dreams and Nightmares: Science and Technology in Myth and Fiction* (Mordecai Roshwald, 2008)

10 Lilith *in a New Light: Essays on the George MacDonald Fantasy Novel* (ed. Lucas H. Harriman, 2008)

11 *Feminist Narrative and the Supernatural: The Function of Fantastic Devices in Seven Recent Novels* (Katherine J. Weese, 2008)

12 *The Science of Fiction and the Fiction of Science: Collected Essays on SF Storytelling and the Gnostic Imagination* (Frank McConnell, ed. Gary Westfahl, 2009)

13 *Kim Stanley Robinson Maps the Unimaginable: Critical Essays* (ed. William J. Burling, 2009)

14 *The Inter-Galactic Playground: A Critical Study of Children's and Teens' Science Fiction* (Farah Mendlesohn, 2009)

15 *Science Fiction from Québec: A Postcolonial Study* (Amy J. Ransom, 2009)

16 *Science Fiction and the Two Cultures: Essays on Bridging the Gap Between the Sciences and the Humanities* (ed. Gary Westfahl, George Slusser, 2009)

17 *Stephen R. Donaldson and the Modern Epic Vision: A Critical Study of the "Chronicles of Thomas Covenant" Novels* (Christine Barkley, 2009)

18 *Ursula K. Le Guin's Journey to Post-Feminism* (Amy M. Clarke, 2010)

19 *Portals of Power: Magical Agency and Transformation in Literary Fantasy* (Lori M. Campbell, 2010)

20 *The Animal Fable in Science Fiction and Fantasy* (Bruce Shaw, 2010)

21 *Illuminating* Torchwood: *Essays on Narrative, Character and Sexuality in the BBC Series* (ed. Andrew Ireland, 2010)

22 *Comics as a Nexus of Cultures: Essays on the Interplay of Media, Disciplines and International Perspectives* (ed. Mark Berninger, Jochen Ecke, Gideon Haberkorn, 2010)

23 *The Anatomy of Utopia: Narration, Estrangement and Ambiguity in More, Wells, Huxley and Clarke* (Károly Pintér, 2010)

24 *The Anticipation Novelists of 1950s French Science Fiction* (Bradford Lyau, 2010)

25 *The* Twilight *Mystique: Critical Essays on the Novels and Films* (ed. Amy M. Clarke, Marijane Osborn, 2010)

26 *The Mythic Fantasy of Robert Holdstock: Critical Essays on the Fiction* (ed. Donald E. Morse, Kálmán Matolcsy, 2011)

27 *Science Fiction and the Prediction of the Future: Essays on Foresight and Fallacy* (ed. Gary Westfahl, Wong Kin Yuen, Amy Kit-sze Chan, 2011)

28 *Apocalypse in Australian Fiction and Film: A Critical Study* (Roslyn Weaver, 2011)

29 *British Science Fiction Film and Television: Critical Essays* (ed. Tobias Hochscherf, James Leggott, 2011)

30 *Cult Telefantasy Series: A Critical Analysis of* The Prisoner, Twin Peaks, The X-Files, Buffy the Vampire Slayer, Lost, Heroes, Doctor Who *and* Star Trek (Sue Short, 2011)

31 *The Postnational Fantasy: Essays on Postcolonialism, Cosmopolitics and Science Fiction* (ed. Masood Ashraf Raja, Jason W. Ellis and Swaralipi Nandi, 2011)

32 *Heinlein's Juvenile Novels: A Cultural Dictionary* (C.W. Sullivan III, 2011)

33 *Welsh Mythology and Folklore in Popular Culture: Essays on Adaptations in Literature, Film, Television and Digital Media* (ed. Audrey L. Becker and Kristin Noone, 2011)

34 *I See You: The Shifting Paradigms of James Cameron's* Avatar (Ellen Grabiner, 2012)

35 *Of Bread, Blood and* The Hunger Games: *Critical Essays on the Suzanne Collins Trilogy* (ed. Mary F. Pharr and Leisa A. Clark, 2012)

36 *The Sex Is Out of This World: Essays on the Carnal Side of Science Fiction* (ed. Sherry Ginn and Michael G. Cornelius, 2012)

The Sex Is Out of This World

Essays on the Carnal Side of Science Fiction

Edited by SHERRY GINN *and* MICHAEL G. CORNELIUS

CRITICAL EXPLORATIONS IN SCIENCE FICTION AND FANTASY, 36
Donald E. Palumbo *and* C.W. Sullivan III, *series editors*

McFarland & Company, Inc., Publishers
Jefferson, North Carolina, and London

ALSO OF INTEREST

Power and Control in the Television Worlds of Joss Whedon,
by Sherry Ginn (McFarland, 2012)

Of Muscles and Men: Essays on the Sword and Sandal Film,
edited by Michael G. Cornelius (McFarland, 2011)

The Boy Detectives: Essays on the Hardy Boys and Others,
edited by Michael G. Cornelius (McFarland, 2010)

Nancy Drew and Her Sister Sleuths: Essays on the Fiction of Girl Detectives,
edited by Michael G. Cornelius and Melanie E. Gregg (McFarland, 2008)

LIBRARY OF CONGRESS CATALOGUING-IN-PUBLICATION DATA

The sex is out of this world : essays on the carnal side of science
   fiction / edited by Sherry Ginn and Michael G. Cornelius.
        p.   cm. — (Critical explorations in science fiction and
        fantasy ; 36)
[Donald E. Palumbo and C.W. Sullivan III, series editors]
Includes bibliographical references and index.

ISBN 978-0-7864-6685-6
softcover : acid free paper ∞

1. Science fiction, American — History and criticism.
2. Science fiction, English — History and criticism.   3. Sex in
literature.   4. Science fiction films — History and criticism.
5. Six in motion pictures.   6. Science fiction television
programs — History and criticism.   7. Sex on television.
8. Extraterrestrial beings — Sexual behavior.   9. Human-alien
encounters.   I. Ginn, Sherry.   II. Cornelius, Michael G.
III. Title: Carnal side of science fiction.
PS374.S35.S46 2012
813'.08762093538 — dc23   2012038704

BRITISH LIBRARY CATALOGUING DATA ARE AVAILABLE

© 2012 Sherry Ginn and Michael G. Cornelius.
All rights reserved

*No part of this book may be reproduced or transmitted in any form
or by any means, electronic or mechanical, including photocopying
or recording, or by any information storage and retrieval system,
without permission in writing from the publisher.*

Cover photograph © 2012 Pavel Aleynikov

Manufactured in the United States of America

*McFarland & Company, Inc., Publishers
   Box 611, Jefferson, North Carolina 28640
   www.mcfarlandpub.com*

Sherry says that this one is for Larry,
with Love always,

and

Michael says that this one, as all things,
is for Joe, with Love

Acknowledgments

Sherry Ginn: I would like to thank Donald Palumbo for his acceptance of this title for the Critical Explorations in Science Fiction and Fantasy series. I approached him at the Popular Culture Association Annual Meeting in 2010 in St. Louis. He was immediately agreeable to the idea as he was well aware of the dearth of materials that had been published since his exploration of sex in fantasy and science fiction in 1986. I would also like to thank Michael G. Cornelius for agreeing to co-edit this collection with me. One of the major reasons I chose him for the job was his experience in the field of popular culture as well as his experience as an English professor. I have learned so much from him during this process and cannot thank him enough for that. I also want to acknowledge my little Madison, who would slip into my study while I was working and lie behind my chair, or lie in the doorway of the study watching me type away, raising her head and making odd-sounding noises, not quite purrs, when it looked like "Mommy" would finally stop working. Finally I want to thank my very patient spouse and partner, Larry Williamson. He truly was patient and understanding as I would rush by with a quick "I have to work" at night and on weekends, especially during the last six months. I have some breathing space now — time to make it up to Larry, play with Madison, and catch up on all of the programs wanting some critical analysis (*Fringe, Game of Thrones, Falling Skies,* and so it goes).

Michael G. Cornelius: After echoing much of what Sherry says above, I'd like to add my kind thanks first to Sherry, for bringing me in on this very interesting project. Working with her was a great joy, and a learning experience to boot. Many kind thanks to Joe, my better half of many years, for his patience and consideration and for listening to many, myriad levels of nerdness. And to Knox, my poor pug, who, rather than spending much quality time on my lap, had to settle for my feet as I hammered away at this. His sacrifice may have been the biggest one of all.

Table of Contents

Acknowledgements viii
Introduction: Sexing Science Fiction
    MICHAEL G. CORNELIUS 1

PART ONE : ALIEN SEX

The Future, in Bed with the Past: Miscegenation in Science
    Fiction Film and Television
    CYNTHIA J. MILLER *and* A. BOWDOIN VAN RIPER 17
Alienating Sex: The Discourse of Sexuality in the Works of
    Octavia Butler
    ANCA ROSU 34
"We pair off! One man, one woman": The Heterosexual
    Imperative in Octavia Butler's Xenogenesis Trilogy
    ECHO E. SAVAGE 50
Love at First Contact: Sex, Race and Colonial Fantasy in
    Star Trek: First Contact
    ALLISON WHITNEY 62
"They teach you that in Whore Academy?" A Quantitative
    Examination of Sex and Sex Workers in Joss Whedon's
    Firefly and *Dollhouse*
    HEATHER M. PORTER 86
The Evil Wet Nurse: Preœdipal Development and Primo Levi's
    Science Fiction
    ROBERT C. PIRRO 102

PART TWO : TECHNO SEX

Patriarchy, Paternity and Papas: Reproductive Technologies and
    Parenthood in Science Fiction
    ERIN GRAYSON SAPP 117

"I have worked hard at her head and brain": Dr. Moreau and the New Woman
 THOMAS G. COLE II 134
"Are we not men?" Degeneration, Future-Sex and *The Time Machine*
 LARRY T. SHILLOCK 152
Space Apes Want Our Women! Primate Lust in American Science Fiction
 MATTHEW H. HERSCH 170
Technology as a Nexus for Homoerotic Desire in Boys' Series Books
 MICHAEL G. CORNELIUS 187
(Inter)Mediated Sexuality in the Science Fiction of J. G. Ballard
 CLARE PARODY 204

Human, Alien, Techno — What Next? Evolutionary Psychology, Science Fiction and Sex
 SHERRY GINN 221

Conclusion: Sexing Science Fiction, Take Two
 SHERRY GINN 238
About the Contributors 243
Index 247

Introduction:
Sexing Science Fiction
Michael G. Cornelius

The *Star Trek: New Frontier* novel series — a sequence of original books featuring the adventures of the U.S.S. *Excalibur* and set contemporaneously to the timeline established by the canonical *Star Trek: The Next Generation* television series — featured a chief engineer named Burgoyne 172, a member of a hermaphroditic species called the Hermat.[1] Much "fuss" is made in the opening books in the series in regard to the manner in which members of the Hermatic species are to be referred — pronoun variants include "s/he" (with a separately accented "h," creating a disyllabic word) for the personal subjective pronoun (he, she); "hish" for the possessive form (his, her); and "hir" for the personal objective (him, her) — a linguistic denotation of the confusion and discomfiture the presence of an individual whose gender construction does not conform to the standard Terran model engendered on the starship.[2] Of course, *Star Trek* being *Star Trek*, the other characters congratulate themselves on being so accepting of a model of gender formation so distinct from their own — a manifestation of the "strange new life" trumpeted so commonly in the opening sequence to every episode of the *Original* and *Next Generation* television series — even if their acceptance comes with two overarching interrogatories that dominates Burgoyne 172's characterization and narrative progression throughout the opening books in the series. The first question — how do "normally" gendered figures contend with a species so distinctly "alien" from what they have encountered before; or, in plainer terms, what to make of "it"? — is reflective of the manufactured Other's insertion into cultures that simultaneously recognize "its" distinctness while also finding that same distinctness threatening, discomfiting, or, at the very least, odd. This is a construct that science fiction has long dealt with, in varying manifestations, to some notable success. The relationships between the alien, the Other, and, by logical ratiocination, the familiar, the commonplace, and the same (what Marianna Torgovnick labels the "controlling subject"), have long been accorded sacred space in science fiction narratives (11).[3] Indeed, one of the hallmarks of the genre itself is the bridging between these differing worlds — sometimes literal, sometimes figurative, both outer space and inner — and, from this perspective, the inclusion of the Hermat species in the *Star Trek* universe (non-canonical as the novelizations may be) is part of a longstanding tradition within the realms of science fiction itself. This is not to posit that the constructed Other always fares *well* while being represented in such narratives; indeed, the obverse is just as, if not more, likely to be true, that the Other represents a terror to be destroyed, curtailed, or contained. Nonetheless, science fiction as a genre has, perhaps more than any other major genre of text and film, considered and explored the interrelationships between same and Other, between incepting baseline culture and interloping presence, between present and (potential) future, as a significant component of the genre's composition from its inception.

From this perspective, the *Star Trek: New Frontier* series is merely reacting in the genre's own naturalistic if conservative way when confronting an Other as "other" as the Hermat. In querying into what "it" is and how to reckon with "it" (or, to be more precise in this case, "hir"), the narrative works to bring into itself this larger pantheon of questions that can, at times, dominate the genre. By following its own dictums "to explore strange new worlds, to seek out new life and new civilizations, to boldly go where no man has gone before," the series can congratulate itself on reckoning with the Other and reflect a presentment of inclusion as notions of how to reckon with "it" and what to make of "it" are replaced by sentiments of "it" simply becoming a part of the team. By demarcating a process through which "it" simply becomes Burgoyne, fellow Starfleet officer, friend, and eventually second-in-command of the *Excalibur*, the novels work to bring the realm of the Other into the larger pantheon of the incepting culture. Thus dominant culture works to both invalidate and celebrate constructs of the Other. Starfleet officers can pride themselves for being "its" friend and, in two cases, "its" lover. Acceptance and inclusion wins out, the Other becomes not-so-Other, and difference is shown to still be only a reflection of our differentiated physicalities. What matters is not in the construct or color of our heart, *Star Trek* would argue, but its contents.[4]

However, lurking behind this shadowy facade of inclusion and the understandable curiosity over Burgoyne the Hermat — over what "it" is and how evolved, compassionate, tolerant Starfleet officers should reckon with "it" — is a far more pressing and inscrutable question that, in the conservative philosophies of the *Star Trek* universe, will only be tacitly asked — or, at least, not directly asked of Burgoyne "hirself," and certainly not visibly demonstrated within the confines of the narrative either. For, indeed, as much as individuals in the series wonder what "it" is, they likewise wonder how "it" *does* "it." The confusion surrounding the double-pronoun here, the two "its" both indicating nameless objects, o/Others that cannot be readily quantified or easily spoken of, is reflective of the larger manner in which science fiction itself grapples with and attempts to codify issues of sexual physicality within the narrative confines of the genre. The other characters in *Star Trek: New Frontier* are naturally curious about how a Hermat would engage in physical acts of sexuality, as, indeed, such curiosities only suggest what any child discovering his/her own sexual organs feels, and likewise signals most humans' innate curiosity about sex.

This curiosity, however, is tempered by an incommunicative reticence on the part of anyone in the text to actually broach the subject of these interrogations — to pose, if you will, the question of how "it" actually does "it." Reticence, in fact, is commonly depicted when it comes to the character of Burgoyne 172. On the back cover of the second *New Frontier* book, *Into the Void*, the text meaningfully and dramatically declares about Burgoyne, "The chief engineer of the *Excalibur*, with the decisiveness of Calhoun, the strength of Shelby, and the gender of both. Burgoyne is a Hermat, and when s/he sets his/her sights on you, s/he isn't an easy ... person ... to refuse" (David). The ellipses here speak volumes about the bifurcated manner in which *Star Trek* views such an alien Other as Burgoyne. Simultaneously creating difference while feigning confusion about it, Burgoyne is cast as a sexually aggressive ... and here the narrative demurs, unsure how to enumerate a figure whose gender does not fall within the familiar "either/or" paradigm that acts as the simulacrum of familiarity against which otherness is measured and how to comprehend a sexuality as potentially differentiated as the one such gender disquietude suggests. The ellipses pronounce confusion about Burgoyne; can a being that is not easily demarcated as male or female still even be considered a "...person..."? Other alien species in the text — such as Vulcans — are easily quantified as "people," but Hermats, with their differentiated constructs of gender, are not so easy to classify.

The hermaphroditic aspect of Burgoyne 172 causes those around "hir" to consider questions of sex and sexual functioning, questions that, in the focused world of *Star Trek* and the broader genre of science fiction, are generally uncomfortable to pose. Interestingly, *Into the Void* uses ellipses at other moments in the text to signal further sexual reticence. Early on in the book, Starfleet Admiral Edward Jellico and *Excalibur* First Officer Commander Elizabeth Shelby are discussing alien worlds when Shelby recalls one particularly interesting encounter:

"Zantos." Shelby made a face. "Wasn't that the world where a survey party got caught by the natives years ago, and they took the leader of the party and cut off his, uhm..." She shifted uncomfortably. "...his..."

"Privileges," Jellico said judiciously [David 14].

Why the need for such judiciousness? In a private conversation between two professional adults, with a host of technically-derived (genitals, phallus, lingam), descriptive (reproductive organ, sexual organ,) and/or euphemistic terms (privates, meat and potato, tallywhacker, or whatever twenty-fourth century parents and teenagers had crafted by then to refer to the male sexual organ/s) available for such expression, why the ellipses? Why does Shelby find it so difficult to simply state "penis"? How evolved has the human species become if it cannot even name the male genitalia? Yet naming the object is exactly the problem here, and the purpose of the ellipses. It is not Shelby or Jellico that are ultimately unforthcoming or reserved; rather, it is the audience — or the authorial perception of the audience — and the audience's role as bellwether of similitude against the alien Other that makes naming even human male genitalia so uncomfortable for the Starfleet officers.

As a species, we wonder endlessly about sex. How to best procure "it"? How to best do "it"? Am I doing "it" right? How do others do "it"? How do members of same-sex couplings do "it"? What things do people do when doing "it" that I would never do, or think to do, or, perhaps, secretly long to do but will never do or admit to doing? Our culture's double-speak and obfuscating language surrounding physical manifestations of sexuality only adds to the confusion. Billion-dollar industries proclaim to exhibit and manifest sexuality (pornography) or to aid in the performance of accoupled sexuality (including pharmaceuticals for everything from Viagra to sensation-inducing lotions, creams, and pills) or even to accentuate the pleasure of singular sexuality (including masturbatory devices for both men and women). These industries clearly thrive, but they thrive largely by maintaining a circumspect profile, allowing a culture ashamed of its own sexual curiosity to still perform these acts quite literally in the dark. This commercialization of sex claims, yes, but it will not *pro*claim; that is to say, it will not manifest publicly, because society conceives that such outward displays of sexuality should frighten, disgust, or shame us. It is not surprising that studies of sexual representation in popular culture demonstrate that manifestations of physical sexuality generally assume "the form of talk *about* sex rather than depictions of sexual behaviors" (Taylor 130, emphasis mine). Thus we as individuals speculate rampantly about sexuality, but keep "it" mostly to ourselves.

Yet if any genre should be capable of publicly speculating about sexuality, it should be science fiction. After all, science fiction falls under the larger generic umbrella of speculative fiction. To posit the genre theoretically, to postulate its functioning under such a weighty aegis, it should appear that speculative fiction is designed to do just as its moniker suggests — to speculate, about futures and fears, about our pasts and our presents, about outer spaces and inner desiderata. This should likewise be true of sex:

> In science fiction, as in life, sexuality is a complicated and remarkably intransigent subject of inquiry, one whose material consequences can be ignored only at the peril of both individuals and cultures ... [a]nd yet sexuality in [science fiction] so often catches us by surprise: we may think, as readers and scholars, that it is not represented at all or, when we do catch a glimpse of it out of the corner of our generically conditioned eye, we may blink at it in bemusement [Pearson, Hollinger, and Gordon 2].

Thus science fiction — though an integral component of speculative fiction — has demonstrated a certain (and well-documented) reluctance to truly hypothesize or reflect upon or about sexual physicality. Too often, sex in science fiction merely replicates what is already reflected to be prurient and possible by and in the incepting culture in which the work originates. This is not necessarily true of sexuality, gender, or even sexual subjectivity — indeed, even the most banal of science fictions like *Star Trek* can revel in representations of alternate and third genders and the sexual confusion that naturally follows — but in especial regard to *the corporeal manifestation* of said sex and sexuality, these same works often refuse to do what their genre suggests they are best designed to do — to speculate about the nature of differentiated, evolved, or, indeed, "alien" forms of sexual pleasure and expression. To put it another way, science fiction, as a whole, has a real problem in *truly* going "where no man has gone before."

There is an inconsistency at play here in works that strive to reflect differentiated forms of sexuality while shying away from representing the actual form such sexualities take. The reader is told over and over again that Burgoyne 172 is hermaphroditic, that s/he has both male and female sexual organs. Yet the actual, corporeal manifestation of these organs — which part can be found where? — and the actual functioning of these organs remains, for the most part, obscured from view, a construct reflected when Burgoyne 172 is summoned to the *Excalibur's* medical bay for a routine physical exam in *Into the Void*. Though summoned by Vulcan Chief Medical Officer Dr. Selar, Burgoyne is disappointed when the doctor assigns another medical officer to conduct "hish" physical. Burgoyne notes:

> There aren't many Hermats in Starfleet, and none at command level aside from me. The Vulcans I know have always had a great inquisitiveness about the galaxy they live in and the people therein. I would be surprised if you, a woman of science, did not share that famed Vulcan drive to satisfy curiosity [David 107].

Selar coolly responds, "I am quite certain my curiosity about the medical uniqueness of Hermats will be more than satisfied by my scrutiny of Dr. Maxwell's no-doubt detailed examination" (David 108). Selar (and by extension, the reader) here represents the controlling subject against which the Other is measured as well as the general reticence from which science fiction often regards the sexual manifestation of said Other. That which makes Hermats "medically" unique is their biology — specifically, their doubled genitalia. Selar, a scientist, prefers to "read about" the manifesting Other rather than "see" or experience it for herself— to physically examine Burgoyne, who offers "hirself" willingly as a specimen of Other for general perusal. Burgoyne aggressively manifests hish sexual congress for all to see. S/he is, for example, the only character in the book unreluctant to make an actual penis joke; when told that another ship has a malfunctioning engine that requires hish "magic touch," Burgoyne replies, "My wand is at the ready, sir" (David 132). Other (single-gendered) crew members chuckle or share a "disapproving glance," but the joke never radiates beyond this point of harmless entry (David 132). Thus, like Selar, we find ourselves content to "read about" Burgoyne's "uniqueness" without ever being presented with any actual manifestation of it. Paradoxically, we are constantly pressed to "see" Burgoyne as Other without being allowed to ever satisfy our curiosity as to exactly how this Other is actually differentiated from "the norm" from a biological perspective.[5]

At its core, the construct of "science fiction" itself is something of a paradox. "Fiction" denotes fantasy, fancy, that which is divorced from "reality." Certainly fiction has always spoken to and explored what is considered to be real or reality, but in its very construction one sees the seeds for a departure from the tangible and into realms that exist beyond this real world. "Science," however, suggests a specific discipline grounded in reality, based on predictable principles of action and inaction. Science is the study of the physical world in all its varied manifestations; it relies on observation, experimentation, and the judicious recording and interpretation of reality and fact. The two together, then, create that aforementioned oxymoron: "science fiction," which, for all intents and purposes, could be translated into "real unreality." More than a genre like fantasy, which creates entirely new realms of possibility, science fiction constructs its possibilities from what is real, from what is, indeed, possible, or conceivably so. The fact that science fiction and its most common manifestations — space flight, technology, alien realms — are so connected to the future, and to our visions and re-visions of the future, suggests that the genre is concerned not with what is *un*real, but rather with what *may* be real, or may soon be real. The flights of fancy that govern science fiction are grounded in the tangible, in the realm of what is possible, real, hoped for, and feared.

Of course, in life and in fiction, few things are more "hoped for" or "feared" than sex, and sex's many manifestations in our world delight, confound, and enrage. Debate about sex, its role and its function, its form and its meaning, permeate every aspect of our culture — philosophically, ideologically, culturally, religiously, politically. Sex is both "real" and "unreal" and, perhaps sometimes, "surreal." It is part of every society, something continually acknowledged and enshrouded, something we are all self-righteous over and simultaneously ashamed of — as a culture, as individuals, and as members of sexually-based relationships.

Perhaps it is this "real unreality" that creates the generic space in which science fiction exists as eager to explore the possibilities of sexual representation while simultaneously desirous to obscure the manifestations of those same possibilities — which is how characters like Burgoyne 172 are created and also why their sexual uniqueness is repressed. In large part because science fiction postulates on the possible, on what may come to pass — what we perhaps fear will come to pass or, conversely, anticipate will come to pass — the genre instinctually recoils when it comes to delving into matters reflective of a topic that society still shackles with significant taboos. Joanna Russ, in a famous 1979 response to an article by Nancy Sahli in *Chrysalis*, laments that "genital activity ... betray[s an] uneasiness with the subject" (168). In her work, Russ is discussing specifically female same-sex erotic relationships, but her observation is applicable on a larger sexual scale. Tellingly, Russ laments in the same piece that "we are forced to talk about female sexuality in general in an alien vocabulary," an apt choice of word ("alien") for a subject matter that invites obfuscation, even for a genre that prides itself on exploration and speculation (170).

It may seem that I am being a bit harsh in regards to science fiction, either in suggesting that all science fiction remains forever prudish (indeed, it does not) or that it acts in ways significantly different from most other genres of literature and film (for, indeed, it does not here as well). It should be stated that the goal of this introduction and collection is not to castigate the genre's handling of manifested sexuality, nor to accuse science fiction of any particular set of "hang-ups" or anxieties not present in the larger society that creates and sustains it. Indeed, science fiction has a proud history of being an inclusive genre — inclusive of Others in regards to race, gender, and orientation — but inclusion is not quite the same as representation, and as Wendy Gay Pearson, Veronica Hollinger, and Joan Gordon observe, "Representation matters" (2). If science fiction is, in some ways, "unreal reality," than it is perhaps time the genre looks to what is truly most real about sex and sexuality — and that which makes society most uncomfortable about it, its corporeal manifestation — and bring not only the manifesting Other into the light, but indeed, the manner in which we ourselves exhibit, celebrate, suppress, and fear sexual congress into the light as well.

This collection, then, looks to understand and explore the sexualized and sexualizing areas of "unreal reality," to note ways in which our culture's continually changing and evolving mores of sex and sexuality are reflected in, dissected by, and deconstructed through the genre of science fiction. The essays herein interrogate, challenge, and affirm the ways in which physical manifestations of sex relate to the genre of science fiction itself. Both of these fashioned notions — sex and sexuality and the genre of science fiction — are at the forefront in these essays, with the goal of recovering the ways in which science fiction has (past,) does (present,) and should (future) consider the modes and means through which sexual congress — and the representation of physical sex and sexuality — is reflected and replicated in science fiction works.

The collection itself is divided into two parts. The first, "Alien Sex," examines the alien Other as a reflection of and redaction to our own ethos in regards to representing acts of physical, sexual conjunction within both the popular and the dominant culture. Human/alien sexual congress has long been a part of the science fiction tradition; as Istvan Csicsery-Ronay, Jr., writes, "It is not rare for human and humanoid aliens to have sex and mate — and to feel the same anxieties about violence and self-loss in the other as in human sexual affairs.... The humanoid alien therefore projects a formidable and generally taboo biological difference on to a being whose difference is actually cultural — in other words, it seeks to establish a natural barrier where there is none" (16). Of course, any student of history can observe that "cultural" difference is no real impediment to sexual congress; indeed, our culture is replete with narratives featuring the sexual exploitation of those deemed culturally — or racially, economically, or ideologically — "different" from, and especially inferior to, the dominant (baseline) culture. The true "Otherness" of science fiction is — as many scholars and critics have observed — rooted in a continually shifting representation of both the individual self and the greater cultural self. As Gwyneth Jones (amongst others) has observed:

> [A]ll the aliens we know so far speak human. They speak our human predicament, our history, our hopes and fears, our pride and shame. As long as we haven't met any actual no kidding intelligent extraterrestrials ... the aliens we imagine are always other humans in disguise: no more, no less [108].

The result of this, as Alcena Madeline David Rogan correctly notes, is that "science-fictional representations of sex acts involving aliens are therefore bound to reinscribe the epistemological and ontological lineaments of the human sexual experience" (443). To put it plainly, the more alien the sexual act or sexual partner, the more familiar, truly, it is.

The essays in this portion of the collection concern themselves with these notions, with human anxiety disguised as alien Otherness and the ways in which manifesting acts of physical sexuality only increase both our anxiety of and alienation toward the (individual and cultural) self. "The Future, in Bed with the Past: Miscegenation in Science Fiction Film and Television" by Cynthia J. Miller and A. Bowdoin Van Riper commences this work by examining cultural attitudes toward — and fears of— miscegenation and the loss of clearly discernible cultural identity. Generally socialized out of existence on Earth (or, at least, en route to being so), in space, in encounters with new alien Others, the old cultural anxieties that relate to intimate interactions between the controlling subject and that which represents difference echoes the racism, colonialism, and xenophobia of Earth's troubled social history (and present).

The next two essays examine the work of one significant science fiction author — Octavia Butler — and, through very differentiated methodologies and purposes, arrive at a similar conclusion in how Butler represents and reflects on manifestations of physical, Other-bound sexuality. Anca Rosu's "Alienating Sex: The Discourse of Sexuality in the Works of Octavia Butler" and Echo E. Savage's "'We pair off! One man, one woman': The Heterosexual Imperative in Octavia Butler's Xenogenesis Trilogy" both use the works of this highly influential genre authority to interrogate dominant-culture norms of sex and sexuality. Rosu suggests that Butler attempts valiantly to deconstruct the paradigm of baseline sexuality, to tear down the "natural barriers" Csicsery-Ronay suggests impede our understanding of both sex and alienness. Savage, on the other hand, writes that Butler's differentiated manifestations of sexual congress are really just more of the same reflection of the human onto the alien Other that Jones writes about, and that the more "inventive" Butler becomes in her depictions of alien sexual physicality, the more they reflect the compulsory heteronormativism of dominant culture. Fascinatingly, both authors reach similar (if analogous) concluding points, but their journey to each conclusion reflects the nascent struggle with the genre of science fiction to balance both the Other and the imperative self, a struggle that, seemingly, is more usually won by the familiar than the strange.

Allison Whitney continues the interrogation of miscegenation; in "Love at First Contact: Sex, Race and Colonial Fantasy in *Star Trek: First Contact*," she explores how this particular film in the *Star Trek* franchise, in its depiction of sexualized/sexualizing women of color, reflects the socionational dynamics of colonial narrative, suggesting still a conservative neocolonialist reading of American cultural history. *Star Trek: First Contact* problematizes both women and the ways in which women are considered by the dominant, baseline culture, crafting a purposeful statement designed to silence the Other before, perhaps, it has an opportunity to demonstrate just how aligned to us it truly can be.

To this point, the essays in the collection have been concerned with what Rogan labels "the limits of representation," which "describes the epistemological limits of speculative thought ... [s]uch inquiry engages the contradictory nature of signification itself: that is, the unsignifiable nature of the real" (443). As much as science fiction may wish to speculate, in some ways the more we cast our eyes upward, to the stars, or forward, to the future, the more we truly cast our gaze directly back at our (individual and cultural) selves. Heather M. Porter's quantitative analysis of prostitutes, demimondaines, and other such "working women" in the Joss Whedon television series *Firefly* and *Dollhouse* suggests that one of the true limiting factors to representation is not so much our speculative imaginations as it is our inabilities to view ourselves — or more precisely, the Others in our own culture — and the sexualization of each in ways that go beyond our own prurient tendencies. Robert C. Pirro also explores the "limits of representation" in his essay "The Evil Wet Nurse: Pre-œdipal Development and Primo Levi's Science Fiction." Pirro's Chodorowan take on the short genre fiction of Primo Levi demonstrates the alien Other within ourselves and our own families, reflecting (in this case) on man's inability to not only relate to his fellow man but, more tellingly perhaps, also with his mother (or to that part of his self formed by his earliest, infantile encounters with a maternal caretaker).

Pirro's essay is also concerned with the ways in which technology manifests as a means to challenge our accepted versions of both the self and the dominant culture, and, as such, is a fitting bridge into the second half of the collection, "Techno Sex." "Techno Sex" examines the ways in which technology alters both the Other and the self and the means of sexual congress. Isaac Asimov — no slouch when it comes to science fiction — writes that the genre innately and continually must deal "with human science, with the continuing ability of human beings to make themselves better understand the universe" (10). The essential key in understanding the relationship between technology and genre, Asimov argues, is rooted in the "continuing ability [of human beings] to alter some parts [of their world/s] for their own comfort and security by the ingenuity of their ideas" (10). Technology, then, is a tool, both a means to an end as well as the manifestation of that same end. Often in science fiction, technology exists as a source of combat or an object of fear; what is often considered the first science fiction novel, Mary Shelley's *Frankenstein*, exhibits technology as flesh, crafting both (technology and the body) as a source of anxiety and a cautionary tale. Pirro's observations about technology in his essay, used as a means to threaten male autonomy, reflect that same disquiet. Generally, though, in relation to manifestations of sexuality, technology works as a tool of a very different stripe. Catherine S. Ramirez, writing specifically about "cyborg identity" but posting an observation that applies to science fiction technology more generally, suggests that notions of technology are based on concepts of "constructionism," a term she also labels as "anti-essentialism" (384). According to Ramirez, technology's main purpose in science fiction is as a tool of shaping: "It reconceives of identity (a static and fixed essence) as *position* (within a particular history, narrative, ideology, and/or social system)" (384, italics original). As such, technology can be used to shape sex — to transfigure sexualities, corporeal physicality, sexual congress, and even sexual expression. Yet to what end? If technology can change who we are — if technology can alter the (cultural and individual) self — then what do we use it to create?

Ultimately, the authors in this section suggest that the limits of technology may not emanate from the tool itself, but rather the imagination of those who wield it. Try as we might to supersede our own sexual limitations, our other limitations draw us back to the realm of the self, the present, and the limited. Erin Grayson Sapp, for example, looks at reproductive technologies in three twentieth-century science fiction novels in her essay "Patriarchy, Paternity and Papas: Reproductive Technologies and Parenthood in Science Fiction." Though these novels are often bent on creating "brave new worlds," Sapp argues that they sacrifice institutions of value in favor of alternatives that, ultimately, seem as limiting as their current incarnations. In "'I have worked hard at her head and brain': Dr. Moreau and the New Woman," Thomas G. Cole II suggests that H. G. Wells' *The Island of Dr. Moreau* uses technology as a means of interrogating and containing both the feminine and the forming New Woman, a manifestation of technology being used to contain, rather than recreate, (sexualizing) identity. Larry T. Shillock also examines Wells' apprehension in regards to identity and technology. His essay "'Are we not men?' Degeneration, Future-Sex and *The Time Machine*" uses Wells' framing of technology to reveal and criticize anxiety about the past and the future, both of which, according to Wells, are rooted in imperfections in his (and our own) present. In traveling to a distant future, Wells' time traveler, as Shillock reveals, encounters de-evolved beings that reflect moral and civil decay, a reflection of not only where the self perhaps emerged from but also where the (cultural and individual) self may be headed. More disquiet about technology and its possible revelations on our past and future is revealed in Matthew H. Hersch's "Space Apes Want Our Women! Primate Lust in American Science Fiction." In his essay Hersch examines our own fears of the loss of collective identity as a result of colonial expansion (past) and genetic manipulation (future). In examining the figure of the "space" ape — a figure that wholly embodies both ancient (pre-evolutionary) pasts and imagined (science fiction) futures—Hersch explores the notion that our fears of technology are rooted in both: a fear of returning to the past and a fear of what may lie ahead in our future.

In each of the above essays, sexual manifestation is reflective of these anxieties: in the asexualized methods of reproduction; in the panther woman's sexualized aggression; in the bifurcated nature of the Eloi and the Morlocks and their means of interrogating the sexual world around them; and in the hands of pre- and post-evolved simians that desire blonde "babes," reflecting both colonial-era and post-colonial fears of the Other. Technology here is the means of achieving, not alleviating anxiety; it shapes identity by further deconstructing it and, consequently, reinforcing it. By Ramirez's account, technology has constructed new identities in these science fiction accounts, but they have been judged lacking, and the retreat to the current dominant culture (though in *Time Machine*, for example, it is the dominant culture that dooms us all) is assured. Technology, however, can also be utilized differently. In my own essay, "Technology as a Nexus for Homoerotic Desire in Boys' Series Books," technology is a means of sexual expression for mid-century figures that would otherwise lack the ability to declare — in any manner — their affection for the other. In boys' series such as Rick Brant, Ken Holt, and Christopher Cool, technology alters identity positively — if perhaps in some ways haphazardly and accidentally — by manufacturing a means through which desire, if not actual sex, can actually manifest in a time period when it would otherwise remain suppressed. The last essay in the section, "(Inter)Mediated Sexuality in the Science Fiction of J. G. Ballard" by Clare Parody, logically concludes "Techno Sex" by revealing technology as the object of desire itself. In Ballard's science fiction, technology is not a means to an end or a way to shape identity but rather the end — and in some ways, the identity — itself. Parody demonstrates that Ballard's characters, in lusting after and over technology itself, create forms of media that are reflective not only of the (cultural and individual) self but that also suggest the inherent problems with these same selves. Technology then becomes a mirror and a means through which the Other becomes most wholly constructed (to borrow Ramirez's term) and actualized.

The last two contributions are written by my collaborator Sherry Ginn. In "Human, Alien, Techno—What Next? Evolutionary Psychology, Science Fiction and Sex," Ginn reiterates a theme of this introduction — the "unreal reality" that acts as an essentialist reduction of a science fictive tenet — but rather than focusing on the more narrative aspect of the genre, as I do here, Ginn focuses on science — specifically, the science of evolutionary psychology — as a means to read the sexual activity of a variety of science fiction works. The result is that Ginn brings the collection back to its roots, sweeping the work from the "unreal" (fiction) back into the realm of "reality" (science), not only reminding us of the genre's origins but also demonstrating that its future lies as much in real-world laboratories as in the imaginations — and beds — of those who generate it. She ends the collection with a conclusion to the book as a whole: "Sexing Science Fiction, Take Two."

There is a pun at work in the title of this introduction. In using sex as a verb, "Sexing Science Fiction" suggests less making science fiction sexualized and more instead determining the gender of the genre itself, as if the authors in this collection are veritably lifting up the skirt of science fiction to see, indeed, that which has been hidden so long. And, in a way, that is in part the goal of this collection of works, to metaphorically pull back the veils that have hidden manifesting sexuality within the science fiction genre to see, indeed, what lies beneath. The more science fiction talks about sex, the more it talks about us, about that culture which creates and consumes it. And the more science fiction is desperate to hide actual manifestations of sexual physicality, the more we demonstrate our own desire to hide from ourselves. Genres that are rooted in speculation should be free to do just that. Yet in positing itself as speculation of the future — for both the cultural and individual self — science fiction has cast itself, in some significant ways, as the potent harbinger not only of things to come, but of the self to come as well. Such speculations make us nervous, and that anxiety is reflected in the "unreal realities" we create when we craft "brave new worlds" or seek out "strange alien life." We may be close; but it seems, perhaps, that we are not quite ready to go — boldly or timidly — "where no man has gone before."

Notes

1. The *Star Trek: New Frontier* series was created by John J. Ordover and Peter David in 1997 and published by Pocket Books. The series featured original characters as well as characters already considered part of the *Star Trek* canon, most notably Commander Shelby, who first appeared in the two-part *Star Trek: The Next Generation* episode "Best of Both Worlds." All told, the series consisted of eighteen original novels, two graphic novels, and nine stories/crossover books, almost all of which were penned by David.

2. In regards to obfuscating gender in species, *Star Trek* had in fact already gone "where no man had gone before" with the introduction of the J'naii in *The Next Generation* episode "The Outcast." In the episode, the *Enterprise* encounters an alien race that claims no distinct gender (whereas the Hermat proudly proclaim both). In the J'naii culture, any outward manifestation of gender or gendered sexuality is considered a criminal act and/or a symptom of an ailment. During the episode, Commander Riker embarks on a relationship with a J'naii shuttle pilot named Soren, a member of the J'naii who had secretly identified herself as female, even though such identifications were taboo in J'naii culture. The relationship is quickly discovered by another member of the J'naii and just as swiftly condemned. Soren is sentenced to psychotectic treatment, which suppresses her urge to express her gender. Tellingly, despite the desire to create a "neutered"/sexless race of aliens, in the episode, the J'naii were all played by women with their breasts taped down (Westmore and Nazzaro 89). Of the episode, producer Rick Ber-

man said in the *Star Trek: The Next Generation Companion*, "We thought we had made a very positive statement about sexual prejudice in a distinctively *Star Trek* [sic] way, but we still got letters from those who thought it was just our way of 'washing our hands' of the homosexual situation" (qtd. in "The Outcast [217]"). Actor Jonathan Frakes, who played Commander Riker, publicly criticized the decision to cast women in the roles of the J'naii; Berman, replying to the controversy, said to the *San Jose Mercury News*, "having Riker engaged in passionate kisses with a male actor might have been a little unpalatable to viewers" (qtd. in "The Outcast [217]"). Of course not only is Soren played by a female actress, but she also self-identifies in the episode as female and, in her desire for sexual congress with those who identify as males, she also self-identifies as resolutely *hetero*sexual. Thus Berman's statement suggesting that the episode dealt with issues of "sexual prejudice" in a "distinctively *Star Trek* [sic] way" is rather apt, since, in reflecting broader trends in science fiction and its treatment of manifesting sexual practice, the episode is reticent, conservative, patriarchal, and ultimately re-affirming of the considered sexual order.

3. In the introduction to their collection *Queer Universes: Sexualities in Science Fiction*, Wendy Gay Pearson, Veronica Hollinger, and Joan Gordon argue that "science fiction ... is intimately concerned with how people live in the world and what makes the world livable for them. Often [science fiction] answers these questions — or extends the sequence of interrogation — by postulating alternative (often future) societies and cultures ... [t]he result is a field that is coming to understand that knowledge of social systems and ontological questions is as necessary to any conception of alternative (future) societies as is knowledge of science and technology per se" (6–7). This common construct in regards to the composition of the science fiction genre often ignores science fiction's contradictory desires in regards to these types of "interrogations" that purportedly engender the thrust of the genre itself, which as much engages in *conserving* existing societal aspects as often as reshaping or re-examining them. It also disregards that the cynosure to this essential act of interrogation lies not in the questioner — in who is doing the interrogation — but rather in the baseline of interrogation, from which the interrogator asks his/her relevant questions. This notion, then, of the familiar and the commonplace as oppositional to the alien Other reflects not on the makers of science fiction but on its consumers. The reader/viewer is the bellwether of sameness and familiarity against which the more "exotic" modes, alien Others, and "alternative societies" are constructed; as such, science fiction is less disposed to outwardly challenge what it perceives to be the quiddity of what is both a point of departure and set of public values — whether real or imagined — in favor of working with both these constructs and those who hold them, thus potentially (and in some instances severely) limiting the shape of the "future" societies that Pearson, Hollinger, and Gordon suggest are essential to the nature of science fiction's generic conventions.

4. *Star Trek* labors diligently to reinforce this notion; indeed, in one *Star Trek: The Next Generation* episode, "The Chase (246)," the *Enterprise* crew, along with a host of Klingons, Cardassians, and Romulans, discovers an archaeological message hidden in their own DNA that reveals that the entire Alpha Quadrant was "seeded" by one mother species in a type of controlled panspermia, indicating that all of the present species originated from the same primary source material. Interestingly, such concepts work to deconstruct notions of Otherness; in suggesting a biological commonality, the *Star Trek* philosophy rejects conceptions of Otherness, negating difference in favor of similarity.

5. To be perfectly fair about this, *Star Trek* does not always present such a rigid view of sexual manifestation. Perhaps the best example of this occurs in the *Star Trek: Voyager* episode "Before and After" where Kes, an Ocampa female, is depicted giving birth through her back. Though the actual shot is quite short, and not revelatory of the moment of birthing, the brief glimpse of biological otherness nonetheless most perfectly captures the notion of difference in sexual congress and manifestation between and among the alien Other and baseline norm. However, the presentation of the birth (as the result of an officially sanctioned heterosexual coupling) and the questions raised but never addressed (is the birth canal depicted also the primary means of inception — i.e., the vagina?) still reflect a reluctance to satisfy sexual curiosity beyond the point of science fiction's usual coyness.

WORKS CITED

Asimov, Isaac. *Isaac Asimov on Science Fiction*. London: Granada, 1983. Print.
"Before and After." *Star Trek: Voyager*. Dir. Allan Kroeker. Syndicated program. 9 Apr 1997.
"The Chase." *Star Trek: The Next Generation*. Dir. Jonathan Frakes. Syndicated program. 26 Apr 1993.
Csicsery-Ronay, Istvan, Jr. "Some Things We Know About Aliens." *The Yearbook of English Studies* 37.2 (2007): 1–23. Print.
David, Peter. *Into the Void*. New York: Pocket Books, 1997. Print.
Jones, Gwyneth. *Deconstructing the Starships: Science, Fiction, and Reality*. Liverpool: Liverpool University Press, 1999. Print.
"The Outcast." *Star Trek: The Next Generation*. Dir. Robert Scheerer. Syndicated program. 16 Mar 1992.
"The Outcast (episode)." *Memory Alpha: The Star Trek Wiki*. Web. 5. Jan 2012.
Pearson, Wendy Gay, Veronica Hollinger, and Joan Gordon. "Introduction: Queer Universes." *Queer Universes: Sexualities in Science Fiction*. Eds. Wendy Gay Pearson, Veronica Hollinger, and Joan Gordon. Liverpool: Liverpool University Press, 2008. 1–13. Print.
Ramirez, Catherine S. "Cyborg Feminism: The Science Fiction of Octavia E. Butler and Gloria Anzalúda." *Reload: Rethinking Women and Cyberculture*. Eds. Mary Flanagan and Austin Booth. Cambridge: The MIT Press, 2002. 374–402. Print.
Rogan, Alcena Madeline David. "Alien Sex Acts in Feminist Science Fiction: Heuristic Models for Thinking a Feminist Future of Desire." *PMLA* 119.3 (May 2004): 442–456. Print.
Russ, Joanna. "Is 'Smashing' Erotic?" *To Write Like a Woman: Essays in Feminism and Science Fiction*. Bloomington: Indiana University Press, 1995. Print.
Taylor, Laramie D. "Effects of Visual and Verbal Sexual Television Content and Perceived Realism on Attitudes and Beliefs." *The Journal of Sex Research* 42.2 (May 2005): 130–137. Print.
Torgovnick, Marianna. *Gone Primitive: Savage Intellects, Modern Lives*. Chicago: University of Chicago Press, 1990. Print.
Westmore, Michael, and Joe Nazzaro. *Star Trek: The Next Generation Makeup FX Journal*. New York: Starlog Communications, 1992.

PART ONE : ALIEN SEX

The Future, in Bed with the Past: Miscegenation in Science Fiction Film and Television
Cynthia J. Miller and *A. Bowdoin Van Riper*

When humans venture to the outer reaches of cinematic space, they carry with them the baggage of entire cultures, filling the "final frontier" with Earth-bound ideologies long-since abandoned or suppressed on an increasingly civilized homeworld. In a universe where the variety in life forms is seemingly endless, sexuality — fascination, romance, longing and lust — triggers anxieties over the mingling of species and the loss of clearly defined identity. These fears of miscegenation, socialized out of existence on Earth, are once again given form in space, infused with ideals and taboos that echo the racism, colonialism, and xenophobia of Earth's troubled social history.

Throughout that history, intimate relationships between racial and social Others have been problematized, both formally and informally, through social sanctions such as ostracism, violence, incarceration, and even death, and attempts at "passing" to circumvent taboos are accompanied by great peril. Desire has signaled destruction; passion prefigured contamination; seduction implied violation. The offspring of such unions — visible and undeniable testimony to the sins of the fathers (and mothers) — are relegated to status that is liminal at best, and often shunted to the margins of society.

In the context of cinematic space, where astounding developments in science and technology are often accompanied by advances in ethics and morality, intimacy is no less complex, and miscegenation is similarly fraught with risk. Indeed, it may be more so, since the range of potential partners is as wide as the science fictional universe, and evolving metaphysical and cognitive abilities expand the erotic repertoire, both consensual and forced. Seductive shape shifters, androids, and clones add new dimensions to "passing," while humanoid and non-humanoid aliens merge into a continuum of difference that ranges from the alluring to the monstrous.

Whether set on Earth or in deepest space, narratives of intimacy between species — or even different categories of life forms — reflect hierarchies, biases, and consequences drawn directly from human history. And similar to narratives drawn from that history, representations of interstellar difference all engage with the social, cultural, and ideological contexts in which they are produced and received. This paper, then, will use miscegenation — sexual intimacy at its most controversial — as a lens through which to examine such issues. It will explore the ways in which — even as science fiction carries the reader outward in space and forward in time — its framing assumptions about sexuality remain rooted in Earth's past.

Earth's Checkered Past

Heavy-laden with social, historical and ideological freight, the term "miscegenation" is, as Jane M. Gaines points out, far from neutral (199). Its very utterance evokes images of "pollution," "corruption," and "trespass" (Lott "Love and Theft" 30). The term emerged in 1864, as part of an anti-emancipation hoax, and carried a warning — not merely about sex across the "color line," as Gaines notes, but about the "frenzy of love in the white woman for the Negro" — of fear, inadequacy, loss of control, and ultimately, of decline in social, political, and economic status (199).[1]

Similarly, contemporary concerns with miscegenation are really part of a much larger constellation of culturally-situated notions about appropriate relationships, encompassing not merely racial, ethnic, and class-based endogamy, but notions of heteronormative, and, at least serially, monogamous sexual pairings as well. This framework of appropriate relationships has informed cinematic portrayals of sexual and romantic couplings since the origins of the medium itself— and it all began with a kiss. As early as 1903, Thomas Edison's one-minute film clip, "What Happened in the Tunnel," playfully teased audiences with the hint of sexual impropriety between races. When the scene opens, an amorous gentleman is seated in a railway car behind a vivacious young woman and her black maid. As he attempts to move toward her with romantic intent, the screen goes black, signifying the train's entry into a tunnel. When the image returns, the woman and her maid have switched seats, and the brazen gentleman finds himself embracing the maid as the two women laugh (Courtney 5–9; Gaines 52–54).

In the decades that followed, however, suggestions of miscegenation in film were no laughing matter. Portrayals of romantic or sexual pairings of whites with blacks, Asians, Latino/as, or Native Americans were increasingly suppressed, supporting and reflecting the proliferation of anti-miscegenation legislation in the wider culture. In 1930, the Motion Picture Production Code specifically prohibited the depiction of interracial sexuality or romance, in the same conceptual breath as it prohibited references to sexual perversion, rape, and child pornography.[2] While many films — such as *The Squaw Man* (1914, 1918, 1931), *Daughter of the Dragon* (1931), and *God's Step Children* (1938) — disregarded this prohibition, or employed racially ambiguous light-skinned actors, their portrayals largely served to uphold "culturally accepted notions of nation, class, race, ethnicity, gender, and sexual orientation," typically functioning as morality tales about the disastrous ends met by those who dared to cross racial or ethnic lines (Marchetti 1; Mapp). Although the Code's edict specified "sex relationships between the white and black races," popular interpretations included other non–Caucasian groups as well, as illustrated in films such as *First Yank into Tokyo* (1945) and *Sayonara* (1957) (Chin and Karthikeyan 1; Fuller 168–169, 205).

The Code's replacement, in 1968, by the Motion Picture Association of America's (MPAA) rating system ended the formal prohibition of depictions of miscegenation in film. Social constraints, however, remained, as American society struggled to come to terms with "sex across the color line" at the culmination of the Civil Rights Era. This persistent resistance to, and resentment of, portrayals of interracial relationships in film — over one hundred years after "miscegenation" was first coined — echoed the fears embedded in the term's origins: "that white women's bodies needed to be protected from what white men perceived as black men's superior sexual potency" (Lott *Class* 57; Tucker 50). These cultural responses to the black body — as simultaneously threatening and fascinating — also extended across genders, casting black women as sexual aggressors or deviants as well. As Jacqueline Bobo, Felly Nkweto Simmons, David J. Leonard, and others note, "the most resilient image [of the black woman] has been that of the jezebel, the 'sexual siren'" (Leonard 48). These portrayals, then, infused cinematic — as well as real-world — perceptions of miscegenation with a sense of physical, as well as social, danger.

The demise of the Code led to numerous films that explored, challenged, and exploited these fears. From early champions of interracial relationships, such as *Guess Who's Coming to Dinner* (1967), to productions that trafficked in lurid sensationalism, such as *Mandingo* (1975), to the troubling realism of films such as *Spike Lee's Jungle Fever* (1991), portrayals of interracial relationships continued to engage with notions of miscegenation throughout the twentieth century. More recent cinematic offerings, such as *Monster's Ball* (2001) and *Something New* (2006), and television programs like *ER* and

Hawthorne, have continued to reflect not only the historical legacy of the term, but also the complex social, political, economic, and psychosexual context of the present day.

While race is, as Adam Roberts notes, a significant concern in contemporary science fiction, representations of race — and thus, we would add, conceptualizations of miscegenation — allow for a more "complex and sophisticated response to the dynamics of difference" that extends well beyond coding the alien as "black" (94). Rendering diversity through narratives of beauty and horror, sensuality and violence, desire and dread, contextualizes difference — what Roberts signposts as "the radically strange" — simultaneously in both power and pleasure (96). Miscegenation in space, with its tales of mutation, hybridity, the unexpected, and the unexplained, often engages with science fiction's potential for exploring the full range of difference, as well as its absence, presenting audiences with an Otherness so profound it retains vibrancy and tension rather than succumbing to simplistic binary oppositions.

In the Image of...

Miscegenation "represents changing social circumstances, whereby visible racial characteristics separate human beings and represent raced identities. People who do not fit any of these categories deeply trouble others" (Lavender 126). However, individuals who only *appear* to fit categories are even more troublesome. Movements that sought to ferret out, and sometimes eliminate, Others in the name of political and ideological security, as well as racial purity, mar Earth's real-world history. Government-sponsored eugenics efforts, the "one drop" rule and other legal impositions of identity, as well as formal and informal retribution for the transgression of racial, ethnic, and other categories of identification have shaped the terrain of inter-group hierarchies and relationships for centuries, and continue into the present day (Malcolmson). Within this context, the ability of individuals from one world to disappear within another becomes the key to resources, opportunities, and survival — and often, to miscegenation as well — and has prompted moral panics across communities, organizations, industries, and entire nations.

When Earth transports its notions of "blood boundaries" and inter-group hierarchies into space, however, the picture grows even more complicated. While the underlying motivations for passing remain familiar — power and privilege, espionage or other forms of information-seeking, sanctuary, and romantic or sexual desire — the means and opportunities for doing so increase exponentially. The rewards and consequences of passing expand in space, as well, as successful passing can ensure the survival of entire species or bring about the extinction or assimilation of others.

The ability of androids, shape-shifters, and aliens to "pass"—to appear, and be accepted as, human—places them in a valued location on the continuum of difference and Otherness that informs notions of miscegenation. The rewards of successful assimilation across species are high, as illustrated in television comedies such as *Mork & Mindy* and *Third Rock from the Sun*, when alien observers find new lives and loves on Earth, or in films such as *Starman* (1984), when Jenny Hayden (Karen Allen) falls in love with a non-corporeal alien who "wears" the cloned body of her dead husband, Scott (Jeff Bridges), or *What Planet Are You From?* (2000), in which alien operative Harold Anderson (Garry Shandling) finds more than simply an opportunity to reproduce when he takes a bride (Annette Bening) on Earth. These ambiguously human/alien characters—like the racially ambiguous heroes prominent in recent science fiction films (Park 197–198)—make social inroads in places where more identifiable Others would be turned away.

The risks of being "nearly human" are also high. Narratives of passing and miscegenation, as Gina Marchetti notes, most closely associate the erasure of difference with self-denial, duplicity, and tragedy (68–71). Less successful aliens, androids, and others are often relegated to the ranks of a sub-human underclass, serving marginalized, utilitarian roles as physical and emotional surrogates. Often isolated, always diminished, they are denied not only human status, but also the personal, social, economic, and political standing of even the least fortunate of their fully-human counterparts. Many serve as no more than exploited, sexualized wage workers, such as the robotic prostitutes in *Westworld* (1973), or the never-seen holographic "companions" in the suites above Quark's bar in *Star Trek: Deep Space Nine*. Others, such as Pris, the "basic pleasure model" replicant played by Daryl Hannah in *Blade Runner* (1982), and Gigolo Joe, the android prostitute played by Jude Law in *A. I.* (2001), are allowed more complete social expression but denied full humanity by design—created with limited emotional ranges that are sufficient for brief, purely sexual encounters with humans but not for enduring relationships.

Even greater ambiguity is experienced by the android Lt. Commander Data (Brent Spiner), of *Star Trek: The Next Generation*, whose quest for humanity is briefly rewarded when he is seduced by Lt. Tasha Yar (Denise Crosby) in "The Naked Now." Her sex drive intensified by an alien virus, Yar enthusiastically beds Data, expressing a desire for "gentleness, and joy, and love," but it soon becomes clear that her interest is short term and purely sexual. When the virus wears off, she tells Data the encounter "never happened"—but it is, for both characters, a relationship between equals (Wilcox 272–274). The robotic whores of *Westworld* or Quark's sexualized holograms may be tools to be used and then set aside — sex toys for the ultimate one-night stand — but Data is already so close to human that his liaison with Yar, and its lingering effect on him, become proof of his emerging humanity (Wilcox 273).

These instances of passing, or attempted passing, are part of a long tradition in cinematic science fiction — from early television's *Twilight Zone* series to the 2011 film *I Am Number Four* — but only a few examples have received significant scholarly attention. Among these, Ridley Scott's *Blade Runner* has been the focus of several discussions that consider the implications of passing and miscegenation. Set in a dystopian near-future society in which "replicants" — androids so flawlessly human-looking that only experts using sophisticated tests can recognize their artificial nature — form a permanent, despised underclass, the film follows Rick Deckard (Harrison Ford), a bounty hunter hired to "retire" a group of replicants who turn renegade, fleeing their masters and seeking out their human maker in order to force him to extend their hard-wired four-year life spans.

In *Black Space: Imagining Race in Science Fiction Film*, Adilifu Nama examines the film in relation to fears of successful assimilation and ultimate "replacement," and explores the ways in which its narrative calls into question taken-for-granted notions of human authenticity (56–60). Here, the passing Other is the product of human minds — science spun out of control — and only successful assimilation with humans will ensure their (even limited) survival. *Blade Runner* personalizes this issue through the sexual and emotional tension it conveys between Deckard and Rachael (Sean Young), a sanctioned replicant who, he discovers, is ignorant of her own status and passing, believing herself to be human. Deckard is simultaneously drawn to and repulsed by Rachael's dual status, and must ultimately choose to recognize only one.

Nama, who along with Isiah Lavender considers the film within the structures of historical black/white racism (Nama 56–60; Lavender 127, 179–182), views *Blade Runner*'s replicants' overt coding as socially and economically exploited, repressed, and denigrated, serving as part of a broader historical web of racial meaning (57). Within this framework, Deckard's passion for the "passing" Rachael clearly serves as a prime example of miscegenation, simultaneously violating blood boundaries separating android/human and black/white. A continued look at miscegenation in space, however, illustrates that these parallels are but one example of Earth's ideological baggage being carried into the future.

Love and the Visible Other

Stories of beings who appear human — whether by construction, accident of biology, or through the carefully maintained subterfuge of passing — minimize the difference between the species, often presenting them as human in all but name. Most of cinematic science fiction's depictions of miscegenation, however, follow a pattern that, Adam Knee argues, is characteristic of fantastic cinema as a whole: emphasizing, rather than minimizing, difference (157–159). This difference becomes the defining element — and in some cases the *only* salient element — in relationships between lovers, exemplifying science fiction's tendency "to present otherness in unitary terms, so that 'humanity' is uncomplicatedly opposed to the 'alien'" and difference is subsumed "within a common-sense notion of what it is to be human" (Wolmark 46). With alien species presented in similarly reductive fashion, miscegenation becomes a union of categories rather than of individual beings.

Leading men in *Star Trek* and its sequels thus routinely find love with alien women who are defined by the qualities that most sharply distinguished their species from humans. On *Star Trek: Deep Space Nine*, for example, Worf (Michael Dorn), a Klingon devoted to the austere simplicity and rigid demands of his species' code of honor, is coupled with Jadzia Dax (Terry Farrell), a Trill who — as seventh host to a sentient, symbiotic organism — sees the world with the eyes of one who has already lived six complete, very different lives. "I can see our lives together will not be easy," Worf remarks to Dax at one point. "True," she responds. "But they'll be fun" ("Sons and Daughters").

Revelations of differences such as these — frequently focused on anatomical and sexual practices — often serve as comic relief from interplanetary drama. Tongue-in-cheek sexual humor in one episode of the television series *Babylon 5* finds Centauri ambassador Londo Mollari (Peter Jurasik) using his meter-long genitalia to cheat at cards ("The Quality of Mercy"), while in another, Narn ambassador G'Kar (Andreas Katsulas) — during an attempt to hire human telepath Lyta Alexander (Patricia Tallman) to bear his child — asks: "Would you prefer to be conscious or unconscious during the procedure? I would prefer conscious, but I don't know what your [grins] pleasure threshold is" ("The Gathering"). Similarly, in an intimate moment in *Cocoon* (1985), the alien Kitty (Tahnee Welch) emits a glowing ball of energy that caroms off walls and ceilings, finally exploding into her human partner, Jack Bonner (Steve Gutenberg), filling him with his own ecstatic glow. His sole response is giddy and breathless: "If this is foreplay, I'm a dead man" (*Cocoon*). Even the crew of the relatively sex-free *Star Trek: Voyager* joins in the fun when Harry Kim (Garrett Wang) and his seemingly humanoid girlfriend Derran Tal (Musetta Vander) shake their heads over the extent to which "the birds and the bees would be confused" by their anatomical differences ("The Disease").

In other contexts, though, "difference" moves from exotic and endearing to address more deeply rooted prejudices and fears. Scenes of Princess Leia

(Carrie Fisher) as a captive of Jabba the Hutt in *Return of the Jedi* (1983) rely on the mere threat of interspecies sexual contact to evoke such fears. Bound by a collar and chain to the massive slug-like alien's throne, Leia is dressed in a revealing "slave girl" costume that marks her as a sexualized plaything. In a scene where Jabba uses Leia's chain to pull her close to his wrinkled face, his protruding tongue makes explicit — both conceptually and visually — the simultaneous fascination with and revulsion over "difference" that is central to cinematic science fiction's stories of miscegenation. Even in comedies, such as *Earth Girls are Easy* (1988), humor is used to soften the revelation that although alien Mac (Jeff Goldblum) appears completely human when shorn of his bright blue fur, his love interest, Valerie Gail (Geena Davis), struggles to see him as anything other than "alien" and different.

Audiences' worst fears of difference and the Other are realized in films such as *Species* (1995) and its sequels: stories of predatory female aliens who mate with, then kill, unsuspecting men. Each human victim — including, in the first film, a member of a team assigned to hunt down the alien — believes they are involved with a beautiful, sexually aggressive woman. Only too late do they realize that their partner is an alien Other capable of sprouting fins from her spine, tentacles from her nipples, or a tongue long and sharp enough to pierce the skull with a single thrust. The growing capability of special effects to depict genuinely *alien* aliens, like those in the *Species* films, enhances cinematic science fiction's ability to "dramatize the conflict between self and other, human and alien" that lies at the heart of the genre (Park 187).

Miscegenation as Social Drama

Miscegenation's ability to elicit a range of visceral responses from members of a community — whether fascination, anxiety, dread, revulsion, or hostility — turns the most private of acts and emotions into social drama acted out on a public stage. Relationships that blur the lines between fundamental social groups are often aligned in the public consciousness with other forces that challenge society, and partners in such couplings are framed as morally unworthy to participate in the community (Coyne 38). These social responses raise complex questions of status for the characters and their offspring, as historian Michael Coyne points out: "It is not so much a question of accommodation as one of assimilation: either they *belong* or they don't" (70).

Much like earthbound relationships across racial, ethnic, and other social boundaries, extraterrestrial couplings are typically defined by their contexts rather than by their participants. Despite enlightened, futuristic sound-bites such as "I find interspecies mating rituals fascinating to watch," boundary-defying relationships are frequently no better received in space than on Earth ("Strange Bedfellows").[3] Nama cites *Star Trek* for adapting its "utopian model of racial diversity and cooperation from the televised *Star Trek* series onto the silver screen" (34). Daniel Leonard Bernardi insists, however, that the relationship between them remains fraught with tension, arguing that a distinct anti-miscegenation thrust prevails (126–131). While mixed-species matings — across a full range of genders and sexual practices — abound in these cinematic tales of outer space, the participants often suffer danger, exploitation, and discrimination similar to that inflicted on their terrestrial predecessors. Although *Star Trek* laid claim to the United States' first televised interracial kiss in 1968,[4] the very *concept* of miscegenation came under attack in the *Star Trek: Enterprise* episode "Terra Prime," over three decades later, when a group of xenophobic humans, seeking to expel all aliens from Earth's solar system, clone a human/Vulcan baby as an example of the dangers of interspecies mating.[5]

Interspecies romance also takes on political significance in the television series *Babylon 5*, when Minbari ambassador and member of the planet's mysterious Grey Council, Delenn (Mira Furlan), undergoes a painful transformation, becoming a Minbari/human hybrid, in order to serve as a "bridge" between the two species. Delenn's ensuing involvement with the human station commander John Sheridan (Bruce Boxleitner) destroys a thousand-year peace on the Minbari homeworld, and causes both Sheridan and Delenn to be reviled and mistrusted by their own species, who believe their representatives' judgment to be tainted by "alien influence." Similarly, in both the cinematic and television versions of *Alien Nation*, the tension of political intrigue, racism, and exploitation complicate inter-species romance between humans and Newcomers, threatening the existence of both races.

Not all inter-species mating threatens to bring about planetary ruin, however. *Babylon 5*'s Narn ambassador, G'Kar, is cast as a somewhat mischievous character with a fetish for human women — a compulsion that his fellow Narns find perverse and distasteful — yet this spin-off of the traditional "aliens want our women" trope adds an element of biting comedy to the program's main narratives of war and survival. G'Kar frequently entertains multiple human prostitutes — to the dismay and disgust of his Narn assistant, Na'Toth (Caitlin Brown) — and is the source (and object) of recurring jokes about his virility and preferences, such as when he asks Na'Toth to investigate the source of a black tulip found in his bed. She replies: "Far be it from me to speculate how *anything* finds its way into *your* bed" ("The Parliament of Dreams").

Similar comic reactions to interspecies love may be found across big and small screens, in television programs such as *Third Rock from the Sun* and *Futurama*, where the robot Bender pays tribute to director Spike Lee in his warning to robot-dating human, Philip J. Fry: "Stay away from our women!

You've got Metal Fever, boy, Metal Fever!" ("I Dated a Robot"). In *Galaxy Quest* (1999), a comic homage to the *Star Trek* television series, informal social sanction takes an even more personal turn when Fred Kwan's (Tony Shalhoub) fellow "crew member" Guy Fleegman (Sam Rockwell) witnesses a passionate embrace between Kwan and his Thermian girlfriend, Laliari (Missi Pyle). Lost in passion, she drops her holographic disguise, revealing her octopoidal tentacles. Fleegman stares, calling, "Fred? Um ... Fred?" and then exclaims, "Eeew! That's just not right!!" (*Galaxy Quest*).

Nobody's Child

Society's disapproval of interspecies miscegenation falls, with particular intensity, upon its offspring. The children of mixed-species humanoid couples face, on screen, the same social challenges as the children of mixed-race or even mixed-ethnicity marriages have traditionally faced on Earth: harassment or outright rejection — by strangers, school-mates, and even relatives — for being "different" or "impure" (Ali 143–166). The children of more extreme forms of interspecies miscegenation, however, are denied even this (admittedly fraught) degree of personhood and cast, instead, as monsters. They are presented — particularly in exploitation films such as *Humanoids from the Deep* (1980) and *Breeders* (1985) — as threats, not simply to the social order, but to the lives of anyone foolish enough to let them live.

Mixed-species characters abound in the *Star Trek* universe: Spock (Leonard Nimoy) in the original series, Deanna Troi (Marina Sirtis) in *Star Trek: The Next Generation*, Tora Ziyal (Melanie Smith) in *Star Trek: Deep Space Nine*, and B'elanna Torres (Roxann Dawson) in *Star Trek: Voyager* among them.[6] All see themselves, to varying degrees, as outsiders among their ancestral species, and are often viewed with varying degrees of suspicion by pure-blooded members in return (Pounds 159–161). As Spock's human mother, Amanda (Jane Wyatt), reminds him in the episode "Journey to Babel": "When you were five years old and came home stiff-lipped, anguished, because the other boys tormented you saying that you weren't really Vulcan. I watched you knowing that inside ... that the human part of you was crying and I cried, too" ("Journey to Babel"). The prejudice and hostility faced by such characters is all the more striking because the *Star Trek* universe is so pointedly egalitarian in its attitudes toward gender, race, and ethnicity (Wilcox 265–267).

The socially precarious position of interspecies hybrids is frequently complicated by physical frailties or eccentricities. Hera Agathon (Illana Gomez-Martinez), the only viable child produced by a program designed to interbreed humans with the biomechanical Cylons in the 2004–2009 iteration of the television series *Battlestar Galactica*, is physically frail but possesses extraordinary regenerative capabilities. The extent to which she will, as she matures, manifest her Cylon heritage in other superhuman ways remains a subject of both anticipation and anxiety among the adults around her. Scorpius (Wayne Pygram), the principal villain in the television series *Farscape* and a rare interspecies hybrid whose parents are both non-human, received a less fortunate combination of traits. Like his Scarran father, he has an unusually high body temperature that rises further when he becomes angry; like his Sebacean mother, however, he is unable to withstand excess heat. He is forced, therefore, to rely on a full-body cooling suit and a calm, calculating — that is, metaphorically icy — personality to keep him himself alive. The physical precariousness of his existence underlines that he is an "unnatural" being, a label applied — by some characters at least — to virtually every interspecies hybrid in cinematic science fiction.

The perceived unnaturalness of miscegenation often forces single-species parents to choose between their mixed-species children and their own well-being, or even the good of the society whose reproductive norms they violated, as two moral mandates — protection of offspring and species loyalty — grapple for primacy. In the three-part alien-invasion miniseries *V: The Final Battle*, when teenager Robin Maxwell (Blair Tefkin) discovers that her boyfriend Brian (Peter Nelson) is an alien in human disguise and the child she is carrying will be a human/Visitor hybrid, she immediately seeks to terminate the rapidly advancing pregnancy. Failing in this, she orchestrates Brian's murder and rejects their child so completely that those around her fear she will also murder it. Eventually, though, Robin's maternal instincts triumph over the fury and disgust evoked by miscegenation. Similarly, Ziyal, a recurring Bajoran/Cardassian character on *Star Trek: Deep Space Nine*, is introduced in an episode where her father, Cardassian military officer Gul Dukat (Marc Alaimo), plans to murder her in order to safeguard his reputation. Ultimately, the Cardassian yields to his paternal emotions and spares his offspring, rather than eradicate the evidence of his inter-species affair ("Indiscretion"). While he saves her life, however, he cannot save her the pain of never fully belonging in either society. Less fortunate is *Farscape* character Lo'Laan (Alison Fox), a Sebacean, who is murdered by her brother over her marriage to the Luxan Ka D'Argo (Anthony Simcoe); her mixed-species child, Jothee (Matthew Newton), is sold into slavery ("Mental as Anything").

Unexpected Others

Hearts — human and otherwise — do what they will, even amidst the advances of a fictional intergalactic future. However, relationships that transgress the borders and boundaries of social identities, species, and even life forms take on new and complex possibilities when a universe already brimming over with opportunities for pairing encounters futuristic technologies. As cultural critic Donna Haraway observes, "Science fiction is generally concerned with the interpenetration of boundaries of problematic selves and unexpected others" (300). Gene-splicing, biomechanical hybridization, symbiosis, holography, and the "downloading" of one organism's consciousness into the body of another all vastly increase the range of hybrid beings that miscegenation can produce, multiplying and intensifying the challenges it poses to individual and group identity. These expansions of scientific possibilities can shift or eradicate categories of race and gender, complicate our understandings of relationships, and even further destabilize the notion of personhood, resulting in great benefits and, sometimes, even greater trauma.

This exploding of categories is one of the most critical issues arising from science fiction's "new" technology-enhanced miscegenation — the creation of a world in which "technology is rapidly making the concept of the 'natural' human obsolete" (Vint 7). As theorist Elaine Graham contends, "What is at stake, supremely, about the implications of digital, cybernetic, and biomedical technologies is precisely what (and who) will define authoritative notions of normative, exemplary, desirable humanity" (11). Or, as Lavender asks, how are we to think about unresolved issues of social identity, such as race, "if the human body cannot be distinguished from a computer simulation or a cybernetic being?" (27). The ability to replicate, merge, or assimilate, then, widens the debate around how and where we locate "humanity" in the individual. The body, personality, self-awareness, abilities to learn and create, and even memories are all subject to manipulation and reproduction, alone or in combination, creating previously unimagined entities.

Following the Cartesian tradition, the body is often conceived as the most easily divorced from human identity. As Sherryl Vint notes, there is a tendency "to speak of the postmodern body as an obsolete relic," and yet, nowhere is the concern over humanity's status more pronounced than in the blending of organic and mechanical (8). Variations on the merging of body and machine range from the purely functional — such as the bio-mechanical child produced in *Demon Seed* (1977) when the sentient computer Proteus imprisons and impregnates its creator's wife (Julie Christie) in order to be fully "alive"— to the wildly imaginative, such as the Leviathan craft Moya in the television series *Farscape*. A self-aware, bio-mechanical spaceship, Moya is so closely physically and psychically bonded to her "Pilot"— a member of a species designated as her companion, navigator, caregiver, and translator — that they can survive only limited periods of separation.

Cinematic cyborgs, hybrid beings whose organic and technological components are even more intricately interwoven, are unsettling in equal measure. Frequently portrayed as evil, they are narratively positioned as threats to identity, authenticity, or even human existence itself—"resolutely anti-human and anti-reproductive" as Jonathan Goldberg notes — but, in fact, cyborgs collectively extend science fiction's contribution to the conversation on miscegenation (243). The humanoid, biomechanical Cylons of *Battlestar Galactica*, for example, see themselves as the metaphorical "children" of humanity, but also as a purer and more advanced life form justified in waging genocidal war against their "parents." The Borg, implacable enemies of the Federation in *Star Trek*, "assimilate" other sentient species by inserting Borg technology to individual members' bodies and importing the distinctive qualities of the species as a whole to the Borg hive-mind. Christine Wertheim argues that this "penetration of self by other is what makes the Borg, to a Western mind raised on the credos of individualism and an absolute distinction of self and other(s) so suspect, so alien, so Other" (75). Existing completely outside any existential dialectic, the radical Otherness of the Borg collective is terrifying — creating a discontinuity that cannot be breached — as it takes "the revaluation of all values to its logical [and incomprehensible] extreme" (Roberts 120, 122).

The insertion of a disembodied consciousness into a new body leaves no doubt of the newly created hybrid being's individuality, but raises complex questions about its uniqueness. In "Booby Trap," Geordi La Forge (LeVar Burton) of *Star Trek: The Next Generation* falls in love with a holographic simulation of Dr. Leah Brahms (Susan Gibney), but finds the "real" Dr. Brahms cold and off-putting when he meets her in person ("Galaxy's Child"). The "Jake Sully" (Sam Worthington) who serves as one of humankind's emissaries to the Na'vi in *Avatar* (2009) is a hybrid of the paraplegic ex–Marine's personality and a fully functional holographic body whose face is, itself, a hybrid of Sully's and that of a Na'vi. The transient electronic "body" of *Star Trek: Voyager*'s holographic doctor (Robert Picardo) is modeled after that of its human creator, holographic engineer Dr. Lewis Zimmerman, and its prickly personality is Zimmerman's as well. Its medical expertise, however, is an amalgam of that possessed by forty-seven of the Federation's leading physicians, and its mind as a whole has been shaped by experiences in the Delta Quadrant that none of its "fathers"— Zimmerman or the doctors — share. He is, therefore, a distinct being—one capable, for example, of falling deeply in love with an alien colleague, Denara Pel (Susan Diol), who the "real" Zimmerman never met, and never will meet ("Lifesigns").

Perhaps the most complex forms of miscegenation in space result from the merging of memories — the essence of individuality — in ways that interweave the emotions and experiences of distinct individuals housed in the same corporeal form. When the symbiote Jolinar, a member of the Tok'ra resistance movement on the series *Stargate SG-1*, is forced to take refuge in Captain Samantha Carter (Amanda Tapping), her personality, memories, and abilities are merged with Carter's own — including the memories of her one hundred-year love affair with her mate, Tok'ra leader Martouf (J.R. Bourne), and his symbiote, Lantash ("In the Line of Duty"). When Carter and Martouf meet, they are immediately drawn to one another, but past and present blur, as neither is able to disentangle the memories and passions of Martouf's relationship with Jolinar and her former host, Rosha, from their current emotions. Martouf senses Rosha/Jolinar in Samantha, while she, in turn, responds to Jolinar's memories of him. The intricacies of their entanglement — romantically combining three species and five distinct personalities in a single pairing — reflects science fiction's redefinition of miscegenation: a radical expansion of its boundaries to include partners other than humans and forms of coupling more intimate and fundamental even than sex.

Conclusion: Contesting the Past

In a genre that is, as Adam Roberts points out, fascinated by encounters with difference, it is not surprising that many of science fiction's icons, images, and narratives call to mind earthbound differences such as race, class, gender, and sexual orientation — or that titles like *Black Space, Race in American Science Fiction*, or *Race in Space* have taken their place alongside volumes on cybernetics, virtual bodies, and technological subjectivities (94). Science fiction often suggests that centuries-old assumptions about difference will follow humankind outward into space and forward into the future, and that, as scholars such as Marc Bould and Micheal Pounds suggest, the future is another form of "racist space" in which people of color (human or alien) remain one-dimensional characters filling traditional, circumscribed roles (Bould 180; Pounds 171–188). Others, such as Roberts, Nama, and Jane Park, illustrate the ways in which science fiction creates a space of "structured absence and token presence," embracing the appearance of diversity and egalitarianism among alien species, while valorizing the white, male, heteronormative values embodied by explorer/heroes (Park 199; Nama 10–41). Still others, such as Lavender and Alondra Nelson, argue for "Afrofuturism" and rail against a future like that forecast by journalist Leon Wynter, in which "historical definitions of whiteness are being absorbed into a 'transracial' order," and racial, ethnic, and gender distinctions are erased by narratives that render the human body infinitely mutable, submerging uniqueness, heritage, and experience in a gray sea of sameness (ctd. in Park 199).

In cinematic narratives of space, ample evidence may be found to support each of these positions. However, the complexities of difference in science fiction narratives of space offer other possibilities as well. Spectacular technologies that make possible assimilation, species blending, the transplantation of consciousness and memory, and biomechanical birth create hybridity and difference in ways that confound and defy traditional categories and conditioned responses. The radical alterity of species such as the Borg; the existential merging of pairings such as Pilot and Moya; the organically transplanted century-long love joining Jolinar, Carter, Rosha, Martouf, and Lantash — all represent a dramatic broadening of the concept of intermingling of species. This process, along with the vast expansion of the range of potential exogamous partners, makes miscegenation possible on a scale undreamed of in other genres. A careful reading of cinematic science fiction's portrayals of miscegenation illustrates the genre's speculative nature, and its ability to contest the past. While the tension of Earth's history continues to shape narratives of the future, it is not without challenge. Overwhelming hybridity of biologies, identities, and sexualities shares "space" with boundaries, categories, and assumptions; new possibilities are "reproduced" alongside old fears, filling the "final frontier" with endless variation that refuses to be contained.

Notes

1. See also Martha Hodes. *White Women, Black Men: Illicit Sex in the Nineteenth-Century South* (New Haven: Yale University Press, 1997).
2. Well over fifty movies featuring romantic or sexual relationships between races were produced prior to the repeal of the Production Code, in addition to numerous Western genre films featuring relationships between white characters and those of Latino/a origin and "half breeds."
3. Spoken by Weyoun (Jeffrey Combs), a Voorta, in the *Star Trek: Deep Space Nine* episode "Strange Bedfellows."
4. "Plato's Stepchildren," episode 3.10, aired 22 November 1968.
5. The baby is cloned from the DNA of Vulcan Commander T'Pol and human Commander Charles "Trip" Tucker III.
6. Spock is of Vulcan/human parentage, Troi is human/Betazoid, Ziyal is Cardassian/Bajoran, and Torres is human/Klingon.

Works Cited

Ali, Suki. *Mixed-Race, Post-Race: Gender, New Ethnicities, and Cultural Practice*. London: Berg, 2003. Print.

Bernardi, Daniel Leonard. *Star Trek and History: Race-ing Toward a White Future*. New Brunswick, NJ: Rutgers University Press, 1998. Print.

Bobo, Jacqueline. *Black Women as Cultural Readers*. New York: Columbia University Press, 1995. Print.

Bould, Mark. "The Ships Landed Long Ago." *Science Fiction Studies* 34.2 (2007): 177–186. Print.
Chin, Gabriel, and Hrishi Karthikeyan. "Preserving Racial Identity: Population Patterns and the Application of Anti-Miscegenation Statutes to Asian Americans 1910–1950." *Berkeley Asian Law Journal* 9.1 (2002): 1–39. Print.
Courtney, Susan. *Hollywood Fantasies of Miscegenation: Spectacular Narratives of Gender and Race, 1903–1967*. Princeton, NJ: Princeton University Press, 2005. Print.
Coyne, Michael. *The Crowded Prairie: American National Identity in the Hollywood Western*. London: Tauris, 1997. Print.
Fuller, Karla Rae. *Hollywood Goes Oriental: CaucAsian Performance in American Film*. Detroit: Wayne State University Press, 2010. Print.
Gaines, Jane M. *Fire and Desire: Mixed-Race Movies in the Silent Era*. Chicago: University of Chicago Press, 2001. Print.
Goldberg, Jonathan. "Recalling Totalities: The Mirrored Stages of Arnold Schwarzenegger." *The Cyborg Handbook*. Ed. Chris Gray, Heide Hables, J. Figuroa-Arriera and Steven Mentor. London: Routledge, 1995. 233–254. Print.
Graham, Elaine. *Representations of the Post/Human: Monsters, Aliens, and Others in Popular Culture*. New Brunswick, NJ: Rutgers University Press, 2002. Print.
Haraway, Donna. "The Promises of Monsters: A Regenerative Politics for Inappropriate/d Others." *Cultural Studies*. Ed. Lawrence Grossberg, Cary Nelson, and Paula Treichler. London: Routledge, 1992. 295–337. Print.
Hodes, Martha. *White Women, Black Men: Illicit Sex in the Nineteenth-Century South*. New Haven, CT: Yale University Press, 1997. Print.
Knee, Adam. "Race Mixing and the Fantastic: Lineages of Identity and Genre in Contemporary Hollywood." *Mixed Race Hollywood*. Ed. Mary Beltran and Camille Fojas. New York: NYU Press, 1988. 157–181. Print.
Lavender, Isiah, III. *Race in American Science Fiction*. Bloomington: Indiana University Press, 2011. Print.
Leonard, David J. *Screens Fade to Black*. Westport, CT: Praeger, 2006. Print.
Lott, Eric. *Love and Theft: Blackface Minstrelsy and the American Working Class*. New York: Oxford University Press, 1993. Print.
———. "Love and Theft: The Racial Unconscious of Blackface Minstrelsy." *Representations* 39 (1992): 23–50. Print.
Malcolmson, Scott L. *One Drop of Blood: The American Misadventure of Race*. New York: Farrar, Straus and Giroux, 2000. Print.
Mapp, Edward. *Blacks in American Films: Today and Yesterday*. Metuchen, NJ: Scarecrow Press, 1972. Print.
Marchetti, Gina. *Romance and the "Yellow Peril": Race, Sex, and Discursive Strategies in Hollywood Fiction*. Berkeley: University of California Press, 1993. Print.
Nama, Adiliuf. *Black Space: Imagining Race in Science Fiction Film*. Austin: University of Texas Press, 2008. Print.
Nelson, Alondra, ed. "Afrofuturism." Special issue of *Social Text* 20.2 (2002). Print.
Park, Jane. "Virtual Race: The Racially Ambiguous Action Hero in *Pitch Black* and *The Matrix*." *Mixed Race Hollywood*. Ed. Mary Beltran and Camille Fojas. New York: NYU Press, 1988. 182–202. Print.
Pounds, Micheal C. *Race in Space: The Representation of Ethnicity in* Star Trek *and* Star Trek: The Next Generation. Metuchen, NJ: Scarecrow Press, 1999. Print.
Roberts, Adam. *Science Fiction (The New Critical Idiom)*. 2d ed. London: Routledge, 2006. Print.
Simmons, Felly Nkweto. "'She's Gotta Have It': The Representation of Black Female Sexuality on Film." *Feminist Review* 29 (Summer 1988): 10–22. Print.
Tucker, Linda G. *Lockstep and Dance: Images of Black Men in Popular Culture*. Jackson: University of Mississippi Press, 2007. Print.
Vint, Sherryl. *Bodies of Tomorrow: Technology, Subjectivity, Science Fiction*. Toronto: University of Toronto Press, 2007. Print.

Wertheim, Christine. "*Star Trek: First Contact*: The Hybrid, the Whore, and the Machine." *Aliens R Us: The Other in Science Fiction Cinema*. Ed. Ziauddin Sardar and Sean Cubbitt. London: Pluto Press, 2002. 74–93. Print.

Wilcox, Rhonda V. "Dating Data: Miscegenation in *Star Trek: The Next Generation.*" *Extrapolation* 34.3 (1993): 265–277. Print.

Wolmark, Jenny. *Aliens and Others: Science Fiction, Feminism, and Postmodernism*. Iowa City: University of Iowa Press. 1994. Print.

Films and Television Episodes Cited

A. I. Artificial Intelligence [2001]. Dir. Steven Spielberg. Dreamworks, 2002. DVD.
Avatar [2009]. Dir. James Cameron. 20th Century–Fox Home Entertainment, 2010. DVD.
Babylon 5. Warner Home Video, 2002. DVD.
  "The Gathering." Pilot. First Broadcast 22 February 1993.
  "The Parliament of Dreams." Season 1, Episode 5. First Broadcast 23 February 1994.
  "The Quality of Mercy." Season 1, Episode 21. First Broadcast 17 August 1994.
Blade Runner [1982]. Dir. Ridley Scott. Warner Home Video, 1997. DVD.
Breeders [1986]. Dir. Tim Kincaid. MGM/UA Home Entertainment, 2001. DVD.
Demon Seed [1977]. Dir. Donald Cammell. Warner Home Video, 2005. DVD.
Farscape. A & E Home Video, 2009. DVD.
  "Mental as Anything." Season 4, Episode 15. First broadcast 20 January 2003.
Earth Girls Are Easy [1988]. Dir. Julien Temple. Artisan Entertainment, 1998. DVD.
Futurama. 20th Century–Fox Home Entertainment, 2003–2004. DVD.
  "I Dated a Robot." Season 3, Episode 15. First broadcast 13 May 2001.
Galaxy Quest [1999]. Dir. Dean Parisot. DreamWorks Home Entertainment, 2000. DVD.
Humanoids from the Deep [1980]. Dir. Barbara Peeters. New Horizons Home Video, 2010. DVD.
Return of the Jedi [1983]. Dir. Richard Marquand. 20th Century–Fox Home Video, 2004. DVD.
Species [1995]. Dir. Roger Donaldson. MGM/UA Home Entertainment, 2001. DVD.
Stargate SG-1. MGM Domestic Television Distribution, 2006. DVD.
  "In the Line of Duty." Season 2, Episode 2. First broadcast 3 July 1998.
Star Trek: The Original Series. Paramount Home Video, 2004. DVD.
  "Journey to Babel." Season 2, Episode 10. First broadcast 17 November 1967.
  "Plato's Stepchildren." Season 3, Episode 10. First broadcast 22 November 1968.
Star Trek: Deep Space Nine. Paramount Home Video, 2004. DVD.
  "Indiscretion." Season 4, Episode 4. First broadcast 23 October 1995.
  "Sons and Daughters." Season 6, Episode 3. First broadcast 13 October 1997.
  "Strange Bedfellows." Season 7, Episode 19. First broadcast 21 April 1999.
Star Trek: Enterprise. Paramount Home Video, 2005. DVD.
  "Terra Prime." Season 4, Episode 21. First broadcast 13 May 2005.
Star Trek: The Next Generation. CBS Video, 2002. DVD.
  "Booby Trap." Season 3, Episode 6. First broadcast 30 October 1989.
  "Galaxy's Child." Season 4, Episode 16. First broadcast 11 March 1991.
  "The Naked Now." Season 1, Episode 3. First broadcast 5 October 1987.
Star Trek: Voyager. Paramount Home Video, 2004. DVD.
  "The Disease." Season 5, Episode 17. First broadcast 24 February 1999.
  "Lifesigns." Season 2, Episode 19. First broadcast 26 February 1996.
Starman [1984]. Dir. John Carpenter. Columbia/TriStar Home Video, 1998. DVD.
V: The Final Battle. Dir. Kenneth Johnston. NBC. May 6–8, 1984. Television.
What Planet Are You From? [2000]. Dir. Mike Nichols. Columbia/TriStar Home Video, 2001. DVD.
Westworld [1973]. Dir. Michael Crichton. MGM/UA Home Entertainment, 1998. DVD.

Alienating Sex: The Discourse of Sexuality in the Works of Octavia Butler

Anca Rosu

Octavia Butler confessed, in more than one interview, that she always wondered how aliens had sex.[1] This may be the reason why sexuality is always a high stake in her novels, and critics never fail to admire her inventiveness in the matter. Yet some find Butler's depiction of sexual relations wanting, in that it does not deal directly with homosexuality. Biologist Joan Slonczewski, for instance, finds the absence of "non-procreative forms of sexuality" in Butler's works "overly conservative" (par. 15). Yet, as Patricia Melzer observes, "homosexuality and heterosexuality become insufficient labels to categorize sexual encounters between five people of two species and three gender/sexes" (86). Melzer follows Eric White, who declares, "Undoing the privileging of genital over other erogenous zones, alien sex is polymorphously perverse" (404). His characterization of alien sex implies a frame of reference in which the "perverse" is a deviation from the "normal," and it is precisely the norms regarding sexuality that become dubious in Butler's work. Slonczewski, Melzer, and White, as most of Butler's critics, mention sex within larger discussions about gender, race, identity, and social issues, which sometimes obscure its full importance for her imagined worlds. It is perhaps necessary to reconfigure the critical discussion of her novels and focus directly on sexuality in order to fully understand how Butler deconstructs ideas about sexual normality prevalent in Western cultures.

As Michel Foucault demonstrates in the first volume of *The History of Sexuality*, the notion of "normal sex" emerged in the seventeenth century as an element of discourse. "Discourse," as he explains in "The Order of Discourse," "far from being that transparent or neutral element in which sexuality is disarmed and politics is pacified, is in fact one of the places where sexuality and politics exercise in a privileged way some of their most formidable powers" (52). Foucault's assertions go against the common view of language as a representation of reality. As Sara Mills put it, "Discourse does not simply translate reality into language; rather discourse should be seen as a system which structures the way we perceive reality" (55). There are multiple discourses in any society, and they are specific to various disciplines: "Discourses must be treated as discontinuous practices, which cross each other, are sometimes juxtaposed to one another, but can just as well exclude or be unaware of each other" (Foucault "The Order of Discourse" 67). The "order of discourse" is thus a complex system in which the discourses of various disciplines intersect and interact with each other, influencing, and sometimes determining, the way a civilization sees its world. What Foucault calls "the discourse of sexuality" is not unitary but consists of a plurality of discourses: "literary, religious or ethical, biological or medical, juridical too — where sexuality is discussed, and where it is named, described, metaphorised, explained, judged" (72).

Science fiction constructs other worlds, with different social structures and alternate orders of discourse. In Butler's work, however, the alternate social structure is so minimalistic as to give the impression that there is no "order of discourse" at all. Her deconstruction of "normal sexuality" is predicated upon an attempt to eliminate the entire set of social perceptions, discursive practices, and power relations comprised in that order. This attempt is ultimately futile, for however otherworldly the subject matter, writing must draw upon a discourse. Nevertheless, the effort is worthwhile, as the discourse of sexuality reemerges within the fabric of Butler's texts in various guises that reveal both its untenable assumptions and the power relations it masks.

Butler's *Patternist* series sprang from the author's interest in telepathy and extrasensory perception — two abilities that bypass verbal communication and enable a social order where discourses seem to have no place. The first novel in this series, *Patternmaster*, takes place at the end of an unexplained turn in human evolution. In a distant future, humanity shares the world with two other species that have evolved from it: the patternists, who are highly intelligent, telepathic, and hierarchically organized; and the clayarks, who are animal-like creatures, physically strong and with keen senses but no exceptional mental capabilities. The patternists' various struggles for power generate the novel's plot. As they communicate directly from one mind to another, the patternists' relationships amount to raw power struggles waged mind to mind. The whole discursive scaffolding of our society is replaced by a much simpler structure: there are no institutions, no moral concerns, and no religion.

This simplified structure leaves out a large part of the discursive mechanisms that regulate sex in our culture, and it raises the question: what happens to the discourse of sexuality if the order that generates it does not exist? Following Foucault, it can be said that, since this complex discourse has a history, its disappearance is not out of the question. Yet the future, as seen in *Patternmaster*, does not reinvent "sex"; rather, it relies on a view of sexual relations reminiscent of the Middle Ages. Referring to medieval society in *The History of Sexuality*, Foucault points out that it was ruled by "blood" rather than "sex" relations: "For a society in which the systems of alliance, the political form of the sovereign, the differentiation into orders and castes, and the value of descent lines were predominant; for a society in which famine, epidemics, and violence made death imminent, blood constituted one of the fundamental values" (147). Although "blood" can be considered natural, indicating genetic heritage, its value in medieval society is mainly symbolic. It establishes who inherits what and functions as a guarantee of maintaining a particular social order. As "blood," sexuality thus plays an overt role in the power structure of the medieval society. Under capitalism, this involvement with power continues, but a whole system of professional discourses works to obscure sexuality's relation to the political and social aspects. Foucault describes the society of "sex" in contrast with the society of "blood": "Through the themes of health, progeny and race, the future of the species, the vitality of the social body, power spoke of sexuality and to sexuality; the latter was not a mark or a symbol, it was an object and a target" (147). With the development of capitalism comes thus a discourse that robs sex/blood of its symbolic value, even as it buries it under a host of symbolic representations.

Butler's future society, where sex functions similarly to "blood," restores sexuality to its status as symbol rather than target of power. The patternists live in "houses," reminiscent of medieval clans, where the strongest mind rules the others. Their sexual behavior seems to bear all the marks of sixties' liberating ideology: people choose their partners according to their inclinations. They express their desires directly and are free to refuse any sexual transaction. There are, however, some notable exceptions, since, under this thin veneer of freedom, lie old restrictions: "The laws were old, made in harsher times. Perhaps it was reasonable, as the old records said, to forbid weak men to sire potentially weak children. But what reason could there be for denying a man access to his chosen one, his first, while permitting him so many others?" (*Patternmaster* 30). Sexual taboos start by controlling reproduction, but they develop into means of pure control. The laws about sex are, above all, ways in which the master of the house, who has rights similar to the *droit-du-seigneur*, expresses his or her power. Hence sexuality regains its place among the symbols of power, subverting the present day discourse, which places sex in the private sphere and thus separates it from the (public) political arena.

As mentioned above, *Patternmaster* presents the readers with a society imaginable by analogy with the power hierarchies of the Middle Ages. In contrast, *Mind of My Mind*, the second book in the series, in which Butler fills in the missing explanation of the patternists' origins, takes place in a contemporary setting, though the characters are all outside the mainstream.[2] They form a fringe society whose rules are established and enforced by the main character, Doro. This abstraction from mainstream social life situates this novel and its prequel, *Wild Seed*, in an unfamiliar social milieu, also deprived of its "order of discourse." The sexual relations in these two texts are as different from the general view on them as they were in *Patternmaster*. More obviously than the patternists, Doro controls reproduction for a large group of seemingly abnormal people. From a mainstream point of view, Doro's sexuality appears, to say the least, eccentric. It violates all familiar sexual taboos of contemporary society: promiscuity, prostitution, adultery, incest, rape, and even child abuse. Frances Bonner finds that "the incest is muted not only by Doro's endorsement of it as part of his breeding plans, but by his 'wearing' different bodies — the body which sleeps with the daughter is not the one which engendered her" (57). Of course, the supernatural elements help dull the edge, as it were, but the abuse is quite obvious and could be excused, in the context of the novel, only by its higher purpose. Doro, however, does not make any excuses for it. As Bonner notes, Doro wants to breed a new race, his own people, among whom his own identity can be validated. Guided by this purpose, he disregards people's desires or interests and robs them of their reproductive rights, as well as their chance at intimacy.

Doro manages to get his people's submission through a mixture of seduction and coercion. Even though she is aware of Doro's manipulations as she submits to him, Mary, his daughter, lover, and protégée, speaks about his "love": "His love ... it lasts as long as I do what he tells me" (*Mind of My Mind* 196). Love thus appears close to a master/slave relationship, conditioned by the submission of the weaker partner. This type of relationship is common between the emerging patternists and the ordinary people, whose minds they are able to manipulate. Doro not only breeds a new race but, in doing so, he also creates a means of subduing and subjecting others.

This seduction/subjection takes the place of love in the sexual relationships that develop between characters. Even when they approach authenticity, sex scenes make the reader doubt the whole notion of love. After an enforced cohabitation with Karl, the husband Doro had chosen for her, Mary decides to claim his love:

> "Why did you stay?"
> "You know why. I wanted to be with you."
> "The husband he chose for you."
> "Yeah." I turned to face him. "Stupid me, falling in love with my own husband" [*Mind of My Mind* 183].

This dialogue could easily come out of a Harlequin romance. As Linda Barlow and Jayne Ann Krentz point out,

> Romance novels are often criticized for certain plot elements that occur over and over again in the genre — spirited young women forced into marriage with mysterious earls and heroes with dark and dangerous pasts who are bent upon vengeance rather than love. It is possible to write a romance that does not utilize these elements; indeed, it's done all the time. But the books that hit the bestseller list are invariably those with plots that place an innocent young woman at risk with a powerful, enigmatic male. Her future happiness and *his* depend upon her ability to teach him how to love [17].

Mary's story follows the general lines of this typical plot, but it is laden with various ironies. Mary is far from being innocent and too cynical to fall prey to romantic feelings. Her offer of love is qualified by her power, which she knows to be greater than Karl's, albeit not yet manifest. Thus the romance becomes an act of subjection disguised as submission — that is, a seduction. In *Seduction*, Jean Baudrillard plays with the idea of a different perspective on the relationships between genders. From his perspective, seduction is a way to change the seat of power and reverse all familiar hierarchies: "Seduction is stronger than power because it is reversible and mortal, while power, like value, seeks to be irreversible, cumulative and immortal" (46). In seduction, the power relation is reversible, allowing the weaker party (in this case, Karl) to take the upper hand, if only temporarily.

Mary succeeds in seducing Karl, and the lovemaking that follows has, again, many of the marks of a romance novel: "We seemed to flow together — frighteningly at first. I felt as though I were losing myself, combining so thoroughly with him that I wouldn't be able to free myself again" (*Mind of My Mind* 184). In this scene, the minds of the two lovers fuse in cerebral union that transcends their personalities and runs on the heels of the romantic idea of merging souls, where the body is just an instrument that enacts a higher love.

In the modern discourse of sexuality, there is no more thorough attempt to mask power interests than the notion of romantic love. In her spirited polemic *Against Love*, Laura Kipnis argues that, contrary to the popular belief that love is natural and an affirmation of individuality, an analysis of its representations in various texts unveils its economic, social, and political underpinnings. Observing the *quasi*-propagandistic promotion of romantic love through art, literature, music, and movies, Kipnis asks, "But if pledging oneself to love is the human spirit triumphal, or human nature, or consummately 'normal,' why does it require such vast PR expenditures?" (34). Kipnis' polemical tone touches the core of deeply entrenched beliefs. Her questions at once expose the assumptions about the nature of romantic love and attribute to it a blatantly ideological function in contemporary society. Thus she reveals a power dynamic in the so-called matters of the heart closely akin to Butler's representations of sexuality.

In this view, not only does romantic love hide the entanglements of power and sex, but it also offers a complex look at relations of power in general. Nancy Armstrong points to the influence of Rousseau's social contract on the (then) new ideology of love: "When it took the form of domestic fiction rather than political theory, however, the [social] contract enjoyed a different fate. The contradictions inherent in theory eventually changed the way in which people understood sexual relationships. It could be said that the social contract lives on as a sexual contract even today" (30). Rousseau's original theory hypothesized a state where the social contract did not already exist, and people decided to enter into one freely. When it comes to the relations between men and women, however, the situation is no longer hypothetical. When getting married, the man and the woman enter an actual contract. Armstrong argues that the novel, as a genre, provided a framework for this contract to be negotiated. It gave women power, but only within the confines of the home. This domestic power was not so much a counterpart of men's public power as it was a consolation prize. Women's insistence on romantic feelings was a way to claim that prize. The notion of love developing at this point in history is, according to Armstrong, qualitatively different from other representations it may have known before. Armstrong also points out that Rousseau's contract was built on contradictions, which were then inherited by the sexual contract. The romance genre is based on the same contradictions, and it invokes love as their imaginary solution.

The *Patternist* series can be regarded as a struggle with and against the ideology of romantic love. Butler adulterates sexual relationships, and this subtle twisting of the familiar images of love unmasks the power mechanisms at the heart of romance. While romance presupposes a permanent and unbreakable contract, in Butler's *Patternist* series, monogamy is hardly achievable, and all the other possible forms of sexuality prevail. Promiscuity, the exchange of partners, and incest all debunk both notions of romantic love and the Freudian family narrative. The immortality of some characters shows a distorting mirror to the claim romantic love is eternal. Butler's attempt to invent a society stripped of discursive encumbrances, such as "love," gives the romantic interludes a different meaning than they would have in a romance novel. If in our society's discourse romance masks the power struggles between sexes, in Butler's novels, the romance reveals its doubtful premises.

Another ironically framed love scene takes place in *Wild Seed*, which takes the story further back in time, when Doro meets Anyanwu. Doro is the mind that jumped out of his body before he died, and continues to jump from body to body, all the while killing the minds he displaces. He has no body, but wears many. In contrast, Anyanwu has a persistent, if changeable, body. She uses her mind to change it at a molecular level, transforming herself into older or younger forms, animals, or even a masculine self. Although her abilities are comparable to Doro's, and her longevity allows her to be his equal over centuries, Anyanwu eventually becomes his victim, too. After an initial disappointment, when he forces her to marry one of his sons, Anyanwu tries to win her freedom by hiding from Doro and living as a man. Inevitably, he finds her again, and in a romantic interlude, he enslaves her completely: "And there was Doro with her, touching her as no one had touched her before. It was as though he touched her spirit, enfolding it within himself, spreading the sensation of his touch through every part of her" (*Wild Seed* 257). The description of the mind contact between Doro and Anyanwu is very similar to the scene between Mary and Karl and has the same ironic overlay. Anyanwu hopes that by allowing him to know her mind, she will become his most special companion. She succumbs to the magic of the moment and becomes compassionate for Doro's solitude. Yet the magic is soon dispelled:

> Not until she rested, pleasantly weary, did she begin to realize she was losing herself. It seemed that his restraint had not held. The joining they had enjoyed was not enough for him. He was absorbing her, consuming her, making her part of his own substance. He was the great light, the fire that had englobed her. Now he was killing her, little by little, digesting her little by little [*Wild Seed* 257].

The union of the two spirits ends with a surrender, in which one of the partners' identity is lost, whereas the other threatens to kill and consume her. Whereas in a romance novel this would be a metaphoric description, here it has to be taken literally, since Doro has the ability to annihilate someone else's mind.

Lewis Call argues that the relationship between Doro and Anyanwu is an acceptable form of slavery, since it is consensual, and Anyanwu learns to deal with Doro:

> In short, she learns to eroticize the power relations which exist between her and Doro. By doing so, she alters the basic nature of their relationship. The erotic power which begins to flow between Anyanwu and Doro becomes entirely distinct from the ethically problematic forms of power which Butler described in the previous *Patternmaster* books. For one thing, this erotic power is far more consensual than the other kind. Anyanwu frequently resists Doro's attempts to incorporate her into his nonconsensual breeding programme. But she willingly becomes his erotic slave [284].

As an analogy, the equation of erotic and master/slave relationships can emphasize one pole or the other, and Call invokes Hegel's master/slave dialectic as his model. Call's point departs significantly, however, from Hegel. Hegel's work has been interpreted in many ways, but the idea that it puts the slave in a desirable position is hard to accept. Call does not entirely miss the irony of the situation, and his argument may serve to highlight the reversibility of romantic relationships. This reversibility does not, however, justify Doro's attitudes or make him a victim. He remains driven by a need to enslave others.

Doro's search for identity has the force of a biological imperative, which finds a literal illustration in *Clay's Ark*, where Butler explains the origins of the clayarks. Eli, the only surviving astronaut of Clay's Ark, a returning spaceship, is infected with an extraterrestrial microorganism, which gives him an extreme sexual appetite: "His body demanded that he go to the woman. He understood the demand, the drive, but he refused to be just an animal governed by instinct" (*Clay's Ark* 18). The presence of the instinctual drive and the control exercised over it put this incident and others like it in a Freudian context where the superego controls the id. The implication is that there is a struggle between the two, and instinct is beginning to win over. Donna Haraway notices a kinship between Butler's scenario and Richard Dawkins' biological theory: "Indeed, *Clay's Ark* reads like *The Extended Phenotype*; the invaders seem disturbingly like the 'ultimate' unit of selection that haunts the biopolitical imaginations of postmodern evolutionary theorists and economic planners" (226). Haraway regards the extraterrestrial microorganism as an invader, looking for hosts to ensure its survival, much like Dawkins' "selfish gene." No fan of Dawkins, however, Haraway finds Butler's work to be an exploration that exposes the assumptions of sociobiology rather than endorsing them.[3]

Together with the "biopolitical imaginations of postmodern evolutionary theorists," *Clay's Ark* also exposes many untenable assumptions about sexuality (Haraway 226). Eli has been conditioned to think of sex as regulated by prohibitions and taboos, which, as Foucault shows, were introduced in the seventeenth century, a period "...characterized by the advent of the great prohibitions, the exclusive promotion of adult marital sexuality, the imperatives of decency, the obligatory concealment of the body, the reduction to silence and mandatory reticences of language" (*The History of Sexuality* 115). The emerging discourse of sexuality consisted of a series of mechanisms meant to ensure the labor force necessary for capitalist development. Among other ideas, it produced a notion of sex that is supposedly rooted in biology, although it clearly caters to the economic needs of early capitalism. Although Eli belongs in a time of sexual liberation, he clings to the notion of channeling sexual energy into marriage. He keeps remembering his dead wife and hesitates to obey the sexual impulses caused by the microorganism. When the biology of the alien microorganism leads to rampant sexual encounters and uncontrolled reproduction, it becomes evident that restricting sexuality to marriage is not a biological necessity but a social one. For instead of producing a disciplined labor force, those driven by the virus' biology generate another species, one which will have no part in perpetuating the capitalist system.

Sara Outterson notes the inner conflicts caused by the extraterrestrial virus: "Yet the horror and self-disgust that the infected humans feel for themselves and for their four-legged, cat-like children cannot prevent them from fulfilling their new biological imperative. They must infect the rest of humanity; they have no choice" (438). The infection the main characters try so hard to contain undermines the social order and destroys the order of discourse. Due to the biology of the microorganism, people regress to atavistic behavior, and violence displaces verbal communication. The biological imperative eradicates thus the very discourse that constrains sex by invoking biology.

If the *Patternist* series works toward eliminating the "order of discourse," the absence of such order is the very premise of the *Xenogenesis* trilogy, since the Oankali aliens do not possess one.[4] Representing this absence is not easy, as the Oankali are revealed to the surviving humans through the mediation of discourse. Among themselves, the Oankali communicate through touch. Touch is also their way to learn and know. Nolan Belk uses Audre Lorde's notion of "the erotic" to describe the kind of knowledge that prevails among the Oankali:

> For Lorde, the erotic nature of the body — that is the body's ability to "know" without thought what it desires — has been too long relegated to the realm of sexuality. Surely it belongs there — and the Oankali who personify the power of the erotic certainly emphasize the importance of a sexual connection. However, the true power of the erotic comes through following its lead against the world of logic that has chosen to ignore it [376].

For Belk, it is important to show that the Oankali do not reduce knowledge to reason, but knowledge of/through the body implies more than the absence of rationality. It renders unnecessary the whole "order of discourse." The relegation of this type of knowledge to sexuality is no longer the issue when the very order in which sex could be defined is not there. In the behavior of the Oankali, sexuality is not different from a lot of other activities. They use their hyper-sensual/sensitive bodies to investigate, to heal, to give commands, or to give pleasure. As Melzer points out, "Oankali sexuality is physically decentralized: sexual activities are not concentrated on sexual organs. Ooloi-produced stimulation includes the whole body surface" (86). Pleasure itself is not necessarily sexual, but polymorphous, to use White's word.

Having no discourse about sex, the Oankali seek only the fulfillment of their biological need to combine with other species and diversify their genetic pool. Yet body knowledge does not help in communicating with the Humans, who can barely bring themselves to touch the Oankali. The genetic trade cannot be forced, and the Oankali have to learn to speak Human languages, as well as transform their bodies to resemble, however vaguely, the Human form. Most of all, they have to struggle and translate their biological imperative into cultural terms specific to Humanity. The order of discourse, in which sexuality is conceptualized, is thus reinstated in the relationship between the Oankali and the Humans.

This relationship has variously been seen as enslavement, colonization, or symbiosis. Christina Braid, for instance, emphasizes the violence of the relationship: "Obsessed with their newfound biological possessions, the aliens treat the Humans like an animal species that is greedily adopted to satisfy alien pleasure" (59). Jim Miller highlights the similarity of the novels with slave narratives:

> These novels mix the typical science-fiction "space alien" story with elements of the slave narrative, the Genesis story, the nature/culture debate, utopian/dystopian tales, captivity narratives, and more. Butler's aliens are both colonizers and a Utopian collective, while the captured/saved humans are both admirable survivors and ugly xenophobes [339–40].

Laurel Bollinger, on the other hand, sees a positive aspect in the relationship and describes it as symbiotic, following Butler's own cues: "Butler uses symbiosis as a tool for establishing that power and submission are finally 'about' subjectivity, and ultimately about intersubjective fusion" (332). All critics, however, highlight the ambiguity of the relationship and its many possible interpretations. It is this very ambiguity that power relations, as represented in the trilogy, share with the representations of sex. Speaking about Butler's short story "Bloodchild," Eva Cherniavsky focuses on the word "trade," which the aliens use to designate their demands from the Humans: "Like *Dawn*, 'Bloodchild' posits a hypothetical mode of material exchange, what Butler calls 'trade,' to investigate the forms of both intimate (familial) and economic relation such a trade would require and enable" (43). The power plays assumed in economic relations extend to intimacy, wrapped as they are in discursive dissimulations.

The genetic trade between the two species in the *Xenogenesis* series assumes thus the familiar representations of sexuality and develops into an interspecies romance. Here is how the ooloi, Nikanj, explains the meaning of the trade to a man:

> "We ... do need you," Nikanj spoke so softly that Joseph leaned forward to hear. "A partner must be biologically interesting, attractive to us, and you are fascinating. You are horror and beauty in rare combination. In a very real way, you've captured us, and we can't escape. But you're more than only the composition and workings of your bodies. You are your personalities, your cultures. We're interested in those too. That's why we saved as many of you as we could" [*Lilith's Brood* 153–54].

What starts as an explanation in a *quasi*-clinical language continues in the language of courtship. The Humans are "attractive," "interesting," and "fascinating." Nikanj assures Joseph that the Oankali are not interested only in their bodies, but also in their cultures, just as any enamored young man would assure a newly found love that she is not only pretty, but also intellectually stimulating. Significantly, Nikanj portrays the Humans as the ones in the position of power. "You've captured us" is a phrase reminiscent of the vocabulary of romantic lovers, who declare themselves conquered, captured, or enslaved. The origin of such phrases in the language of war becomes ironically obvious, since, for some of the Humans, there *is* a war going on, where *they*, and not the Oankali, are the captives.

The Oankali could perform the genetic trade without physical intervention, since they have created copies of the humans that can be used for the purpose, but they insist on the physical contact, on the exchange of pleasure, which, as Sheryl Vint has shown, serves no procreative purpose. Rather, Vint finds that Oankali reproductive processes closely resemble in vitro fertilization (IVF):

> Although the moment of conception is separated from sexual activity in both IVF and Oankali reproduction, in both examples — as IVF is currently used — there remains a relationship of sexual desire between the parents. However, this is not necessary to the practice of reproduction in either case, and could be used as a ground from which to argue for the separation of sexuality and reproduction, undermining discourses which rely on the "natural" status of sexual reproduction to restrict expressions of sexual desire to those activities which lead to reproduction [81].

Vint refers to the discourse of sexuality persisting from the seventeenth century on, which makes reproduction the purpose of sex. Yet this discourse is not limited to the invocation of biology as a way to restrict pleasure. Although its purpose is marriage and the production of children, romance, an important version of that discourse, emphasizes pleasure and feelings. The discourse of romance is re-established by the Oankali for the benefit of the courted humans. The courtship itself seems unnecessary since the oolois have the power to chemically induce Humans to do anything. Yet like any romantic lover, the ooloi is not satisfied with blind submission but indulges in elaborate rituals of seduction to gain consent. Lilith, the heroine of *Dawn*, who is otherwise unsentimental, finds Nikanj's invitation to join it and Joseph on the bed irresistible: "She thought there could be nothing more seductive than an ooloi speaking in that particular tone, making that particular suggestion…. She did not pretend outwardly or to herself that she would resist Nikanj's invitation — or that she wanted to resist it" (*Lilith's Brood* 161). Unlike Eli in *Clay's Ark*, Lilith is not only driven by a biologic, albeit alien, impulse, but she is also seduced. It should be noted as well that, although Butler always insisted that the ooloi is a third sex, and Laurel Bollinger likened it to the placenta in its role as a mediator between self and other, in these romantic scenes, the ooloi appears definitely masculine (340). As Cherniavky points out, "In part, the novelty of interspecies trade lies in the way that a feminized posture of psychic and corporeal receptivity becomes the new standard of human commercial functionality, to the detriment of industrial capitalism's gender and sexual disciplines" (43). It is not only the women but the men as well that are used for reproduction and the engendering of the new species. This upsets the men more than it does the women, though some do surrender to the seductions of the ooloi.

The use of clinical vocabulary in the process of negotiating sex is added to the romantic conventions to resurrect the discourse of sexuality in a new guise. Here is how Nikanj explains the sexual pleasure it has shared with the Humans: "'Interpretation. Electrochemical stimulation of certain nerves, certain parts of your brain.... What happened was real. Your body knows how real it was. Your interpretations were illusion. The sensations were entirely real. You can have them again — or you can have others'" (*Lilith's Brood* 188). The ooloi's efforts to communicate reiterate one of the moments in Foucault's *History of Sexuality*. The development of a clinical vocabulary about sex served not only to bring unusual sexual behavior into discourse but also to elicit pleasure for the clinician involved in extracting the particulars:

> The power which thus took charge of sexuality set about contacting bodies, caressing them with its eyes, intensifying areas, electrifying surfaces, dramatizing troubled moments. It wrapped the sexual body in its embrace. There was undoubtedly an increase in effectiveness and an extension of the domain controlled; but also a sensualization of power and a gain of pleasure [44].

This insight reveals the ulterior motives of the medical discourse and, at the same time, it describes with uncanny accuracy the courtship of two Humans by another ooloi, Jodahs. Its story is complicated by the fact that it is a Human/Oankali construct in dire need of Human sexual partners. Jodahs uses medical discourse to seduce the two siblings it stumbles upon in its wanderings, starting with a persuasive diagnosis:

> "Why do you say he would go blind or deaf?" Jesusa demanded. "He may not. You don't know."
> "Of course, I know. I couldn't touch him and not know. And I know there was a time when he could see out of his right eye and hear with his right ear. There was a time when the mass on his shoulder was smaller and his arm wasn't involved at all. He will be blind and deaf and without the use of his right arm — and he knows it. So do you" [*Lilith's Brood* 621].

In a parenthetical remark, Cathy Peppers invites us to "note the use of romance discourse in a scene where [Jodahs] seduces a human mate" (60). In addition to being romantic, Jodahs' courtship of Tomas and Jesusa is performed almost exclusively through medical talk. It diagnoses their diseases and explains how it is uniquely qualified to heal them. The two Humans, who are otherwise determined not to divulge their secrets, confess to Jodahs in the manner patients reveal their sexual habits to the doctors mentioned by Foucault. As a result of the exchange, Jodahs finds out about the community of survivors that escaped the Oankali sterilization. It finds out about the incest and the inbreeding, and it eventually enables the Oankali to "save" the villagers from the ills of their stubborn resistance.

Jodahs acts according to its biological imperative, and the fact that the story is narrated by it gives readers a glimpse into its own feelings, which are a mixture of medical curiosity and desire: "The smell-taste-feel of Jesusa, the rhythm of her heartbeat, the rush of her blood, the texture of her flesh, the easy, right, self-sustaining working of her organs, her cells, the smallest organelles within her cells — all this was a vast, infinitely absorbing complexity" (*Lilith's Brood* 678). Yet the desire to heal is mixed with the desire to possess. The sentence starts as a romantic declaration of love, gushing with metaphors; however, it rapidly turns into a clinical description and becomes frightfully literal. The clinical discourse used to seduce also has the effect of giving the ooloi pleasure. As in its diagnosis of Tomas, Jodahs proceeds without permission, penetrating Jesusa's cells with unrestrained curiosity. It is difficult to judge Jodahs by human moral standards. It does nothing wrong, according to its ethos based on a biological imperative, which does not allow it to have an identity until it finds mates. Its sibling, less fortunate than Jodahs, wanders aimlessly and transforms to the point of becoming a slug with no biological identity. In this instance, sexuality is the main component of identity. As in the case of Doro, the ooloi establishes its identity at the expense of the identities of the beloved ones.

Beyond the romance conventions that are exposed as power plays, and beyond the medical discourse that blatantly targets sexuality, the *Xenogenesis* trilogy also literalizes the biological basis of sex and exposes it as an untenable assumption. The Oankali are aware that Human sexual bonds are not biological:

> "But Human mates can walk away from one another," Dichaan said. "They never lose the ability to do that. They can leave one another permanently and find new mates. Humans can take the mates from other Humans. There's no physical bond. No security. And because Humans are hierarchical, they tend to compete for mates and property" [*Lilith's Brood* 595–96].

Dichaan's explanation of the sexual relationships among Humans shows they belong in "the order of discourse" and lack the biological bond. It is the

Oankali who exemplify what it would be like if sexual relations were only biological: groups permanently fixed for the purpose of reproduction. Yet it is precisely these groups that the Humans reject, in spite of their desire to have children. The idea of letting themselves be slaves to their biology is repulsive to those who resist the Oankali, and even to those who have accepted the trade. The sexuality of the aliens is perhaps why Butler's representations give the impression of supporting conservative ideas. Slonczewski points out that "the Oankali are not our opposites, but rather an extension of some of humanity's most extreme tendencies.... Humans[,] in the traditional Western Christian view, consider procreation the sole function of sexuality. The Oankali ... basically share this view" (par 14). Her objection is based on the assumption that the Oankali are intended as an ideal alternative to humanity. Yet Butler's invocation of biology only demonstrates that such a reduction is far from acceptable in Human terms.

As Butler's aliens reinstate, at least partially, the discourse of sexuality — the romance, the clinical discourse, and the relations of power comprised in them — the repressed discursive order returns, but it is, in more ways than one, alienated. The notion of sexuality that emerges from her work is a paradigm for power struggles in which players vie for control. This notion adds itself to the existent discourse, for even as they reflect critically on the discourse of sexuality, Butler's works become part of it. Foucault characterizes discourse as, "both an instrument and an effect of power, but also a hindrance, a stumbling-block, a point of resistance and a starting point for an opposing strategy" (*The History of Sexuality* 101). Butler's contribution to the discourse of sexuality is one such point of resistance.

Notes

1. Examples of these include interviews with Butler in 1998, 2000, and 2006, as well as interviews by Potts and Sanders. See Works Cited for complete information.

2. The *Patternist* series contains four novels, which are prequels rather than sequels to each other. I have discussed them in the order of publication, using the originals as my bibliographic references, since Butler's thinking on sexuality and other matters evolved as she matured as a writer. The novels have been published in a single book entitled *Seed to Harvest* (2007), which deploys them in the order of the events.

3. Sociobiology is based on the controversial assumption that human behavior is rooted in biology. It is, however, a more nuanced approach than social Darwinism. Richard Dawkins' *The Selfish Gene*, for instance, proposes the idea that the struggle for survival takes place at the level of the gene rather than of the entire organism. People, as well as animals, can display behavior that goes counter to their own interests, if such behavior ensures the survival of the species. Butler's work is definitely influenced by such theories, but her biology-related metaphors are much looser, and her political position is closer to that of the critics of sociobiology, such as Donna Haraway.

4. The trilogy containing the novels *Dawn* (1987), *Adulthood Rites* (1988), and *Imago*

(1989) has been called *Xenogenesis* by Butler's critics. It derives from the initial title of the first novel, *Dawn: Xenogenesis*. The trilogy was published in a single book as *Lilith's Brood* in 2000. I have used this latest edition for my bibliographic references but called the trilogy *Xenogenesis* to maintain the tradition created by the critics I have quoted.

Works Cited

Armstrong, Nancy. *Desire and Domestic Fiction: A Political History of the Novel*. New York: Oxford University Press, 1989. Print.
Barlow, Linda, and Jayne Ann Krentz. "Beneath the Surface. The Hidden Codes of Romance." *Dangerous Men and Adventurous Women*. Ed. Jayne Ann Krentz. Philadelphia: University of Pennsylvania Press, 1992. 15–30. Print.
Baudrillard, Jean. *Seduction*. Trans. Brian Singer. New York: St. Martin's Press, 1990. Print.
Belk, Nolan. "The Certainty of the Flesh: Octavia Butler's Use of the Erotic in the *Xenogenesis* Trilogy." *Utopian Studies* 19.3 (2008): 369–89. Print.
Bollinger, Laurel. "Placental Economy: Octavia Butler, Luce Irigaray, and Speculative Subjectivity." *LIT: Literature, Interpretation, Theory* 18.4 (2007): 325–352. Print.
Bonner, Frances. "Difference and Desire, Slavery and Seduction: Octavia Butler's *Xenogenesis*." *Foundation* 48 (Spring 1990): 50–62. Print.
Braid, Christina. "Contemplating and Contesting Violence in Dystopia: Violence in Octavia Butler's *Xenogenesis* Trilogy." *Contemporary Justice Review* 9.1 (2006): 47–65. Print.
Butler, Octavia E. *Bloodchild and Other Stories*. 2d ed. New York: Seven Stories Press, 2005. Print.
_____. *Clay's Ark*. New York: Warner Books, 1984. Print.
_____. "Interview with Octavia Butler." *Papercut by Woo Themes*. Addicted to Race. 6 Feb. 2006. Web. 23 Jan. 2011. <http://www.addictedtorace.com/2006/02/06/atr-15-%E2%80%93-feb-6-2006-voicemail-206-203-3983-addictedtoracegmailcom/.
_____. *Lilith's Brood*. New York: Aspect/Warner Books, 2000. Print.
_____. *Mind of My Mind*. New York: Aspect/Warner Books, 1977. Print.
_____. "Octavia Butler 1998." *Index Magazine*. Index Worldwide. Index Magazine. 1998. Web. 26 Jan. 2011. http://www.indexmagazine.com/interviews/octavia_butler.shtml.
_____. "Octavia E. Butler: Persistence." *Locus Online*. Locus Magazine. June 2000. Web. 23 Jan. 2011. http://www.locusmag.com/2000/Issues/06/Butler.html.
_____. *Patternmaster*. New York: Aspect/Warner Books, 1976. Print.
_____. *Wild Seed*. New York and Boston: Aspect/Warner Books, 1980. Print.
Call, Lewis. "Structures of Desire: Erotic Power in the Speculative Fiction of Octavia Butler and Samuel Delany." *Rethinking History* 9.2/3 (2005): 275–296. Print.
Cherniavsky, Eva. *Incorporations: Race, Nation, and the Body Politics of Capital*. Minneapolis: University of Minnesota Press, 2006. Print.
Dawkins, Richard. *The Selfish Gene*. 2d ed. New York: Oxford University Press, 1989. Print.
Foucault, Michel. *The History of Sexuality. An Introduction*. Vol. I. New York: Random House/Vintage, 1990. Print.
_____. "The Order of Discourse." *Untying the Text: A Post-Structuralist Reader*. Ed. Robert Young. Trans. Ian McLeod. London: Routledge and Kegan Paul, 1981. 48–78. Print.
Haraway, Donna J. *Simians, Cyborgs, and Women: The Reinvention of Nature*. New York: Routledge, 1991. Print.
Kipnis, Laura. *Against Love: A Polemic*. New York: Pantheon Books, 2003. Print.
Melzer, Patricia. *Alien Constructions: Science Fiction and Feminist Thought*. Austin: University of Texas Press, 2006. Print.
Miller, Jim. "Post-Apocalyptic Hoping: Octavia Butler's Dystopian/Utopian Vision." *Science Fiction Studies* 25.2 (1998): 336–360. Print.
Mills, Sara. *Michel Foucault*. London: Routledge, 2005. Print.

Outterson, Sarah. "Diversity, Change, Violence: Octavia Butler's Pedagogical Philosophy." *Utopian Studies* 19.3 (2008): 433–456. Print.
Peppers, Cathy. "Dialogic Origins and Alien Identities in Butler's *Xenogenesis*." *Science Fiction Studies* 22.1 (1995): 47–62. Print.
Potts, Stephen W. "'We Keep Playing the Same Record': A Conversation with Octavia E. Butler." *Science Fiction Studies* 23.70 (Nov. 1996). Web. 23 Jan. 2011. http://www.depauw.edu/sfs/interviews/potts70interview.htm.
Sanders, Joshunda. "Interview with Octavia Butler." *In Motion Magazine. Art Changes*. 14 Mar. 2004. Web. 23 Jan. 2011. http://www.inmotionmagazine.com/ac04/obutler.html.
Slonczewski, Joan. "Octavia Butler's *Xenogenesis* Trilogy: A Biologist's Response." June 2000. Web. 23 Jan. 2011 http://biology.kenyon.edu/slonc/books/butler1.html#top Digital file.
Vint, Sherryl. *Bodies of Tomorrow: Technology, Subjectivity, Science Fiction*. Toronto: University of Toronto Press, 2006. Print.
White, Eric. "The Erotics of Becoming." *Science Fiction Studies* 20 (1993): 394–408. Print.

"We pair off! One man, one woman": The Heterosexual Imperative in Octavia Butler's Xenogenesis Trilogy
Echo E. Savage

> *No wonder we need aliens.*
> *No wonder we're so good at creating aliens.*
> *No wonder we so often project alienness onto one another.*
> *This last of course has been the worst of our problems — the human alien from another culture, country, gender, race, ethnicity. This is the tangible alien who can be hurt or killed.*
>   OCTAVIA BUTLER, "THE MONOPHOBIC RESPONSE"

In a 1997 interview with Charles H. Rowell, Octavia Butler declared that as she embarks upon new projects she finds herself, time and again, motivated by the desire to "tell a good story about a strange community of people," but noted that, of course, this is not all she is attempting to do (63). Along with telling good stories about strange groups of people, Butler's work is consistently concerned with telling good stories about *estranged* groups of people — people whose experience as the societal Other precludes them from easily accessing positions of social power and agency. Writing within the genre of science fiction allows Butler to do more than simply tell stories — it allows her to access a space of unbounded potential for re-visioning alternate realities that invert and unseat established frameworks of power. In Butler's fictional worlds the estranged are offered a subjectivity that is systematically denied them in the empirical reality from which she writes. It is important to recognize, however, that there is a utility in this work that is ambitious beyond the desire to simply tell a good story or imagine chimerical futures. Kodwo Eshun warns that "it would be naïve to understand science fiction ... as merely prediction into the far future, or as a utopian project for imagining alternative social realities" (290). Certainly, however, envisioning different realities in futuristic settings is imbued with a political valence, for conceptualizing alternative ways of being is at the center of any effort to mitigate an unsatisfying reality. Eshun addresses this aspect of the genre by citing William Gibson's belief that science fiction functions as a vehicle through which to "preprogram the present," adding that the genre is particularly concerned with "engineering feedback between its preferred future and its becoming present" (290). Butler's devotion to her work is heavily tied to her investment in affecting the "becoming present" Eshun mentions. The revised reality Butler hopes to realize is one that witnesses a long-awaited erasure of institutional oppression based on class, race, and gender. However, her vision is not without its blind spots. In this essay I intend to apply a queer reading to Octavia Butler's Xenogenesis Trilogy in order to illuminate and interrogate the ways in which Butler, while successfully destabilizing received notions of gender roles, racialized experience, and the role and perception of the societal Other, simultaneously leaves notions of obligatory heteronormativity relatively unquestioned and unchallenged.[1] As a consequence, I believe a new set of questions arises concerning what is involved in (and what may result from) constructing a blueprint for the becoming present or preferred future that seems unable to envision a space for the queer presence in social communities.

Lamentations over the lack of homosexual representations in science fiction are not particularly new criticisms of the genre; nevertheless, it is particularly noteworthy that Butler's propensity to undermine inequitable or persecutory power structures ultimately fails to challenge heterocentric notions of the human experience.[2] At the center of the Xenogenesis Trilogy is the issue of what Butler terms the "human contradiction"—the volatile mix of human intelligence with what Butler sees as an ultimately fatalistic biological and societal drive to function hierarchically. It is this contradiction that, over the course of terrestrial time, causes the human race to implode, creating global nuclear warfare and causing the near annihilation of the entire species. The few survivors remaining on earth are taken from the ravaged planet by a group of extraterrestrials called the Oankali, who are interested in genetically engineering the human species and their offspring to preserve the complexity of humanity. Once aboard the Oankali ship, the humans are kept unconscious in cocoon-like pods for over two hundred years, at which point they are awakened and begin a grooming process orchestrated by their alien rescuers that is intended to prepare them to both accept alien counterparts and, with their help, evolve into trustworthy stewards of the planet and the species. As the Oankali work to orchestrate the regeneration of humanity, they account for their subjects' predisposition for the human "contradiction" and labor to modify it by hybridizing human offspring (constructs) using a combination of human and Oankali genetic material. Ostensibly, they succeed in this endeavor — the new species of individuals that results is carefully "mixed" to retain only the best, most evolved traits of its respective human and Oankali lineages. For all intents and purposes, the "contradiction" is (throughout the course of the novels) slowly erased. However, I aim to trouble this triumph by arguing that the fact that Butler's communities remain structured in strictly heteronormative ways points to the reinscription of new societies with (selected) old prejudices.

Because Butler is a self-proclaimed feminist as well as the science fiction genre's most prominent black female writer, the critical reception of her work is often inflected by what might be understood as the tacit promise it makes to revise regressive and oppressive notions of race and gender. While critics are frequently quick to commend her work toward this end, many are just as quick to take Butler to task for the means by which she attempts narrative revisions of the position and power of the gendered or raced body, citing essentialist leanings as an unnecessary evil in her imagination of alternate subjectivities. Nancy Jesser, in her essay "Blood, Genes, and Gender in Octavia Butler's *Kindred* and *Dawn*," takes issue with what she understands to be Butler's commitment to biological essentialism, but situates her concerns as primarily relevant to representations of the gendered body rather than the raced body. Jesser asserts that while Butler "undermines racial essentialism as corrupt and unscientific, [she] retains a commitment to a qualified essentialist stance toward the biologically sexed body" (39). Consequently, Jesser cautions against readings of Butler's work that acknowledge progressive re-visions of racial (ir)relevance and then mistakenly imagine a functional correspondence between race and gender which infers that a destabilization of essentialist notions is transferable from one to the other. This is certainly not meant to imply that categorical notions of gender do not matter to Butler, but rather to point toward a need to uncover the ways in which they matter *differently* in the context of her fiction.

In her excavation of Butler's narrative priorities, Jesser posits that for all of the attention given to undermining and unsettling established ideas about, and fears of, difference (racial, experiential, or even inter-species), the one sociobiological variable that remains relevant in Butler's utopias is sex, especially as it relates to reproduction. Ultimately, she notes, "Butler does little to destabilize the scientific reifications of sex/gender and little to dismantle a normative heterosexuality that demands stable sex/gender positions" (40). While the validity of this criticism resonates with a number of Butler's works, it seems important to allow that in the same way that categorical notions of race and gender matter differently within her work, so, too, might reinforcements of the heteronormative matter differently from one text to the next. For example, it may not be constructive to level the same criticisms at *Kin-*

dred—a novel thoroughly tied to ideas of immutable history—that are justifiably brought to bear upon *Dawn* and, for my purposes, the whole of the Xenogenesis Trilogy—novels set in a distant, post-apocalyptic future.

Dawn begins the work of recreating communities of humans out of those few survivors of the war that the Oankali could save from imminent death. After collecting and safely storing pre-war humans in a sort of suspended animation, the Oankali can "awaken" them one by one and organize them into new communities. True to the form of revisionist creation myth, the protagonist of *Dawn* is a woman named Lilith, and she is chosen by the Oankali to aid in the work of acclimating pre-war humans to what will be a very different post-war existence. As she awakens each individual, it is Lilith's job to ensure that they have an understanding of what has occurred, where they are, and what they need to anticipate in order to prepare themselves for meeting the Oankali. As a former anthropologist, Lilith is well-suited for a relatively quick acclimation to interactions with the alien Other, signified, quite literally, by the intervening extraterrestrials. Lilith's adaptability is a byproduct of her propensity for ethnographic approaches to the unfamiliar; this leads toward a hopeful figuring of the human potential to overcome fear of the unfamiliar through rational thought.

To be sure, most of the humans awakened by the Oankali do not possess Lilith's rational, analytical nature. Many of the pre-war humans are terribly unsettled by the "blank" slate of the ungendered, completely (extraterrestrial) alien body, and quickly ascribe to it (and to those humans who interact with it) the identity and experience of what, in their history, might be considered the "terrestrial" alien—the deviant homosexual. The precedent that is established in this exchange—the superiority of the heteronormative—serves to shape the function of the resister villages (populated by those unwilling to accept the presence of the Oankali in Earth's future), the trade villages (populated by those who accept and even welcome the fusion of human culture and genes with Oankali culture and genes), and the contentious and often violent interactions between the two throughout the entirety of the trilogy. In developing this observation throughout the course of my essay, it is my intention to approach an understanding of its import and implications by considering questions raised by Eshun's work of whether it is the function of the science fiction genre not to predict the future, but to shape the progression toward it by offering new possibilities for ways of being and ways of knowing. What does an aggressive insistence upon heteronormative existence in speculative fiction indicate about the importance of allowing for the validity of alternate subjectivities of varied sexualities in societies of the future or even the becoming present? Butler successfully erases the existence of racially or ethnically-based prejudices in her creation of futuristic colonies on Lo, Earth, and Mars, which can be understood as her effort to inform a *realistic* future that follows suit. So, what does it mean that her work in the Xenogenesis Trilogy is decidedly uninterested in undermining, and is perhaps even perpetuating, an insistence upon the heterosexual experience?

In "Utopia, Dystopia, and Ideology in the Science Fiction of Octavia Butler," Hoda M. Zaki posits that Butler's work is not easily (or accurately) read as primarily utopic or dystopic because her fiction consistently evidences a necessary interplay between the two. While the books of Xenogenesis proffer a future society unafflicted by racial enmities, Zaki notes that, "[f]or Butler, there is a pervasive human need to alienate from oneself those who appear to be different — i.e., to create Others" (241). Because this need is at the core of Butler's conception of human hierarchical behavior, it functions as a predisposition that will inevitably reassert itself. Consequently, "the end of racial discrimination must coincide with the rise of some kind of similar discrimination based upon biological differences, which accordingly continue to play a role in future social orders" (241). For Zaki, the waning need to establish a racialized other in Xenogenesis occurs by virtue of the collective fear of the extraterrestrial Other, and the Oankali offer an extreme example of readily observable difference that is easily inducted into the empty space in human orders of power that the raced body formerly occupied. Indeed, the "resister" humans' insistence upon segregation between the species is a dominant narrative thread throughout the books of the series. After all, there is perhaps nothing more alien than the literal, extraterrestrial alien. Yet, I would offer two observations that serve to complicate the simplicity of this assertion. First, it would be remiss to understand the Oankali as the new "raced" Other, for "raced" bodies abound in Butler's new colonies though, ostensibly, the erasure of racialized tensions in futuristic societies is at the center of her project. To read the Oankali through the lens of race prejudice is to, perhaps, undermine Butler's intentions. Second, although the pre-war humans are made notably nervous by the presence (and intentions) of the Oankali, the most unsettling, confusing, and threatening beings are the ooloi members of the community. These ungendered, highly-sexualized beings confound and entice their human counterparts — they confuse notions of discrete gender identities and destabilize conceptions of biologically encoded sexualities. By calling to the surface conflicting human responses of attraction and disgust, the ooloi become the expressly sexualized Other. Consequently, it is my assertion that with the erasure of racial anxieties in Xenogenesis comes the concomitant development of tensions derived from a heteronormative imperative. This occurs primarily because, although the ooloi are genderless, the sexual confusion they cause the pre-war humans to experience requires a framework for interpretation, and while it is certainly *possible* for humans to develop new frameworks to accommodate the unfamiliar, Butler emphasizes that it is also human nature to fall back on pre-established (if often archaic) modes of thinking.

Arguably, highly homophobic tendencies in the text are specific to resister humans. In *Dawn* it is Gabe Rinaldi who is the first to attempt to explain the human insistence upon gendering the un-gendered ooloi, and in doing so he illuminates what appears to be the humans' reflexive impulse to justify fear of the unfamiliar Other by inscribing it with an identity they already know how to hate. In her essay "Alien Cryptographies: The View from Queer," Wendy Pearson offers that a typical trope of the science fiction genre can be found in the storyline that revolves around a human fear of being unable to easily identify the alien in a human community. She notes that essential to the ability to police the boundaries of the normative is the ability to identify that which constitutes the non-normative: "one must be able to identify 'the enemy'" (7). Certainly, the pre-war humans in *Dawn* have no difficulty identifying the alien in the Oankali — they exhibit obvious non-human physical characteristics (notably, their tentacles and scales) that prominently mark their foreignness. Yet, identifying the alien in the ooloi proves a bit more challenging. Though they too retain extraterrestrial physical adaptations (including smaller, filament-like tentacles), theirs remain rather camouflaged by decidedly human likenesses. The fact that the ooloi are members of the Oankali species is, on the one hand, enough to identify them as expressly alien in one capacity, but this fact does not account for the uncanny feelings of anxiety and discomfort they arouse in the humans who begrudgingly find them alluring (feelings that are not aroused through interactions with the non-ooloi Oankali). Pearson argues that, "unlike the differences of race and biological sex, sexual difference is often invisible," making the fear of the "passing" queer in heteronormative societies tantamount (6).[3] For the ooloi, race, biological sex, and sexual difference are all relatively invisible: as obviously alien as the ooloi are in one sense, they simultaneously function as the feared "invisible alien" Pearson discusses. Thus, the sexual anxiety they incite in Butler's human ranks renders them ideal entities for the inscription of a version of queer identity that pre-war societies find fearsome but, just as importantly, familiar.

Gabe explains that while the men on the training floor have been told — and can rationally understand — that the ooloi are not male, the experience of sexual congress with one leaves the human male feeling "taken like a woman," which is an assault on the tenets of inflexible masculine heterosexuality that justifies violent reaction (203). When a man is feminized in this manner, he is stripped of the control that he has been socialized to believe is solely his within sexual interactions. Gabe states that the human male "knows all the sex that goes on is in his head. It doesn't matter ... someone else is pushing all his buttons. He can't let them get away with that" (203).[4] It is important to note, however, that in the process of attracting human males the ooloi do not actually "get away" with anything. They do not assault them, or force them to participate in any interaction that they have not willingly chosen to be part of. Rather, they *seduce* the humans. They engage in them a desire — a longing, even — that is completely unfamiliar, publicly observable, and thus terribly unsettling. Traci N. Castleberry, in an essay examining the role of a third sex in science fiction and its function in *Xenogenesis*, states:

> Human society is hierarchical with men at the top of that hierarchy, and they believe that giving in to the Oankali, no matter how much their bodies want it, means submission and therefore losing their masculinity. That very idea is at the root of homophobia in today's society... [16].

It is Castleberry's position that the third sex (which, in Butler's text, is manifest in the un-sexed or gender neutral ooloi) at once attracts human counterparts physically while repelling them mentally. Indeed, the pre-war humans — especially the males — quickly respond to their own feelings of desire for a very alien sexuality with feelings of disgust for themselves and hatred for the Other who ignites what they experience as perverse desire. Gabe's explanation of the human male's experience of anxiety over potential emasculation highlights the expressly homophobic nature of what his fellow resisters see as necessary, retaliatory violence. In understanding the manifestation of homophobic tendencies within Butler's heternormative society, is important to recognize that Gabe's speech about the brittle nature of human masculinity occupies a position in the novel that is flanked on either side by scenes of grave violence — a violence that I believe can be accurately interpreted, in both instances, as sexually based.

Peter, another pre-war human awakened on the Oankali ship, is certainly affected by Gabe's malaise, and his death, though accidental, is the unfortunate result of his frantic attack upon the ooloi he mates with and then quickly comes to abhor once his attraction to it translates into disgust with himself. Peter becomes convinced that he has been caused "to demean himself in alien perversions. His humanity was profaned. His manhood taken away," and he responds by attacking his ooloi and beating it extensively with his bare fists (192). It is important to note that although Peter was subsequently killed by his ooloi, his death was accidental. As he savagely beat the ooloi (who did not attempt to fight back or purposefully defend itself), his fist struck a sensitive portion of the ooloi's body and triggered a reflexive fatal sting. After Peter's death, Butler notes that his ooloi became immediately catatonic with grief, "and it seemed to be as dead as the human it was apparently mourning" (193). While violent outbursts among the newly awakened humans on the training floor are not uncommon, Peter's assault upon his ooloi is the first altercation to be heavily underwritten by the markers of homophobic anxiety. What Gabe later refers to as being "taken like a woman," Peter understands as a submission to "alien perversions." Although the ooloi are sexless, genderless, and never explicitly referred to as homosexual beings, the phrases noted above, used by human males to describe physical interactions with them, bear striking resemblance to the rhetoric bandied about by anti-gay establishments seeking to call sympathizers to action. While Peter sets the tone for violent reactions against the ooloi, his resulting death constructs him as a sort of martyr for the cause of fiercely protecting what appears to be an increasingly anxious human heterosexuality. This paves the way for what I read as the fear-induced murder of Joseph that takes place near the end of *Dawn*. However, Joseph's death occurs not at the tentacles of an alien being, but rather at the hands of his fellow humans, who are intent on excising what they understand as threats to the natural, heteronormative order.

Joseph's role in the pilot group of reanimated humans is an important one. Through his relationship with Lilith he occupies a position of relative power, as he is allowed information and input that is not available to other newly awakened humans. Yet because a relationship with Lilith also means a relationship with her ooloi, Nikanj, Joseph is identified as a willing participant in the triadic sexual relationship that resister humans view as especially deviant and perverse. In fact, the only blatantly homophobic slur in the entirety of *Xenogenesis* is uttered against Joseph, and he learns of it as Nikanj expresses concern for his safety after overhearing him hatefully referred to as a "faggot" by one of the other human males (159). After Lilith explains to Nikanj what the word means, Nikanj is confused by the accusation and responds by telling Lilith that the other humans "know he's not that. They know he's mated with you" (160). For all that the Oankali understand about human desires and behavior, about their hierarchical drives and propensity for violence, Nikanj's assertion highlights an Oankali ignorance of what Lilith, as a pre-war human, would understand all too well—that knowing rationally that Joseph is "not that" is not the same as understanding emotionally that he is not a threat. This reality becomes painfully clear only after Joseph is brutally murdered, and Lilith stands with Nikanj surveying the grisly scene of his death:

He had been attacked with an ax.
[Lilith] stared, speechless, then rushed to him. He had been hit more than once— blows to the head and neck. His head had been all but severed from his body. He was already cold.
The hatred that someone must have felt for him... [223].

Nikanj confirms Lilith's suspicions that Curt, one of the more volatile members of the group, is the man responsible for Joseph's death. It tells Lilith that it believes the murder was not wholly intentional, and that it shares with

Lilith a responsibility for Joseph's death because their mutual love for him caused the resister humans to question his very humanity.[5] Nikanj's feelings of culpability are specific to the "strengthening" power it imparted to Joseph to protect him against harm, for when Curt observed Joseph's minor injuries begin to heal themselves before his eyes it was only then that he attacked him brutally with the ax. It is my assertion that the moment Curt witnesses Joseph's wounds healing, the "alien perversions" Joseph has embraced become visible on his body and call forth a violent disgust within Curt, much like the disgust Peter felt before launching his own angry attack upon the subject of his discomfort. The parallels between these two events (both born of anxiety over the sexual Other), as well as Butler's inference that the second bears the markers of a hate-based crime, points to the potential allegorical function of the encounters as narratological revisions of what is contemporarily understood as "gay bashing." Moreover, the deaths of Peter and Joseph seem to punctuate Butler's solid establishment of a compulsory heterosexual existence in both human and alien societies that, because it remains relatively stable throughout *Dawn* and the books of Xenogenesis that follow, bears the troubling markers of an essentialism Butler's critics frequently cite as a disappointing aspect of her otherwise progressive fiction.

Michelle Erica Green situates herself in firm opposition to Butler's critics on matters of essentialism. It is her perspective that Xenogenesis is nothing short of "a scathing condemnation of the tendency of humans to hate, repress, and attack differences they do not understand" (166). She argues that Butler works to transform the utopian mode, consistently "challeng[ing] various forms of cultural hegemony" and thus "adapt[ing] it for the purposes of social critique" (167). Certainly, the ways in which Butler attends to the revision of racially- and gender-based hierarchies of power within this futuristic trilogy highlights her own misgivings about the fate of a species with such an antipathetic relationship with difference. Xenogenesis is, in this sense, a sort of cautionary tale: learn to accept and value difference or risk extinction. Where Green smartly observes Butler's diligence in undermining and, thus, critiquing racism, patriarchy, and even humanism, she fails to attend to the implications of the fact that Butler does not undermine heteronormativity. Furthermore, although she does acknowledge that "the only subset of individuals ... who receive any real group hostility are 'faggots,'" she quickly dismisses the importance of this observation by allowing for its inevitability given the biological imperative to procreate (187). Green seems to imply that a reliance on heterosexual default identities should not be considered particularly problematic, since so much of the narrative attends to "the dream of reproducing the species" (187). This is a slippery slope, for an understanding of Butler's heterocentric approach to post-war societies as undeserving of critique based on issues of biology risks undermining the work she has done elsewhere in the text to flout biological arguments for racial or gender inequity. Green's argument is additionally reductive in its failure to acknowledge that biological reproduction is already altered and revised among the post-war human ranks to prevent procreation on Earth that is not Oankali-assisted.

All reproduction on Earth is orchestrated by the Oankali ooloi. It is the ooloi's job to sample reproductive cells from human men and women and effectively "mix" them with Oankali genetic material within its own body before implanting the fertilized embryo back into the mother. Although it is generally the case that two "heterosexual" pairs of parents (one pair human, one Oankali) have decided as a group that it is time to have "construct children" — children that all four of them will raise — it is established early on that this preferred family structure is not actually a necessary one. Lilith is impregnated with the first construct child to be born into the colony when she is effectively single. Though the child she will bear is also Joseph's child, she is not made pregnant until after his death, when she has no human partner at all. It is my assertion that the mechanics of reproduction Green cites as a biological reinforcement of compulsory heterosexuality in Butler's post-war societies in Xenogenesis are exactly what *could*, quite easily, allow for the existence of the varied sexualities that are conspicuously absent throughout the novels. Because the creation of healthy post-war children begins within the body of a veritable surrogate through a scientific "mixing" of DNA, the only aspect of reproduction that remains biologically necessary is the *existence* of men and women from which to collect genetic material; any imperative for them to couple heterosexually is effectively negated. On the one hand, it is perhaps possible to theorize this reality as a progressive movement in the right direction — removing the biological need for heterosexual relationships troubles socially mandated male/female parings. On the other hand, Butler offers no representations of non-heterosexual pairings anywhere in Xenogenesis, leaving any potential for revised notions of the hetero-imperative unrealized.

In "(Re)reading Queerly," Veronica Hollinger notes that despite the fact that science fiction functions "as a literature of cognitive estrangement," rendering the genre particularly suited to narrative revisions of normative experience, "heterosexuality as an institutionalized nexus of human activity remains stubbornly resistant to defamiliarization" (24). Hollinger argues that this continues to be the case in part because of a "totalizing ideological hold" that a privileged heterosexuality maintains on contemporary societies, which makes envisioning an alternate reality, even in an alternate future, difficult (24).[6] Because Butler is so adept at the work of destabilizing conceptions of what is normal and natural, the fact that Xenogenesis fails to shirk the markers of heteronormative inculcation rings curious. Certainly Butler succeeds in imagining functional revisions of family structures that embrace the Other. She creates a society of humans that are compelled to accept difference because the survival of the species depends upon a willingness to adapt to new, unfamiliar ways of being. *Dawn* is Butler's own book of genesis for a future that can only exist after humans revise the grave mistakes that cost them so dearly the first time around. Ostensibly, hers is a demand for more sustainable social structures that reject the bigotry, hatred, and inequity that delimit human potential. Yet, an early declaration made by Curt that everyone must pair up, "one man, one woman," resounds as a vehement assertion that a functional society is a "straight" society. The narrative adherence to this mandate throughout the trilogy (ooloi intermediaries aside) implicates Butler in the perpetuation of hierarchies that privilege the essentially heterosexual experience on the same pages that theoretically aim to indict hierarchical behavior as unevolved and destructive.

Eshun asserts that "powerful descriptions of the future have an increasing ability to draw us toward them, to command us to make them flesh," and Butler's devotion to the genre indicates that she is invested in accessing that potential (291). Her work in Xenogenesis clearly aims to offer a narrative intervention in the becoming present that undermines human justifications for subjugating and persecuting that which is different. While it is important to acknowledge her successes toward this end, it would be imprudent to ignore those shortcomings that threaten its full realization. Yet, my indictment of Butler's contribution to the social, literary, and futuristic stronghold of the heteronormative imperative should not be understood as an effort to devalue the important contributions she makes to the steady destabilization of other oppressive power structures equally in need of methodical deconstruction. While I cannot rightly speak to Butler's personal and political leanings, I do believe that her work evidences a conviction that oppression is interlocking — that the maintenance of one form of prejudice nourishes an insidious human predisposition to create, then persecute, societal Others.[7] The questions I pose here intend to call attention to the need for more discursive, deliberate efforts in the genre of science fiction to make space in the future for representations of queer subjectivity that exist as comfortably — and free from the threat of systemic violence — as heterosexual identities do today.

Notes

1. In this essay, I will focus specifically on the first novel in the trilogy, *Dawn*. However, I will frequently refer to the trilogy as a whole (collected in my main source text, *Lilith's Brood*), for a number of the concerns I raise are exemplified initially in *Dawn*, but maintained through *Adulthood Rites* and *Imago* as well.

2. For further discussion of critical responses to compulsory heterosexuality in the science

fiction genre, a genre that consistently fosters re-imaginations of subjectivity and difference, see Pearson and Hollinger.

3. Pearson continues, in a footnote, to say that "[t]he difficulty of ascertaining who is and who isn't homosexual, within a conceptual framework that renders the homosexual/heterosexual dyad as *the* axis of difference, preoccupies science, which seeks 'objective' proof of this difference..." (19–20). It is my assertion that we see this desire reiterated in the humans' experience with the ooloi, but that the absence of gender markers complicates an arrival at objective proof of sexual difference. Because the homosexual/heterosexual dyad remains in Butler's new societies, the pre-war humans have only this framework within which to fit the ooloi existence. Thus, as the sexual Other, they come to represent a homosexual presence.

4. Though I have included Gabe's pronouncement as illustrative of the collective male experience of sexual congress with the ooloi, the "he" Gabe indicates in these lines refers specifically to another resister named Curt. While this is not a discussion I intend to take up in this essay, it is perhaps not coincidental that Curt is not only the first to demand that the humans of the pilot group pair off in heterosexual units, but he is also the man responsible for Joseph's murder later in the novel. This occurs after Joseph is called a "faggot" by one of the more militant members of the group — a member whose identity Butler never expressly reveals, but who I assume to be Curt based on Butler's characterization of his volatility.

5. At the center of arguably any hate-based violence is the inability of the perpetrators to see their victims as human. Indeed, part of the objective of hate-based violence is to even further dehumanize individuals that threaten normative identity in an effort to reassure the perpetrators of their own superiority and the stability of their social power.

6. Hollinger cites Michael Warner's assertion that "Het [sic] culture thinks of itself as the elemental form of human association, as the very model of inter-gender relations, as the indivisible basis of all community, and as the means of reproduction without which society wouldn't exist" (24).

7. The epigraph I have chosen for this essay, excerpted from Butler's "The Monophobic Response," indicates as much. Sadly, it also indicates Butler's oversight of the human alien from another *sexuality* as the "tangible alien who can be hurt or killed"— equally vulnerable to serious, often violent oppression (415).

Works Cited

Butler, Octavia E. *Lilith's Brood.* New York: Warner Books, 1989. Print.
_____. "The Monophobic Response." *Dark Matter: A Century of Speculative Fiction from the African Diaspora.* Ed. Sheree R. Thomas. New York: Warner Books, 2000. 415–416. Print.
Castleberry, Tracy N. "Twisting the Other: Using a 'Third' Sex to Represent Homosexuality in Science Fiction." *The New York Review of Science Fiction* 21.5 (2009): 13–17. Print.
Eshun, Kodwo. "Further Considerations of Afrofuturism." *CR: The New Centennial Review* 3.2 (2003): 287–302. Print.
Green, Michelle Erica. "'There Goes the Neighborhood': Octavia Butler's Demand for Diversity in Utopias." *Utopian and Science Fiction by Women: Worlds of Difference.* Ed. Jane L. Donawerth, Carol A. Kolmerten, and Susan Gubar. Syracuse: Syracuse University Press, 1994. 166–89. Print.
Hollinger, Veronica. "(Re)reading Queerly: Science Fiction, Feminism, and the Defamiliarization of Gender." *Science Fiction Studies* 26.1 (1999): 23–40. Print.
Jesser, Nancy. "Blood, Genes and Gender in Octavia Butler's *Kindred* and *Dawn.*" *Extrapolation* 43.1 (2002): 36–61. Print.
Pearson, Wendy. "Alien Cryptographies: The View from Queer." *Science Fiction Studies* 26.1 (1999): 1–22. Print.
Rowell, Charles H. "An Interview with Octavia E. Butler." *Callaloo* 20.1 (1997): 47–66. Print.
Zaki, Hoda M. "Utopia, Dystopia, and Ideology in the Science Fiction of Octavia Butler." *Science Fiction Studies* 17.2 (1990): 239–51. Print.

Love at First Contact: Sex, Race and Colonial Fantasy in *Star Trek: First Contact*

Allison Whitney

Star Trek: First Contact (Jonathan Frakes, 1996) opens with a dream. The first shot is a close-up of an eye, an image that in science fiction usually indicates the imminent transformation of the subject, often through an encounter with the sublime. The camera pulls back to reveal that the eye belongs to Captain Jean-Luc Picard (Patrick Stewart), who is wearing his Starfleet uniform but standing in the regeneration alcove of a Borg drone. An alien species of cyborgs whose cybernetic implants keep them in a state of total and dependent interconnection, the Borg collective represent one of the more significant threats in the Star Trek universe. As the dream continues, Picard quickly vanishes into the collective via an effects shot where the camera pulls back to reveal the vast and intricate structure of a Borg spacecraft. Picard then appears in his persona as Locutus — the name he assumed once assimilated by the Borg in a two-part episode of the *Star Trek: The Next Generation* television series, "The Best of Both Worlds." He looks into the camera and utters the words, "I am Locutus of Borg. Resistance is futile" (*First Contact*). What follows is a sequence detailing the physical transformations of his assimilation process, concluding with a close-up of a drill about to penetrate his eye — the very eye that initiated the scene. Picard wakes from this nightmare, but when he moves to the sink to wash his face, he experiences a literal return of the repressed. He looks in the mirror, only to watch in horror as a Borg implant erupts from his cheek. Picard awakes again — a dream within a dream — only to discover that his nightmare has proved prophetic when he receives a message from Starfleet that the Borg are invading the Federation.

The Borg embody colonialism in its most monstrous form, assimilating any civilization they encounter and absorbing the bodies, minds, and cultures of individuals into their collective "hive mind." As they begin their invasion, they state their intentions clearly, transmitting their message to every ship they encounter: "We are the Borg. Lower your shields and surrender your ships. We will add your biological and technological distinctiveness to our own. Your culture will adapt to service us. Resistance is futile" (*First Contact*). They race through Federation territory, destroying starships and colonies along the way, but when they reach Earth, Picard uses his knowledge of Borg technology to help the fleet destroy their ship. With their mission in jeopardy, the Borg's strategy for assimilation takes a curious turn when they create a "temporal wake," allowing them to travel back in time to assimilate the Earth in the twenty-first century. The *Enterprise* crew peer through this rupture in time and see the Earth as it will appear in the "new" future, but now, instead of a utopian sanctuary, they see the nightmare scenario of a Borg planet, its atmosphere poisoned, its population assimilated, and its green and blue surface turned gray and black, covered in a web of electrification. Faced with this vision of horror, Picard orders his crew to follow the Borg back through time to "repair whatever damage they've done" (*First Contact*). Yet the "damage" that they seek to repair is not only to the obviously corrupted planet. As the story unfolds, it becomes clear that what needs rescuing is not just the past, but also the historical record of the past and the myths of personality and civilization that stem from that record.

In her *Sight and Sound* review of *Star Trek: First Contact*, Leslie Felperin comments on this larger threat to the Star Trek ethos:

> If Star Trek is a kind of ongoing American epic, it would seem to be entering a baroque, self-questioning phase here. Even Zefram Cochran, a character who first appeared in the original series, wants to run from his destiny as the inventor of warp drive and saviour of humanity. History is colder than death, and it sends a chill through the cast of characters. The first series' cold-war warriors with ray guns have given way to the Next Generation's technocratic peacekeepers, who are centre-stage in this film after the handing of the baton to the crew in *Star Trek Generations*. Captain Kirk and crew seldom had any self-doubts that they were in the right; Picard et al, on the other hand, are racked with doubts [49].

Indeed, absent the ideological foundations of the Cold War, Star Trek's utopian narratives of exploration lose much of their moral authority. Further, the Star Trek worldview, which relies on the notion that contact with a new civilization invariably initiates an age of enlightenment, and where mutually-beneficial cultural exchange is the norm, started to come under particular duress in the 1990s, in large part because of the public debate surrounding the 500th anniversary of Columbus' 1492 journey to the "New World." As Kent Ono explains in his book *Contemporary Media Culture and the Remnants of a Colo-*

nial Past, in the mid–1990s many popular texts were inspired by the Columbus quincentenary to commemorate, celebrate, or condemn the conduct of European explorers and colonists. Some responses to the anniversary brought to the fore more complex and disturbing details of the destructive effect of European contact on native civilizations, while others defended traditional narratives, often in the name of preserving the personal, ethnic, and national identities that depend on them. For example, in a chapter on the 1995 animated film *Pocahontas* (Mike Gabriel and Eric Goldberg), Ono and his co-author Derek T. Buescher discuss how this film idealizes the colonization of the Americas by articulating the story as a neocolonialist romance. Ono and Buescher argue that this film's romanticized narrative constitutes the Disney Corporation's "answer" to the revision of colonial history (90). I would argue that *Star Trek: First Contact* offers a similar response to postcolonial thought, as the heroes risk their lives in order to preserve the utopian narrative of first contact with alien intelligence that is so integral to the origin story of their civilization. As Felperin's review suggests, the primary mission of the *Enterprise* crew is to cast aside their existential doubts, and they do so by affirming that colonialism can be a just and heroic endeavor. Further, their mission to rescue their own history not only resonates with a larger cultural desire to romanticize the conquest of the New World, but also, like *Pocahontas*, employs romantic and erotic dynamics in order to accomplish the goal.

Nicholas Mirzoeff has noted that much of *Star Trek: First Contact* "is concerned with trying to differentiate the Federation's benign neocolonialism from the aggressive imperialism of the Borg," and I would argue that the film anchors this differentiation in its comparison of two female characters who develop intimate relationships with the film's heroes (215). First, there is the Borg Queen (Alice Krige), whose superior technology, expansive knowledge, and sexual power present a deadly challenge to the Federation's positive model of colonialism. The Borg Queen not only embodies the threat of female leadership, but also, by kidnapping members of the crew, she allows the film to draw upon the tradition of the "captivity narrative"—stories of white explorers captured by "natives"—in order to distance the Federation from her violent and terrifying brand of colonial expansionism. Second, the film introduces Lily (Alfre Woodard), an African American woman who, although she plays a central role in the first contact scenario, is conspicuously absent from the historical record of the event. While her character initially invites a progressive reading—she is the engineer who built the spacecraft that will achieve the first warp-speed flight—Lily's role in the story turns out to be far more conservative. As she develops a close emotional connection with Picard, her behavior recalls romanticized narratives about Native American women, whose actions affirm the white male heroes' agency, power, and fame, all the while effecting their own erasure from history so as to preserve the patriarchal narrative and the power structure on which it depends.

In order to understand the film's employment of these female figures and their sexuality, it is important to address the relationship between time travel and the concept of the primal scene fantasy — Freud's term for fantasies of observing parental intercourse. In "Time Travel, Primal Scene and the Critical Dystopia," Constance Penley argues that time travel stories often incorporate some form of primal scene, utilizing the unique spatial/temporal qualities of this narrative premise to rehearse the fantasy of watching, listening to, or even orchestrating one's own conception. Penley discusses science fiction scenarios where characters have an opportunity to direct their own primal scene by ensuring that their parents meet, fall in love, and consummate their relationship so that they might be born (121). *Star Trek: First Contact* also uses time travel to fulfill a primal scene fantasy, but here, it is not for an individual hero, but an entire civilization. The Borg travel back in time to Earth in the twenty-first century in an effort to destroy the Federation before it begins, disrupting the moment when humans make first contact with emphatically rational and beneficent aliens — the Vulcans — an event that initiates the utopian era of social and scientific progress that is the basis of the Star Trek franchise. By disrupting this first contact narrative — in effect, the moment when the Federation is conceived — the Borg intend to substitute their own primal scene, creating a future civilization in their own image.

The Borg strategy makes explicit use of sexuality, both when the Borg Queen attempts to seduce the android crewmember Data (Brent Spiner), promising him sexual pleasure to secure his help in conquering the Earth, and later in the film, when Picard's flashback reveals that his experience with the Borg also entailed an erotic relationship with the Queen. For example, when Picard enters the Engineering section in an effort to rescue Data from captivity, the Queen addresses him as "Locutus" and reminds him, "We were very close, you and I. You can still hear our song," followed immediately by a flashback image of the Queen sensually touching Picard's mouth (*First Contact*). Picard recalls their encounter during his assimilation, noting that it "wasn't enough that you assimilate me. I had to give myself freely to the Borg, to you," continuing that she did not want him to be merely a drone, but rather a "counterpart" (*First Contact*). Picard goes so far as to offer himself as a Queen's consort in exchange for Data's freedom, saying, "It's not too late. Locutus could still be with you ... let Data go and I will take my place at your side" (*First Contact*). The film's prolonged deliberations on both Data and Picard's erotic relationships with the Queen suggest that her vision of a transformed civilization seems to require forms of heterosexual bonding (acknowledging, of course, that Borg-android sex is far from normative). While the Queen will not literally give birth as a result of her relationships with either Data or Picard, it seems that in order to conceive a new Borg civilization, the historical narrative must be re-written to include a new set of "parents."

Faced with the Borg's threat to their civilization's origin story, the *Enterprise* crew must orchestrate a primal scene that is consistent with their historical record. Their enactment of the "correct" version of history is supported by Picard's relationship with Lily, a character who performs many of the functions ascribed to native women in colonial narratives, as cultural interpreters, practical helpers, and even potential intimate partners of white male explorers. Lily's position in the narrative is consistent with the ways women of color, and particularly native women, have been treated by mainstream Eurocentric history. Lily provides white male characters with the technical and emotional support they need to fulfill their roles as "heroes," but the film makes it clear that Lily's value is contingent on her never overshadowing the heroes' exploits, nor demanding her rightful place in the historical record. While Lily and Picard do not have an explicit romance (just as Picard and the Queen do not have literal intercourse), a mutual attraction is implied, and their relationship resonates with Picard's romantic history with other female characters. It seems, therefore, that the film organizes its visions of colonialism around these two female characters and the divergent primal scenes they might represent. On the one hand, Picard's submission to the Borg Queen will lead to a narrative of genocide and destruction, while on the other, his relationship with Lily will ensure a utopian future.

The film's early images of Picard's assimilated body and the corrupted Earth reveal that not only is the future at stake, but so is the self-image of the Federation. In his dream, Picard looks in the mirror to see himself become a monster; minutes later, the *Enterprise* crew have a glimpse of the Borg's revised Earth from a perspective directly above North America. While it is standard practice in American science fiction cinema for the United States to appear at the center of the planet, in this case, the imposition of this frightening image on North America is particularly suitable. The Borg, by revising history, have taken an edenic territory that represented liberty, abundance, opportunity, and natural beauty, and transformed it into a space of death, cultural destruction, and environmental degradation. One could argue that, from a Native American perspective, this image of an assimilated territory, overtaken and radically transformed with genocidal consequences, is actually quite valid, since for aboriginal cultures the arrival of European explorers was hardly a positive development. If one takes Ono and Buescher's approach of reading texts like *Star Trek: First Contact* as a response to mid–1990s revisions of North American history that tended to emphasize the experience of marginalized groups, then the experience of horror felt by the *Enterprise* crew, who see their home planet transformed from dream to nightmare, is analogous to the threat felt by those whose cultural identity is bound up with traditional notions of colonialism as a heroic and just enterprise.[1]

In the film, the threat is compounded by the fact that Picard still carries Borg implants in his body—implants that were too deeply embedded to remove after his assimilation. It seems that these devices allow Picard to retain a level of connection with the collective. For example, when Picard awakes from his dream to a message from Starfleet, he actually interrupts the Admiral's report, saying, "Yes, I know, the Borg," suggesting that his dream was not merely the work of his unconscious, but a form of subliminal communication (*First Contact*). Similarly, just as the Borg begin to generate their temporal wake, Picard turns to Counselor Troi (Marina Sirtis) and tells her, "I can hear them," meaning that he is able to pick up on their transmissions (*First Contact*). The film's emphasis on Picard's intimate physical connection with the Borg, a connection he both utilizes and seeks to sever, can be read in two fashions. On the one hand, the image of his body as a colonized territory is terrifying, and his mission in the film is to prevent the Borg conquest on a macro scale. On the other hand, the implants force Picard to see himself cast in the role of colonialist monster. Similarly, North America appears as a colonized dystopia, while it is also implicated as an imperialist force. The film's premise thus holds up a mirror to North America, whose reflection explicitly threatens its memory of a glorious colonial past. It is the job of the *Enterprise* crew to restore that image, specifically by orchestrating their culture's primal scene, and thereby rescuing their historical narrative of first contact.

The dual nature of the Borg threat, to both colonize and implicate in colonialism, speaks to a larger pattern in the film. At first glance, the film seems to be plagued by inconsistencies, as the roles of explorer/colonist and native/colonized are traded among characters, with many individuals playing multiple and conflicting roles. For example, as members of Starfleet, the *Enterprise* crewmembers are explorers, but as (mostly) humans, they are also identified with the natives of the soon-to-be-contacted Earth. Similarly, the Borg are clearly colonialists with an expansionist agenda, but they also take on the role of "savages" in the film's evocations of captivity narratives.

The captivity narrative is a genre of colonial literature detailing the sometimes factual, sometimes fictionalized experiences of white colonists and explorers captured by either Native Americans (referred to as Indians), or in the case of Barbary captivity, Africans. Captivity narratives offer accounts ranging from enslavement, torture, and murder to assimilation and eventual acceptance as a member of the native community. In *Star Trek: First Contact*, Data and Picard's imprisonment by the Borg Queen draws heavily from this literary tradition. To be clear, captivity narratives are by no means monolithic, nor do they express a singular message, but rather, they reveal and have been employed for varied ideological ends at different points in history. For example, in her introduction to *Women's Indian Captivity Narratives*, Kathryn Zabelle Derounian-Stodola explains that the narratives are by no means static, but rather, "each individual text reveals variations on, and even reversals of, gender and cultural archetypes concerning identity" (xxi). Similarly, Paul Baepler explains in *White Slaves, African Masters: An Anthology of American Barbary Captivity Narratives* that accounts of captivity vary tremendously in both content and tone (18). What is consistent, however, is that the popularity of captivity narratives and the inverted world-view they represent — where white figures are dominated by a racial Other — tend to become more popular at moments of historical upheaval. For example, Baepler notes that the demand for Indian captivity narratives increased during the period of the Revolutionary War; when colonists "increasingly viewed themselves as captives to a tyrannical king," stories that had been out of print for decades found a new readership (24). Later, Barbary captivity narratives developed during the first decades of the nineteenth century, when the slave population in the United States was increasing rapidly, as was the anti-slavery movement (25). Baepler describes the Barbary narrative's "semiotic plasticity," as it was used in contradictory ways, both to portray the "barbarity" of the Africans and also to critique slavery in North America (31). In the case of *Star Trek: First Contact*, the film capitalizes on captivity's semiotic plasticity so that the *Enterprise* crew, and the idealized vision of North America they represent, might confront the horrors of colonialism while also resisting the terrifying power of the Other and thus purging themselves of culpability.[2]

In the film's opening sequence, Picard's dream recalls his experience as a captive from the television series' two-part episode "The Best of Both Worlds." Picard was kidnapped and assimilated by the Borg, who explain that since human society is hierarchical, they plan to use Picard, re-named Locutus, as an authority figure who can facilitate their conquest of the Federation. The first episode begins with the *Enterprise* responding to a distress call from a colony called New Providence, located on the far reaches of explored space. When they arrive, they find that not only have the colonists disappeared, but the colony has been literally ripped from the planet's surface. This destruction of New Providence, whose name clearly resonates with early American history, signals the beginning of a Borg invasion. Once Picard is captured and assimilated, the *Enterprise* faces an even more disastrous situation, for not only is their captain in mortal danger, but the enemy now possesses all of Picard's knowledge of Federation technology, culture, and military strategy. Eventually the crew rescues Picard, and they turn the tables on their enemy by using Picard's reciprocal knowledge of Borg systems to win the day.

Picard's experience reflects two common elements of Indian captivity narratives: the captors' integration of captives into their societies, and former captives using their knowledge of the captors' culture against them in conflict. As Christina Snyder explains in *Slavery in Indian Country: The Changing Face of Captivity in Early America*, captivity was a standard practice of Native American societies, where, by acquiring members of other groups, they could profit from captives' language skills, technologies, and other forms of practical and cultural knowledge (110). While some captives were kept as slaves, others were adopted by their captors, undergoing a ritual re-birth that transformed "strangers into kin" (110). In many respects, this is analogous to Borg colonial strategy, where they fully absorb the cultures they encounter, promising those they intend to conquer that "we will add your biological and technological distinctiveness to our own" (*First Contact*). Once individuals are assimilated, they become fully Borg, and yet the progressive evolution of Borg civilization is dependent on absorbing the cumulative knowledge of those individuals. In a sense, the culture and material of the original civilization survives, but in a form that is rendered indistinguishable from the collective. Just as Native Americans "rarely sought the total destruction of an enemy people," we may regard the Borg tactic of assimilation as resonant with Native American practices of cultural integration and advancement through captivity (Snyder 113).

Whereas some captives became integrated into Native American societies and found fulfillment in their new lives, others escaped captivity, and later used their knowledge of their captors' cultures to wreck vengeance against them. In the former case, for example, Hanna Hale, who was captured as a child during the American Revolution, grew up among the Creek people, married a Creek man, and raised a family. In an effort to reclaim her for white society, her relatives kidnapped her in 1798, but she later insisted on returning to the Creek Nation (Snyder 108). Indeed, in many respects, women had greater property and personal rights in Native communities, and "when offered the rare opportunity to choose between societies, often elected to remain in Indian country" (Snyder 109). Meanwhile, Joseph Brown, who was captured by the Chickamaugas in 1788, but later freed in a prisoner exchange, had no desire to return to Indian life. Rather, he used his knowledge of his former captors' territory and practices to guide a 1794 military expedition against them (Snyder 153–54).

This variety of responses to captivity is reflected in *Star Trek: First Contact*, where Picard's history with the Borg raises questions about his loyalty and proves at once a boon and a liability both to the Borg and to the Federation. Picard is contacted by Starfleet Command and informed of the invasion, but instead of asking Picard to use his experience with the Borg to help deter the attack, as he had done previously, Starfleet Command instead orders him to take the *Enterprise* far from the action, to the edge of the Neutral Zone. Puzzled by this turn of events, Commander Riker (Jonathan Frakes), the *Enterprise*'s second-in-command, approaches Picard in his ready room. Riker asks why the *Enterprise* has been sent to such a remote location, and Picard explains that Starfleet regards his history with the Borg as a liability:

> PICARD: Let's just say that Starfleet has every confidence in the *Enterprise* and her crew, they're just not sure about her captain. They believe that a man who was once captured and assimilated by the Borg should not be put in a position where he would face them again. To do so would introduce an unstable element to a critical situation.
>
> RIKER: That's ridiculous. Your experience with the Borg makes you the perfect man to lead this fight [*First Contact*].

Starfleet's concerns reflect the dynamics of some Indian captivity stories, like Hanna Hale's, where captives, given the opportunity to rejoin white society, prefer to remain with their Indian communities, having formed intimate bonds with members of the tribe. Starfleet fears that Picard will do the same; in effect, they fear that the image from Picard's dream, where his repressed Borg elements burst forth, will become manifest if he is unable to resist their influence. However, the *Enterprise* does not remain out of the action for long; once they listen to panicked transmissions from the fleet, who are clearly no match for the invaders, they decide to violate their orders and race to the rescue. Much like in Joseph Brown's case, Picard's experience with the Borg provides him with valuable knowledge and tactical information that he uses to defeat them in battle. Picard is able to give the remains of the fleet accurate information about how to attack the Borg ship, and he is able to hear enough of their transmissions to predict their next move.

After the *Enterprise* pursues the invaders back in time to twenty-first century Earth, the Borg secretly transport themselves aboard the *Enterprise*. Soon thereafter, on-board systems begin to malfunction, crewmembers begin to disappear, and Picard starts to detect Borg transmissions via his implants. In an effort to impede the Borg takeover, Data prevents their seizing control of the main computer by locking it out with an encryption code. This encourages the Borg to kidnap Data and try to persuade him to give up the code, and this is where the scenario takes a decidedly eroticized turn. When Data is captured, he wakes up restrained to a table in Engineering. He notices that the Borg are trying to decipher the encryption, and he informs them that not only is this impossible, but also that he is invulnerable to assimilation. Their response comes in the form of a female voice, that of the Borg Queen, who assures him that as an "imperfect being, created by an imperfect being," he must have a weakness, and it is only a matter of time before they find it (*First Contact*). Curious about his captor, Data asks "Who are you?" Her response is "I am the Borg," which Data immediately identifies as a contradiction (*First Contact*). Indeed, as a collective, the Borg have no concept of individual identity — they are of one mind, and even their bodies are functionally indistinguishable via their cybernetic implants — so the Queen's statement of "I am the Borg" seems to go against a central premise of Borg civilization. Indeed, this film makes several significant deviations from earlier representations of Borg technology and social organization, most notably by introducing gendered dynamics that better serve the film's evocations of the primal scene, as well as its exploration of captivity.

When the Borg were introduced in the *Star Trek: The Next Generation* episode "Q Who?," they represented easily the most disturbing alien culture in the Star Trek franchise, in large part because they confounded notions of individual human psychology. While other Star Trek villains are motivated by greed, aggression, or misunderstandings that are soon remedied by the Federation's enlightened philosophies, the Borg are insatiable, unstoppable, and represent the antithesis of individualism and self-determination. Furthermore, the Borg expand their empire not through the idealized, mutually beneficial contact touted by the Federation, but rather by a process wherein the individual subject is lost and the conquered civilization is rendered indistinguishable within the Borg hive mind. It is not made entirely clear if the Borg *can* reproduce sexually, but it is clear that they neither experience desire, nor form interpersonal, "romantic" relationships, at least not in any form that is sensical to us.[3] Further, when the crew first encounters a Borg drone in "Q Who?," Q (John de Lancie), an omnipotent being who enjoys tormenting Picard and his crew, comments on the Borg's lack of a gender system: "Interesting, isn't it? Not a he, not a she, not like anything you've ever seen" ("Q Who?")[4]

To be fair, the Queen does clarify that she is not a member of the collective; rather, she *is* the collective. Although she appears in the form of an individual, she is not distinct from the whole, but represents its totality, albeit in a surprisingly gendered and desirous manner. I would argue that the introduction of a female identity and erotic drives in this film, particularly through the figure of a Queen, facilitates the seemingly contradictory roles that the Borg play as agents of colonial narratives. On the one hand, her tactics equate the Borg's mission with the sexual domination that is so often integral to colonialist conquest, thus solidifying the Borg's association with the violence and exploitation of imperialism. On the other hand, the Queen's sexuality also allows the Borg to play the role of the sensual savage, whose mystery and eroticism tempt white explorers to renounce civilization. The notion of Borg desire also allows Data and Picard to be tempted by the promise of what amounts to a marital bond with the Queen, recalling the way kinship bonds would encourage captives to reject their culture of origin and remain in their captors' societies.

As the Queen introduces herself to Data, her head and robotic spinal column descend from the ceiling and come to rest in an explicitly female body. She talks to Data about the ongoing evolution of Borg civilization, but Data challenges her, stating that the Borg "do not evolve. They conquer" (*First Contact*). She retorts that they accomplish this via assimilation, in a process that brings the assimilated "closer to perfection," and that Data only resists because he has not been properly "stimulated" (*First Contact*). Data's emotion chip, which he chose to have implanted in the previous film, *Star Trek: Generations* (David Carson, 1994), but which he has since deactivated in order to better handle the anxiety of the Borg attack, is suddenly turned back on. The Queen then reveals that she is adding organic skin to Data's body, transforming him from an android into a cyborg, like herself. She makes it immediately clear that she is doing this in an effort to control Data with the promise of sensual pleasure, blowing on the patch of new skin and giving him his first experience of goosebumps. As Data gasps with pleasure at this new sensation, the Queen playfully asks, "Was that good for you?" (*First Contact*).

Data's situation as the explorer seduced by the mysterious Other resonates with some of the accounts of colonial-era whites and their sexual experiences in the wilderness. For example, Richard Slotkin describes how in William Byrd's account of exploring Indian territory, *Histories of the Dividing Line*, likely composed in 1728, the possibility of sexual relationships and/or intermarriage with native women was a crucial part of the colonial experience. For these surveyors, as they "penetrate the land ... the darkening of the landscape is paralleled by their meetings with a series of erotic figures and temptations, each one more vile than the last," and while Byrd resisted these temptations, many frontiersmen did not (218). If Data is analogous to such a "frontiersman," his resistance to the Queen does indeed seem to wear down over time and in direct proportion to his increasing quantity of organic flesh. Realizing that the Queen is using this biological element to control him, he attempts escape, only to be overwhelmed by pain when a drone slashes his new skin, and to realize the depth of his predicament when the Queen goads him to "tear the skin from your limb as you would a defective circuit," something he is unable to do (*First Contact*). The Queen's seduction continues, leading to a humorous conversation about Data's "fully functional" sexual capacities, and prolonged kisses that clearly represent much more.[5] The Queen's seduction, on a practical level, is motivated by an attempt to retrieve the encryption code that will allow the Borg to fully take control of the *Enterprise* and use its weapons to disrupt first contact. However, she does state that this is only one of the Borg's goals, and that their efforts represent a larger project to enhance their civilization. This returns us to the notion of time travel as a facilitator of the primal scene fantasy — here, the sexual bond between Data and the Queen might lead to a renewed manifestation of the Borg, one driven by the notion of cyborg "perfection," itself a dark inversion of the Federation's ideals of independence and self-actualization.

Later in the film, after Picard has decided to initiate the *Enterprise* auto-destruct in a final effort to save first contact, his Borg implants allow him to hear Data calling for help. He remains on board to attempt a rescue, and heads down to Engineering, where he encounters the Queen. She addresses him as Locutus, using an angry tone, and we see a brief flashback to the image from Picard's dream, with the drill about to penetrate his eye. As is mentioned above, the Queen recalls the closeness of their relationship, and as Picard begins to remember, the flashbacks continue, including a shot of the Queen caressing his face. Picard bargains for Data's freedom by volunteering himself as a Queen's consort, remembering that it was not enough for him to be assimilated by force, but rather that the Borg wanted him to freely submit to their will. Picard continues that she wanted more than a drone, but rather an equal, a partner. This is one of many instances where the film makes a departure from traditional representations of the Borg. Previously, there was never any question of the assimilated being a willing party, nor was there any notion of personal relationships within the collective. Indeed, the Borg mantra "Resistance is futile" suggests that submission is neither requested nor desired, and that the feelings of the assimilated are irrelevant. Again, this change in Borg strategy reflects not only the assimilationist element of captivity narratives, but also the film's rehearsal of the primal scene, where Picard offers to take Data's place as the father figure in the conception and birth of a new era in Borg civilization.

In the end, however, both Data and Picard reject the Queen's advances, finally killing her in a particularly gruesome scene. First, Data ruptures the tanks of plasma surrounding the warp core, which, as is explained earlier in the film, instantly liquefies all organic matter. As cyborgs, the Borg cannot function without their organic components, and the Queen literally melts in the plasma, leaving only the mechanical portions of her body behind. Finally, Picard picks up the remains of her still-twitching mechanical skull and spinal cord and angrily snaps her neck — the final act in what Dean Conrad describes as the film's "display of patriarchal power" (94). Tudor Balinisteanu notes that in this film, the Federation is "shown as the kind of progressive society envisioned in theories of sociocultural evolutionism rooted in the idealisms of the Enlightenment" while the Borg represent an "alternative social order that relies on female leadership" (396). The explicitly violent and personal manner in which Picard kills the Queen expresses a visceral rejection of this "female leadership" and the colonial narratives it represents — captivity scenarios where Picard, a white male authority figure, is rendered vulnerable. Picard not only thwarts the Queen, but he also rejects the Borg part of himself that remained "colonized" after his assimilation. Similarly, Data is also restored to his original "pure" state when the organic portions of his body, which, in the Queen's words, allowed him to be "tempted by flesh," melt away in the plasma (*First Contact*).

The film's use of a Queen figure allows a differentiation of colonial narratives by introducing a gendered division between the now-feminized Borg and the idealized narrative of first contact that is not only dominated by male heroes, but actually depends on the systematic purging of female presence and influence. While it is true that in Star Trek narratives there are female leaders, and gender equality is presented as part of the enlightened nature of Federation culture, the leadership in *Star Trek: First Contact* is explicitly masculine, to the point where female figures are actively excised from history. This process of elimination of both the Borg's monstrous version of imperialism and the threats connoted by Data and Picard's experiences of captivity are achieved in part by contrasting the Queen with Lily, a character who plays into another set of colonial narratives, where native women serve as physical, emotional, and cultural helpers to white men.

The film's mission to restore the historical record, as well as Picard's physical and psychological integrity, are much dependent on Picard's relationship with Lily, who helps him evade the Borg, retain his persona as leader, and mitigate his descent into vengeance. Their relationship supports the utopian contact scenario through a specific dynamic of race and gender that conforms to some of the romanticized images of native women in American history. Lily is an engineer who not only designs and builds the spacecraft that allows first contact, but also performs many of the roles ascribed to native women, "as saviors and guides of white men and agents of European expansion" (Kidwell 98). The assistance these women proffered to colonists was not only invaluable to their progress, but it was even idealized as part of a larger destiny, whose ultimate goal was to establish a new and white-dominated society. As Robert Tilton explains in his analysis of the various iterations of the Pocahontas story, nineteenth-century versions of the narrative clearly argued that "Pocahontas had rescued Smith, and by implication all Anglo-Americans, so that they might carry on the destined work of becoming a great nation" (55). Further, as Frederic W. Gleach explains in an essay on the popular myths surrounding Pocahontas, once Native Americans had been sufficiently disempowered through marginalization, forced relocation, or extermination, the mainstream culture shifted from a focus on captivity narratives to a more romanticized view of "Indian" characters (435). Lily's role in the film is consistent with this shift, and she embodies the nostalgic image of the benevolent native woman whose destiny is to assist white colonists, often with the ironic twist of her thereby aiding the destruction of her own culture. Whereas Lily is of course African American rather than Native American, her status as a twenty-first century human positions her as a "native" of the Earth, while her narrative functions are remarkably consistent with figures like Pocahontas. Just as the narrative of Pocahontas' rescuing Smith was used to romanticize the conquest of Native American cultures, and to implicate aboriginal people in their own oppression, Lily's role in the narrative is to facilitate the first contact scenario, but in a manner that ensures her own erasure from history. Even though Lily's efforts are instrumental to the construction of the spacecraft and the success of the mission, she is apparently unknown to twenty-fourth century historians, who attribute the first contact event to the genius of an individual white man. Furthermore, members of the *Enterprise* crew, in spite of their futuristic and enlightened world-view, do not seem to notice Lily's exclusion from history, nor do they challenge it in any respect. Rather, Picard uses Lily's social and historical invisibility to protect the first contact scenario.

The Borg's revision of history hinges on their attempts to kill a man named Zefram Cochran (James Cromwell) and to destroy his space ship, the *Phoenix*. First contact will occur when the *Phoenix* becomes the original human-built spacecraft to travel at warp speed, catching the attention of Vulcan scientists who happen to be passing through the solar system. When Cochran's character is introduced, he is staggering out of a bar, accompanied by Lily, who encourages him to stop drinking and go to bed so he will be in good enough shape to fly the spaceship the following day. It seems that Lily not only keeps Cochran's drinking and carousing under control so he can complete his work, a role common to the women behind "great men," but she is also the engineer who built the *Phoenix*. At first glance, Lily's level of technical expertise seems progressive, as the role of aerospace engineer is not generally associated with African American women. Indeed, Alfre Woodard's casting in this role would appear to be consistent with a larger Star Trek practice of valorizing gender and racial equality.

However, there is a significant problem with this reading of Lily's role as progressive. The *Enterprise* crew seems to have memorized the first contact narrative down to the smallest detail, including exact times, locations, and even gestures. Further, they mention that the *Enterprise* computer contains extensive information about the first contact incident, including the full technical specs of the *Phoenix*. And yet, nobody from the twenty-fourth century recognizes Lily as a historical figure. While they are downright giddy about meeting Cochran, at no point does anyone identify Lily or acknowledge her accomplishments. Further, while La Forge (Levar Burton), the *Enterprise* Chief Engineer, talks about having attended Zefram Cochran High School, Lily's character is never even given a last name. In some respects, Lily's anonymity is consistent with the erasure of women, and especially women of color, from history, and particularly the history of science and technology. Indeed, much feminist recovery work has focused on revealing the identities of women whose contributions to scientific discovery have been overlooked or attributed to their male colleagues. Yet the seemingly enlightened twenty-fourth century characters never make any indication that they are going to revise their accounts of first contact to include Lily's contributions. Indeed, at no point in the film does anyone from the future question the accuracy or completeness of any part of the historical record. The only character who does so is Cochran himself, but only to express his insecurity about being heralded as a hero — an insecurity that he overcomes in part thanks to Lily's emotional support. Throughout the film, Lily's multiple competencies and her historical invisibility support the heroic exploits of two white male explorers, Cochran and Picard, with whom she shares a level of emotional intimacy. Lily offers them, as necessary, the technical expertise, psychological support, and ethical discernment needed to complete their missions, while also allowing them to share her invisibility when necessary.

Lily's exclusion from history begins during her first encounter with the *Enterprise* crew. Shortly after the Borg arrive in the twenty-first century, they try to destroy the *Phoenix* by firing upon the missile silo where it is under construction. Several *Enterprise* crewmembers beam down to assess the damage and find Cochran, and as they are exploring the silo, Lily assumes that these trespassers are behind the attack, and begins shooting at them. Picard tries to explain that "we're here to help" but Lily replies by shouting "Bullshit!" and continues firing her machine gun (*First Contact*). Since Data is impervious to gunfire, he assures Picard that he can handle the situation, offering greetings to Lily even as she is riddling him with bullets. Lily then collapses, and Dr. Crusher (Gates McFadden) soon discovers that she is suffering from radiation poisoning caused by the Borg's damage to the *Phoenix*. Crusher insists on bringing Lily back to the ship for treatment, reassuring Picard that she will keep her unconscious in order to conceal their twenty-fourth century origins from her and not disrupt the historical timeline.

When it comes to Lily's symbolic functions in the narrative, Crusher's removing her from the scene distances her both physically and conceptually from her creation, the *Phoenix*. As the sequence in the silo continues, the camera makes a dramatic movement up the side of the *Phoenix*, starting from an extreme low angle that emphasizes its great height, then moving up to a platform where Picard and Data are standing. They begin a conversation about historical irony, noting how Cochran re-purposed a weapon of war — a nuclear missile — to inaugurate an era of peace. Picard also explains the importance of material presence and tactile contact in humans' understanding of the "real." While running his hand up and down the *Phoenix*, Picard explains to Data that while he has seen the ship on display at the Smithsonian, he was never able to touch it. Intrigued by the suggestion that touching something can make it seem more real, Data begins to stroke the *Phoenix* as well, at which point Troi, observing them from above and noting the suggestiveness of the scene, asks sarcastically, "Would you three like to be alone?" (*First Contact*). While missiles easily lend themselves toward phallic associations, Troi's joke, in combination with the camera movement's emphasis on the vertical immensity of the *Phoenix*, draws the viewer's attention to the explicit masculinity of the scene. Indeed, Troi's witticism rests on the fact that all three of the parties in this scene are gendered male. Picard and Data immediately pull their hands away, and Picard inquires as to whether Cochran has been found. Troi says there is no sign of him, and Picard replies, "He has to be here. There was nothing more important to him than this ship. This flight — it was his dream" (*First Contact*). Troi reminds Picard that Cochran may have been killed, and Picard despairs that the future may have died with him. The true historical irony is that Picard's description of Cochran, as a dedicated innovator who would do anything to realize his vision of technological progress, applies more logically to Lily. Indeed, it is Lily, not Cochran, who was actually with the *Phoenix*, and who was prepared to defend it by force. Yet Lily's exclusion from history persists, in part thanks to Crusher's medical evacuation — as they beam up, Lily de-materializes, and thereby reifies the narrative of Cochran's solitary achievement, leaving behind the *Phoenix* and the "realness" its material presence provides. Once Lily is removed, the mission to enact an emphatically white and masculine vision of history can proceed.

Crusher succeeds in treating Lily's radiation sickness, but just as they are ready to return her to the planet, the Borg begin to attack the *Enterprise* sick bay, and Crusher is forced to wake Lily so they can escape. Confused and frightened, she flees the medical staff and ends up encountering Picard, who has since returned to the ship. Picard must try to explain to the terrified Lily, in short order, the existence of time travel, interstellar transportation, and extraterrestrial life. They eventually encounter a number of Borg drones, and Picard hatches a plan to lure the drones into a trap and acquire their neural processors, which he might use to learn more about the Borg's strategies. Without mentioning this plan to Lily, he fires his phaser to provoke the drones to follow them into the holodeck — a holographic simulation system that creates immersive environments. Picard chooses the holographic novel "The Big Goodbye," where he takes on the role of a 1940s private eye named Dixon

Hill. The holodeck scene takes place in a nightclub, straight out of a film noir or hardboiled detective novel, where Picard and Lily behave as though they are a couple on a date. Lily dances with Picard, and becomes one of his "broads" in the storyline, even experiencing a moment of rivalry with another female character in the scene. Picard picks a fight with some holographic gangsters, and while Lily distracts an assailant by hitting him with a champagne bucket, Picard grabs his machine-gun, and, having deactivated the holodeck's safety protocols, uses it to kill the Borg drones.

On one level, the holodeck scene appears to be an amusing fantasy, drawing upon the popularity of the Dixon Hill stories from the *Star Trek: The Next Generation* television program. However, on another level, by placing Lily in the anachronistic position of being a white man's date in a 1940s American nightclub, the scene also reveals many of the internal contradictions of this film and of Star Trek in general when it comes to the representation of race. Indeed, while Star Trek narratives appear to valorize a multi-racial and multicultural future, where all forms of prejudice have dissipated, Daniel Bernardi argues that Star Trek's "liberal-humanist project is exceedingly inconsistent and at times disturbingly contradictory," re-producing racist stereotypes and hierarchies by dismissing the significance of difference (211). Further, David Golumbia notes that in spite of Star Trek's assertions of egalitarianism, non-human characters consistently seek to become part of a homogenized white human culture. For example, Data, in spite of his super-human strength, vast intellectual abilities, and potential immortality, aspires to become human — not "alive," or a member of any other sentient alien species, but specifically human (90). Characters who are marked as Other by virtue of race, species, disability, gender, or other factors are deployed as representatives of "difference" when it is convenient for narrative and thematic purposes, but Federation culture remains strangely monolithic. In Lily's case, the film simultaneously draws attention to her racial difference by making her the only non-white character in the scene, while also dismissing that difference by ignoring the scene's historical fallacy.

Once inside the holodeck, Lily embodies the paradoxical invisibility and hyper-visibility that are so often imposed on women of color, who, even as their voices and agency are systematically overlooked, are also scrutinized for their difference. On the one hand, Lily's beauty (she looks great in that dress) and capacity to adapt to new situations make her blend in easily with the glamorous context of the nightclub and assist Picard in escaping the Borg's notice. In this respect, her visibility helps make Picard "invisible" long enough to gain a tactical advantage. Meanwhile, this scene also demonstrates Lily's historical invisibility, and Star Trek's tendency to deny the significance of race, precisely because her race is never addressed. The audience is aware that in the real 1940s, an interracial couple at an American nightclub would attract a level of negative attention that is not manifest in this scene. Of course, one could argue that the lack of segregationist attitudes is simply a result of this being a recreational simulation; it is unlikely that Picard would program racist attitudes into his game of make-believe. However, as Picard is activating the holodeck, the film offers a close-up of the control screen listing an array of possible scenes, including the Champs-Elysée, The Café des Artistes, a twentieth-century comedy club, a relaxing wading pool, and a horseback riding adventure. In many respects, any of these might provide easier cover for an interracial couple than a 1940s nightclub, and yet, Picard chooses "The Big Goodbye." Of course, that program's criminal underworld is more likely to provide Picard with a machine gun than, say, the wading pool, but given the seemingly infinite flexibility of holodeck programs, it is conspicuous that Picard chooses one that makes Lily's race all the more visible to the audience.

There are precedents for this kind of anachronistic racial dynamic in *Star Trek: The Next Generation*. For example, in the episode entitled "Clues," Guinan (Whoopi Goldberg), who is the *Enterprise* bartender, joins Picard in the Dixon Hill holodeck program, and, like Lily, her race is never acknowledged. Even more astonishing, in another time-travel narrative, the two-part episode "Time's Arrow" where the *Enterprise* crew travel to the late nineteenth century to investigate evidence of extraterrestrial visitors, meeting Samuel Clemens/Mark Twain along the way, Guinan (who is there independently of the *Enterprise*, as she comes from an alien species with very long life-spans) appears to be living within white society in a manner that would have been impossible for a black woman in that historical context. Again, this discrepancy is never addressed. On the surface, instances like these might appear to have a progressive component — indeed, it may be productive to imagine worlds where individuals are accepted in any social context regardless of race and gender. However, Star Trek's re-imagining of the historical past stripped of its racial politics ultimately supports a conservative, even retrograde worldview. By highlighting Lily's race, and then insisting that it does not matter, the film indicates that nostalgic visions of the past, particularly the American past, can only function once race is rendered invisible. Indeed, this requirement is consistent with the larger agenda of *Star Trek: First Contact* to enact a fantasy of colonialism while denying its destructive history.

Another important consequence of Picard's holodeck selection is that it forces Lily to conform to the narrow roles afforded to women in 1940s narratives, and particularly in film noir. Needless to say, there is no "female engineer" character in "The Big Goodbye," so Lily instead takes on the default position of Picard's romantic partner. Lily's limited options are consistent with the general rigidity of female characterization in Star Trek, and Golumbia has noted that while white male characters frequently apply their skills "other than at their central command station," female characters rarely translate their skills with such fluidity, resulting in fewer opportunities for character development (88). In Lily's case, the film refuses to make room for her to perform multiple roles — she cannot be both an engineer and one of Picard's "broads." In effect, by drawing her into the holodeck, Picard gives her a paradigm in which to interact with him, and in many respects, it sticks. The conspicuous denial of Lily's race makes the artificiality of her role all the more visible, but as she adapts to "The Big Goodbye," Lily quickly assumes a position that echoes her relationship with Cochran, in that she starts to provide Picard with the practical assistance, psychological support, and moral discernment that he needs to be an effective leader. For example, after shooting the Borg drones with the machine gun, Picard lunges toward one of them to bludgeon its clearly lifeless corpse. Lily intervenes, saying, "I think you got him!" (*First Contact*). Lily looks on in horror as Picard starts to eviscerate the body in search of the neural processor, finally calling his attention to the fact that the dead drone is a former *Enterprise* crewmember, one Picard identifies as Ensign Lynch. Lily is shocked at Picard's casual response to his crewmate's fate, and will later remind Picard of this incident in an effort to make him turn away from vengeance and regain his status as a rational leader.

Lily's responsibilities as moral compass and intimate confidante recall Picard's relationships with other female characters from the television series, particularly Crusher and Guinan, each of whom had a romantic connection with Picard. In both cases, the series makes strong suggestions of an erotic dynamic, but the characters never state directly if and how they have acted on those desires. In terms of these women's functions within the narrative, it seems that their emotional intimacy allows them to challenge Picard on ethical matters and provide him with moral guidance. For example, Guinan does not appear in this film, but viewers familiar with *Star Trek: The Next Generation* would know that when the Federation has their first contact with the Borg in the episode "Q Who?," Guinan serves as the cultural interpreter, explaining to Picard how her own people were scattered around the galaxy after their culture was all but destroyed by the Borg — a narrative that is easily linked to that of the African diaspora specifically, and the plight of colonized and displaced peoples in general. In a later episode, "The Best of Both Worlds: Part 2," Guinan explains to Riker that her relationship with Picard is romantically intimate, describing it as "beyond friendship, beyond family..." ("Best of Both Worlds: Part 2"). This is only one of several moments in the television series where her sexual relationship with Picard is implied (Roberts 130). Meanwhile, there are numerous episodes where Crusher and Picard interact in ways that go beyond the boundaries of mere friendship, including "The

Naked Now," where they flirt openly, "Attached," where they experience telepathic communication that reveals romantic feelings, and "All Good Things...," where they marry in an alternate timeline. Again, this closeness continually places both women in a position to challenge Picard on moral and ethical matters, and in *Star Trek: First Contact*, this function appears to transfer to Lily. A level of emotional intimacy quickly develops between Lily and Picard, and while the film is as coy as the television program as to the romantic tone of their relationship, they do share a kiss at the end of the film, and there is a suggestion that they might pursue the relationship further were it not for the centuries that separate them.

As the Borg assimilate more and more of the ship, Picard appears to lose his emotional stability, acting more out of a desire for vengeance than in the best interests of his crew. Faced with this crisis in leadership, Lily uses her emotional connection with Picard to restore him to reason. For example, the Klingon crewmember, Worf (Michael Dorn), who has particular expertise in military strategy, challenges Picard's decision-making, telling him that his past traumatic experiences with the Borg are clouding his judgment. Instead of considering Worf's position, Picard calls him a coward, and Worf angrily retreats. Meanwhile, Crusher initially supports Worf's position, but she too relents, and far more quickly than is typical of her character, telling Lily that "once the Captain has made up his mind, the discussion is over" (*First Contact*). It is left to Lily to help Picard come to his senses, quell his desire for revenge, and act as a rational leader. As an intimate outsider, and filling the role of "native helpmate" in the film's colonial narrative, it is Lily's job to question Picard's motives and his idealized notions of his culture's "evolved sensibility," but only for purposes of allowing him to be an effective hero, rather than offering a larger critique of the Federation's utopian self-image (*First Contact*).

After Picard refuses Worf's recommendation to abandon and destroy the *Enterprise* as a way of eliminating the Borg, and instead orders his crew to fight hand-to-hand in what is clearly a losing battle, Lily follows him to the boardroom where he is trying to modify a phaser. Lily tells him that the crew thinks his plan is suicidal, but they are afraid to challenge him. Picard explains his course of action by telling Lily his captivity narrative, explaining how he was stripped of his individuality, linked to the hive mind, and turned into "one of them," and he argues that his experience with the Borg affords him unique knowledge of how to defeat them (*First Contact*). It is true that Picard's captivity gives him unparalleled understanding of the Borg, but it is clear that the traumatic experience of being a captive has also compromised his judgment. At this moment, it appears that Starfleet's initial assessment of Picard, the former captive, as an "unstable element" is indeed valid. By the time Lily confronts Picard in the boardroom, it is clear that Worf and the others are right that his thinking is distorted, but it is Lily who restores Picard to mental health by allowing him to exorcise the trauma he experienced as a captive. Lily hears about Picard's traumatic experiences, and correctly assesses his motivations: "It's so simple. The Borg hurt you, and now you're going to hurt them back" (*First Contact*).

Picard is enraged at the suggestion that he is acting out of vengeance, but Lily refuses to back down, finally shouting at him, "Captain Ahab has to go hunt his whale!" (*First Contact*). The analogy to *Moby Dick* is apt, not only because Picard shares Ahab's obsessive drive for revenge, but because the nature of Ahab's injury — the loss of a leg and its transparent reference to castration — is easily compared with the physical violation that Picard suffered when captured by the Borg. Picard pauses at Lily's Melville reference, and she continues, angrily, "You do have books in the twenty-fourth century?" (*First Contact*). Her tactics seem to demonstrate a profound understanding of Picard's character, as an intellectual who is more likely to be swayed by a philosophical argument or literary reference than by brute force. Interestingly, when Picard begins to quote *Moby Dick*, Lily confesses, "Actually, I never read it" (*First Contact*). Lily's lack of literary knowledge serves an important function — again, Lily's role is not to be credited for her own talents and accomplishments, but strictly to provide Picard with the emotional and psychological checks and balances that allow him to maintain his heroic role in the narrative. By referencing Ahab, Lily allows Picard to move beyond the role of damaged and traumatized captive and to become his "old self" again — effectively regaining the rational and ethical clarity that is the marker of his utopian civilization. As David Greven points out in *Gender and Sexuality in Star Trek*, the revelation that Lily can conjure enough literary references to appeal to Picard's intellectual side, but not enough to be his equal in erudition, is a deeply troubling moment in the narrative, as it denies the "intellectual, thinking life of African Americans and women in one fell swoop" (137). Picard finally activates the ship's auto-destruct, and Lily leaves the *Enterprise* with the rest of the crew while Picard stays behind to rescue Data. Once she returns to Earth, Lily transfers her supporting function back to Cochran, helping him execute his role as a heroic figure. At the moment of first contact, when the Vulcan ship lands in the appointed spot, Riker urges Cochran to step forward, saying that the aliens are "going to want to meet the man who flew that warp ship" (*First Contact*). As Cochran walks toward them, he pauses beside Lily, who takes his hand. It appears at first that they are going to go forward together, but instead he leaves her behind. Lily is yet again giving him the emotional sustenance he needs to fulfill the appointed role of "great man," while she remains invisible in the background.

It is interesting that Cochran is the only character in *Star Trek: First Contact* who ever challenges the historical narrative. Not comfortable with being cast in the role of hero, he consistently resists the time-travelers' accounts of his greatness. From the moment that the *Enterprise* crewmembers inform him of his place in history, he continually objects to their visions of "Zefram Cochran," stating, "This other guy you keep talking about, this historical figure? I never met him. I can't imagine I ever will" (*First Contact*). At one point, when Cochran is expressing doubts about the success of the mission, Riker quotes his future self back to him, saying, "Don't try to be a great man, just be a man. Let history make its own judgments" (*First Contact*). In some respects, Cochran's objections to his heroic image allows the film to acknowledge that historical narratives are constructed through a process of exaggeration and omission, as it is clear that many elements of Cochran's personality, and the processes that allowed first contact to take place (most notably, the contributions of twenty-fourth century time-travelers), are not recorded in the history books. First contact would not have occurred were it not for Lily's technical and emotional labor and the strategic interference of the *Enterprise* crew, but Lily becomes invisible when Cochran leaves her behind, while the twenty-fourth century characters literally vanish as they beam up. The film seems to admit that the real mechanics of history remain invisible and that the dominant narrative conceals whole truth, and yet, the film does not offer a critique of history, but rather an endorsement of the exclusionary process. While one might wonder if Lily would have been recognized by history if she could "just be a man," the film does not regard her invisibility as a problem. Rather, her marginalization, and that of the women and people of color she represents, seems crucial to the correct order of things.

In orchestrating their civilization's primal scene, the *Enterprise* crew restores order by removing many levels of nuance from the historical record. Picard's mission is to repress not only his own ambiguous identity as a former captive, but also to suppress the complexities of contact scenarios, here represented through the Borg's dual role as both imperialist monster and savage captor. *Star Trek: First Contact*'s romantic and sexual dynamics, rooted in two very different female characters, permit an exploration of both the utopian and nightmare scenarios of first contact, scenarios that, in the mid–1990s, had especially prescient political implications. The Borg, with their sexually rapacious Queen and their strategic uses of captivity, threaten the Earth with a revision of history, one whose new narrative is one of darkness, domination, and genocide — a narrative that is both compelling and frightening precisely because it corresponds so closely with the history of colonialism. Meanwhile, the heroic *Enterprise* crew, with the assistance of their native female helpmate, rescues their own civilization by enacting and affirming an idealized first contact scenario, one that is largely dependent on the racial Other's technical competence, emotional intelligence, and ultimate invisibility. Rather than using the public debate surrounding the history of the Americas to embrace a more complex vision of first contact, the film instead silences dissenting voices, rejects or conceals female leadership, and treats the mainstream historical record as gospel. Although the film begins with the white male hero seeing his mirror image corrupted by a memory of colonial violence, it concludes with the successful restoration of the historical myth, where the natives are willing and receptive, the explorers are vindicated, and the native women who facilitate their own conquest demand no place in the history books.

Notes

1. While not all of the crewmembers are humans, it is fair to describe the Earth as a "home planet" for members of the Federation, since it is the center of their organizational structure. Further, the major non-human members of the crew either have a human parent (Troi), were raised by humans (Worf), or aspire to become human (Data).

2. The use of captivity as a narrative device was well established in the *Star Trek: The Next Generation* television series. In several episodes members of the crew were held captive by aliens, such as "The Samaritan Snare," where La Forge is held by aliens who want to use his engineering expertise, or "The High Ground," where Crusher is kidnapped by terrorists so she can give medical treatment to their people. Meanwhile, in "Suddenly Human," the crew encounters human children who have been raised in alien captivity, and must face the challenges of re-integrating them into Federation culture.

3. In "Q Who?" there are infants who appear to be born as entirely biological beings, with cyborg implants introduced later in development, but this process is not explained in detail, nor is it clear whether these infants are captives from assimilated peoples, or are born of the Borg themselves. The television series *Star Trek: Voyager* would come to elaborate on processes of Borg reproduction, but only in episodes that aired after the release of *Star Trek: First Contact*.

4. It is true that subsequent Borg narratives do attribute gendered qualities and pronouns to individual Borg drones, but only when they are separated from the collective. Examples include Hugh (Jonathan Del Arco), from the episode "I, Borg," and Seven of Nine (Jeri Ryan), who appeared on *Star Trek: Voyager*, but only in seasons produced after the release of *Star Trek: First Contact*.

5. This description of Data as "fully functional" refers to Data's sexual experiences in episodes from *Star Trek: The Next Generation*, including an encounter with crewmate Tasha Yar (Denise Crosby) in "The Naked Now."

Works Cited

"All Good Things…" *Star Trek: The Next Generation*. Dir. Winrich Kolbe. 23 May 1994. Paramount, 2004. DVD.

"Attached." *Star Trek: The Next Generation*. Dir. Jonathan Frakes. 8 November 1993. Paramount, 2004. DVD.

Baepler, Paul. *White Slaves, African Masters: An Anthology of American Barbary Captivity Narratives*. Chicago: University of Chicago Press, 1999. Print.

Balinisteanu, Tudor. "The Cyborg Goddess: Social Myths of Women as Goddesses of Technologized Otherworlds." *Feminist Studies* 33.2 (Summer 2007): 394–423. Print.

Bernardi, Daniel. "'Star Trek' in the 1960s: Liberal-Humanism and the Production of Race." *Science Fiction Studies* 24.2 (July 1997): 209–225. Print.
"The Best of Both Worlds: Part One." *Star Trek: The Next Generation*. Dir. Cliff Bole. 18 June 1990. Paramount, 2004. DVD.
"The Best of Both Worlds: Part Two." *Star Trek: The Next Generation*. Dir. Cliff Bole. 24 September 1990. Paramount, 2004. DVD.
"Clues." *Star Trek: The Next Generation*. Dir. Les Landau. 11 February 1991. Paramount, 2004. DVD.
Conrad, Dean. "*Femmes Futures*: One Hundred Years of Female Representation in SF Cinema." *Science Fiction Film and Television* 4.1 (2011): 79–100. Print.
Derounian-Stodola, Kathryn Zabelle. "Introduction." *Women's Indian Captivity Narratives*. Ed. K. Z. Derounina-Stodola. New York: Penguin, 1998. xi–xxviii. Print.
Felperin, Leslie. "Star Trek First Contact." *Sight and Sound* 7.1 (January 1997): 48–49. Print.
Gleach, Frederic W. "Pocahontas: An Exercise in Mythmaking and Marketing." *New Perspectives on Native North America: Cultures, Histories, and Representations*. Ed. Sergei A. Kan and Pauline Turner Strong. Lincoln: University of Nebraska Press, 2006. 433–455. Print.
Golumbia, David. "Black and White World: Race, Ideology, and Utopia in 'Triton' and 'Star Trek.'" *Cultural Critique* 32 (Winter 1995-1996): 75–95. Print.
Greven, David. *Gender and Sexuality in* Star Trek: *Allegories of Desire in the Television Series and Films*. Jefferson, NC: McFarland, 2009. Print.
"The High Ground." *Star Trek: The Next Generation*. Dir. Gabrielle Beaumont. 29 January 1990. Paramount 2004. DVD.
"I, Borg." *Star Trek: The Next Generation*. Dir. Robert Lederman. 11 May 1992. Paramount, 2004. DVD.
Kidwell, Clara Sue. "Indian Women as Cultural Mediators." *Ethnohistory* 39.2 (Spring 1992): 97–107. Print.
Mirzoeff, Nicholas. *An Introduction to Visual Culture*. London: Routledge, 1999. Print.
"The Naked Now." *Star Trek: The Next Generation*. Dir. Paul Lynch. 5 October 1987. Paramount, 2004. DVD.
Ono, Kent A., with Derek T. Buescher. "Civilized Colonialism: *Pocahontas* as Neocolonialist Narrative." *Contemporary Media Culture and the Remnants of a Colonial Past*. New York: Peter Lang, 2009. 89–112. Print.
Penley, Constance. "Time Travel, Primal Scene and the Critical Dystopia." *Alien Zone: Cultural Theory and Contemporary Science Fiction Cinema*. Ed. Annette Kuhn. London: Verso, 1990. 116–127. Print.
"Q Who?" *Star Trek: The Next Generation*. Dir. Rob Bowman. 8 May 1989. Paramount, 2004. DVD.
Roberts, Robin. *Sexual Generations: "Star Trek: The Next Generation" and Gender*. Urbana: University of Illinois Press, 1999. Print.
"Samaritan Snare." *Star Trek: The Next Generation*. Dir. Les Landau. 15 May 1989. Paramount 2004. DVD.
Slotkin, Richard. *Regeneration Through Violence: The Mythology of the American Frontier, 1600–1860*. Norman: Oklahoma University Press, 2000. Print.
Snyder, Christina. *Slavery in Indian Country: The Changing Face of Captivity in Early America*. Cambridge: Harvard University Press, 2010. Print.
Star Trek: First Contact. Dir. Jonathan Frakes. Paramount, 1996. Film.
Star Trek: Generations. Dir. David Carson. Paramount, 1994. Film.
"Suddenly Human." *Star Trek: The Next Generation*. Dir. Gabrielle Beaumont. 15 October 1990. Paramount 2004. DVD.
Tilton, Robert. *Pocahontas: The Evolution of a Narrative*. Cambridge: Cambridge University Press, 1994. Print.
"Time's Arrow — Part 1." *Star Trek: The Next Generation*. Dir. Cliff Bole. 24 September 1990. Paramount, 2004. DVD.

"They teach you that in Whore Academy?"
A Quantitative Examination of Sex and Sex Workers in Joss Whedon's *Firefly* and *Dollhouse*

Heather M. Porter

Sexual content can be found in great abundance on television, where it fulfills a variety of narrative functions. Sex can be a versatile tool for the storyteller; it can make political and social statements, or even commercial statements (in the form of ratings). It is also, of course, a direct and potentially provocative way to express a variety of human experiences, from the intimacy between lovers to the violence and power of rape to the consequences and responsibilities of teenage sex. The television works of Joss Whedon demonstrate this representational versatility toward sexual functioning. The images and reasons for sex in the Whedonverse are as varied and complicated as the characters that inhabit these worlds. From the virginal slayer of season one of *Buffy the Vampire Slayer* to the Actives programmed for sex in *Dollhouse*, Whedon's works manifest a range of sexual experiences. Of Whedon's works, *Firefly* and *Dollhouse* present the broadest spectrum of sexual depictions due to the wide and varied background of the adult characters in the shows. The inclusion of sex workers in these series — Inara the Companion in *Firefly* and Echo the Active in *Dollhouse*— adds complexity to the sexual thematic material. In the introduction to *Prostitution: An International Handbook on Trend, Problems and Policies*, Nanette J. Davis states, "An underlying theme in the exploration of comparative features is that prostitution serves as a critical symbol for every woman's position is society" (ix). In this case, the depiction of the sex workers in Whedon's works stands as a reflection of the other female characters and their positions in their universe. This essay will utilize a content analysis to examine depictions of sex in *Firefly* and *Dollhouse*. Then, using the results, I will closely investigate the portrayal of the sex workers in these two shows and how they compare to the other characters in each series.

A Review of Sex and Sex Workers in Joss Whedon's Television Series

Joss Whedon's first television creation, *Buffy the Vampire Slayer*, began in 1997 on the WB, with its spin-off *Angel* premiering in 1999. The concept of *Buffy* was simple: in a world filled with vampires, demons, and other forces of darkness, one girl has the strength and power to defeat them; she is the Slayer. On the whole, *Buffy* projected a very simplistic and conservative view of sex. In *Televised Morality: The Case for Buffy the Vampire Slayer*, Gregory Stevenson comments,

> The place that sexuality occupies within *Buffy's* moral vision is neither a hedonistic one nor a moralistic one. *Buffy* fits comfortably within a western secular morality that says sex outside of marriage is viable in principal as long as it is governed by love [201].

Yet even subsumed within this "western secular morality," there are dangers and consequences to the sexual acts depicted on *Buffy*. This is most concretely illustrated when Buffy and her boyfriend, the ensouled vampire Angel, have sex for the first time in the episode "Surprise" (2.13). In the next episode, "Innocence" (2.14), it is revealed that the moment of true happiness that Angel experiences when consummating his relationship with Buffy broke the curse that had originally restored his soul, reverting him to his vampire self, the murderous Angelus. Angelus' first act after this rebirth is to kill a prostitute in an alley. Before revealing his new nature to Buffy, he taunts her about their sexual encounter, referring to her as a "pro." Buffy spends the rest of the season dealing emotionally and psychologically with the aftermath of this sexual encounter.

In *Buffy*, prostitutes are quite often presented as vampires and, in the case of the series *Angel*, as demons. *Buffy* introduces the vampire Darla, who was a prostitute dying of syphilis when she was turned into a vampire (*Angel* "Darla" 2.7). In the *Buffy* episode "Into the Woods" (5.10), Buffy's college boyfriend Riley visits a vampire prostitute, paying her to bite him, so that he can feel as if he is needed. Buffy's disgust at his behavior leads to their relationship's dissolution. The image of the prostitute as a demon is also illustrated in the *Angel* episode "War Zone" (1.20); as he tries to help a client who is being blackmailed, Angel visits Madame Dorion's, a demon brothel where female demons serve both human and demon clients.

Sexual encounters in the *Buffy*verse either serve to change the characters, by having them mature or face their inner "demons," or lead them into more committed relationships (making them "good" in the sense of Stevenson's "western sexual morality"). This theme of sex being positive only within the confines of a committed relationship is illustrated in the *Angel*verse as well, wherein the complexities of manifesting sexual agency, sexual mores, and sexual corporeality are suppressed in favor of a more rigid, more generically-common "black and white" vision of sex and sexuality. Yet this overtly simplistic examination of sexual relationships would soon be replaced with more complex visions in Whedon's later television creations.

The series *Firefly* and its eventual movie conclusion, *Serenity*, provided a more encompassing perspective on sex than either *Buffy* or *Angel*. *Firefly* takes place in the twenty-sixth century, and its created world is a generic mixture of science fiction and the American Western. Its sense of sexual values also seems to combine a futuristic sophistication with old-fashioned ideals. For example, Zoe and Wash are a happily married couple and are shown to have a healthy and active sexual relationship. Conversely, Shepherd Book lives a vow of chastity, though he does not judge the sexuality of the other characters, as one might expect from a preacher. In the pilot episode, Kaylee begins to harbor what appears to be an innocent crush for Dr. Simon Tam. When Jayne, another member of Serenity's crew, makes an offensive remark about Kaylee and her crush, he is banished from the dinner table (*Firefly* "Serenity"1.1). Later in the series, the viewer discovers that Mal's first sight of Kaylee occurred while she was having casual sex in the engine room of *Serenity*. Mal's response to catching Kaylee illustrates the series' handling of sexual situations. Mal is generally depicted as having a prudish attitude toward sex. However, he makes no judgment against Kaylee for the incident. He immediately hires her when she demonstrates more mechanical expertise than *Serenity*'s current mechanic, her sexual partner in that encounter ("Out of Gas" 1.8). Ultimately, Kaylee's sex life does not affect Mal's view of her. He judges her on her knowledge and abilities and defends her from inappropriate remarks.

Probably the boldest indication that Whedon's sexual attitudes matured with *Firefly* is the inclusion of the "Companion" Inara, a sex worker who has set up shop in one of *Serenity*'s shuttles. In this universe, a Companion is an educated man or woman trained in the arts of seduction. A Companion must be registered with a Guild and is highly regarded in society. Guild law dictates that Companions such as Inara choose their clients and control the conditions of their interactions. Inara's presence on *Serenity* gives respectability to the ship. Many scholars and fans viewed the Companions as an allusion to the geisha culture of Japan; however, it should be noted that traditional Geishas were not prostitutes. As Leigh Adams Wright observes,

The Companion's high social status demonstrates a fundamental change in the world as we know it — that not just purchased sex, but purchased company should not only be acceptable, but *respected* as a profession is a marked departure from Western modes of interaction, where selling one's emotional time has always been viewed with suspicion if not downright scorned, from prostitutes to actors [32].

The episode "Heart of Gold" (1.13) provides the best examples of *Firefly*'s attitudes toward sex, Companions, and whores. The episode depicts a whorehouse under attack by the local town bully, Rance Burgess. Inara enlists Mal and the crew to help the women and men of the whorehouse. Nandi is the madam of the whorehouse, a friend of Inara's and a former Companion. Inara tells Mal that Nandi is not a Companion; rather she is a whore, naming a distinction between the two types of sex workers in the world of *Firefly*. Nevertheless, Mal and his crew protect the sex workers and appear to respect them. Mal even engages in sexual relations with Nandi, who gives herself freely to him. It is not a business transition but an act of mutual attraction. This is the first and only time that Mal is shown manifesting actual physical sexuality during the short run of the series. However, the series is insistent in depicting Mal spending time getting to know Nandi prior to the coital act. Although theirs may not be a relationship, there is more of a connection between them than just casual sex. This interaction is juxtaposed with that of Jayne, who also has sex with one of the prostitutes, though more directly, as payment for defending the whorehouse. Still, no judgment is implied; Jayne fights beside the same woman as an equal during the final battle of the episode. In fact, the manner in which these sex workers heroically stand their ground provides an uncharacteristic amount of humanity and dignity to prostitutes that is rarely found on television. Overall, *Firefly* presented an intriguing attitude toward sex acts occurring between its characters and their sex worker mates. Sex is both paid for/not paid for, but the commoditization of sexuality is no more remarked upon than any other act of commerce. In other words, it is significant for its seeming insignificance.

Dollhouse, on the other hand, appears to diverge from the previous series' views on sexuality. *Dollhouse* is about an organization, the Rossum Corporation, which runs a number of facilities around the world known as Dollhouses. In these Dollhouses, "volunteers" or Actives have their memories erased and replaced with a personality of the paying customers' choosing. When the Actives return from their engagements, these "false" personalities are erased and the Actives are returned to a passive, doll-like state. In this state, the Actives live in the Dollhouse, waiting for their next assignment, until the end of their five-year contract with Rossum. Actives often have sex with clients while on engagements. Imprinted with personalities tailored to the client's needs and requests, the Actives believe that they love the client and are choosing to be with them. Adelle Dewitt, director of the Los Angeles Dollhouse, explains this to a client in one episode ("The Target," 1.2), telling him that the Active will not be pretending during their encounter; the Active will actually be in love with him. Yet, given that these Actives are *programmed* to think this way, the series clearly depicts that will and choice are not part of the sexual expression. This programming of love, and the resultant loss of free will, is in direct contrast with the image of the Companion in *Firefly*.

It is this moral obfuscation that made *Dollhouse* one of Whedon's most problematic series. Catherine Coker acknowledges this, noting,

> *Dollhouse* has become Joss Whedon's most controversial work yet, with many fans, viewers, and critics troubled by the images and aspects of human trafficking and prostitution depicted on the show. Female characters are regularly menaced and abused, often sexually, both within and without the confines of the Dollhouse and the assignations it arranges [226].

Unlike *Firefly's* Companions or even its respected sexual workers, *Dollhouse* presents the subordination of the female in the act of sexual congress. In a very tangible way, every manifestation of sexuality is an act of rape, since the Actives have no ability to provide actual consent to the sex acts subjected to them and their bodies.

Because of its basic premise, *Dollhouse* frequently depicts sex and, because the majority of sexual acts occur between an Active and a client, this sex can, from one perspective, also be considered prostitution. The clients have paid for their fantasies made flesh, and the Actives (unknowingly) deliver. Even in cases that appear to indicate a healthy relationship, it merely an illusion. For example, Paul Ballard, a former FBI agent who seeks to expose and bring down the Dollhouse, develops a sexual relationship with his neighbor, Mellie. The viewer soon learns that Mellie has been programmed by the Dollhouse to get close to, and spy on, Paul. Ballard does not pay for her, nor has he asked for her services, but there is still an element of prostitution in the sense that Mellie has been "given" to Paul, albeit without his awareness.

Whedon himself has commented on the interconnections between prostitution, coercion, and *Dollhouse*:

> I believe that prostitution is not, in concept, repulsive. I believe that people are gonna want to have sex for a long time.... What interests me is that urge and what we do with it. People will always want to give up their power on some level. It's a nightmare and a fantasy. The nightmare is I have no will. And the fantasy is I have no responsibility or memory of what I've done [Press, qtd. in Lavery and Burkhead 187].

This perhaps is the issue that is addressed by *Dollhouse*; not the morality of prostitution, but rather the notion of sexual commoditization and prostitution always reflecting acts of non-consensual sex.

Content Analysis of Sex on Firefly *and* Dollhouse
METHODOLOGY

Numerous studies have examined the sexual content of television programs, ranging from sexual and violent portrayals in movie rental previews (Oliver & Kalycarmon), heterosexual scripts of primetime television (Kim, et al.), to television sexual content as it relates to teenagers' sexual expectations (Martino, et al.). Laramie D. Taylor, of the University of Michigan, examined the effects of sexual content on television on the attitudes and beliefs of viewers through a combination of content analysis and interviews with subjects. This research showed that visual depictions of sex on television, such as on-screen sexual encounters, did not seem to affect the beliefs of the research subjects. However, verbal sexual content, such as discussions between characters about sex and sexual experiences, did influence the beliefs of the same test groups.

In another study, the Parents Television Council (2002) reviewed programs for sexual content in two main categories: visual sexual content and verbal sexual content. In the study, programs were recorded from sweeps week in November of 1998, 2000, and 2002 on the six major networks broadcasting at that time (ABC, CBS, NBC, FOX, WB, and UPN) in order to track changes in sexual content. This study showed a decrease in sexual content in programming during the first two hours of prime time, between 8 P.M. and 10 P.M. More importantly, this study also delineated a methodology for measuring sexual content that was later expanded in the group's 2007 study "The Alarming Family Hour." Though the PTC has their own biases and questionable motives for these studies, their thorough methodologies provide a means of quantifying depictions of sexual content on television and film.

A 2003 report by the Kaiser Foundation, a non-partisan research group, entitled "Sex on TV" also examined sexual content, including sexual behavior and sexual talk. This study categorized incidents of sexual behavior into six types, ranging from physical flirtation through depicted acts of sexuality. The study also categorized incidents of sexual talk into six degrees of behavior, ranging from sexual comment to expert advice. The study found that almost all types of shows, excluding reality shows, included sexual content, though very few showed sexual responsibility. This study also provided an important baseline for describing sexual content on television while also contributing measures for tracking sexual content (Kunkel, et al.).

Deborah Fisher, Douglas Hill, Joel Grube, and Enid Gruber also published a study that examined sex across television networks and genres. They found very few genres consistently offered programs free of sexual content during the peak viewing times for teens (8 P.M.–10 P.M.). This study also created very specific measures for sexual coding, including the identification of sexual incidents, coding each incident by sexual behaviors, relationship status, explicitness, sexual talk, and sexual responsibility.

These aforementioned studies provide the foundation for the methodology of this present research, allowing me to create a set of parameters to examine sexual content on *Firefly* and *Dollhouse*. These parameters were expanded to include coding to examine prostitution as it applies to *Firefly* and *Dollhouse*.

For the purposes of the present research, a sexual incident is defined as an onscreen simulated sexual encounter, act, performance, nudity, or suggestive behavior, such as two characters "making out" at the end of a date. It also includes the discussion of sex, sexual behaviors, sexual attraction, sexual references, jokes, clinical discussions, or any other allusions to sexual topics. Examples include conversation between characters about the sexual desirability of another character or when two characters discuss a past sexual encounter. An incident occurs in a program during an uninterrupted segment or scene where a segment is defined as one that begins and ends when the action cuts away to another segment, event, scene, or commercial, such as when two characters are rolling around on a bed kissing and petting, then the camera pans up and goes to black. A segment such as this is counted as one incident. A return to the segment after such a break, such as coming back to the previous two characters now naked under sheets in bed, is counted as a separate incident because a casual viewer could observe one scene but not the other.

Each character involved in an incident was recorded for each incident. The initiator of the sexual incident was also coded. In the case of a sexual act, the initiator of the act is determined according to perception of that scene in isolation. For example, in the case of a verbal sexual incident, the instigator would be the person who initiated the conversation or told the joke as determined by viewing the scene in isolation. The gender of the initiator was recorded along with a brief description of the scene. Incidents were coded into three major categories, each with sub-categories: visual non-sex sexual content; visual sexual content; and verbal sexual content. Incidents with more than one type of content were coded as one incident and all appropriate categories are marked.

Visual Non-Sex Content. Visual non-sex content is defined as sexual visuals with no sexual contact or behaviors. This includes discreet nudity, nudity non-sexual, nudity sexual, provocative dress, undressing, and provocative actions.

- *Discreet nudity*: nudity that is covered by a bed sheet, clothing held up, or blurring of obvious nudity.

- *Non-sexual nudity*: nudity that occurs in a non-sexual environment and not for other characters to view, such as getting dressed or showering alone.
- *Sexual nudity*: nudity that is meant to be seen and is intended to give sexual pleasure to another character or characters. One character finding another character naked in bed is an example.
- *Provocative dress*: dressing in a manner to invoke a sexual response, including short skirts, lingerie, or low cut clothing revealing cleavage.
- *Undressing*: the removal of clothing regardless of the context. This could be someone undressing to take a shower alone or a character dropping a robe to entice another character.
- *Provocative actions*: suggestive actions such as dancing, performance and sexual exhibition where there is no touching between any characters.

Visual Sexual Content. Visual sexual content is onscreen depiction of sexual contact. This includes physical flirtation, kissing, petting or groping, implied sexual congress, depicted sexual congress, oral sex, kink and bondage.
- *Physical flirtation*: touching non-sexual parts of the body to invoke a sexual response. This could be shown in a character stroking or running his/her fingers along another character's arm.
- *Kissing*: romantic kissing or deep kissing. Affection exchanges between family or friends are excluded from this definition.
- *Petting/groping*: touching sexual areas with clothing on.
- *Sex implied*: an off-screen sexual act that is implied through an action in the scene, such as waking up naked in bed together, or showing the initiation of a sex act before cutting away or falling out of frame.
- *Sex depicted*: onscreen sex with or without coverings. This includes shots like close-ups of feet under sheets or moans emanating from writhing forms under sheets.
- *Oral sex*: depictions of oral sex that is either implied or depicted on screen.
- *Kink*: incidents of spanking, humiliation, or other forms of sadomasochistic sex acts.
- *Bondage*: coded when bondage is shown as a part of sex such as when hands are tied, handcuffed, or shackled.

Verbal Sexual Content. Verbal discussions of a sexual nature include direct conversations, indirect conversations, humor, sexual references, sexual specifics and offers of sex.

- *Direct conversations*: conversations that are upfront and explicitly discussing sex.
- *Indirect conversations*: conversations that make implications or innuendos about sex, sex acts, or sexual body parts.
- *Humor*: jokes of a sexual nature.
- *Sexual references*: comments about sex, but not specifically discussing sex, such as a character saying, "You know what I mean."
- *Specific sexual conversations*: about specific sexual experiences.
- *Offers of sex*: verbal sexual offers of sex either direct or by innuendo.

All of these conversations are also coded as casual or clinical. Casual sexual discussions are discussions of a sexual nature with friends, colleagues, or others that are not medical discussions or medical questions. Clinical discussions include conversations with medical professionals, classroom lectures on sex, or asking medical-type questions to friends or parents.

When a sexual act occurs, the relationship between the partners is also analyzed, including relationship status, power in the relationship, healthiness of the relationship, and attitude towards the encounter. Relationship between sexual partners defines the relationship between those engaged in a sex act. These relationships are defined as either:

- *Married*: a legally married couple or domestic partnership/implied marriage or long-term relationship cohabiting.
- *A couple*: a dating couple, but not married; an established relationship.
- *Casual relationship*: not in a relationship, though the partners may know each other as friends, acquaintances or colleagues, or are just strangers who just met and have had no previous relationship.

Power in the relationship is the demonstration of power dynamics between the people involved and who is in control of the situation. This includes such criteria as who was on top in the sexual encounter and if the encounter was rape or other sexual assault. Healthiness defines the overall good that the partnership has for the participants. The relationship is coded as healthy if both partners are shown to be positive toward the relationship and the relationship is depicted as in the best interest of both parties. The relationship is coded as unhealthy if it shown as being detrimental to either of the participants. If the relationship shows one partner in control and happy but the relationship is harmful and hurtful to the other partner, the relationship is coded as unhealthy. The attitude of the participants toward the incident was also noted: did they respond to the event in a positive or negative way? Did they appear happy or upset about it?

Specific coding was developed to examine prostitution in *Firefly* and *Dollhouse*. Prostitution is coded when money or goods were exchanged for sex or sexual favors. In the case of prostitution, the client and provider were coded by gender. Also coded was who chose whom. Specifically, was it the prostitute who chose the client, or did the client chose the prostitute? The provider's ability to refuse and the provider's awareness of prostitution were also coded. The provider's ability to refuse includes being able to choose not to participate at any time or to choose not to participate with a specific client. Awareness of prostitution is specific to *Dollhouse,* as many of the Actives are programmed to believe that they are in relationships with the clients and do not know that they are participating in acts akin to prostitution.

Using the parameters outlined above, all episodes of the series *Firefly* (14) and *Dollhouse* (26), as well as *Firefly*'s sequel film *Serenity*, were examined and coded. The episodes of all series included aired and unaired episodes in chronological order as determined by Whedon and ordered on the DVDs of each series. Opening credits of shows and "previously on" recaps were not included in coding.

Results

Interesting trends resulted from the analyses of *Firefly* and *Dollhouse*. A total of 274 sexual incidents were observed in the two series, an average of 6.52 incidents per episode. The Parents Television Council reported that, across the six networks examined, there was an average of 3.76 incidents of sexual content per hour in 2007. This means that *Firefly* and *Dollhouse* were averaging 43 percent more sexual incidents than the overall network television average. It should be noted that neither series was on the air in 2007; however, given the available data and considering the seven-year gap between the premieres of *Firefly* and *Dollhouse*, these numbers can determine relative trends in television as well as act as a central fulcrum between which both series can be posited. *Firefly*, as a series, had a total of ninety sexual incidents, or an average of 6.00 per episode. *Dollhouse* totaled 178 incidents of sexual content, for an average of 6.85 per episode. Thus *Dollhouse* averaged almost one more incident per episode than *Firefly* and 46 percent more than the television average. Of the 274 total incidents, 118 incidents included visual sex, 123 incidents included visual non-sex, and 197 incidents included sex talk.

The 197 incidents of sex talk or verbal sex varied over the subcategories and between the two series. There were seventy-four direct references to sex or the sex act and 105 indirect references or innuendos. There were also ninety-eight references to sex, and fifty-seven specific mentions of sexual acts. On average, more sexual references occurred in *Firefly* than *Dollhouse*. *Firefly* averaged

2.88 sexual references per episode compared to *Dollhouse* at 2.00. Twenty-five offers of sex occurred in the entire series of *Dollhouse*, versus twenty-six offers in *Firefly*, which had half as many episodes. All verbal sexual incidents were coded as either discussions of a casual nature between regular people or discussions of a clinical nature between a person and a doctor or someone seeking medical advice. Of the incidents coded, all but ten fell into casual discussions. The ten clinical discussions all occurred on the series *Dollhouse*. However, there was more sex talk on *Firefly* (4.81 incidents per episode) than on *Dollhouse* (4.62 incidents per episode).

The incidents that included visual non-sex varied significantly between the two series. There were forty-seven incidents of discreet nudity, with only fifteen occurring on *Firefly*, such as Mal seated naked on a rock in the episode "Trash" (1.11). There were a total of thirty-three incidents of non-sexual nudity, which includes a scene in which Echo is covered in gauze to cover her private parts while doctors steal her spinal fluid in the episode "The Hollow Men" (2.12). A total of twenty-three incidents of sexual nudity occur between both series, such as the scene in which Saffron appears naked in Mal's room as she tries to seduce him in "Our Mrs. Reynolds" (1.6). Sexual nudity is, on average, nearly identical between the two shows (0.54 per episode on *Firefly* and 0.56 per episode on *Dollhouse*). Thirty-six incidents of undressing were observed, with thirty-three of these occurring on *Dollhouse*. *Dollhouse* also provided more incidents of provocative dress and provocative actions than *Firefly*. *Dollhouse* had 2.00 incidents per episode of provocative dress and .92 of provocative action, compared to *Firefly*'s 1.19 of provocative dress and 0.31 of provocative action. Such incidents in *Dollhouse* also tended to be a bit more provocative than the ones shown in *Firefly*. Whiskey's very sexualized dance in "Omega" (1.12), for example, is considerably more provocative when compared to the legs-only shot of the women dancing in the bar as seen in the movie *Serenity*.

Of the 118 incidents of visual sex recorded, only forty-seven included sexual activity. Of those, nine depicted onscreen sexual activity, such as with Inara's first appearance in the series, as she is shown having sex with a client (*Firefly* "Serenity"1.1). The remaining thirty-eight incidents were implied sex, such as the shot of Echo waking up naked in bed with a man in the *Dollhouse* episode "Instinct" (2.2). The majority of the visual sex depicted fell into the categories of kissing or physical flirtation, with sixty-six and eighty-six, respectively. The opening scene of "Objects in Space" (*Firefly* 1.14), when Simon and Kaylee are lightly touching each other as they talk, is an example of this physical flirtation.

Additional information was coded for all incidents of visual sex. Of the sexual incidents depicted, thirty-three incidents occurred between married partners and forty incidents occurred between strangers. The remainder occurred either between couples or casual acquaintances. The initiator of the sexual activity was shown in a position of power or control 103 times, although the partner was also shown in a position of power or shared power sixty-six times. With regard to power in these sexual encounters, there were ten incidents of depicted rape, and rape was discussed an additional twenty times. Of these depicted rapes, nine were shown in *Dollhouse*.

Prostitution is a major theme in each of these series, which is why there are, on average, 1.38 incidents of prostitution per episode. The topic of prostitution is mentioned an average of 1.33 times per episode. Prostitution occurs in almost every episode of each series and is mentioned fifty-five times (from a total of forty episodes). However, it is the portrayal of prostitution that is as significant as the frequency of its occurrences. As would be expected, in forty-eight of the fifty-eight incidents, the client is male and the provider is female. There are five incidents in which the client is female and the provider is male, two in which the client and the provider are both female, and none in which the client and provider are both male. A bigger distinction between these two series concerns the depiction of *how* the provider is chosen and whether they have the right to refuse the client. The Companion of *Firefly* is shown to choose her client in twelve incidents. The other five incidents of prostitution in *Firefly* occur with "regular" prostitutes, not Companions. These women do not choose their clients, and in all but two incidents, do not have the ability to refuse the client. The Actives of *Dollhouse* are involved in forty-one incidents of prostitution and, in all but six of these, they do not know that they are being sold for sex. In the incidents in which they are aware that they are participating in prostitution, they are programmed as prostitutes. Thus the question of what they do or do not know is unclear. In *Dollhouse*, the Actives also have no ability to refuse the client in most cases. Of the forty-one incidents of prostitution in *Dollhouse*, only six times is the provider shown to have the ability to refuse. It should be noted, however, that it is their programmed personality refusing, and not the actual person.

Conclusions

Depictions of sex in the Whedonverse are varied from series to series and character to character. Overall, sex is shown to be a positive part of a healthy and committed relationship between two people who care for each other. *Buffy* and *Angel* laid the ground work for this idealized relationship and for the repercussions of not conforming to it. *Firefly* and *Dollhouse* challenged these ideals for sexual relationships. *Firefly* depicts sexual relationships through all its characters, with each member of the *Serenity*'s crew, except for River Tam and Shepherd Book, shown in sexual congress. These sexual relationships are depicted as positive in most cases, entered into willingly with a partner who the main characters have spent time with prior to the sexual act, but with whom they may or may not have committed relationship. There are incidents of sex shown as "bad" as well. For example, the prostitute Chari, in "Heart of Gold" (1.13), is shown in a position of submission when she is forced to perform oral sex on Burgess in front of his men. For the most, part, however, *Firefly* depicts sexuality with an "evolved" version of Stevenson's "western secular morality" model — stretching the bonds, but not breaking them.

The image of the Companion is perhaps the one clear divergence from the means in which sex previously manifested in Whedon's works. The Companion of *Firefly* is shown to have a healthy relationship toward sex. The incidents of sex and prostitution that involve Inara are shown as positive for both the client and the provider. Inara holds the power in these relationships and always has the choice to reject the client or walk away at anytime. In one instance, Inara tells Mal, "One of the virtues of not being puritanical about sex is not feeling embarrassed afterwards. You should look into it" ("Heart of Gold" 1.13). The Companion is presented as a strong, educated woman who trades her company, including sex, as her profession. The crew of *Serenity*, with the exception of Mal, accepts Inara as a Companion without degrading her or her work. Surprisingly, Shepherd Book easily accepts Inara and her profession with very little comment, even jokingly offering her a sermon on her "wicked ways" when bringing her dinner. It is only Mal who is shown to have an issue with Inara's profession. Mal's somewhat puritanical views on sex and his obvious feelings for Inara underlie his negative remarks. Mal's defense of all of the whores at Nandi's compound indicates that his affront to Inara as a Companion could likely be attributed to his own feelings for her.

Dollhouse provides a skewed view of the prostitute — the prostitute that does not know she is a one. The Actives in Dollhouse, as Adelle Dewitt comments, get to be both the whore and the virgin ("A Love Supreme" 2.8). They are sold as sexual toys to clients of means and then "wiped" clean and left in a childlike state until they are needed again. Given that sex and power are the main themes of *Dollhouse*, it is no surprise that there are more sexual incidents in this show than on *Firefly*. In addition, there are more graphic scenes, serving to reinforce the fact that the Actives have little to no power over these incidents. The graphic incidents and loss of power are shown even further in the nine incidents of rape on *Dollhouse*, all of which were committed against Actives. On *Firefly*, rape is mentioned as a threat twice, once in regards to Reavers raping people to death ("Serenity" 1.1) and once when Jubal Early asks Kaylee if she has ever been raped as a means to intimidate her ("Objects in Space" 1.14). There is one incident of implied rape on *Firefly*, committed against a prostitute.

Overall, sex on *Dollhouse* and *Firefly* indicate a change in attitude toward sex in Whedon's works, but not in the morality underlying these acts. *Dollhouse* provides the most extreme depictions of sex, illustrating sexual slavery and possible rape. *Dollhouse* contains almost double the incidents of sexual content than the national television average per hour and, in almost seventy percent of these incidents, at least one of the participants is a programmed Active. *Firefly*, on the other hand, depicts an above average amount of sex, but these acts are evenly divided between sexual incidents that involve commoditized sex and sex between couples in committed relationships. *Firefly* shows an idealized world with regards to sex; even the most puritanical characters do not judge others for their sexual choices. The sexual incidents occurring in relationships between committed couples are shown to be just as positive as most of the sexual incidents occurring in casual relationships or in the majority of the paid transactions.

These changes in attitude toward sex and the relationship between the images of sex shown by Inara and Echo illustrate a change in Whedon's works with respect to his depictions of sex. Davis writes, "Attempting to gain an authentic understanding of the status and life chances of prostitutes is the first step in enhancing the position and status of all women" (ix). *Firefly* and *Dollhouse* take this one step further. The Companion and the Active are dichotomies of one another; they are perfect reflections of the worlds in which they live and those worlds' views toward sex and, not only women, but people as a whole. Inara is in control of her world, living in the idealized situation for a prostitute. As a Companion she can choose who she is with, where she works, and what she does. The same is true of the crew of *Serenity*; any member of the crew can leave at any time and is not judged on who they are or what they do, only on their actions and abilities.

Echo as an Active is in the completely opposite situation. She has no control over her life and is at the mercy of those who run the Dollhouse. She is the ideal prostitute with no power, no choices, and no free will. This lack of control over one's life and choices is not limited to the Actives in the Dollhouses. Adelle's power is as easily stripped as Echo's when her superiors at Rossum remove the Los Angeles Dollhouse from her directorship ("Meet Jane Doe" 2.7).

The overall theme that emerges is that, ultimately, "good" sex is not necessarily about commitment and love. It is about choice. In sexual relationships where both partners chose the relationship, the sex is "good." In sexual relationships with a powerless partner, or one who did not choose to be there, the sex is "bad." This pattern of choice is held throughout Whedon's works.

Inara and the universe of *Firefly* allow for such choices while Echo and the universe in *Dollhouse* illustrate the lack of choice. Gone is the attitude of the *Buffy* and *Angel* series that "good" sex can only exist in committed relationships. With this change in the determination between "good" and "bad" sex, *Firefly* and *Dollhouse* demonstrate a maturing attitude toward sex in Whedon's works.

WORKS CITED

Coker, Catherine. "Exploitation of Bodies and Minds in Season One of *Dollhouse.*" *Sexual Rhetoric in the Works of Joss Whedon.* Ed. Erin B. Waggoner. Jefferson, NC: McFarland, 2010. 226–238. Print.
Davis, Nanette J., ed. *Prostitution: An International Handbook on Trends, Problems and Politics.* Westport, CT: Greenwood Press, 1993. Print.
Fisher, Deborah A., Douglas L. Hill, Joel W. Grube, and Enid L. Gruber. "Sex on American Television: An Analysis across Program Genres and Network Types." *Journal of Broadcasting & Electronic Media* 48.4 (2004): 529–553. Web. 6 June 2011.
Kim, Janna L., C. Sorsoli, Katherine Collins, Bonnie Zylbergold, Deborah Schooler, and Deborah Tolman. "From Sex to Sexuality: Exposing the Heterosexual Script on Primetime Network Television." *The Journal of Sex Research* 44.2(2007): 143–158. Web. 6 June 2011.
Kunkel, Dale, Erica Biely, Keren Eyal, Kristie Cope-Farrar, Edward Donnerstein, and Rena Fanrich. "Sex on TV: Content and Context A Biennial Report to the Henry J. Kaiser Family Foundation." Kff.org. 2003. Web. 12 June 2006.
Martino, Steven C., Rebecca Collins, Marc Elliott, David Kanouse, and Sandra Berry. "It's Better on TV: Does Television Set Teenagers Up for Regret Following Sexual Initiation? (Influence of Television Sex) (Report)." *Perspectives on Sexual and Reproductive Health* 41.2 (2009): 92–99. Web. 6 June 2011.
Oliver, Mary Beth, and Sriram Kalyanaraman. "Appropriate for All Viewing Audiences? An Examination of Violent and Sexual Portrayals in Movie Previews Featured on Video Rentals." *Journal of Broadcasting & Electronic Media* 46.2 (2002): 283–300. Print.
Parents Television Council. "The Alarming Family Hour...No Place for Children." Parentstv.org. 2007. Web. 9 Dec. 2009.
_____. "Sex Loses Its Appeal: A State of the Industry Report on Sex on TV." Parentstv.org. 2002. Web. 31 May 2011.
Press, Joy. "Joss Whedon Just Wants to Be Loved." Interview from Salon.com, February 11, 2009. Salon Media Group. *Joss Whedon Conversations.* Ed. David Lavery and Cynthia Burkhead. Jackson: University Press of Mississippi, 2011. 184–189. Print.
Stevenson, Gregory. *Televised Morality: The Case for* Buffy the Vampire Slayer. Lanham, MD: Hamilton Books, 2003. Print.
Taylor, Laramie D. "Effects of Visual and Verbal Sexual Television Content and Perceived Realism on Attitudes and Beliefs." *Journal of Sex Research* 42.2 (2005): 130–137. Web. 6 June 2011.
Wright, Leigh Adams. "Asian Objects in Space.*" Finding Serenity: Anti-heroes, Lost Shepherds and Space Hookers in Joss Whedon's* Firefly. Ed. Jane Espenson with Glenn Yeffeth. Dallas: BenBella Books, 2004. 29–36. Print.

Television Episodes and Films Cited

Angel: Seasons 1–5. The DVD Collector's Limited Edition Set. 20th Century–Fox Home Entertainment, 2007.

"Darla." Season 2, Episode 7. Writ. Tim Minear. Dir. Tim Minear.
"War Zone." Season 1, Episode 20. Writ. Garry Campbell. Dir. David Straiton.
Buffy the Vampire Slayer: The Complete Second Season. 20th Century–Fox, 2000. DVD.
"Innocence." Episode 14. Writ. Joss Whedon. Dir. Joss Whedon.
"Surprise." Episode 13. Writ. Marti Noxon. Dir. Michael Lange.
Buffy the Vampire Slayer: The Complete Fifth Season. 20th Century–Fox, 2003. DVD.
"Into the Woods." Episode 10. Writ. Marti Noxon. Dir. Marti Noxon.
Dollhouse: The Complete First Season. 20th Century–Fox, 2009. DVD.
"Man on the Street." Episode 6. Writ. Joss Whedon. Dir. David Straiton.
"Omega." Episode 12. Writ. Tim Minear. Dir. Tim Minear.
"The Target." Episode 2. Writ. Steven S. DeKnight. Dir. Steven S. DeKnight.
Dollhouse: The Complete Second Season. 20th Century–Fox, 2010. DVD.
"The Hollow Men." Episode 12. Writ. Michele Fazekas, Tara Butters and Tracy Bellomo. Dir. Terrance O'Hara.
"Instinct." Episode 2. Writ. Michele Fazekas and Tara Butters. Dir. Marita Grabiak.
"A Love Supreme." Episode 8. Writ. Jenny DeArmitt. Dir. David Straiton.
"Meet Jane Doe." Episode 7. Writ. Maurissa Tancharoen, Jed Whedon and Andrew Chambliss. Dir. Dwight Little.
Firefly: The Complete Series. 20th Century–Fox, 2003. DVD.
"Heart of Gold." Episode 13. Writ. Brett Matthews. Dir. Thomas J. Wright.
"Objects in Space." Episode 14. Writ. Ben Edlund and Jose Molino. Dir. Vern Gillum.
"Our Mrs. Reynolds." Episode 6. Writ. Joss Whedon. Dir. Vondie Curtis-Hall.
"Out of Gas." Episode 8. Writ. David Solomon. Dir. Tim Minear.
"Serenity." Episode 1 (Parts 1 and 2). Writ. Joss Whedon. Dir. Joss Whedon.
"Trash." Episode 11. Writ. Joss Whedon. Dir. Joss Whedon.
Serenity. Dir. Joss Whedon. Universal Studios, 2005. DVD.

The Evil Wet Nurse: Preœdipal Development and Primo Levi's Science Fiction
Robert C. Pirro

> *I believe that I chose [the pseudonym Damiano Malabaila for my collection* Natural Histories*] casually; it is the name of a merchant by whose shop I would pass twice daily on the way to and from work. Then I noticed a relationship between the name and the stories.... Malabaila means "evil wet nurse" and it now seems to me that many of my stories give off a vague odor of spoiled milk, of nourishment that is no longer such, in short, of adulteration, contamination, of evil-doing.*
>
> PRIMO LEVI, ECHI 37

It is primarily due to his testimonies as Holocaust witness and survivor, *Survival in Auschwitz* and *The Drowned and the Saved*, that Italian writer Primo Levi remains a major presence in the imagination of both popular and scholarly readers. The claim of his writing to a permanent place in both Italian and world literature is additionally founded on the critical and popular receptions of his lightly fictionalized, richly imagined autobiographical reflections on the nature and rewards of work as seen through his own university training and career experience as an industrial chemist (*The Periodic Table*) and through his encounters, while on a business trip to the Soviet Union, with a Piedmontese derrick rigger (*The Monkey's Wrench*).

Much less noticed or celebrated have been Levi's efforts as a short story writer of science fiction and fantasy, efforts which started in 1942 before his deportation and continued until the end of February 1987, less than two months before his death.[1] If these works — published in English translation in *The Sixth Day* (stories selected from *Storie naturali* 1966 and *Vizio di forma* 1971), *A Tranquil Star* (stories selected from *Lilìt e altri racconti* 1981), and *The Mirror Maker* (stories selected from *Racconti e saggi* 1986) — represent a major part of Levi's literary output and stand as a favored mode of storytelling expression, their significance to his legacy as a writer remains unclear since assessments of the nature and larger meaning of this sprawling legacy vary.

Following the lead of Levi's epistolary declaration regarding *Storie naturali*, that there was "a continuity, a bridge between the Lager and these inventions," some scholars argue that his short fiction expands upon concerns he first broached in his Auschwitz writings (*Opere* 1435). Nancy Harrowitz reads "Versamina," Levi's tale of the wartime discovery by a German chemist of a drug that confounded pleasure and pain, as referring back to "the role of science in the execution of the Holocaust" (71). Lucie Benchouiha notes several ways that Levi's faux fairytale, "Sleeping Beauty in the Fridge," a story about a woman who escapes from a state of cryogenic suspension, evokes the dehumanizing conditions of Levi's camp experience (366).

Other analyses, including those by Giuseppina Santagostino and Roberto Farneti, focus on how Levi's stories tend to blur (and invite reflection on) the line between human agency and natural processes. For Robert Gordon, Levi's retelling of the golem story in "The Servant" takes as its theme "the profound difficulty of setting the boundaries of the human" (179). Jonathan Usher sees Levi as engaged in writing "around the problem of new life consistently" and finds in his science fiction stories an urge "to be freed from the weight of the flesh" (204, 206).

Gender is at issue in Ilona Klein's consideration of Levi's science fiction plots that are driven by technological discoveries. Klein observes that in most of them, "Levi lets women resist technology" (118). Charlotte Ross offers a somewhat more extensive consideration of gender as a context for "stories that slip in and out of conventional genre categories, oscillating between narrating what appears to be purely fictional, and what feels uncannily close to our lived experience" (105). Suggesting that the story of technologically-facilitated rape in "Sleeping Beauty in the Fridge" "has an undeniably feminist edge," Ross argues that Levi's short fiction "highlights the concentration of technological power into often unscrupulous male hands" (112). Yet while both Klein and Ross refer to stereotypically gendered patterns of behavior exhibited by characters in Levi's short fiction, they do not offer a systematic survey of those behavioral patterns across his writings, nor do they attempt to explain those patterns by reference to Levi's life. In reflecting on his choice of pseudonym for *Natural Histories* in terms of infantile nutrition gone sour, Levi invites a psychologically-informed analysis of preœdipal relations and their power to shape childhood and adult emotional experience and perceptions. As this essay will show, Levi's science fiction oeuvre can be seen as being both entangled in preœdipal images of the maternal and engaged in a struggle to understand the nature of that entanglement and test its limits. From the perspective of theories of preœdipal experience, Levi's tendency to configure scientific discovery in maternal terms, as the substratum out of which male autonomy is made possible and from which the greatest challenges are posed to that autonomy, takes on special significance. The key to this essay's approach to Levi's science fiction, then, is to understand these pieces as attempting to address the problems of male autonomy in a modern technological world using metaphors, allegories, and motifs related to that earliest episode of human struggle for autonomy, precœdipal relations with the mother.

This approach both builds on, and reveals the limits of, the interpretation of Levi's family dynamics offered in Carole Angier's biography, *The Double Bond: Primo Levi, a Biography* (2002). Precœdipal relations encompass infant and toddler perceptions of, and responses to, primary care and nurturance. This stage of development is *pre*-œdipal in the sense that it precedes the œdipal stage, when issues of genital sexuality and sexually charged possession are salient. In the precœdipal stage, babies are orally fixated and engaged in processes of rudimentary individuation. Focusing for the most part on issues of œdipal sexuality, Angier's biography slights the influence of the precœdipal stage on Levi's struggles with issues of dependence and autonomy. Deploying the psychological notion of the double bind or "a crippling conflict between contradictory or unfulfillable requirements which you can neither escape nor win," Angier draws upon the testimony both of Levi's fictionalized alter egos and his friends to argue for his lifelong "torment over sex and love" (xviii, 80). This torment purportedly originated in his highly fraught relationship to his mother, with whom he lived for his entire life except for brief interruptions while he worked two wartime jobs, during his internment at Auschwitz, and for the first few months of his marriage to Lucia Morporgu. According to Angier, Levi's mother puritanically rejected her much older and (eventually) adulterous husband and loved her son Primo "possessively, controllingly, and only as long as he was in her own image, and not his father's" (63). Soon after his marriage, Levi would return with his wife to his mother's apartment, and the two remained there to raise their children and pursue their respective careers. As Angier describes it, Lucia's strict guardianship over Levi's time when he wasn't working or writing would serve as an excuse for his highly ambivalent feelings toward women: "he still both longed for women and feared them but now he could blame someone else for his fear" (527). His guilt-ridden acquiescence to the limits set by his wife is, in turn, linked by Angier to "Primo's first bondage, to his mother" (527).

Offering an illuminating (if single-minded) consideration of the impact of family and gender relations on Levi's life and work, Angier's approach nevertheless mostly ignores the possible influence of the precœdipal environment of mother/infant relations upon his literary engagement with issues of male autonomy.[2] Only once does Angier broach the possibility that Levi's earliest period of relationship with his mother contributed to his later "woman problem." Singling out "Vilmy," a tale from *Formal Defect* about the travails of an Englishman who has become addicted to the milk of his cat-like pet, Angier argues that the story evokes a hopeless desire. On one hand, she interprets the creature as a symbol of "women, who had always inspired in Primo both intense desire and intense fear" (571). On the other hand, she suggests the "vilmy" stood for the "bad mother, who leaves her child with 'an almost pathological bond' to her, because she has never given him what he needs.... That need is hopeless, because it is the infant's need, and could only have been satisfied in the past, which is irretrievably gone" (571). While thought-provoking, this allusion to infantile relations with the mother is not developed. As a result, Angier's grasp of the psychological bases of the "woman problem" from which Levi purportedly suffered and the possible connections of that psychological context to his science fiction stories' engagement with issues of personal autonomy remains incomplete.

Maternal Presence and Infantile States in Levi's Science Fiction

> PAOLA VALABREGA: *When you write about families, I've noticed that you concentrate more on the father-son than on the mother-son relationship. What is the reason for this?*
> PRIMO LEVI: *The reason is very simple. My mother is still alive, you can hear her walking around, and you don't write about the living* [PRIMO LEVI, "INTERVIEW" 140].

In both his writings and in interviews, Levi avoided reflecting on the nature of his relationship to his mother. In a rare moment of self-exposure during a 1982 interview, "Levi told a journalist that he could not remember a 'single kiss or caress' from his mother" (Thomson 21). The biographer who reported this confessional outburst gave its substance little credence: "This is a rather hostile overstatement and perhaps characteristic of men who are overly attached to their mothers" (Thomson 21). Students of Levi's early life generally report that his mother was devoted to her young children, if also rather undemonstrative in her affection towards them (Thomson 21; Angier 51). As was typical of middle-class Piedmontese matriarchs of the early twentieth century, his mother enjoyed the help of a family servant, Silvia Meneghalli, described by Ian Thomson as "the sure center of [Levi's] world," to whom he was "deeply attached" and in response to whose presence and care he formed "his first word, 'Cia'" (probably Levi's pre-toddler attempt at articulating "Silvia") (21). The emotional importance of "Cia" makes sense in light of what is known about the preoedipal stage of life when mothers and/or mother figures "provide nearly exclusive care and certainly the most meaningful relation to the infant" (Chodorow 78).

If Levi never reflected in writing about the nature and significance of his relationships to the women who provided primary care and nurturance in his earliest years, he did provide at least two glimpses into the preœdipal experiences of one of his family members. In *The Periodic Table*, Levi refers to his maternal grandmother, "Grandmother Fina, one of the four sisters everyone called Fina: this first name singularity was owed to the fact that the four girls had been sent successively to the same wet nurse [in Italian, *balia*] in Bra whose name was Delfina and who called all her 'nurslings' by that name" (15). In marked contrast to the tone of this reference is the family story told "*sotto voce*, and with a shudder" of the terrible fate of one of his maternal grandmother's twenty-one brothers: "when he was still with his wet nurse, [he] had been devoured in his crib by a pig" ("Grandfather's" 73). This latter account of deficient wet nursing gives one pause and raises the question whether Levi's choice of Malabaila (evil wet nurse) as a pseudonym for *Natural Histories* was coincidental. The choice of this *nom de plume* seems all the more overdetermined upon consideration of the many references, direct and indirect, in his stories to maternal states — e.g., pregnancy, parturition, nursing — and evocations of infantile feelings — e.g., of being overwhelmed by maternal affect and provision (or their lack), and of oscillating between those states of merger and separation that are characteristic of the infant's development from an initial perception of "itself as merged or continuous with ... its mother or caretakers" toward a rudimentary sense of separate existence (Chodorow 61). Interestingly, Levi's science fiction stories are almost entirely bereft of *actual* mothers, however thickly populated they are by manifestations of the maternal. Instead of mothers, Levi offers mother substitutes, usually men who, through their creative will and often with the help of scientific training and technology, assume maternal powers, to the detriment of themselves and others.

In "The Mnemogogues," among the earliest of his short story efforts (written in 1946) and the one he chose to place at the head of *Natural Histories*, the mother is absent even as the plot seems driven in large part by the evocation of a maternal presence. In the story, a recently graduated medical doctor arrives in a backwater town to take over the practice of an elderly municipal doctor. In their introductory meeting in the doctor's office, the older man, who had spent the free hours of his decades-long practice experimenting with chemicals and producing mixtures whose scents powerfully evoke past memories, invites his younger charge to sniff a few samples of his "mnemogogues: 'arousers of memories'" (14). In response to all but the last of the samples, the younger doctor identifies chemical scents or offers guesses that approximate the deeply personal experiences the elderly doctor had been trying to recapture:

elementary school, a period of caring for a dying diabetic father, a hospital internship, youthful mountain-climbing jaunts. Only the last sample, which the young man picks out randomly and sniffs unbidden, leaves him speechless and blushing. The elderly doctor "curtly" expounds, "This is neither a place nor a time, it is a person" (17). The next scene has the young man departing from the old man's office "amid the pine trees furiously climbing up the steepest slope, trampling on the soft underbrush … feel[ing] his muscles, lungs and heart working at their full power … [until with] the blood throbbing loudly in his ears … he stretch[es] out on the grass … [and feels himself] washed clean" (17).

It is hardly a stretch to interpret the passage as a metaphor for sexual passion and release set off by an encounter with a highly stimulating and deeply personal scent: "a light airy smell of clean skin, powder, and summer" (17). Such an interpretation would track well with Angier's portrait of Levi as suffering severely from sexual insecurities and sublimating his desires in forms of intense activity. It would also be consistent with an œdipal reading of the story's basic premise: a younger man's replacement of an older man. In this regard, the story's opening passage, which includes an explicit allusion to a maternal figure, is of no small significance. In the passage, the young man arrives in town intending to remain incognito before the start of his official duties, but his plan is foiled: "from the tobacconist's smile, at once deferential and maternal and slightly mocking, he'd understood that he was already the 'new doctor'" (11). The pressure the young man feels from the tobacconist to claim his new title and authority can be read as alluding to œdipal fantasies of maternal preference for son over father. At the same time, the young doctor's perception of the maternal smile as blending subservience and ridicule harkens back to a toddler's perception of the mother as indulgently setting limits on the toddler's agency. The preœdipal resonances of that smile are further highlighted with reference to Lacan's postulation of a mirror stage in infantile development, according to which the mother's mirroring of the infant's facial expressions provides an intimation to the infant of a coherent subjectivity that it is only just beginning to consolidate (Rose 30). Thus, the state of the protagonist's subjectivity in the preœdipal stage of development is explicitly made an issue in the story protagonist's response to this maternal gaze. He feels irritation, "something along the lines of the birth trauma, he concluded without too much coherence" (11).

According to Nancy Chodorow, in societies where fathers and other adult males tend to be out of the house for significant periods of each day, "the wife is likely to turn her affection and attention to the next obvious male — her son," experiencing him "as a definite other — an opposite-gendered and sexed other" (104, 105). Chodorow's conclusion that mothers tend to see their baby sons as sexual others and push them from a preœdipal into an œdipal framework earlier than baby daughters might also explain why the knowing maternal smile and the future it seems to hold for the doctor feels to him like a "huge and everlasting nuisance" (11).

Scholars of preœdipal experience have suggested that a baby's internalization of "a very primitive image of the mother, still fragmented into 'bad' and 'good' parts, still suffused with intense and powerful affect, still focused on eating and being consumed" can lead to immoderate fears of female entrapment later in life (Pitkin 192). The "spider's long thread" that the story protagonist notices hanging from the ceiling of the doctor's office suggests that preœdipal issues of emergent but incomplete and threatened subjectivity are at play in "The Mnemogogues" (12). Levi, who suffered from arachnophobia, recognized the spider web's symbolic meaning of maternal entrapment and re-incorporation:

> The capturing technique of the spider who covers with filaments the prey caught in the web supposedly turns it into a maternal symbol: the spider is the enemy-mother who envelops and encompasses, who wants to make us reenter the womb from which we have issued, bind us tightly to take us back to the impotence of infancy, subject us again to her power ["Fear" 156].

If "The Mnemogogues," with its ambiguous allusions to maternal presence, yields to œdipal as well as preœdipal readings, "Recuenco: The Nurse," with its strikingly explicit evocation of issues of primal hunger and nurturance in highly polarized terms, invites a much more one-sidedly preœdipal reading. In a remote rural village afflicted by famine, stories circulate among the inhabitants of a long ago visitation by "the Nurse," an airborne bringer of relief whose precipitous dispensation of nutrition comes in the form of an overwhelming torrent. One day, Sinda, a shepherd boy accompanying the rag tag herd of village goats to a distant and sparse pasture, notices over the sea a large airborne object headed in the direction of the village: "Sinda ran because he hoped-feared that the thing was the Nurse, who comes every hundred years and brings abundance and slaughter; he wanted to tell everyone, so they should prepare, and he also wanted to be the first to bring the news" (184). Reaching the village square to call out a warning just as the Nurse arrives, Sinda is enveloped in a maelstrom of noise and wind: "[S]uddenly the nourishment, the celestial milk, poured in white spurts from the pipes" (186). After the visitation, Sinda gets up from the ground to observe how "the milk poured thickly down all the inclined alleys and streamed from the few roofs that had not collapsed. The lower part of the village was flooded: two women had drowned, and so had many rabbits and dogs, and all the chickens" (186). Enough of the milk-like liquid was pooled in the flooded ruins of the village to provide the surviving inhabitants with sustenance for a year. Despite leaflets of warning, ten famished villagers die in the days following the Nurse's visit, all from eating too much, too fast.

The story is not lacking in references to the author's concentration camp experience. Levi had, for example, witnessed after the arrival of Soviet troops how some camp inmates "died of their rescue, their starved stomachs collapsing under the shock of a sudden abundance" (Angier 369). Auschwitz is not, however, the sole plausible biographical source for Levi's description of a nutritive experience that is both desperately wished for and potentially deadly.[3] Preœdipal development, with its characteristic oscillations between feelings of merger and feelings of separation, introduces each human being to the possibility of the "dissolution of self, of losing boundaries between self and others" (Pitkin 191). Insofar as the main "other" in the preœdipal oscillation between feelings of merger and feelings of separation is a mother, she (and, later, women generally) will embody that threatening possibility of loss of self. In the narrative build up to the arrival of *la Nutrice* (the Nurse, from the Italian verb, *nutrire*: to nourish), the text offers up several references to objects metaphorically associated with maternity — gourd, oven, sea, moon (182–183). These references, taken together with the scenario of an abrupt and overwhelming intake of a milk-like substance that both satisfies and endangers, are consistent with universal and highly-charged infantile experiences of mothering, of suddenly and inexplicably having urgent needs met and just as suddenly and inexplicably not having them met, of feeling boundaries form and then just as suddenly collapse.

In "Recuenco: The Rafter," the sequel to "Recuenco: The Nurse," Levi configures the appearance of the maternal within the framework of modern science and technology. The Nurse turns out to be an airborne tanker carrying a load of processed, protein-rich, milk-like fluid. Four such vehicles, or Rafters, manned by crewmen from technologically advanced countries, patrol the globe and, in response to chemical sensors that detect human bodies in a state of starvation, bring relief. For reasons of efficiency, the "milk" is distributed in only three minutes from udder-like holding bays in the form of a deluge that often kills some of those it is meant to succor. The needy populations to whom the "milk" is distributed are described by a Rafter crewman in terms that arguably infantilize the recipients as "lazy, improvident and good for nothing" (192). Whereas "Recuenco: The Nurse" suggests how the emotionally-charged and deeply intimate infantile experience of breast-feeding can be re-imagined as an event whose polarized meanings — life-saving sustenance *and* overwhelming force — can only be contained within the bounds of communal myth, "Recuenco: The Rafter" encourages emotional distancing from that event through its presentation of the feeding process as rationally planned and scientifically organized. The men who oversee this process are technicians of limited intellectual and moral imagination who do their jobs in an impersonal and routine way.

The Recuenco pieces exemplify a narrative pattern in Levi's science fiction wherein men deploy advanced technology in ways that evoke highly polarized infantile experiences of maternal powers and functions. Sometimes, as with "Recuenco: The Rafter," these translations of preoedipal experience into futuristic scenarios of scientific endeavor and technological adaptation have the effect of toning down the emotional resonance of what originally are highly fraught infantile states of response. Other times, the effect is to ratchet up that emotional resonance for the purpose of conveying a point. "Angelic Butterfly," one of Levi's most powerful tales of Nazi evil, exemplifies the latter effect by relating a scenario in which a man attempts to appropriate the maternal power of creation.

In "Angelic Butterfly," a team of Allied officers on the trail of Leeb, a Nazi scientist, make their way through the ruins of Berlin to a locked and abandoned apartment where they find, "a layer of foul rags, wastepaper, bones, feathers and fruit peels ... large reddish brown stains ... [and] a small heap of an indefinable material, dry, white and gray, smell[ing] of ammonia and rotten eggs" (20). A week later, at a meeting with their commanding officer and a staff scientist, they discover that the apartment had been requisitioned for conducting experiments on four unfortunate concentration camp inmates. Those experiments were based on Leeb's hypothesis that "angels are not a fantastic invention nor supernatural beings nor a poetic dream but our future, what we will become if we lived long enough, or subjected ourselves to his manipulation" (23).

The result of Leeb's ambition to develop humans to their fullest potential was a generation of previously unknown beings, traces of whose existence at the apartment include feathers, guano, and blood stains containing human hemoglobin. The story ends with the testimony of a neighborhood girl who, the day after a bombing raid blew out the apartment windows, saw four vulture-like beings, "ugly beasts roost[ing] on four poles placed across the room halfway up" (24). In the desperate conditions of the war's closing days, a mob of homeless and famished neighbors, invited into the apartment by the "male nurse," got hold of the mutated experimental subjects and, "slaughter[ing] them with clubs and knives, cut them into pieces" (25).

If Levi, during his time of incarceration at Auschwitz, was not aware of the experiments being conducted by Nazi doctors on camp inmates, he had surely learned of those experiments by the time he composed "Angelic Butterfly." However, whereas the horrific program of Nazi medical experimentation is a plausible narrative jumping off point for "Angelic Butterfly," it is not necessarily the only basis for its frisson. The plot does not primarily turn on the presentation of the results of a botched experiment on human subjects. Rather, the story's frisson is generated by the spectacle of infantilized beings, reduced to a state of utter dependence and lacking the capacity of language ("They let out terrifying cries") or control over their bodily functions (as the pile of guano on the floor attests), being devoured by a mob at the behest of the "nurse" in whose care the poor creatures had been left (24). The reader's visceral reaction is elicited, in other words, by the story's indirect evocation of the "primitive mother" who, processed through the infantile imagination, cannibalizes her newborns (Pitkin 192). With this image, Levi signals the final collapse and moral bankruptcy of the Nazi attempt to transcend the maternal function of birthing by generating new and higher humans.

While "Angelic Butterfly" achieves its effect by evoking the primitively-imaged mother who first gives life and then reincorporates it, "The Servant," a science fiction tale that also takes male creation as its central theme, offers a less polarized depiction of the mother. In Levi's reworking of the story of Rabbi Löw's creation of a golem to defend the Jewish community of medieval Prague, a male figure (Rabbi Arié) seeks to create new life in an environment in which the absence of actual mothers is strongly over-determined: "it is also said that he got married four times, that four times he became a widower" (203). Arié's creation protocol withholds two dimensions of human life, one physical, one spiritual, from the golem. Firstly, Arié chooses not to grant his creation a reproductive organ: "Below the waist, the golem was truly golem, that is a fragment of chaos: underneath the suit of mail, which hung all the way to the ground like an apron, one could glimpse only a sturdy tangle of clay, metal and glass" (206). Secondly, Arié seeks to deprive his creation of will: "He denied him blood, and with blood he denied him will, Eve's curiosity, the desire for enterprise..." (206).

To the extent that the golem is a creation of clay, it is noteworthy that Levi construes the first deprivation explicitly in terms of a polarity between divine and animal: "the waist is a frontier, only above the waist is man made in God's image, whereas below it he is a beast" (206). Interestingly, the image of a hybrid creature divided at the waist was one favored by Levi in his writings. Levi drew upon mythic notions of centaurs as ungovernable in their sexual passion to fashion one of his pieces in *Storie Naturali*, "Quaestio de Centauris." In an interview he gave on the occasion of the release of that short story collection, Levi characterized himself as a "centaur," ostensibly to capture his sense of being divided between his work as an industrial chemist and his work as a writer ("Science" 85). In considering the Jewish diasporic condition in *The Periodic Table*, Levi draws the conclusion that "man is a centaur, a tangle of flesh and mind, divine inspiration and dust" (9).

Angier reads the ending of "The Servant," in which Arié inadvertently attempts to work the golem on the Sabbath and thereby places it between the conflicting imperatives of serving its master and obeying the Mosaic prohibition against work, as referencing the double bind Levi felt in his own life (693). That bind pitted Levi's deep aversion to the "dark unconscious and animal sides of himself" against powerful desires for release of those sides of himself (Angier xix). In addition to this œdipal reading, "The Servant" also invites an interpretation that exploits its preœdipal resonances. Lacking genitals, the golem can be located in the preœdipal stage where rudimentary individuation rather than (sexual) possession is the focus of development. That orality is more at issue than genital concerns in the case of the golem is further indicated by the fact that the creature is activated only "when the case with the Name was slipped between his teeth" (206).[4]

Levi's treatment of the other form of deprivation that the golem suffers, Arié's withholding of the passion of willfulness, also lends itself to a preœdipally-imaged interpretation. To the extent that willfulness presupposes a being who recognizes itself *as* a self, as individuated from its environment and capable of having, and acting on, desires, Arié's wish to withhold will from his creation would correspond to a mother's wish to keep her child in an infantile state. Such a wish is unrealistic, of course, and a mother knows this. She also wants her baby to grow and develop a sense of self and a capacity for purposive activity. As a result, the mother's attitude to the baby is fraught with ambivalence and conflict, wanting the baby always to be her baby, to be an extension of herself, and yet also looking forward to her baby's development into a separate and independent person. In regard to this dimension of preœdipal relations, Arié's own ambivalence toward signs of willfulness in his creature is significant. He initially and very deliberately attempts to deprive his creature of will, and yet, when he is later faced with evidence that his attempt has failed, he is not altogether displeased. Thus, when the golem refuses to move after the rabbi puts an axe into its hands and orders it to chop small logs into firewood, Arié does not feel anger:

> "Come now, chop!" Arié ordered, and deep laughter tickled his heart without appearing on his face. The monster's laziness and disobedience flattered him because these are human, innate passions; he had not inspired them in him, the clay colossus had thought of them by himself: he was more human than Arié had meant him to be [208].

Egged on by his master to do his bidding, the golem eventually starts to work, though not in the way Arié had intended. The creature discards the axe and begins to chop the wood with his hand in an "angry and mechanical" manner (208). The rabbi is puzzled by the unforeseen way in which the golem has acceded to his command. Levi tries to capture the quality of Arié's puzzlement by analogizing it to a parent's painful discovery that a child is not an extension of the parent:

> Why had he refused the hatchet? He thought about it for a long time ... and yet for at least a half an hour the solution eluded him. He persisted in his search: the golem was his work, his son, and it is a painful goad to discover in our children opinions and acts of will different from ours, distant, incomprehensible [208].

That preœdipal issues of establishing and maintaining viable boundaries around a rudimentary self are fundamentally at issue in "The Servant" is finally suggested at story's end by the fate of the golem's body: "Arié touched him with one finger and the giant fell to the ground and was shattered. The rabbi collected the fragments and stored them in the attic of the house on Broad Street in Prague" (210). In describing the bodily disintegration of the golem in "The Servant," Levi gestures to the possibility of boundary collapse that occurs to human beings for probably the first time in the preœdipal stage. As has been discussed, such gestures are common in Levi's science fiction oeuvre: the dismemberment of Leeb's experimental subjects, the inundation of Sinda's village. And as with many of his other science fiction stories, in "The Servant," Levi accords the maternally-coded role of mediating the infant's highly charged experiences of boundary fluctuation, helpless dependence, and urgent physical need to a man and his technology: Rabbi Arié and his kabalistic magic.[5]

Conclusions

Although Levi may have remained mostly silent about the mother/son relationship in his explicitly autobiographical writings, this analysis of his science fiction stories suggests that this relationship left its peculiar mark on his literary imagination. Even in those stories where the narrative is ostensibly not about familial relations, dramatic energy is mustered through contact with infantile images of the maternal. To the extent that Levi's science fiction tales revisit infantile perceptions of preœdipal experience, they invite the reader to reconnect to emotionally fraught issues of individuation, dependence, and need. How these issues are resolved at the preœdipal stage of development has lasting effects for a person's later sense of autonomy. Since women typically assume the role of primary caretaker of male babies and children, and thereby come to stand for a form of commanding presence that is both comforting and overwhelming, autonomy is often felt by men to be threatened by the women around them as well as by the qualities of the mother, such as attentiveness to the needs of others and emotional openness, that they have internalized as babies and children. Yet while Levi's stories draw upon maternal images in order to solicit the reader's emotional investment, they do not invest women characters with motherhood. Where female characters appear, in stories such as "The Measure of Beauty," "Buffet Dinner," and "Bureau of Vital Statistics," they most often play the role of wives, potential lovers, daughters — anything but actual mothers. Instead, evocations of the maternal in Levi's writings tend to be associated with ill-considered, wrongheaded, or, at the least, questionable uses of technology by men who, in aggrandizing maternal powers, pose a threat to the autonomy of themselves or others. So, in relation to questions of autonomy, the maternal in Levi's science fiction is masculinized even as it mostly retains its negative connotation.

It may well be that Levi did not give up negative images of the maternal presence because the close, continuous, and intense relationship he maintained with his mother for his entire life did not allow him the requisite emotional distance. The extreme deprivations he suffered at Auschwitz, particularly over issues of nurturance, bodily integrity, and dependence, may have conditioned him to see the threats to human autonomy posed by men in the modern world through the prism of experiences he dimly remembered but to which he remained emotionally connected. Whatever the cause of his reliance on motifs related to infantile experience of maternal presence, they afforded him a way to articulate one of the major ironies of the experience of human autonomy in late modernity — as science progresses and technologies advance, people feel both more empowered and less in control, exhilarated at what they increasingly can do and deeply anxious about what increasingly can be done to them. Whether or not Levi intended it, his peculiar way of imagining the future invites his readers to reflect upon the prospects for human autonomy in late modernity through images that evoke the earliest struggles for autonomy in precedipal relations of care. In doing so, his science fiction writings point the way to a better understanding of why autonomy will remain a treasured — if also sometimes elusive — goal in the literature of science fiction, as well as in modern life.

Notes

The author thanks Cassandra Haag for her research assistance.

1. The two fantasy stories included in *The Periodic Table* under the headings "Lead" and "Mercury" were written in 1942. Levi completed "Interview with a Spider" at the end of February 1987. See Angier (178–181; 703–705).

2. See, for example, the review by Marcus, who takes Angier to task for her book's "tyrannical teleology" (69).

3. In offering up a scenario of emergency response to starvation, Levi possibly had in mind reports of food crises in underdeveloped regions of the world that were in the news during the

period (late 1960s) when he composed these stories. In response to a 1981 interview question about "Recuenco: The Nurse," Levi responded, "Besides my own experience of hunger, you only have to read the newspapers to know that a third of the world's population is undernourished. I don't think you have to have been in Auschwitz to be aware of the problem of hunger" ("Interview" 143).

4. In many of the earliest versions of the golem story, activation of the golem entails the ritual enunciation of sacred words and letters (Bilski and Idel 10–12). One of the precursor versions of the Rabbi Löw story refers to an amulet hanging upon the neck of the golem, upon which is written the word *emet* (truth). Removal of the amulet results in the golem's dissolution into dust (31). In other golem stories, *emet* (truth) is inscribed on the forehead or written on a parchment attached to the golem's forehead (32).

5. Levi describes the rabbi's use of sacred texts and spells explicitly in terms of modern technology. His story is "an ironic reworking of the legend of Golem, imagin[ing] that the Rabbi Löw knew the secrets of genetics and computer science, and thus Golem, his own creature, was nothing but a robot" ("Itinerary" 164).

Works Cited

Angier, Carole. *The Double Bond: Primo Levi; a Biography*. New York: Farrar, Strauss and Giroux, 2002. Print.
Benchouiha, Lucie. "The Perversion of a Fairy Tale: Primo Levi's '*La Bella Addormentata nel Frigo*.'" *Modern Language Review* 100 (April 2005): 356–366. Print.
Bilski, Emily, and Moshe Idel. "The Golem: An Historical Overview." *Golem! Danger, Deliverance and Art*. Ed. Emily Bilski. New York: The Jewish Museum, 1988. Print.
Chodorow, Nancy. *The Reproduction of Mothering: Psychoanalysis and the Sociology of Gender*. Berkeley: University of California Press, 1978. Print.
Farneti, Roberto. "Of Humans and Other Portentous Beings: On Primo Levi's *Storie Naturali*." *Critical Inquiry* 32 (Summer 2006): 724–740. Print.
Gordon, Robert S. C. *Primo Levi's Ordinary Virtues: From Testimony to Ethics*. Oxford: Oxford University Press, 2001. Print.
Harrowitz, Nancy. "Primo Levi's Science as 'Evil Nurse'." *Memory and Mastery: Primo Levi as Writer and Witness*. Ed. Roberta Kremer. Albany: SUNY Press, 2001. 59–73. Print.
Klein, Ilona. "'Official Science Often Lacks Humility': Humor, Science and Technology in Levi's *Storie Naturali*." *Reason and Light: Essays on Primo Levi*. Ed. Susan Tarrow. Ithaca, NY: Western Societies Program Occasional Paper, 1990. 112–126. Print.
Levi, Primo. "Angelic Butterfly." *The Sixth Day and Other Tales*. Tr. Raymond Rosenthal. London: Michael Joseph, 1990. 19–25. Print.
———. "Buffet Dinner." *A Tranquil Star*. Tr. Alessandra Bastagli. New York: W.W. Norton, 2007. 136–142. Print.
———. "Bureau of Vital Statistics." *A Tranquil Star*. Tr. Alessandra Bastagli. New York: W.W. Norton, 2007. 123–128. Print.
———. *Echi di una voce perduta: Incontri, interviste e conversazioni con Primo Levi*. Eds. Gabriella Poli and Giorgio Calcagno. Milan: Mursia, 1992. Print.
———. "The Fear of Spiders." *Other People's Trades*. Tr. Raymond Rosenthal. New York: Summit, 1989. 154–157. Print.
———. "Grandfather's Store." *Other People's Trades*. Tr. Raymond Rosenthal. New York: Summit, 1989. 70–73. Print.
———. "Itinerary of a Jewish Writer." *The Black Hole of Auschwitz*. Tr. Sharon Wood. Cambridge, England: Polity, 2005. Print.
———. "Interview for a Dissertation (1981): Paola Valbrega." *The Voice of Memory: Primo Levi, Interviews 1961–1987*. Eds. Marco Belpoliti and Robert Gordon. New York: The New Press, 2001. 136–147. Print.

———. "The Measure of Beauty." *The Sixth Day and Other Tales*. Tr. Raymond Rosenthal. London: Michael Joseph, 1990. 71–79. Print.
———. "The Memnogogues." *The Sixth Day and Other Tales*. Tr. Raymond Rosenthal. London: Michael Joseph, 1990. 11–18. Print.
———. *The Periodic Table*. Tr. Raymond Rosenthal. New York: Schocken Books, 1984. Print.
———. "Recuenco: The Nurse." *The Sixth Day and Other Tales*. Tr. Raymond Rosenthal. London: Michael Joseph, 1990. 182–187. Print.
———. "Recuenco: The Rafter." *The Sixth Day and Other Tales*. Tr. Raymond Rosenthal. London: Michael Joseph, 1990. 188–194. Print.
———. "Science Fiction I: Storie naturali. Interviews with Edoardo Fadini (1966–1971)." *The Voice of Memory: Primo Levi, Interviews 1961–1987*. Eds. Marco Belpoliti and Robert Gordon. New York: The New Press, 2001. 84–86. Print.
———. "The Servant." *The Sixth Day and Other Tales*. Tr. Raymond Rosenthal. London: Michael Joseph, 1990. 203–210. Print.
Marcus, Millicent. Review of Carole Angier's *The Double Bond*. *Italica* 80:1 (Spring 2003): 67–72. Print.
Pitkin, Hanna. *Fortune Is a Woman: Gender and Politics in the Thought of Niccolò Machiavelli*. Berkeley: University of California Press, 1984. Print.
Rose, Jacqueline. "Introduction — II." *Feminine Sexuality: Jacques Lacan and the Ècole Freudienne*. Eds. Juliet Mitchell and Jacqueline Rose. New York: Pantheon, 1985. Print.
Ross, Charlotte. "Primo Levi's Science Fiction." *Cambridge Companion to Primo Levi*. Ed. Robert S. C. Gordon. Cambridge: Cambridge University Press, 2007. 105–118. Print.
Santagostino, Giuseppina. "*Destituzione e Ossessione Biologica Nell'Immaginario di Primo Levi*." *Letteratura Italiana Contemporanea* 37 (1992): 127–145. Print.
Thomson, Ian. *Primo Levi: A Life*. New York: Henry Holt, 2003. Print.
Usher, Jonathan. "Levi's Science Fiction and the Humanoid." *Journal of the Institute of Romance Studies* 4 (1996): 199–216. Print.

PART TWO: TECHNO SEX

Patriarchy, Paternity and Papas: Reproductive Technologies and Parenthood in Science Fiction

Erin Grayson Sapp

Just as the literature of science fiction is a contradictory marriage of fact and fantasy, it also performs the essential yet oxymoronic function of presenting fictional characters with "real" human emotions. Frederick Pohl champions the assessment of change as a "diagnostic trait of science fiction," and Donald M. Hassler and Clyde Wilcox celebrate the experimental space in which utopian theories can be "fleshed out" by authors of science fiction (7, 1). An essential aspect to the success of these textual laboratories is the narrative insight of the reader into the "true" thoughts and feelings of a story's unreal inhabitants of hypothetical societies. While manifestos of political theory are limited by their social agendas, actors within science fiction plots have the anonymity to exhibit unpopular, controversial, and embarrassing perspectives on their full environment. June Deery recognizes that this "nonrealism" can be used "to perform a vital social function, which is to offer a testing ground ... where the social consequences of new and projected technologies can be extrapolated in an intuitive, holistic, and empathetic manner" (88). The instantiation of proposed political and scientific conditions within the highly developed social, familial, and emotional environment of a protagonist can reveal necessary physical and emotional sacrifices often unacknowledged in utopian theoretical assessments.

Works of science fiction that play with sex and gender can rearrange demographics, family structures, and even human anatomy to produce newly formatted social hierarchies, community organizations, and interpersonal relationships. Like much of feminist theory, science fiction can imagine the necessary, potential, or likely changes that would produce socio-political conditions in which women would be liberated from patriarchal oppression. For both sexes, conditions that result in gendered advantages would have to be sacrificed for the realization of equality, and the forfeitures required of women have been documented and debated. However, given that gender equality would necessarily require a weakening of male power relative to that of women, there is little room in the scholarship of sex and gender studies for a mournful or sympathetic assessment of the aspects of contemporary life men would have to forfeit. As characters in science fiction texts experience and assess these changes, readers gain insight into contradictory emotional and affective sacrifices bundled with otherwise logical maneuvers for what is understood as the greater good. In the works of Marge Piercy, Theodore Sturgeon, and Katherine Burdekin, for example, both female and male characters struggle to reconcile nostalgia for traditional parenthood roles with support for the abolition of patriarchal domination. Ultimately, texts by these three authors question the possibility and value of separating the "Papa" from the patriarch.

Written in three different socially and politically charged decades of the twentieth century, Piercy's *Woman on the Edge of Time* (1976), Sturgeon's *Venus Plus X* (1960), and Burdekin's *The End of This Day's Business* (composed around 1935 but first published in 1989) reflect the anxieties and debates of their respective intellectual climates, but each presents a utopia in which women have been freed from gendered inequity through uniquely alternative systems of human reproduction. In each novel, the traditionally dual parental roles of mother and father are obsolete. Characters with knowledge of the books' contemporary cultures evaluate and react to the societal and familial sacrifices that allowed these utopian communities to develop, and at least one character from each story struggles with the unpopularity of and inherent contradictions in nostalgia for the family structures universally understood to have fostered the oppression of women. In particular, each book invites the reader to contemplate the affective consequences of the elimination of individual male father figures in the process of toppling patriarchal power structures. These are stories in which the conscious decisions of the human mind, through either technological or conspiratorial developments, have created worlds without "daddies"; through insight into characters' internal battles, the reader is prompted to consider not only what men would have to sacrifice, but also what all of society would lose, if patriarchy and paternity were eradicated through alternative means of human reproduction.

There exists a prolific and growing body of theoretical literature either critiquing or celebrating the increasing use of available technologies in the creation of human life while also predicting future uses of additional foreseeable technological alternatives, such as cloning and artificial wombs. As developments in procreative sciences continue, and these technologies become more widely used in a growing variety of combinations and applications, the Western world is flirting with vast ideological, cultural, and social change. As the method of becoming a parent changes, the meaning of being a parent cannot remain fixed. As technology increasingly enables the creation of children (and therefore parents) to be removed from the marital bedroom and into the medical laboratory, gendered roles, responsibilities, and positions of power become relocated as well. And as science fiction literature enacts utopian theories, exercises revolutionary thought, and addresses anxieties over today's societal ills, it also acknowledges potential problems with or sacrifices necessary for seemingly "ideal" solutions; one area in which such critical speculation is timely and fruitful is that of the changes occurring in and still awaiting the institutions of parenthood.

Various groups and movements under the banners of feminism and women's rights have consistently failed in repeated attempts to offer a language or definition that would provide a "woman-centered way of understanding motherhood," and the diversity of perspectives on maternity are also reflected in feminist attitudes toward reproductive technologies (Rothman 313). Grossly understated, feminist analyses of conceptive technologies appear to be "caught in an opposition between liberation and oppression" (Zipper and Sevenhuijsen 120). Women who view their sex's "value as child-bearers" as the "last power" women retain in relation to men describe the male-dominated fields of science and medicine as working toward usurping control of human reproduction from the female body (Rowland 368). Jalna Hamner warns that reproductive technologies are being developed under the guise of helping individual women, while these procedures are actually seizing control of women's bodies and reproductive capacities "in the interest of their [men's] continuing power domination over women" (441). In addition to fears that the male sex will become "the procreator of the species" and the female sex will become "obsolete as childbearers," concerns about the commercialization of reproductive bodily materials and services are also raised in feminist literature (Klein 66, 70). Renate Duelli Klein sees "technodocs" as reducing female bodies to "living laboratories" as women's reproductive systems are dismembered, marketed, and reassembled as standalone products (65–66). Andrea Dworkin refers to the commercialization of conceptive anatomy as another form of female prostitution in which women are "reproductive commodities," and Gena Corea describes the reproductive engineering of cattle as an extant model of how a "reproductive brothel" would operate (187, 39).

However, other feminist theorists view reproductive difference as the foundation of women's oppression and celebrate alternatives to traditional pregnancy, childbearing, and nursing. In *The Second Sex*, Simone de Beauvoir champions progress in reproductive science as granting the individual woman increased "control over her own person"; she describes the ability of "humanity to master the reproductive function" as leading to women's "freedom from reproductive slavery" (139). Anita Röper contends that "until human beings are produced in laboratories instead of having to be brought into the world by women ... the notion of 'equal rights' will remain an unrealizable dream" (quoted in Hauke 42). Similarly, Nancy Breeze questions the idea that women would be giving up a great power to men if parthenogenesis becomes a reality, asserting that "two thousand years of morning sickness and stretch marks have not resulted in liberation for women or children" and that "a Petri dish ... could turn out to be your best friend" (400). Breeze argues that women should guard against the misuse of new reproductive technologies but not oppose the entire field indiscriminately.

This latter stance has been influentially posited by Shulamith Firestone in *The Dialectic of Sex: The Case for Feminist Revolution*. Firestone, like many other feminist theorists, locates the source of women's oppression in nature; the responsibility of the female sex to gestate, bear, and nurse children results in women being physically and economically dependent on the male half of the adult population because of the bodily demands and limitations of childbearing. In her view, women have "maintained the species in order to free the other half for the business of the world" (232). It follows from such thought that the achievement of extra-uterine gestation and communal child-rearing would be "the freeing of women from the tyranny of their reproductive biology" (Firestone 233). Firestone also calls for the economic independence and contribution of all members of society as well as complete freedom of sexual activity for all (men, women, and children) in order for social equality to be achieved (232–237).

Firestone's utopian projection has an intriguingly similar theoretical parallel and speculative enactment in Marge Piercy's 1976 science fiction novel, *Woman on the Edge of Time*, which presents a woman witnessing two potential futures, one utopian and one dystopian, the materialization of each hinging upon what occurs in the protagonist's present day. The utopian future, regarded clearly as such, mirrors Firestone's calls for communal work and service, sexual freedom for all, extra-uterine conception and gestation, and a dually-sexed responsibility for child rearing. Furthermore, Connie, the tourist witnessing the future in 2137, is accompanied by a knowledgeable guide, Luciente, who constantly and thoroughly explains the motivations for and consequences of the many momentous decisions that led to the (at least comparatively) utopian societal organization of Luciente's Massachusetts village community of Mattapoisett.

Among the features of this future community that Connie struggles to understand and accept are the means of creating, nursing, and rearing babies. The "brooder" is a warehouse of anonymous and diverse genetic material out of which embryos are formed at specific times: when someone dies, the community agrees to create another life, and three "co-mothers" volunteer and are approved as guardians. Men and women take on these roles as mothers, and at least two of a child's three mothers — of either sex — will breastfeed via hormonal stimulation. Pregnancy is no longer required of anyone, though the experience of nursing is open to all. The theme of *choice* in parenting that defines reproduction in Mattapoisett reflects the debates of the 1970s over women's bodily independence, contraception, abortion, child care funding, maternal job security, forced sterilization, and rape. That the time traveler from Piercy's present day is overwhelmed by these policies highlights the depth and breadth of the inequities the people of Mattapoisett have overcome.

It is Connie's difficulty comprehending these arrangements and Luciente's patiently detailed explanations that allow Piercy to address nearly the full range of feminist stances on the institution of motherhood as well as the sacrifices imperative for the creation of the utopian Mattapoisett. Connie has borne a beloved daughter but has endured having her permanently removed by Child Services. Initially, Connie is greatly angered by the claims of these men and women that they are *mothers* or that they understand the joys of motherhood. She questions how someone could make such a claim having "never carried a child nine months heavy under her heart ... never borne a baby in blood and pain" (106). Connie reasons that if someone gets a "canned child" ready-made "out of a machine," the "kid isn't really your child" (104, 106). Connie is disgusted by the presumptions of these "co-moms" and wonders, "What do they know of motherhood?" (106). This practice angers Connie so greatly that it breaks her connection with the future, and she returns suddenly to her present day tearfully thinking of her hatred for the community of Mattapoisett (106). This brief abhorrence does not reflect Connie's true impression of these people, whom she has admittedly befriended, but rather the painful absence of her own daughter and her growing envy of this utopian life.

Furthermore, Connie's instinct to safeguard the unique maternal abilities of her sex/gender also emerges as she is infuriated upon witnessing a male experience the ecstasy of breastfeeding a baby. She remembers the distinctive physical and emotional pleasure it brought her to have her daughter feed from her nipple: "Her breasts ached with remembrance" (134). Connie hates to view a man being able to share this joy that, in her world, only biological, female, birth mothers experience. She cannot comprehend how the females of Mattapoisett "had abandoned to men the last refuge of women" (134). The justification Luciente provides does acknowledge, in a Firestonian fashion, that true equality cannot exist as long as nature's designation of only one sex to gestate, bear, and nurse offspring is sustained: "It was part of women's long revolution.

When we were breaking all the old hierarchies" (105). This explanation is worded, however, in terms of the surrendering of a great power in the interest of universal equality rather than as a relief to be rid of a heavy burden. "Finally," there had been "that one thing" women had to sacrifice; they had given up their sole power "in return for no more power for anyone" (105). Connie suffered greatly in her own time because of her sex and ethnicity, but had also known the satisfaction and reward of biological motherhood; her character is situated precisely between the sacrifice and promise of the interpersonal equality of Mattapoisett. While many aspects of this community are extremely difficult for Connie to comprehend and accept, ultimately she makes great sacrifices, even committing murder, in a radical attempt to ensure the materialization of this potential utopian future.

Piercy's book proposes that regardless of whether or not child-bearing is seen as a gift or a curse, it is the limitation of this act to only half the population that will inevitably result in inequity between the sexes. Advances in science, medicine, and technology have, by Luciente's time, progressed to the point of nullifying the fundamental difference between males and females that has spawned ideologies of binary oppositions and a universal focus on difference rather than similarity between the sexes. In this way, Piercy establishes a Firestonian utopia in which the loss of biological and female-specific motherhood is addressed and mourned, but the resulting equality of all persons is ultimately determined to be worth the sacrifice.

What is not addressed in Piercy's novel is the sacrifice (or riddance) of the sex-specific institution of *fatherhood*. The joys of social and nursing motherhood are exalted as a rewarding option for those individuals who desire the role; the loss to women of the experience of corporeal gestation is grieved, and the satisfaction of men to nurse and nurture babies is celebrated. No mention of the invalidation of fatherhood is made. On the other hand, Luciente declares that if women did not share motherhood with men, "males never would be humanized to be loving and tender. So we all become mothers" (105). As Natalie Rosinsky points out, "this aspect of life in Mattapoisett ... acknowledges gynocentric tradition and values" (101). It is conspicuous that both men and women "become 'mothers' rather than fathers or parents" (Rosinsky 101). This aspect of Mattapoisett is consistent with Sara Ruddick's labeling all forms of "child-tending" work as definitively acts of "mothering," a concept which is "gender-inclusive" yet distinctive from the concepts of *parenting* and *fathering* (229–230). There is no acknowledgment of a loving, nurturing, and *valuable* institution of fatherhood as unique and gender-specific. This striking neglect can be noted similarly in the overwhelming majority of feminist literature concerning reproductive technologies and motherhood. It is precisely this void which Thomas Laqueur addresses in "The Facts of

Fatherhood." The potential consequences for the institution of fatherhood of the currently available reproductive technologies and continuing studies in the field are significant but unpredictable. Moreover, advances in procreative medicine are critical for Firestonian thinkers, who locate the oppression of women in motherhood, as well as thinkers like Laqueur, who witness the plethora of ongoing debates about the meanings of motherhood and lament the degree to which male parenthood is ignored or undervalued.

It would be consistent with much of feminist theory to argue that obviating the institution of male fatherhood would displace the foundation of patriarchy; it is the relative status of female mothers to male fathers that renders motherhood oppressive. Firestone describes women as "the slave class" that sustained the species so that men were able to tend to the "creative aspects" of life, which resulted in the physical dependence of women on men (232). If reproductive science could remove the need for a female womb, and therefore diffuse the responsibilities of childbearing across "society as a whole," this parental dualism would not exist (Firestone 233). As Gerda Lerner has documented, the power structure of patriarchy has as its legacy the absolute power of the father over his wife and children (89–90). It follows that the equalizing of all parenting roles would result in a balance of power between the sexes.

There is, however, a second — less radical and less optimistic — consequence to the loss of the traditional institution of fatherhood; the nullification of paternity necessitates saying farewell to "daddies." As structural inequalities of the traditional nuclear family are increasingly cited, there is little room in nonfictional literature for any nostalgia for "dad" hood. Laqueur's "The Facts of Fatherhood" opens with a seeming disclaimer that he writes "in a grumpy, polemical mood" about the absence of an academic investigation into the "cultural consequences for fathers" during the waning of patriarchy (205). His analysis does not, however, present a valuation of the positive aspects of the institution as his introductory paragraphs might imply. Instead, he proposes a "labor theory of parenthood in which emotional work counts" that downplays differences between motherhood and fatherhood as well as the relevance of biology (205). He campaigns for all parental ties to be acknowledged and understood according to essentially a single measure of emotional bonding. Writing in response to reproductive technology altering familial definitions, Laqueur's focus is more on removing all possible parental ties from traditional conceptions rather than endorsing any gender-specific attributes of fatherhood.

More regretful and nostalgic sentiments concerning the changing definitions of fatherhood are given voice in Theodore Sturgeon's *Venus Plus X* (1960), in which fictional males identify the sacrifices inherent in attempts to achieve gender equality through altered reproductive practices. The book continually alternates between two storylines, one following a presumed time traveler through a futuristic land and the other witnessing the daily lives of a mid–twentieth-century American couple with children. In the narrative, both the cultural tourist and the suburban father struggle to reconcile their support for gender equality with a coexisting nostalgia for sexual difference. First published at the height of the Cold War, this novel reflects fears surrounding the spread of communism and its efforts to achieve equality through *sameness*. Sturgeon's two male protagonists are able to express contradictory emotions and honest perspectives that are difficult to defend, one of which is a desire to be "Dad."

One of these characters, Charlie Johns, finds himself among what he understands to be a new species of humankind, the Ledom, which began as a natural mutation from *Homo sapiens* but has outlived the extinction of this ancestor race. These dually-sexed individuals seek to get from Charlie an honest opinion of their species and society from a *Homo sapiens* subject by teaching him about all aspects of their culture. This education involves a complex mixture of their interpretation of human history and their philosophy of how and why their new race is superior. Their society is clearly presented to Charlie as utopic and without conflict or interpersonal inequalities.

As the Ledom explain to Charlie that their mutation has eliminated the only natural and true difference that had existed between men and women — their biological reproductive capacities — they also reveal their critical perspective on gendered *social* parenting. Because every Ledom has male and female reproductive organs and abilities, the aforementioned singular difference, which had been exploited and enhanced into far greater social differentiations and inequalities, does not exist. It is further explained to Charlie that the exaggeration of this difference into the social parenting roles of motherhood and fatherhood led to father-dominated populations in which a father-god was worshipped and children emulated only one of their parents instead of being influenced by the best qualities of both (173–174). This argument is consistent with Firestone's assessment that traditional parental roles lead to boys and girls only developing half of their psyches (232–233). The Ledom interpret inherent danger in the opposition between a mother-image and father-image.

Furthermore, the Ledom guard heavily against the consequences of worshipping the past rather than the future, such as occurs in religions of a father-deity. The *Homo sapiens* population from whom the Ledom species was spawned had nurtured the race and established their quarantined, hidden environment for them, but these forefathers removed their identities from the history and education of the Ledom society so that they could not be worshipped, as fathers had been within the *Homo sapiens* cultures. The deity worshipped by the Ledom is the Child, and all aspects of the past are necessarily foregone, both the beautiful and the dangerous. The loss of the beautiful parts of history is regarded as a sacrifice necessary to maintain the equality enjoyed in their society (Sturgeon 174).

Meanwhile, Herb and Jeanette Raile of Begonia Drive repeatedly discuss the details of their new style of parenting, as they try to be "a new kind of people" rearing children as "a team" that is external to "this big fat Thing you read about, the father image, the mother image" (82). Jeanette refers to Herb as her "buddy-buddy-hubby" and chastises him for proposing "that father image is supposed to be worth something" (82). When Herb imagines his daughter recounting her life story and saying that she "did-unt have a mom-my and dad-dy like the other lit-tul boys and girruls" but rather that she had "a Committee," Jeanette attributes his nostalgia for traditional fatherhood to his feeling "way down deep" that he needs "to be big" (82). Jeanette's analysis is consistent with the Ledom's explanation of parental differentiation and the existence in mankind of a "desperate necessity to feel superior" (165).

When Herb is watching his daughter Karen sleep and imagining her future, he is deeply angered by the horribly insulting things men can say about and do to women, and he aches to protect her from the hatred and discrim-ination of the world he knows. He wants her tiny hands to one day "take hold of reins," and the reader understands that Herb's status as a father is precisely what fuels his commitment against sexual discrimination (149–151). By cher-ishing fatherhood, Herb both strengthens his desire for gender equality and invokes accusations that he covets the power of patriarchy. Herb contemplates his position on Karen's parental "Committee" and concludes that there is something naturally and fundamentally different about "father-love" (150). Like Laqueur, Herb questions why so little has been written on the subject, despite the plethora of literature on motherhood. He marvels at the potency of fatherly love when it is a force that is quite inexplicable. He reasons that maternal love "makes sense" because the baby is a part of the mother's body for so long, but when he considers the power of fatherly love making "an oth-erwise mild and civilized man go clean berserk," he cannot decide where that force originates (150). He also remembers how "after a while this father-love thing begins to spread out" and cause a man to feel that type of care toward all children (150). This private remembrance of Herb's personal experience of fatherhood contrasts strongly with Luciente's declaration that it was only by making men co-mothers that they were made capable of being "loving and tender" (Piercy 105). Herb knows the bonds of fatherhood to be a truth, some-thing instinctive that suffuses a man when he becomes a dad.

This type of "knowledge" of what is "natural" and "factual" within sexual difference and human reproduction is also argued by Charlie Johns as he struggles to voice and defend his own unpopular views to the Ledom. Although he has reported to his hosts that he finds their race to be the greatest occurrence in world history, he quickly and passionately reverses his stance upon discovering that the Ledom do not result from an evolutionary mutation but are surgically altered at birth. Learning that he is not in the future but rather in some isolated environment of his present day, Charlie becomes disgusted with the population and what he considers their perversions. When he explains his outrage by arguing, "A mutation would have been natural," he is asked how a *Homo sapiens* defines "nature" or if there are rather "degrees of 'nature'" (200). His Ledom hosts question the very basis of Charlie's objection to "artificial" reproductive technologies, that "a gene-changing random cosmic particle" is somehow "more natural than the force of the human mind" (200).

The Ledom system of universal reproductive surgery actually alters the only "natural" difference they acknowledge to have ever existed between male and female *Homo sapiens*. Herb, Charlie, and the Ledom agree that there is a natural and fundamental difference between paternity and maternity. It is only their assessment of its value or danger and the justification of—or objection to—its sacrifice where disagreement occurs. The Ledom do not consider their system of reproduction a sacrifice but rather a successful experiment in achieving interpersonal peace. Charlie objects to what he sees as the artificial and continual medical interference to achieve equality through sameness. Herb struggles to reconcile his support of women's equality with the value he finds in the instinctive, natural, and unique bonds of fatherhood.

The Ledom's criticism of Charlie's use of the word *natural* resembles Donna Haraway's assessment that there no longer exists a real divide between *natural* and *artificial* given the common and expanding technological, scientific, and medical manipulation of the human body (163–165). This probing invites an assessment, from both Charlie and the reader, of the status and implications of reproductive technologies in the present day. The contemporary field of medically-assisted conception in the West initially developed out of efforts to help infertile couples have their own "natural" children through technological intervention; yet from their introduction these processes have incited passionate debates over the resultant modifications of the traditional familial organization. Although Firestone predicts that the liberation of the female sex from the oppression rooted in reproductive biology cannot occur outside of a socialist economy, the current trends in capitalist production suggest freedom of a different kind for women (248–249). Defining a category inclusive of reproductive technologies, Haraway explains that although *cyborgs* are "the illegitimate offspring of militarism and patriarchal capitalism," such creations "are often exceedingly unfaithful to their origins" (151). Thus reproductive sciences arguably intended to sustain or even intensify patriarchal family linkage may have unintended and very different consequences.

The medical field of assisted reproduction, designed originally to recreate traditional nuclear families, has fragmented the work of human procreation to the point that an entirely new spectrum of parenthood definitions is needed. Because the corporeal materials and services necessary for the birth of a child have been divided into the smallest possible units (egg, embryo, uterus, and sperm), a woman's specific type of mothering identity or role depends upon which elements or services she contributes. Martha E. Giminez has assembled a list of seven distinct motherhood roles based on a woman's social, genetic, and/or gestational connections to a child, and her list does not include the maternal act of breastfeeding (344).

Despite this pluralization, "motherhood" will undoubtedly retain its conceptual meaningfulness and a degree of gender specificity because of the essential activities that, for the foreseeable future, must be performed by a female body. Most significantly, until extra-uterine gestation becomes a reality, this institution will remain fundamental. That being said, even in Piercy's utopian future with test tube babies and bi-sexual child nursing and rearing, the three parents are not called "co-parents" but "co-mothers." Motherhood suggests a more intimate role in reproduction that lessens its likelihood to fall into strict gender neutrality.

Fatherhood, on the contrary, is in jeopardy of losing its status as a unique, meaningful, and gender-specific institution as the multiplication of motherhood statuses eclipses and effectively subsumes any biological or social connections a male parent could claim. Through various means, women are able to achieve with their children genetic/social connections commensurate with those of male parents. Furthermore, these technologies make it possible for a woman to "father" a baby by having another woman (such as a lesbian partner) bear the former's genetic child through embryo transplant, resulting in the offspring having a biological link to both women, one gestational and one genetic. Also, in lesbian couples, the act of insemination can take on a meaningful "fatherly" significance if one woman injects donated sperm into the vagina of the other. This aspect of impregnation adds yet another dimension to the increasingly complicated distinction of the fathering role. More significantly, this multiplication of precise parental categories and relationships finds the limited possible ties between a male parent and his child interchangeable with proportionate classifications along the growing spectrum of motherhood roles. As Laqueur has documented with examples, legal, social, and medical precedent confirms that "fatherhood ... is not limited to men" (217).

Herb's three-year-old daughter in *Venus Plus X* comes to this realization when her mother is explaining that both Karen and her brother Davy came from their Mommy's "tummy." Karen replies that one of them should have come "out of Daddy's tummy" (104). When she learns that "mommies get babies in their tummies" but fathers never do, she immediately concludes, "Well then ... we don't need daddies then" (105). When probed by her mother about women needing men to perform various forms of labor while women reproduce, such as "to go to the office and bring back lollipops and lawnmowers and everything," Karen agrees but ultimately concludes there is not a need to have "daddies" in order to "make babies" because "Daddies can't make babies" (105). While Jeanette attempts to carefully explain that fathers do "help" in reproduction through "a very special kind of loving," Karen's unwittingly perceptive suggestion is never fully debunked (105).

This concept, that sperm is necessary for the continuation of the human race but fathers are not, is instantiated in a speculative fiction work by Katherine Burdekin, *The End of This Day's Business*. Although not published until 1989, this book was written around 1935 and reflects critical feminist anxieties about masculine militarism in the uncertain Western political climate between World Wars I and II (Patai 159). As noted by Daphne Patai, this book shares with Burdekin's later novel *Swastika Night* (1937) and Virginia Woolf's contemporaneous *Three Guineas* (1938) an emphasis on the relationship between fascism and patriarchy but stands alone as a work of speculative fiction in which fascism and matriarchy exist in a distantly future society (161).

By 6250, the women of Earth have come into power and strategically reorganized the political and social structure of society. The deliberate elimination of fathers has been achieved through sexual promiscuity and secrecy of paternity because early female leaders saw more threat than benefit in the continuation of that institution. Fathers were no longer necessary for economic support because of the communist economy nor for physical protection since the world had long been civilized after the end of masculine leadership. Furthermore, this role held no religious significance as God the Father was not a recognized deity of their matriarchy. Burdekin's protagonist Grania, like Charlie's Ledom guide, explains that during various periods in human religious history, fathers were worshiped by their children in a dangerously godlike fashion. By 6250, the women ruling Earth have strategically rid the world of the power structures of fascism and patriarchy.

The early foremothers of these female leaders understood from Freudian teaching that the triadic relationship between the father, mother, and child determines how the child comes to understand gendered relations and, more specifically, whether male children or female children develop "sex shame" (Burdekin 89–91). Because fatherhood is unacknowledged, mothers are known as the "*sole* providers" of life and love, and the result is the understood inferiority of the male sex, who can "never be Mothers" and are therefore considered "of less importance" (91). In Grania's time, pregnancy is regarded as a source of pride and honor, and it serves as "the proof that you are a real woman, and not a barren creature rather like a man" (99). Men are also ashamed to show their bare chests because of the limitations of their anatomy, whereas women wear evidence of their fertility proudly.

Furthermore, this society values genetic and social motherhood equally, and it is not uncommon for women to rear other children as their own if the birth mother chooses. For example, Grania's biological son, Neil, refers to her as his "think-Mother" but *feels* Grania's sister Carla as his mother because she is the woman he knew as his mother until he was in his twenties (19). While all aspects of maternity — pregnancy, nursing, and child rearing — are seen as honorable and enjoyable, the act of fathering a child is not acknowledged by anyone in society. Men see sexual acceptance by women to be an important mark of the masculinity that is expected of them but would never think to claim paternity because it is given no importance in their culture.

It is not merely unpopular or taboo for a woman to educate a man in world history and the power struggles that led to their contemporary matriarchy; it is illegal and punishable by death. Grania takes that risk and ultimately martyrs herself to plant the ideological seed that would eventually bring an end to her "day's business" of complete female leadership at the expense of male psychical development. She admits to Neil, her primary male pupil, that the male leadership of the past, which "was always emotional and always based on physical force," brought violence, oppression, and destruction (61). Furthermore, logically she knows it would be "the safest thing for the whole race that women should rule forever," but she is certain that the "safe, reasonable, uncruel, loveless, and *dull*" existence created by women is wrong (104–105). She believes that both men and women have the potential to be much happier than the current social and political structures allow them to be.

A relatively small number of women in the novel had been previously executed for similar crimes, but these women explained that they had committed this treason in order to give a lover "more spirit" (138). Unlike Grania, who believes the tyrannical rule of women has run its course and should be reformed, these previous traitors had merely sought to give a specific man, a single lover, insight into the capabilities of men in order to uplift him. Grania's motivation, however, is revealed subtly throughout the book to be largely founded in her desire for a return of fatherhood. Much like young Karen predicted in Sturgeon's novel, reproduction in Grania's society relies on men as sexual partners (sperm donors) and physical laborers, but Earth's futuristic female rulers have realized and exploited the concept that male "daddies" are not necessary for babies.

It is the unrealized potential for affection and bonding between a father and child in which Grania sees a great value that is being squandered. Emotional ties between a father and a child are forbidden in Grania's society, and yet evinced through the thoughts, actions, and conversations of Burdekin's characters. Paternal bonds are portrayed as instinctual and powerful yet inexplicable, a characterization consistent with Herb's understanding of fatherly love in *Venus Plus X*. In Burdekin's novel, however, the specter of patriarchal domination has been removed, and the aspects of fatherhood these characters experience are the residual affective elements. Whereas Herb is unable to convincingly separate his need "to be big" from his sentimentality for "dad" hood, in Grania's world no man is capable of feelings of gendered superiority (Sturgeon 82). In this way, Burdekin's text offers a speculative glimpse at the concept of fatherhood and its significance, devoid of struggles for power.

The idea of paternal bonds as instinctive is instantiated through both Grania and Neil. For example, Grania's thoughts during her flight to Germany for her execution reveal her lifelong connectedness to her own father, even before she was aware of his identity. She recalls always being fascinated with Germany, the German language, and thoughts of visiting the country. It was only because of her determination to live there that her mother told her about her German father, so that she would not become involved with him in any way. The news of her heritage made her "quite indecently interested in this German father" and she inquired about far more than her mother would divulge (125–126). Despite her imminent execution, Grania feels sentimental and "slightly giddy" when landing in the country she refers to as "mein Vater's Land" (133–134).

Similarly, before Grania tells Neil that Andreas is his father, the reader witnesses Neil concluding that Andreas is not only the man he likes most but actually the only man he feels he never dislikes. After learning of his paternity, Neil feels "love, something more than liking, come into him" upon seeing Andreas again (21). When Grania, Andreas, and Neil walk as a group toward the May Day festivities, Andreas considers their appearance together in public "scandalous," but Neil is so excited and proud to be walking between "his known progenitors" that he stumbles, sways, and repeatedly bumps his parents (24–25). Neil senses "a warm *human* sympathy flowing" between the three of them "like the beating of a heart" (24). Although Neil has stated with certainty, "No one could ever *feel* a father," even if the identity was known, he begins to believe he does "feel" that bond with Andreas (17). Both Grania and Neil have instinctively known and valued a paternal connection prior to confirmation of paternity.

Neil's "feel" mother, Carla, also comments on this "quite unusual" fondness Neil has always had for Andreas, almost as if he had always known the truth (36). She suspects his feelings for Andreas could be similar to how men had felt about their fathers long ago, when paternity was publicly acknowledged. Grania assures her, however, that Neil "has no Old Word filial respect or fear of him [Andreas]" (36). Indeed, by the time Neil is made aware of his father, Andreas is considerably old and feeble. Neil exhibits fear *for* Andreas rather than *of* him, and desires to put himself between Andreas and the world and to protect this father from any discomfort. This compulsion clearly does not stem from any learned system of filial duty or obligation but strictly from affective bonds.

When Neil is walking between his parents, he thinks of himself as the "very kernel of a proud and valuable whole," and it is largely Grania's realization of the *value* of fatherhood that fuels her campaign to end the psychical enslavement of men (24). She clearly does not want to see a return to patriarchal dominance, but she believes the sacrifices necessary for their perfect stability and peace have forced the population to live numbly. One key area in which Grania identifies a missing source of fulfillment and love is the institution of fatherhood. Many types of loving relationships have been obviated during the period of women's rule, such as "spiritual sex-love," which was apparently a higher priority to Grania's criminal predecessors (92). For Grania, however, it is also a wholeness of familial knowledge and the possibility of fatherly love for which she gives her life.

Like Piercy and Sturgeon, Burdekin instantiates potential outcomes of transitions in human reproduction that remove patriarchal domination, and her characters grapple with the social and affective sacrifices that are inherent in the redefinition of parenthoods. *Woman on the Edge of Time* and *Venus Plus X* enact theories of feminist utopias in which the removal of reproductive difference through technology has been achieved, and the protagonists are able to acknowledge and experience contradictory emotions regarding the nullification of traditional parenting roles. *The End of This Day's Business* creates a potential future where social, genetic, and nursing motherhood roles are exalted yet fatherhood does not exist and paternity is unacknowledged. This fictional world, in which the sexual hierarchy has been reversed by the elimination of daddies, provides an imaginative testing ground consistent with reproductive technological advancements that fall short of parthenogenesis.

In these novels, the force of patriarchal domination has been overturned through changes in reproductive practice, and both male and female characters experience honest, unpopular, and controversial emotions in response to the loss of traditional parenthood roles. In each, equality necessarily results from sacrifices, yet these can be forfeitures of power, love, or some seemingly inseparable combination of the two. Connie and Herb struggle with surrendering genetic motherhood and traditional fatherhood, respectively, for gender equality, whereas Grania weighs the risk of restoring patriarchal domination against the perpetuation of a society devoid of paternal bonds.

While theoretical nonfiction allows scholars to rationalize drastic societal changes needed to achieve interpersonal equality, the fictional worlds created in science and speculative fiction works give voice to the "irrational" affective results of enacted utopian thought. The application of this practice to reproductive science and fatherhood is especially timely, as little is more unpopular or scarce in contemporary literature than sympathetic acknowledgment of the sacrifices required of men for gender equality to exist. As reproductive technologies advance and definitions of all parenthoods adapt, traditional male fatherhood is systematically under-acknowledged if not forgotten. Science fiction provides a space to enact exaggerated possibilities and therefore recognize some of the most basic contradictions of the human condition. Both male and female characters are seen to play out the consequences of eradicating patriarchy by invalidating paternity. Even fictional characters, like scholars, find it hard to separate the patriarch from the "Papa," and yet exploring the eradication of both raises warnings that there may be difficulty in dismissing daddies.

Works Cited

de Beauvoir, Simone. *The Second Sex*. Trans. Constance Borde and Sheila Malovany-Chevallier. New York: Alfred A. Knopf, 2010. Print.

Breeze, Nancy. "Who Is Going to Rock the Petri Dish? For Feminists Who Have Considered Parthenogenesis When the Movement Is Not Enough." *Test Tube Women: What Future for Motherhood?* Eds. Rita Arditi, Renate Duelli Klein, and Shelley Minden. London: Pandora Press, 1984. 397–401. Print.

Burdekin, Katherine. *The End of This Day's Business*. New York: City University, 1989. Print.

_____. *Swastika Night*. 1937. London: Lawrence and Wishart, 1985. Print.

Corea, Gena. "The Reproductive Brothel." *Man-Made Women: How New Reproductive Technologies Affect Women*. Eds. Gena Corea, et al. London: Hutchinson, 1985. 38–51. Print.

Deery, June. "The Biopolitics of Cyberspace: Piercy Hacks Gibson." *Future Females, The Next Generation: New Voices and Velocities in Feminist Science Fiction Criticism*. Ed. Marleen Barr. Lanham, MD: Rowman and Littlefield, 2000. 87–108. Print.

Duelli-Klein, Renate. "What's 'New' About the 'New' Reproductive Technologies?" *Man-Made Women: How New Reproductive Technologies Affect Women*. Eds. Gena Corea, et al. London: Hutchinson, 1985. 64–73. Print.

Dworkin, Andrea. *Right Wing Women: The Politics of Domesticated Females*. London: The Women's Press, 1983. Print.

Firestone, Shulamith. *The Dialectic of Sex: The Case for Feminist Revolution*. New York: William Morrow, 1970. Print.

Giminez, Martha E. "The Mode of Reproduction in Transition: A Marxist Feminist Analysis of the Effects of Reproductive Technologies." *Gender and Society* 5.3 (1991): 334–50. Web. 30 October 2011.

Hamner, Jalna. "A Womb of One's Own." *Test Tube Women: What Future for Motherhood?* Eds. Rita Arditi, Renate Duelli Klein, and Shelley Minden. London: Pandora Press, 1984. 438–448. Print.

Haraway, Donna. *Simians, Cyborgs, and Women: The Reinvention of Nature*. New York: Routledge, 1991. Print.

Hassler, Donald M., and Clyde Wilcox. "Introduction: Politics, Art, Collaboration." *Political*

Science Fiction. Eds. Donald M. Hassler and Clyde Wilcox. Columbia: University of South Carolina Press, 1997. 1–6. Print.
Hauke, Manfred. *Women in the Priesthood?* Trans. David Kipp. San Francisco: Ignatius Press, 1988. Print.
Laqueur, Thomas W. "The Facts of Fatherhood." *Conflicts in Feminism.* Eds. Marianne Hirsch and Evelyn Fox Keller. New York: Routledge, 1990. 205–221. Print.
Lerner, Gerda. *The Creation of Patriarchy.* New York: Oxford University Press, 1986. Print.
Patai, Daphne. "Afterword." *The End of This Day's Business.* New York: City University, 1989. Print.
Piercy, Marge. *Woman on the Edge of Time.* New York: Fawcett Crest, 1976. Print.
Pohl, Frederick. "The Politics of Prophecy." *Political Science Fiction.* Eds. Donald M. Hassler and Clyde Wilcox. Columbia: University of South Carolina, 1997. 7–17. Print.
Rosinsky, Natalie M. *Feminist Futures: Contemporary Women's Speculative Fiction.* Ann Arbor: University of Michigan Research Press, 1984. Print.
Rothman, Barbara Katz. "Comment on Harrison: The Commodification of Motherhood." *Gender and Society* 1.3 (1987): 312–16. Web. 30 October 2011.
Rowland, Robyn. "Reproductive Technologies: The Final Solution to the Woman Question?" *Test Tube Women: What Future for Motherhood?* Eds. Rita Arditi, Renate Duelli Klein, and Shelley Minden. London: Pandora Press, 1984. 356–370. Print.
Ruddick, Sara. "Thinking About Fathers." *Conflicts in Feminism.* Eds. Marianne Hirsch and Evelyn Fox Keller. New York: Routledge, 1990. 222–232. Print.
Sturgeon, Theodore. *Venus Plus X.* 1960. New York: Vintage Books, 1999. Print.
Woolf, Virginia. *Three Guineas.* 1938. New York: Harcourt, Brace, Jovanovich, 1966. Print.
Zipper, Juliette, and Selma Sevenhuijsen. "Surrogacy: Feminist Notions of Motherhood Reconsidered." *Reproductive Technologies: Gender, Motherhood, and Medicine.* Ed. Michelle Stanworth. Oxford: Polity Press, 1987. 118–138. Print.

"I have worked hard at her head and brain": Dr. Moreau and the New Woman
Thomas G. Cole II

An important series of debates in late nineteenth-century Britain concerned "the woman question," and subjects such as suffragism, property, marriage, and women's biological "nature" were the center of these debates. The prevailing, patriarchal view was based on both tradition and science, each supporting the other. Traditionally, women were caregivers and supportive spouses, and scientific writings, such as those of the first eugenicist, Francis Galton, confirmed such orthodox views by arguing that women's rightful social obligations were largely reproduction and motherhood. Restricted to gender roles based upon theories of complementarity, women were forced to make louder demands for better rights, and by the 1880s and 1890s women were regularly writing essays and novels that entreated a reevaluation of the woman question.

In her 1894 essay "The New Aspect of the Woman Question," Sarah Grand coined the phrase "New Woman," a description signifying a figure progressive women used to distinguish themselves from traditional women. "New Woman" quickly became a catchphrase for pundits and suffragettes alike. The New Woman made demands such as the right to vote, divorce, and have careers. Though the image of the knickerbockers-clad bicyclist became a boilerplate icon, the New Woman also read novels and periodicals. She became the subject of satire, caricatured in publications such as *Punch*, but she also contributed answers to the woman question. Although they were debarred from formal education, many New Women educated themselves even in the physical sciences, as one New Woman iterates (Fawcett 126). According to Londa Schiebinger, by the end of the eighteenth century botany had become "fashionable" and "appropriate for women's leisure hours" (*Nature's* 29, 37).

Similarly, these New Women utilized scientific reasoning, drawn from Darwin, in their political discussions.¹ The pursuit of science influenced many in the upper class to the extent that several men and women cultivated gardens and kept curios — archaeological trinkets, dissected insects, or fossilized bones. In a word, science was "popular" (*Nature's* 3).

The popularity of science can likewise be seen from the fact that the first "scientific romances" were published in the 1800s (James 27–8). Beginning with Mary Shelley's *Frankenstein* and *The Last Man* in the 1810s and 1820s, through Jules Verne's novels in the 1870s, and culminating with H.G. Wells' romances in the 1890s, science fiction had come to fruition in *fin-de-siècle* Britain (though the term "science fiction" itself would not appear until the 1920s) (James 28). These texts comprise the early canon of science fiction, though the genre itself is difficult to define, as many have argued.² Indeed, attempts to define the genre retroactively often become bogged down in taxonomic rules that need continual tweaking.

Criteria for defining science fiction that critics *can* agree on, however, include the presence of "historical processes of technological and political change" (Seed xv). Thus, according to David Seed, science fiction takes place in an altered space and time and primarily focuses on the ramifications of techno-political change.³ This tripartite definition of space, time, and techno-political change, therefore, allows Wells' *The Island of Doctor Moreau* (1896) a space within the genre of science fiction rather than in its usual placement in the Gothic genre. Though *Moreau* has been included within the genre of science fiction, notably in Darko Suvin's *Victorian Science Fiction in the UK*, its Gothic credentials are more obvious and alluring to readers and critics. Yet as science fiction, the text reopens discussions of politics and science by unshackling itself from the well-known stereotypes of horror, terror, and romance of the Gothic. Wells' *Moreau*, steeped in popular science and reflecting contemporary discussions in British political and scientific communities, portrays a *fin-de-siècle* reaction to the changing topography of women's rights vis-à-vis the New Woman. Wells' text utilizes science fiction to offer political ripostes to the woman question. The text implicitly argues for the consequences of a continued stasis of women's rights and also demonstrates the anxiety produced by politically empowered New Women, which might disrupt the contemporary and masculine order. The novella also suggests that a change in the rights of women will occur, however much enfranchised men may protest it.

Although *Moreau* can be read as advancing charges of feminine animality and women's unrestrained sexuality, or suggesting that animals and women share a closer connection than do men to either, these interpretations fail to incorporate both an understanding of science fiction and the historical context of the woman question. Therefore, *Moreau*, legitimately situated in the genre of science fiction, reflects contemporary popular science and also functions as commentary on the woman question. Furthermore, Wells' *Moreau* exhibits the established gendering of science and medicine in the nineteenth century, especially in light of the fact that from the eighteenth century forward the realm of science categorically eliminated women both as practitioners and from its intellectual aims (Schiebinger *Nature's* 3). In this period, the object of scientific study became ever more feminized. Thus, owing to the conspicuous absence of any human female characters in *Moreau*, a "feminine" element surfaces in the figure of the puma. The resurgence of the feminine extends not simply to the puma but also to the geography of the island, specifically the language used to describe its natural landscape. Readers can perceive aspects of a gendered system of cataloguing the natural world embedded within Wells' prose, for the very act of going into the woods and collecting and recording specimens takes a gendered form: a feminine object in the hands of a masculine scientist. Furthermore, the text exemplifies the gendering of women and nature that characterized much of the contemporary debate over the New Woman. By understanding the relationship between the New Woman and *Moreau*, critics and readers can better see English men's anxieties manifesting in the contemporary popular science of Wells' story and the anti-women's rights movement.

The popularity of *Moreau* has remained strong enough to garner three film adaptations and several literary discussions. Compared to H.G. Wells' other early tales, however, it receives less attention, and because of its seeming amorphousness, critics such as Roger Bozzetto, R.M.P., and Russell Taylor as well as Mason Harris descry its kaleidoscopic value for scholars and readers alike to intuit many facets of the story. Others have approached the text from a postcolonial perspective, tracing out the implicit racialization in the novella.[4] Some critics offer a psychoanalytic reading, contemplating the jungle as a monstrous feminine that engulfs the white male protagonists, as in Elaine Showalter's essay "The Apocalyptic Fables of H. G. Wells." Still others argue for its Gothic qualifications, situating it in the long line of nineteenth-century male birth tales. Frequently, however, *Moreau* fits into essays as a small example. For example, Steven Lehman provides a psychoanalytic reading of male womb envy that focuses on *Frankenstein* where *Moreau* is addressed briefly in an addendum.

Whereas many critics avoid any discussion of women or plunge into larger defenses of masculinity, others such as Showalter, Galia Benziman, and Coral Lansbury deal directly with the feminist issues of the text. Benziman offers an interpretation that closely resembles Lehman's; however, Benziman's methodology employs the historical framework of the rise of gynecology and also historicizes three texts in the Gothic tradition (*Frankenstein*, Robert Louis Stevenson's *The Strange Case of Dr. Jekyll and Mr. Hyde*, and *Moreau*). Because Drs. Frankenstein, Jekyll, and Moreau aim to reproduce a child without a woman, their tasks necessitate constant trial and error, thereby resulting in a self-reflexive definition of themselves. Benziman enumerates the latency of self-reflexivity in the earlier nineteenth-century stories and its increased emergence in later tales of the century. Again, however, Benziman aligns her reading with both Gothic conventions and a male-centered interpretation.

Lansbury, on the other hand, links the vivisected animal, the working class, and feminists of *fin-de-siècle* Britain together as an oppressed group under the condescending aegis of imperial-minded Englishmen. She maintains, "progression from cruelty to animals to the murder of women was consistently used as a theme by male novelists," and she views the puma in *Moreau* as a conflation of the worker, feminist, and vivisected animal, who all refuse to submit (*Old* 143).[5] Showalter, too, recognizes the puma as the New Woman. She provides a concise analysis of *Moreau*, primarily making use of its cannibalistic and human experimentation taboos, while simultaneously arguing that it exemplifies the "imperial gothic" (227).[6] Showalter's thesis ultimately views the text as Gothic and mostly disregards the feminine puma.

The lines between Gothic and science fiction are blurry, especially in regard to *Moreau*: the puma as some monstrous feminine upholds a Gothic reading, while science fiction is more effective for understanding the puma as a figure for the New Woman of the 1890s. Furthermore, what constitutes Gothic for some critics could be counted as science fiction for others. For example, Harris, who speaks of *Moreau* as a "revival of Gothic fiction," would agree with David Punter's assessment of *Moreau* as a typical Gothic text (Harris 99; Punter 13). Punter defines the Gothic in this way:

> [I]t seems to me impossible to make much sense out of Gothic fiction without continual recourse to the concept of paranoia.... Second, Gothic ... is intimately [connected] with the notion of the barbaric. This emerges in a number of forms: as fear of the past ... as fear of the aristocracy ... as fear of racial degeneracy ... and more recently as fear of the barbaric.... And third, I have tried throughout to draw attention to the very wide-ranging concern among Gothic writers with the nature of taboo [183–184].

Punter's definition of the Gothic seems more in line with science fiction than may first seem evident. Indeed, Brian Aldiss writes, "Science fiction is the search for a definition of mankind and his status in the universe which will stand in our advanced but confused state of knowledge (Science), and is characteristically cast in the Gothic or post–Gothic mode" (qtd. in Seed ix). Thus, critics and readers alike can observe a crisscrossing of genre lines, such that where Punter sees Gothic, Aldiss finds science fiction.

What seems more relevant, though, is that the title of Punter's book, *The Literature of Terror: A History of Gothic Fictions from 1765 to the Present Day*, vastly expands the Gothic timeline. For many, the literature in this time frame includes Gothic as well as science fiction (and all its related subgenres), and in regard to Punter's second criterion of the Gothic, he determines,

> Time and time again, those writers who are referred to as Gothic turn out to be those who bring us up against the boundaries of the civilized, who demonstrate to us the relative nature of ethical and behavioural codes, who place, over against the conventional world, a different sphere in which these codes operate at best in distorted forms [183–184].

This type of definition often also fits science fiction. Seed, paraphrasing Brian Nellist, concludes, "Science fiction repeatedly looks forward so as to look back" (xiii). Again, critics find themselves entrenched in a battle over genre.

The contention between Gothic and science fiction, however, is important with regard to *Moreau*. If *Moreau* is a text about a white man on an island in the Pacific or about the barbarism of vivisection, one can certainly make the argument that many have made regarding its postcolonial attributes or psychosocial taboos, familiar in the Gothic. Yet these interpretations overlook the emphasis Wells places on its contemporary setting. Vivisection is closely related to 1890s feminism, and therefore feminism is implicated.[7] Because science fiction involves the types of distortions in time and space that herald socio-scientific change that are perceptible in *Moreau*, the label "science fiction," rather than "Gothic," allows a fuller understanding of the story's external rhetorical situation. Some critics have suggested *Moreau* is science fiction but have neither answered why nor substantiated the reason for their choice. Nevertheless, *Moreau* does fit within Fredric Jameson's view of science fiction, a schema that adds breadth to the descriptions that Aldiss and Seed provide. Specifically concerning the narrative form, Jameson asserts,

> Yet such narrative categories [constituent parts of the narrative form] are themselves fraught with contradiction: in order for narrative to project some closure (a narrative must have an ending, even if it is ingeniously organized around the structural repression of endings as such). At the same time, however, closure or the narrative ending is the mark of that boundary or limit beyond which thought cannot go. The merit of SF [science fiction] is to dramatize this contradiction on the level of plot itself, since the vision of future history cannot know any punctual ending of this kind, at the same time that its novelistic expression demands some such ending [283].

Moreau adheres nicely to Jameson's description, as it perplexes a normal narrative arc in more ways than one. *Moreau* opens with narrative confusion. The book is written from the point of view of the main character, Edward Prendick, yet Prendick does not initiate the story; the "Introduction" is a frame narrative, written by Prendick's nephew. The two authorial voices force the reader to grapple with a grafted text, a characteristic that equally epitomizes Moreau's experiments. The nephew writes, "The following narrative was found among his papers by the undersigned, his nephew and heir, but unaccompanied by any definite request for publication" (Wells "Introduction" 174).[8] That the nephew publishes his uncle's story without the "definite request for publication" suggests Prendick did not want to be around when his story became public. Immediately at the outset, then, the reader is confronted with two authors, a narrator, and an "editor," as well as their diverse intentions.

Moreau takes the form of a flashback by the protagonist. This flashback colors the entire story, making it a double frame narrative. Often jarring the reader out of the present, Prendick offers prefatory comments to the action, annotations to the events, and endnotes on what has just happened. Thus, readers confront a story constantly in revision. They also learn from the nephew's prologue that a ship recently visited the island and that the sailors and captain found no trace of what Prendick claims. The entirety of the story then occurs outside historical time and before the chronological time of composition. It also occurs in a place that retains no verifiable evidence of the narrative. Oddly enough, this is what Prendick fears: that he will get his story wrong by leaving out salient details that confuse his reader. Clarity is essential to the telling of this tale, for when he is rescued and relates his story of the island to his rescuers, they suspect he might be insane. Prendick writes, "Neither the captain nor the mate would believe my story, judging that solitude and danger had made me mad; and fearing their opinion might be that of others, I refrained from telling my adventure further" (Wells *Island* 102). Therefore, when Prendick later recounts his time spent on the island he wants to tell the truth soberly and anonymously so as to avoid any unwanted scrutiny.[9]

What readers find within the text form is evidence of an unstable storyline. In his attempts to create an account that is both legitimate and coherent — one that could serve as a scientific treatise or reliable account of the facts, like Darwin's own trip to the Pacific aboard the HMS *Beagle*— Prendick actually calls attention to the nature of his narrative's constructedness. The aim for supreme order, characteristic of a scientific mode, falls flat, revealing the various parts that constitute the story.

This constructedness lends more to Jameson's model. He writes, "this ultimate 'text' or object of study ... is a *construct*: it exists nowhere in 'empirical' form, and therefore must be re-constructed on the basis of empirical 'texts' of all sorts" (283, emphasis original). Because there can be no master narrative suggests that *Moreau*— a constructed text — is science fiction. Moreover, distortions of time and space are also in play in *Moreau*, following Seed's definition. Jameson reiterates the third condition of the time, space, and techno-political triangle through the concept of defamiliarization: "SF [science fiction] has concealed another, far more complex temporal structure: not to give us 'images' of the future ... but rather to defamiliarize and restructure our experience of our own present, and to do so in specific ways distinct from all other forms of defamiliarization" (286). With the absence of women in *Moreau*, a feminist reading is less than obvious, yet the debates surrounding the woman question are present in the defamiliarized setting and guise of the puma. Thus, the concept of defamiliarization, a crucial facet of science fiction according to Jameson, makes possible a fuller reading of *Moreau*, especially in regard to its feminist issues.

Moreau offers a place without any women — human women, that is. The only women that populate the nameless island are among Moreau's hybrid forms that defy classification, mirroring the problematic genre of the text. The rejection of anything "feminine" and the male-dominated, homosocial order mirrored the ideological push occurring throughout the eighteenth and nineteenth centuries (Schiebinger *Nature's* 9).[10] Yet the feminine reemerges in at least two places in the book: in the geography of the island and in the catastrophic end of Moreau's experiment. Because nature and women are linked within the novella's ideology, the feminine return comments upon the ideology of nineteenth-century science as well as the contemporary discourse on women's rights. What seems different about the island is not readily apparent. The reader learns of a white male scientist who experiments upon humanoid creatures. The location of the island, following Prendick's descriptions of his ships' routes, is very near Galapagos. In effect, *Moreau* functions as a microcosm of British imperialism — with a white European governor and his colonial subjects — but also reenacts the setting of a naturalist going into the wild to collect samples and experiment in the field à la Darwin. Furthermore, the description of the geography offers more than just a landscape. Prendick provides an ekphrastic description: coming into "a broad bay flanked on either hand by a low promontory," Prendick appears in the "embrace" of a large pair of legs (Wells *Island* 17). He observes, "It was low, and covered with thick vegetation," before looking "up to a ridge, perhaps sixty or seventy feet above the sea-level." He describes further: "Half way up was a square enclosure.... Two thatched roofs peeped from within this enclosure" (17).[11] Fascinatingly, here Prendick recounts an array of objects that suggest female bodies, namely the vagina and breasts.

Showalter also suggests that Prendick's description of the island — "Presently the ground gave, rich and oozy, under my feet" — marks it as feminine (Wells *Island* 46; Showalter 80). Like the previous passage about thatched roofs, this sentence alludes to an interpretation of the landscape as feminine.

The "thick vegetation" of the first passage appears again when Prendick decides to wander into it. He writes, "I strode through the undergrowth that clothed the ridge behind the house, scarcely heeding whither I went; passed on through the shadow of a thick cluster of straight-stemmed trees beyond it ... descending towards a streamlet that ran through a narrow valley" (Wells *Island* 26). This entrance into the vaginal passage of the geography foregrounds the feminization of the island and Prendick's access into the gendered feminine world.

In order for the reading of the island as the female body to work within a science fiction perspective, one must remember that science fiction defamiliarizes what is commonplace and recasts it in a strange new light (Jameson 286). Thus, the New Woman debate, too, gets embedded into this bizarre isle of horrors. Though the New Woman is not yet in Parliament, university, or hospital, she is emerging in the environment around the white Europeans — Moreau, Prendick, and Montgomery. The clearest mark to signal these readings is the female body imagery. That the first image of the island takes the form of the female body, one that foreshadows Moreau's experimentation on another female body, instantiates a general focus on female bodies in the geographic environments of the novella. Readers first become aware of the gesture toward bodies and geography in the introduction when Prendick sets sail from Callao, a "guano port in Peru, near Lima" (Wells "Introduction" 174). After the *Lady Vain*, another feminine setting and symbol, sinks, Prendick is rescued by a ship called the *Ipecacuanha*, the name of a commonly used drug that induces vomiting. That this combination of the uncanny in reference to the threatening, feminine landscape of the island and the forceful nausea commences the story, according to Kelley Hurley, makes the reader aware of ulterior meaning (104). Whether it is the faces of the creatures that Prendick cannot describe or the foreboding island itself, there is something else looming, just below the surface, waiting to break out.

Though they never see the beginning of Prendick's journey, Wells' readers do get an account of what happened before the encounter with Moreau. Prendick begins, "I do not propose to add anything to what has already been written concerning the loss of the *Lady Vain*. As everyone knows, she collided with a derelict when ten days out from Callao" (Wells *Island* 1). Readers learn that the boat on which Prendick was sailing, whose name denotes an ostentatious or arrogant woman, sunk when it hit another boat, one abandoned by its crew. The derelict boat and the *Lady Vain* function here as foreshadowing of the eventual derelict laboratory island, as a symbol of technology gone awry, and as two worlds violently colliding into one another. This unmanned technology hits and sinks the *Lady*, quite literally suppressing the feminine symbol, much like the scientific community in Britain treated women and femininity in general.

Jane Caputi suggests that there is an ongoing war carried out under patriarchy against feminine symbols or forms (*Goddesses* 315). That the *Lady Vain* is the first casualty of *Moreau* signals an aggressiveness toward feminine symbols. The contempt for women becomes even more apparent as the story progresses. Cast from the safety of the *Lady Vain*, Prendick is forced into a dinghy with two other men and one flask of water in the endless ocean. Prendick continues, "The longboat [of the *Lady Vain*], with seven of the crew, was picked up eighteen days after" it sank, "and the story of their terrible privations has become quite as well known as the far more horrible *Medusa* case" (Wells *Island* 1). Here, readers learn that the conditions of the other lifeboat are comparable to the aptly named *Medusa*, a ship whose life raft harbored sailors that eventually resorted to cannibalism. Prendick and his two fellow survivors also contemplate drawing straws to see who will become the cannibalized: "The water ended on the fourth day, and we were already thinking strange things and saying them with our eyes" (2). Thus thrown into nature, much like Kurtz in Joseph Conrad's *The Heart of Darkness*, published less than a decade later, these men resort to cannibalism and revert to animalistic tendencies.

The movement from human to animal also becomes a topic of study for Moreau and parallels Prendick's actions. When Prendick arrives on the island, and even after he leaves, the language he uses to describe himself casts him as animal. At one point he falls out of the hammock, which "deposited me upon all-fours on the floor," and later eats food that "contributed to the sense of animal comfort which I experienced" (35). When he discovers Moreau's torture of animals, Prendick runs off and is eventually cornered and caught by Moreau, literally becoming the hunted animal. In order to evade Moreau, he hides in the undergrowth of the island and at one point suffers injury, "a torn and bleeding ear" (47). The diction lends Prendick animalistic qualities, and the plot likewise shows him scurrying through the forest, cutting himself, and crawling on all fours, wherein he eventually "fell in with these monsters' ways" (95). Even later, after he has been saved and is back in England, he remembers, "I too must have undergone strange changes. My clothes hung about me as yellow rags, through whose rents showed the tanned skin. My hair grew long, and became matted together. I am told that even now my eyes have a strange brightness, a swift alertness of movement" (98). Thus even safely returned to England, he still exhibits animalistic inclinations. This switch to the animal only occurs once Prendick goes to the island — a womanless, ersatz society. Moreover, the predisposition toward the animal is what Moreau finds difficult to eradicate from his creations. Just as Prendick becomes more animalistic in his motor functions because of his experiences on the island, Moreau equally cannot control all aspects of his experiments. This lack of control is especially the case when the feminine puma attacks. Harris argues that one of the horrors of *Moreau* lies in its connection to the real debates about vivisection in the 1890s. Moreau's methods would be an all-too-common image for Wells' readers. Charges of godlessness and sadism characterized the staunchest anti-vivisectionists' criticism. Because "opposition to vivisection was often associated with a religious hostility toward science," many of the critiques included suggestions of immorality on the part of these male "godless Darwinists ... who enjoyed inflicting pain" (Harris 100). The latter included Wells' teacher, T.H. Huxley. Bodily pain, then, was a motivating factor in forging the anti-vivisectionist movement. Moreover, a majority of anti-vivisectionists were women. As Lansbury argues, these women saw the plight of the vivisected animal as comparable to their own struggle against a male-dominated Britain. Frances Power Cobbe, founder of the British Union for the Abolition of Vivisection, was also a suffragette who lobbied for the first anti-vivisection bills in Parliament (Otis 32). Thus, anti-vivisectionists and feminists frequently were one and the same.

Though *Moreau* is explicitly about the woes of vivisection, it also participates in discussions of nineteenth-century science and politics. One of the lessons embedded in the text relates to what Caputi argues regarding the relationship between patriarchy and evolution, or even popular science: "Patriarchal men, whatever their intentions or pretensions, *cannot* control the process of mutation; and change, or mutation, is, after all, essential to life" (*Gossips* 276, emphasis original). Another lesson is that nature becomes gendered in the hands of male scientists. Though these "patriarchal men" attempt to describe nature accurately and objectively, their science becomes unavoidably ideological. They import their prejudices about women into their scientific findings, for they wanted to see, as Schiebinger notes, "nature as the guiding light for social reform" (*Nature's* 4). Yet nature and society do not necessarily match up with the interests of science.

According to Benziman, "The invention of gynecology at the beginning of the [nineteenth] century led to what historians of medicine sometimes refer to as the medicalization of the female body" (378). The notion of women as objects thus emerged not only from the social or political context but also from the medical one. As objects of study, the female subject saw a larger gulf separating her from the male scientist. The same manner in which women were relegated to specific places, namely sequestered in the home, and forced to perform only the chores associated with childrearing and the household, extended to science and medicine. Schiebinger writes, "For the most part, academic study of sexual differences was designed to keep women in their place" (*Has* 112). In this "experimental medicine," they were still placed in subordinate positions (Harris 100). The perspective of conquering the woman physically and overcoming nature through science links woman and nature together, especially in the way men of science viewed them.

This power dynamic appears not only in the science of the time but also in political debates over the New Woman. Mona Caird's essay "Marriage," published in 1888 in a prominent periodical, *The Westminster Review*, participates in the discussion of women's nature as informed from the viewpoint of science. She writes, "There is no social philosophy ... which does not lapse into incoherence as soon as it touches the subject of women. The thinker abandons thought-laws which he has obeyed until that fatal moment; he forgets every principle of science previously present to his mind" (186). Caird here identifies what Schiebinger similarly notes almost a hundred years later: "In many cases, ancient prejudices were merely translated into the language of modern science" (*Nature's* 38). Modern science became a contributor to the orthodox view that women ought not partake in voting, education, or the business of the country in general. Modern science thus took on the project of conquering a feminized nature. Caird utilizes a well-known dog metaphor in her essay, linking women and animals together, in order to illustrate the illogical stance men have taken toward women's rights. "We chain up a dog to keep watch over our home," she insists, "we deny him freedom, and in some cases, alas! even sufficient exercise to keep his limbs supple and his body in health" (186). Caird recasts the woman question, conflated here with the dog's dilemma, as a question of humanity and decency: "Humane people ask his master: 'Why do you keep that dog always chained up?'" (187). Caird's logic derives from her position as woman and anti-vivisectionist and connects women to nature. She sees both as the inferior target in masculine, British science and politics.

Science also provided men with another benefit, argues Lehman: "Science," as a controllable replacement for the role of a female spouse, could "provide a vessel for the germination of the future hopes of men without the emotional risks run in relationships with women" (55). Married to science, the thinker could still view his work as something conquerable. This theme is also at work in Wells' depiction of Moreau's scientific labor. In one of the most important chapters, entitled "Dr. Moreau Explains," Prendick discovers Moreau's motivations for experimentation. Prendick first remonstrates Moreau for his gruesome actions, making the same arguments that anti-vivisectionists leveled at scientists. However, Prendick eventually accepts the fact that Moreau's impetus is scientific whimsy but also an insatiable desire to conquer that which plagues him. Moreau says, "So for twenty years altogether — counting nine years in England — I have been going on; and there is still something in everything I do that defeats me, makes me dissatisfied, challenges me to further effort. Sometimes I rise above my level, sometimes I fall below it; but always I fall short of the things I dream" (58). This desire to triumph indicates both a patriarchal and scientific form of domination — something that becomes commensurate in *Moreau*. Moreau's own portrayal of his work suggests his existence is wholly consumed by it. In fact, it defines him. Thus, defeat in his scientific work is not acceptable. Caputi argues, "because the feminine represents a fundamental threat to the success of a male's individuation, masculine subjects seek to control and dominate the feminine, resulting in rape and other forms of abuse" (*Goddesses* 184). Moreau cannot give up because he loses his superiority as a man and a scientist.

Moreau's relentlessness is indicative of his masculine and scientific endeavor, one that cannot endure loss. As Caputi notes, "rape" and "abuse" — both forms of torture — are manners in which patriarchy dominates the feminine. They are likewise the avenues for Moreau in his work.[12] The language he uses to describe his project leaves little room for anything but a view of him as a doctor of death or a cruel god[13]:

> "Each time I dip a living creature into the bath of burning pain, I say, 'This time I will burn out all the animal; this time I will make a rational creature of my own!' After all, what is ten years? Men have been a hundred thousand in the making."
> He thought darkly. "But I am drawing near the fastness. This puma of mine..."
> After a silence, "And they revert. As soon as my hand is taken from them the beast begins to creep back, begins to assert itself again" [Wells *Island* 59].

Moreau's violence necessitates the backlash of the feminine puma. Though there are "more than sixty of these strange creations of Moreau's art" on the island, they compose the inferior end of a power relation (61–62). In effect, they stand as the feminine counterpart in the male-controlled scientific power spectrum.

Similar to Schiebinger, Benziman argues that "modern science was traditionally gender-biased; its enlightened, rational methodologies were perceived as masculine, and its object of research — nature — as feminine" (379). Thus, the work that Moreau performs establishes a gendered binarism between himself and his subjects. As he becomes more and more possessed by his failed labors, he comes to view his creations with disgust. Moreau says, "They only sicken me with a sense of failure" (Wells *Island* 59). The only creature Moreau operates on during Prendick's stay is the puma, and until the discussion he has with Prendick the puma remains genderless. However, after Prendick and the reader learn of Moreau's indifference the puma becomes gendered — almost unnoticeably. Moreau says, "I have some hope of this puma. I have worked hard at her head and brain —" and trails off (59). This puma is simultaneously the creature into which he has poured his greatest efforts and who also signifies his greatest sense of failure.

The inimitable factor that Moreau cannot grasp, that which defeats him, is the feminine. Because Moreau is the active pursuer of a new creation and his subjects are the passive objects of his study, each becomes gendered accordingly. His torture and lack of understanding of the need for the feminine ultimately lead him to his own demise. Benziman stresses, "Since nature — now challenged by man's scientific progress — is conceived of as feminine and maternal, to surpass it is also to defeat the female body" (381). The infringement by Moreau on feminine labor obliges a return of the repressed feminine by the end of the main action (Lehman 54).

"Then suddenly something happened," writes Prendick (Wells *Island* 75). The puma "met its persecutor with a shriek almost like that of an angry virago" (75). Characterized as an evil shrew and spirit, the now-gendered puma reacts with ferocity. Her vengeance echoes Caird's dog metaphor. Caird writes, "*He* [the dog] has no revenge in his power; he must live and die, and no one knows his wretchedness. But the woman takes her unconscious vengeance, for she enters into the inmost life of society. She can pay back the injury with interest" (187, emphasis original). The dog, the puma, and the New Woman all strike back at Moreau.[14]

Wells probably knew of the oft-used dog metaphor, the same one used in Caird's essay on marriage as well as the metaphor Grand employed in her essay "The New Aspect of the Woman Question." Grand, echoing Caird, exhorts,

> When we hear the "Help! help! help!" of the desolate and the oppressed, and still more when we see the awful dumb despair of those who have lost even the hope of help, we must respond. This is often inconvenient to man, especially when he has seized upon a defenceless victim whom he would have destroyed had we not come to the rescue and so, because it is inconvenient to be exposed and thwarted, he snarls about the end of all true womanliness, cants on the subject of the Sphere, so that we cannot be stirred into having our sympathies aroused by his victims when they shriek, and with shades over our eyes that we may not see him in his degradation, we shall be afflicted with short hair, coarse skins, unsymmetrical figures, loud voices, tastelessness in dress, and an unattractive appearance and character generally, and then he will not love us any more or marry us [144–5].

The figure of the "defenceless victim"— the shrieking dog and the puma— hearkens back to the opening of Grand's essay and one of the labels given to the die-hard suffragettes, "Shrieking Sisterhood" (141). The puma enters the fray as the New Woman, a shrieking sister. Her shrieks of pain align her with the rhetoric deployed against the New Woman. Moreover, the women that refuse to submit are "afflicted" with a slew of horrible traits that are analogous to Moreau's creatures. They are described as the unattractive, shorthaired monsters whom no one will marry. For example, the only creature Prendick claims he "hated from the beginning" was a "particularly hateful (and evil-smelling)" female (Wells *Island* 63). He similarly indicates, "the females ... had in the earlier days of my stay an instinctive sense of their own repulsive clumsiness, and displayed in consequence a more than human regard for the decencies and decorum of external costume" (64). If a woman resists she becomes the dejected icon Grand summons — the ugly woman who will have to conceal her monstrousness.

The descriptions of the puma coalesce with the argot of the women's movement. Yet the connection becomes even clearer in Prendick's final portrayal of the puma: "I threw up my arm to defend myself," he continues, "and the great monster, swathed in lint and with red-stained bandages fluttering about it, leapt over me and passed" (75–6). The puma clad in bandages and bleeding — an itinerant wound — runs past Prendick, returning to the natural world from which she originated. Lansbury writes, "All the themes of women, vivisection, and animals are drawn together in this explosive and prophetic image of anger and revenge" ("Gynaecology" 437). Yet what Moreau has done to her in his torture will not allow the puma to be simply released. This puma eventually kills Moreau and causes the death of Montgomery; she also permanently scars Prendick, who will be unable to reassimilate to life in England. Her acts will stand as a lesson to both Prendick and those who read his tale of Moreau's horror of vivisection and scientific dominion.

The action following the puma's escape is all reported to Prendick, who then relates it to his reader. After the puma flees into the jungle, Moreau and Montgomery follow in pursuit. The forest again becomes personified, and Prendick "stared inland at the green bush that had swallowed up Moreau and Montgomery" (77). The feminine landscape now has the ability to attack, to exact its revenge against Moreau. Readers hear of gunfire and of Montgomery's fruitless searches for Moreau. What ensues is a chaos that contrasts against the grim order that Moreau tried to create through his science. The feminine puma brings about new chaos, leading to the deaths of Moreau, Montgomery, and many of the creatures on the island. Similarly, in the ten months Prendick remains on the island after Moreau dies, the beasts begin to revert back to their former types. Though the chaos on the island eventually reaches a point of equilibrium, the trauma Prendick endures persists until his death. When once back in England, he writes, "I could not persuade myself that the men and women I met were not also another Beast People, animals half wrought into the outward image of human souls, and that they would presently begin to revert" (102). Fearing that everyone is now one of Moreau's beasts, Prendick moves to a quiet country home surrounded by books.

Moreau stands as a cautionary tale, warning against the horrors of science, and as a commentary on the debates of the 1890s, including vivisection and women's rights. Commenting on the "New Women of the fin de siècle and the feminist anti-vivisectionists" as well as "the hubris contained in the belief of many of Wells' contemporaries that the biological and social sciences could eliminate the unknown or the excessive from the calculus of humanity," *Moreau* summarizes the worries of science run amok (Showalter 79; Christensen 577). Explicit in the text is the masculine supremacy of logic and science, taking form in Moreau's experiments against nature and animals as well as Prendick's writing of a text. Implicit in the text is the feminized landscape and nature that eventually returns to wreak disaster against the masculine scientist. Wells' text thus both posits the problem of masculine science and offers an image of the response from the rejected feminine.[15]

The feminist message in the text, disguised as the barbaric experiments of a mad scientist's quest for pure creation, is dependent upon defamiliarization. Without recognizing the novella as science fiction, a reading of *Moreau* as proto-feminist would be less than obvious. Rather than taking place in England, though an island itself, *Moreau* transpires on an unfamiliar, fictive isle. In lieu of women, there is a puma. In place of society, there is a Beast People, who are fashioned in light of science, complete with a god named Moreau and his laws. Cleverly disguised, *Moreau* functions as a science fiction text that nonetheless critiques anti-feminist perspectives of the 1890s.

Notes

1. One woman, H. E. Harvey, writing in 1897 and explicitly drawing from Darwinian logic, claims, "I think anyone who looks at social questions from a scientific point of view will admit that the only right which we really recognize is the right of the strongest" (168).
2. See Wegner 4–10.
3. Like Seed's definition, Mark Rose creates a formula of time, space, machine, and monster in his discussions of science fiction. See Mark Rose, *Alien Encounters: Anatomy of Science Fiction* (Cambridge: Harvard University Press, 1981).
4. See Christensen 576–577.
5. Laura Otis views the relationship between anti-vivisectionists and women's rights activists as closely related through the latter's involvement in the initial laws and trials regarding vivisection, specifically David Ferrier's court case.
6. As others have done, Showalter quotes Patrick Brantlinger's *Rule of Darkness: British Literature and Imperialism, 1830–1914* (Ithaca: Cornell University Press, 1988), 227.
7. I use the word "feminism" regarding women's rights in the 1890s, as do many critics, though I should point out that the term would not have been used at the time. Also, Otis' essay on Wilkie Collins' *Heart and Science* and Wells' *Moreau* makes the feminist and anti-vivisectionist connection.
8. Throughout the essay, I quote primarily from the Dover publication of *Moreau*. However, the Dover edition omits the "Introduction" from Prendick's nephew. Therefore, I quote twice from Houghton Mifflin's edition of Shelley and Wells' *Frankenstein* and *Moreau*, which includes the nephew's introduction.
9. This is another characteristic of science fiction, according to Patrick Parrinder: "A catas-

trophe is an occurrence of such magnitude that it can only be confirmed retrospectively. It needs an audience, or at least a sole surviving interpreter" (61).

10. Otis points out that in the original draft of *Moreau*, "Wells gave Moreau a wife and assigned her a significant role in the work. His decision to edit her out of the published version suggests a rethinking of Moreau as a more self-oriented scientist" (51). The definitive elimination of a wife (and therefore women from *Moreau*) mimics the same exclusion that Schiebinger indicates of women from science.

11. My reading of the "feminine" island is similar to Anne McClintock's analysis of a map in H. Rider Haggard's King Solomon's Mines. See Anne McClintock, *Imperial Leather: Race, Gender, and Sexuality in the Colonial Contest* (New York: Routledge, 1995), 1–3.

12. Otis writes, "Mary Ann Elston reports that science was depicted as rape in anti-vivisection literature, and women 'were explicitly invited to identify themselves with the animals'" (48). See Mary Ann Elston, "Women and Anti-vivisection in Victorian England, 1870–1900," in *Vivisection in Historical Perspective*, ed. Nicolaas A. Rupke (New York: Routledge, 1990), 263.

13. For Dr. Moreau as a Dr. Death figure, see Elana Gomel's "From Dr. Moreau to Dr. Mengele: The Biological Sublime." For Dr. Moreau as God, see Gorman Beauchamp's "*The Island of Dr. Moreau* as Theological Grotesque."

14. Lansbury reads the puma as the New Woman. She does not argue, however, for the gendering of science and nature in *Moreau*, nor does she accommodate Caird and Grand's essays. See Lansbury *Old* 151 and also "Gynaecology" 437.

15. Regarding Wells' personal view of vivisection, Harris cites an early reviewer and friend of Wells who suggested that Wells was pro-vivisection but utilized the anti-vivisectionist standpoint as an effective "source of horror" (100). Whether Wells was a feminist is debatable. Writing about a decade after *Moreau* in *First and Last Things* (1908), Wells writes, "I declare for the conventional equality of women, that is to say for the determination to make neither sex nor any sexual characteristic a standard of superiority or inferiority, for the view that a woman is a person as important and necessary, as much to be consulted, and entitled to as much freedom of action as a man" (265). However, Sylvia Hardy, the first female Chair of the H. G. Wells Society, comes to the conclusion, "that although H. G. Wells *did* make a contribution to the feminist cause ... his portrayal of women ... reveals ... a deep-seated reluctance to come to terms with women as free, equal human beings" (61, emphasis original).

Works Cited

Beauchamp, Gorman. "*The Island of Dr. Moreau* as Theological Grotesque." *Papers on Language and Literature* 15.4 (Fall 1979): 408–17. *Academic Search Premier*. Web. 6 July 2011.
Benziman, Galia. "Challenging the Biological: The Fantasy of Male Birth as a Nineteenth-Century Narrative of Ethical Failure." *Women's Studies* 35.4 (2006): 375–395. *Academic Search Premier*. Web. 6 July 2011.
Bozzetto, Roger, R. M. P., and Russell Taylor. "Moreau's Tragi-Farcical Island." *Science Fiction Studies* 20.1 (1993): 34–44. *JSTOR*. Web. 6 July 2011.
Caird, Mona. "Marriage." 1888. *A New Woman Reader: Fiction, Articles, and Drama of the 1890s*. Ed. Carolyn Christensen Nelson. Peterborough, Ontario: Broadview Press, 2001. 185–199. Print.
Caputi, Jane. *Goddesses and Monsters: Women, Myth, Power, and Popular Culture*. Madison: University of Wisconsin Press, 2004. Print.
_____. *Gossips, Gorgons & Crones: The Fates of the Earth*. Santa Fe: Bear & Company, 1993. Print.
Christensen, Timothy. "The 'Bestial Mark' of Race in *The Island of Dr. Moreau*." *Criticism* 46.4 (2004): 575–595. *Academic Search Premier*. Web. 6 July 2011.
Conrad, Joseph. *The Heart of Darkness*. New York: Penguin, 1994. Print.

Darwin, Charles. *The Origin of Species by Means of Natural Selection or The Preservation of Favoured Races in the Struggle for Life*. 1859. New York: Avenel, 1979. Print.
Fawcett, Millicent Garrett. "The Appeal Against Female Suffrage: A Reply. I." July 1889. *A New Woman Reader: Fiction, Articles, and Drama of the 1890s*. Ed. Carolyn Christensen Nelson. Peterborough, Ontario: Broadview Press, 2001. 124–130. Print.
Galton, Francis. "Hereditary Talent and Character." *Macmillan Magazine* XII (1865), 157–166. Web. 6 Jul 2011. http://galton.org/essays/1860-1869/galton-1865-macmillan-hereditary-talent.html
Grand, Sarah. "The New Aspect of the Woman Question." 1894. *A New Woman Reader: Fiction, Articles, and Drama of the 1890s*. Ed. Carolyn Christensen Nelson. Peterborough, Ontario: Broadview Press, 2001. 141–146. Print.
Gomel, Elana. "From Dr. Moreau to Dr. Mengele: The Biological Sublime." *Poetics Today* 21 (2000): 393–421. *Academic Search Premier*. Web. 6 July 2011.
Hardy, Sylvia. "A Feminist Perspective on H.G. Wells." *The Wellsian* 20 (Winter 1997): 49–62. Print.
Harris, Mason. "Vivisection, the Culture of Science, and Intellectual Uncertainty in *The Island of Doctor Moreau*." *Gothic Studies* 4.2 (2002): 99–115. *Academic Search Premier*. Web. 6 July 2011.
Harvey, H. E. "Science and the Rights of Women." Aug. 1897. *A New Woman Reader: Fiction, Articles, and Drama of the 1890s*. Ed. Carolyn Christensen Nelson. Peterborough, Ontario: Broadview Press, 2001. 168–170. Print.
Hurley, Kelley. *The Gothic Body: Sexuality, Materialism and Degeneration at the* fin de siècle. Cambridge: Cambridge University Press, 1996. Print.
James, Edward. "Science Fiction by Gaslight: An Introduction to English-Language Science Fiction in the Nineteenth Century." *Anticipations*. Ed. David Seed. Syracuse: Syracuse University Press, 1995. 26–45. Print.
Jameson, Fredric. *Archaeologies of the Future: The Desire Called Utopia and Other Science Fictions*. New York: Verso, 2005. Print.
Lansbury, Coral. "Gynaecology, Pornography, and the Antivivisection Movement." *Victorian Studies* 28 (1985): 413–437. *JSTOR*. Web. 6 July 2011.
_____. *The Old Brown Dog: Women, Workers, and Vivisection in Edwardian England*. Madison: University of Wisconsin Press, 1985. Print.
Lehman, Steven. "The Motherless Child in Science Fiction: *Frankenstein* and *Moreau*." *Science Fiction Studies* 19.1 (1992): 49–58. *JSTOR*. Web. 6 July 2011.
Otis, Laura. "Howled Out of the Country: Wilkie Collins and H.G. Wells Retry David Ferrier." *Neurology and Literature, 1860–1920*. Ed. Anne Stiles. New York: Palgrave Macmillan, 2007. 27–51. Print.
Parrinder, Patrick. "From Mary Shelley to *The War of the Worlds*: The Thames Valley Catastrophe." *Anticipations*. Ed. David Seed. Syracuse: Syracuse University Press, 1995. 58–74. Print.
Punter, David. *The Literature of Terror: A History of Gothic Fictions from 1765 to the Present Day*. New York: Longman, 1996. Print.
Schiebinger, Londa. *Has Feminism Changed Science?* Cambridge: Harvard University Press, 1999. Print.
_____. *Nature's Body*. Boston: Beacon Press, 1993. Print.
Showalter, Elaine. "The Apocalyptic Fables of H. G. Wells." *Fin de Siècle/Fin du Globe: Fears and Fantasies of the Late Nineteenth Century*. Ed. John Stokes. Hong Kong: St. Martin's Press, 1992. 69–84. Print.
Seed, David. Preface. *Anticipations*. Ed. David Seed. Syracuse: Syracuse University Press, 1995. ix–xvi. Print.
Suvin, Darko. *Victorian Science Fiction in the UK: The Discourses of Knowledge and Power*. Boston: G. K. Hall, 1983. Print.
Wegner, Phillip. *Imaginary Communities: Utopia, the Nation, and the Spatial Histories of Modernity*. Berkeley: University of California Press, 2002. 4–10. Print.

Wells, H. G. *First and Last Things*. New York: Putnam, 1908. Print.
_____. "Introduction." *The Island of Doctor Moreau*. In *Making Humans: Complete Texts with Introduction, Historical Contexts, Critical Essays*. Ed. Judith Wilt. Boston: Houghton Mifflin, 2003. Print.
_____. *The Island of Dr. Moreau*. New York: Dover, 1996. Print.

"Are we not men?" Degeneration, Future-Sex and *The Time Machine*

Larry T. Shillock

> *Three possibilities of life await ... [for] each living being: either it remains primitive and unchanged, or it progresses toward a higher type, or it backslides and retrogresses. The factors underlying the stable state force the animal to remain as it is; those underlying the progressive tendency make it more elaborate; while the factors of degeneration, on the other hand, tend to simplify its structure.*
>
> — EUGENE S. TALBOT, *DEGENERACY* 13

It has long been a commonplace of science fiction scholarship that Charles Darwin's work had a generative role in the writings of H. G. Wells. "Without Darwin," Frank McConnell remarks, "there may literally not have been an 'H. G. Wells,'" since "evolutionary theory profoundly informed almost every aspect of his thought" (53). When Wells wrote his most accomplished scientific romances during the 1890s, J. P. Vernier explains, evolution was "the ruling force in the universe his fancy was creating" (83). Biographer David C. Smith goes so far as to reject an array of source texts for *The Time Machine* (1895), Wells's first and most successful short novel, before concluding that "what Wells was doing in this book was putting evolutionary theory into fictional practice. That was all" (48). While central to *The Time Machine*, evolutionary progression is but one of two temporal models that Wells borrows from nineteenth-century science to constitute his narrative authority. The other model is degeneration, a point that Wells makes as part of sending his newly published work to Thomas H. Huxley, a scientist whose ardent defenses of modern biology caused him to be labeled Darwin's bulldog. In a letter to Huxley, Wells explains that "[t]he central idea [in the book] — of degeneration following security — was the outcome of a certain amount of biological study" (qtd. in Geduld 5). The respectful letter to his teacher concludes in mid-thought, but not before it implies that the novel's conception owes a debt to the more pessimistic ideas in Huxley's *Evolution and Ethics* (1894) as well. A disciplinary lineage thus extends from Darwin to Huxley to Wells and, we might anticipate, from evolution, broadly construed, to evolution, broadly defended, to evolution and degeneration, broadly represented. Degeneration — the last of these lineages — is of special interest to readers of *The Time Machine* because the characters encountered in it have somehow declined, over almost countless generations, in ways that make the Time Traveller evolutionarily superior to them. Thus an eminent scientist from the distant past meets figures in the far-distant future that have become less complex than he, a conjoining of past and future that treats the idea of humankind's progressive improvement — an idea significant to late Victorians — dismissively. Bringing a model of psycho-sexual degeneration to the scientific romance enables Wells to displace anxieties associated with *fin-de-siècle* British masculinity onto the Eloi and Morlocks. In the process, the Time Traveller demonstrates his own attenuated capacity for desire by rejecting the possibility of future-sex in favor of scientific study and, ultimately, brute violence.

The Evolution and Decline of Man

The Time Machine begins on a quiet Thursday evening in a home near London. Following dinner, seven men sit before the fireplace drinking champagne. Wells names them, in order, as the Time Traveller, the Psychologist, Filby, a Very Young Man, the Provincial Mayor, the Medical Man, and Hillyer. With two exceptions, the characters are types more than individuals, with most reflecting masculine success stories. The professionals among them are defined by occupation, whether it be in the fields of science, medicine, or politics; Filby, a difficult person, by what he will not accept; the Very Young Man, by his youth; and Hillyer, by what he recalls as narrator. Strategically, Hillyer transcribes what the unnamed Time Traveller claims to have done on his travels. A frame narrative results as Wells produces what Hillyer has heard the Time Traveller narrate (in the present) to groups of men about what he learned as a scientist in the past (which, for much of the romance, is the future). The two narrator/characters and twice-told tale create a structure that is more like a lecture, at times, than a conventional third-person novella. It follows that understanding *The Time Machine* may depend less on a particular version of events or an author's imaginative authority than on which mediating discourse — fictional, scientific, or psycho-social; and what time period — past, present, or future — readers would tend to privilege.

As the fire burns and his guests relax, the Time Traveller holds forth. He prefaces his remarks by saying that he intends "'to controvert one or two ideas that are almost universally accepted'" (31). The first of these relates to the foundations of geometry. Speaking as if to students, the Time Traveller remarks, "Any real body must have extension in *four* directions: it must have Length, Breadth, Thickness, and — Duration" (32). Human consciousness, it follows, requires that a temporal dimension supplement the dimensions of space, since awareness of phenomena occurs in time. To show that travel through time as well as space is not impossible — the second idea he plans to controvert — our narrator/hero brings a small, clock-like contraption from his laboratory. Rather than turn on what he names as a time machine, he has the Psychologist depress a lever on the model. Announced by a burst of wind, the contraption disappears before their eyes, purportedly into the future.

What began as a private lecture has become a lecture/demonstration. The shift from speech to experiment propels the plot by confusing the Time Traveller's guests — a confusion which must be investigated and resolved if the events begun that evening are to coalesce into a suitably scientific narrative. Unsure of what they have witnessed, several guests label the demonstration a trick, and one asks if the model's disappearance may be likened to the ghost that the Time Traveller conjured at Christmas. Mystified, Hillyer cannot decide whether to believe the guests who disbelieve their eyes or his host's explanation. "The fact is," he comments in his capacity as narrator, "the Time Traveller was one of those men who are too clever to be believed: you never felt that you saw all around him; you always suspected some subtle reserve, some ingenuity in ambush, behind his lucid frankness" (37). Given its mode of address, the opening scene depicts the Time Traveller as a master of rhetoric and experimentation, capable, with equal facility, of lecturing on arcane matters of math and science and building unprecedented inventions. His is thus a science of the literary present, perhaps even of the future, while the naming of his guests recalls the science of the past — specifically, Linnaeus' taxonomies. The scene also shows him to be clever to a fault, and so what he does cannot be accepted on its face by others. Hence Wells represents him as being less a scientific or literary figure than an amalgam whose words call to the work that his audience and readers alike must do to grasp what he has done. Hillyer signals how difficult such work will be by hailing us directly: "You read, I will suppose, attentively enough; but you cannot see the speaker's white, sincere face in the bright circle of the little lamp, nor hear the intonation of his voice" (41). Consequently, our reading will likely produce a partial, and difficult to accept, knowledge.

On the following Thursday evening, a new audience gathers at the Time Traveller's home. The Medical Man and the Psychologist are in attendance, a fact which signals their relevance to the plot, as of course is Hillyer. Replacing Filby, a Very Young Man, and the Provincial Mayor are new types: i.e., a

Journalist, the Editor of a newspaper named Blank, and a Silent Man. Oddly, the party's host is absent. As the mutton his servant has prepared cools on the table, the men discuss the previous week's demonstration. We are meant to take their role in the story seriously, since *The Time Machine* identifies the Medical Man and Hillyer as members of the Linnaean, a learned society where, in 1858, Darwin and Wallace first made public their papers naming the role of natural selection in evolution. The Medical Man also has an unspecified relationship with Tubingen, a German university which helped to develop and institutionalize the modern laboratory. Interrupting the discussion, a pale and bloodied Time Traveller enters and, without explaining his tardiness, directs the others to eat.

After dinner, the men adjourn to the smoking room where their host, no longer "'starving for a bit of meat,'" admits that his experience in the future accounts for his wounds (39). The Time Traveller then agrees to tell what occurred there on the condition that he be uninterrupted — a request which deprofessionalizes his already depersonalized guests. Since they have agreed to not speak, the Medical Man and the Psychologist cannot diagnose patients (much less the Time Traveller), the Journalist cannot report on what he hears, and the Editor cannot edit his reporter's work or speak, as is his habit, in ironic headlines. Only the Silent Man and Hillyer remain true to type. Consequently, the frame narrative positions these characters as audience, which figures the Time Traveller as expert, makes his a multi-disciplinary story (i.e., part scientific fact, fiction, and autobiography), and indicates that readers, following the example of the guests, are to respond to performer and performance with masculine silence verging on fascination.

The Time Traveller, we soon learn, brought little with him to the future other than his remarkable means of conveyance. His most useful possession — a keen grasp of evolutionary theory and the scientific method — is conceptual. Indeed, even as he hurtles forward, wrestling with the "hysterical exhilaration" produced by time travel, he wonders "'[w]hat strange developments of humanity, what wonderful advances upon our rudimentary civilization'" await him (42). Following Darwin, the Time Traveller believes species to have descended from a single tree of life and developed progressively. *The Origin of Species* (1859) foregrounds the tension between individual differentiation, brought about through the competitive pressures associated with living on an "entangled bank" with other organisms, and the shared characteristics that come, via reproduction, to shape an entire species (125). Expanding upon this tension between competition and sex, Darwin observes "that the structure of every organic being is related, in the most essential yet often hidden manner, to that of all other organic beings, with which it comes into competition for food or residence, or from which it has to escape, or on which it preys" (127).

What evolution enables science to know, in advance, is the mechanism of change; what remains occluded from the immediate view of scientists is just such a structural interdependence of species.

The Time Traveller arrives in the year 802,701 A.D. to the sound of thunder. He sees little more than a grey mist and unremarkable foliage before the storm slows enough to reveal a "colossal figure"—that of a marble sphinx—before him. "'It was greatly weather-worn,'" he reports, "'and that imparted an unpleasant suggestion of disease'" (44). The sphinx is an impossible species—part lion, in its haunches, part bird, in its wings, and part woman, in its features. Greek legend represents it as a figure of mystery and taboo as well as a sign associated with interpretive possibility. Markers of time and disease, not deadliness, set this sphinx off from its surroundings. Its presence fascinates our hero, arresting his gaze for what could be thirty seconds or even, he admits, one-half of an hour. The narrative so emphasizes this time-out-of-mind experience that readers are left wondering what the Sphinx augurs for the future of the future.

To this point, the Time Traveller has scarcely gotten his balance in a foreign space/time, and yet is certain that evolution has influenced humans for thousands of years. Working quickly, he reasons from a known mechanism (i.e., natural selection) to its unknown, though determinate, effects. Only two evolutionary outcomes come to mind: nature has either been subdued by man or has triumphed over him. If nature is now civilized, the Time Traveller hypothesizes, man must have become unmanly and feminine; if man is more natural, men must have become cruel and passionate. In either case, our scientist is at risk, since he is likely to appear to such beings as "'some old-world savage animal, only the more dreadful and disgusting for our common likeness — a foul creature to be incontinently slain'" (44). Even though his journey is first-order science, the Time Traveller's ethnocentrism is of standard, late–Victorian issue, since his focus on the status of man requires the uneasy co-existence of evolved and primitive beings (Torgovnick 3). In a clever inversion, however, *The Time Machine* empties our exemplary modern scientist of his humanity and repositions him as a "savage animal." It recalls as well the gender anxiety that marked the British *fin de siècle*. As Karl Miller explains, "Men became women [then]. Women became men. Gender and country were put in doubt. The single life was found to harbor two sexes and two nations" (209). Thus does Wells begin to question the boundaries between persons and genders that Victorians preferred to keep inviolable.

Soon the skies clear, and our anxious man from the past meets "'a fragile thing out of futurity'" (45). Wells means us to see this first encounter from within the discourse of masculinity, and so his character description is adamantly physical: "He was a slight creature — perhaps four feet high — clad in a purple tunic, girdled at the waist with a leather belt" (44–45). Entranced anew, the Time Traveller adds, "He struck me as being a very beautiful and graceful creature, but indescribably frail. His flushed face reminded me of the more beautiful kind of consumptive — that hectic beauty of which we used to hear so much." The Eloi is one of perhaps ten such "exquisite creatures." All are males who coo in a melodious, patently simple, language. Indistinguishable from each other, the welcoming party's members possess a "'Dresden-china type of prettiness,'" with curly hair, no whiskers, minute ears, petite mouths, pointed chins, and large eyes (45). When an Eloi asks if their visitor journeyed from sun to earth via a peal of thunder, the Time Traveller senses that the Eloi may be stunted in intelligence as well as masculinity.

Scholars have long seen traces of aestheticism in these descriptions and imagined Wells to have Aubrey Beardsley, Oscar Wilde, and others in his sights. Yet there are no *fin de siècle* Manly Women, or even Womanly Men, no moral perversity, no fine arts or decadent language, or no heights of paradox, in evidence here. Absent, too, is turn-of-the-century exhaustion; in its place — from the first — resides a childlike, underdeveloped happiness. Indeed, the Time Traveller emphasizes that the Eloi are fragile, slight, beautiful, graceful, frail, petite, soft, playful, consumptive-like. To say they stand in for a self-involved dandy from the period that gave us *The Yellow Book*— that secular bible of aestheticism — is to misunderstand the Eloi, the cosmopolitan dandy, or both. Readers thus sense a different kind of decline is signaled in these gendered assessments, one predicated on ideas tied to degeneration.

The Time Traveller tells us as much when, stunned, he says that the future he had envisioned while creating his machine involved inhabitants "'incredibly in front of us in knowledge, art, everything'" (46). Apparently he was wrong — which, from the perspective of a narrative's early pages, is exactly right for his audiences. Matters cannot be as simple as our hero thinks; however scientific, his initial hypotheses must not be adequate to his experience. If they were, the plot would be shorn of unanticipated obstacles to test our narrator/hero and solicit the narrative desire of readers (Brooks 48). Indeed, to this point in the story, our scientist may be correct in his method alone and be, like those who listen to and identify with him, at the mercy of a partial, time-bound understanding. Thus he has little choice but to amend his evolutionary optimism with ideas from elsewhere in science and we, energized by his efforts to know the future, follow along.

Like evolution, the theory of degeneration focuses on variation and the problem of extinction, posed so dramatically by pioneering geologists like Sir Charles Lyell. As the nineteenth century began, degeneration typically meant variation. Somewhat later, it would indicate atavism or savage regression. Bénédict Augustin Morel would turn degeneration to the purposes of assessing psychiatric and social decline during the 1830s. In his studies of rural and urban families, he found that individuals became ill in response to harsh working conditions, poor hygiene, and powerful stimulants. Their illnesses took a myriad of forms, including epilepsy, hysteria, imbecility, idiocy, and insanity. What made *degenerescence* so degenerative was its capacity to impact a single organism as well as its hereditary endowment. A man's alcoholism, for instance, might compel the son and daughter he fathered to become neurotic. Their children, in turn, might display a host of more debilitating symptoms, provided that the transmissible germ did not skip generations. Degeneration was thus a progressive condition with retrogressive outcomes. If French medicine, psychiatry, and such emerging disciplines as criminology and sexology benefited from a theory of morbid heredity, so, too, did literature. The circle of writers associated with Emile Zola seized upon the model of degeneration proposed by Morel and used it to structure character development and plot. In the hands of the Naturalists, characters often degenerated rather than improved over time, and narratives trended towards death rather than resolving themselves in the marriages that so appealed to nineteenth-century readers. An emphasis on illness and even atavism thus displaced the reproduction of family afforded by marriage plots. In double plots with a contrastive mix of character trajectories, late-century narratives often assumed the chiasmatic shape of an "X," given that characters could either decline and become simpler over time or survive to reproduce and thereby contribute a measure of their hereditary endowment to more complex offspring. That geometrical "X" occurs precisely when one person's trajectory — whether from higher to lower or lower to higher — crosses another's, quite opposite, developmental path. In all, *degenerescence* was the disorder of disorders — the master category of socio-sexual pathology — for the most advanced branches of French medicine and art. Little wonder that it was but a short step for cultural critics to shift from diagnosing families as ill to defining entire societies as degenerate, which Max Nordau would famously do in 1895, the year in which Wells finished revising his scientific romance.

The Science of Science Fiction Sex

The Time Traveller leaves the present so that he might know the future. In the process, he applies ideas from his own time — no matter the subject — to the present/future he studies, "'proceeding,'" in his words, from "'the problems of our own age'" to matters affecting the Eloi (62). Interpreting the future on the basis of past conceptual schema is of course a mainstay of science fiction. Displacing present day problems to the future is no less genre specific.

In response to such an imagined future, readers not only want to know how the future looks and how its inhabitants interact, but also what will come of the intractable problems confronting their lived present. Behind such interest is a kind of literary wish fulfillment, a utopian sense that the inhabitants of the future might somehow fix what we cannot. Often, announcing the problems as having been solved is about all that a science fiction writer accomplishes. Almost as often, the contemporary problems get restaged but go unresolved or worsen. A compromise formation informs the genre in both cases, since science fiction characteristically excites anxiety and optimism only to defend against them by showing that resolutions to the intractable problems that confront readers will not occur in (our) time.

The problem worrying the Time Traveller, once he realizes that other human-like organisms inhabit the future too, is that of descent. Apparently, *Homo sapiens* diverged into two sub-species, the Eloi and Morlocks, long ago — but how? Judging from their appearance, the Morlocks have spent countless generations underground, in the dark, among their own kind. Since they tend to surface rarely, and largely at night, their vision has declined. True to the science of his day, the Time Traveller holds that organisms which do not use a physical trait tend, over long stretches of time, to have it degenerate. Thus, the Morlocks's eyesight, to borrow from Talbot's influential views, has become "adapted to less varied and less complex conditions of life" (32). We are meant to see that the Morlocks, like the Eloi, became less complex overall.

After identifying the Morlocks as the Eloi's hired help, the Time Traveller traces their current interdependence to the nineteenth century and its use of underground spaces for rail stations, workrooms, restaurants, even housing. Taken to its logical (if extreme) conclusion, this tendency would have led to factories being built below the earth "'till industry had gradually lost its birthright in the sky'" (62). Such a process would have been exacerbated above ground by wealthy men and women — who, even in the *fin de siècle*, walled off their London and country properties from lower-class intruders. It follows that the gulf separating the laborers from the owners, those suffering terrible existences below from those enjoying pampered lives above, must have widened as the Morlocks progressively declined and intermarriage ended. In this way, the Time Traveller concludes, humans permanently split into new, but irreconcilable, branches on the tree of life. The Eloi's development apparently involves not merely a "triumph over Nature," as he first proposed, but over fellow humans as well.

Once again, a soon-to-be-disproved hypothesis complicates the plot. The Eloi did not merely best the Morlocks but became dependent upon the industrial labor they performed. To explain this change, the Time Traveller reasons that the Haves and Have-nots (his terms) must have reached economic equilibrium at some point — what Talbot, in the earlier frontispiece, would term a state of stasis that "force[s] the animal to remain as it is" and Wells, in his letter to Huxley, calls "security" (qtd. in Geduld 5). Those who were rich had ample leisure; those poor who worked had, at least, lodgings and sufficient food. Thus a kind of evolutionary equilibrium predominated. Eventually, the Time Traveller asserts, the Upperworlders would likely have become feeble, attractive, and narcissistic because, like the British aristocracy, the Underworlders labored for them. It follows that any disruption of the food supply would have led to Necessity imposing its deadly logic less on those who lived above ground, since they could easily harvest animals, grains, and fruit, than those who lived below the earth. To make the case that Necessity is brutal but also compensatory, Wells evokes an expert from his own past. Following Huxley, who idiosyncratically follows Darwin on human descent, he asserts that "'human intelligence and vigour'" are adaptive responses to "'[h]ardship and freedom'" — the "'conditions under which the active, strong, and subtle survive and the weaker go to the wall; conditions that put a premium upon the loyal alliance of capable men, upon self-restraint, patience, and decision'" (51). Here the Time Traveller assumes that competition is so forceful in nature that it leads to a counterweight in society — what Huxley calls ethics in his "Prolegomena" (26–33). Given his masculinist focus on active, strong, subtle, loyal, restrained, patient, decisive men, it is a wonder that women need contribute to civilization at all. In fact, he adds, once threats to children abate in some undetermined future, a sentiment "'will grow, against connubial jealousy, against fierce maternity, against passion of all sorts; unnecessary things now, and things that make us uncomfortable, [these are] savage survivals, discords in a refined and pleasant life'" (51). How the Time Traveller sees the Upperworlders may also be inferred from his extensive portrayal of Weena, an Eloi whom he rescues after she has a muscle cramp while bathing and is swept down a stream. Aghast, the scientist undresses, wades in, and secures her. In the process, he perceives "'the strange deficiency in these creatures'" (58). Weena's physical weakness is the first of two such deficiencies. The second is the implicit disregard in a culture that treats a threat to one member — despite her crying for help — as of no concern to others, most or all of whom are men. Clearly, the rescue scene has its melodramatic elements, since a helpless female of indeterminate age must await the intervention of an older, stronger, smarter, and more decisive male. We might therefore expect that a Victorian audience, whose masculine self-regard had been rattled by the New Woman, with her call for sexual freedom, and suffragists, who were campaigning for the vote, to be reassured by such forcefulness (see, e.g., Showalter 38–40). However, the rescue has erotic as well as aggressive aspects, since our hero and the victim he saves are naked. Having gotten "'my little woman, as I believe it was,'" to shore, the Time Traveller massages her arms and legs, which "'soon brought her around.'" Shortly thereafter, Weena responds to seeing her rescuer "'with cries of delight and presented me with a big garland of flowers — evidently made for me and me alone'" (58).

Wells and his narrators play this scene in ways that will not alienate Victorian readers. There are no wry allusions to *fin-de-siècle* exhaustion, as evidenced by the swimming prowess of an Eloi, no prurient sense that sex occurs in the gap between a paragraph devoted to rescue and another to exhilaration. To be sure, flowers aplenty are passed from woman/child to man and back again, but they are figured as gifts rather than as the sexual organs of plants. More telling for today's readers, the Time Traveller has a female from the distant future unclothed before him and he grants readers no visual details of her body — despite having represented the terrain and architecture of the year 802,701 A.D. at length. Thus, as an anthropologist of the future, he disappoints. What he describes in the place of her secondary sex characteristics is "'a queer friendship'" marked by chaste cuddling, frequent, reciprocal kissing, and physical proximity. The Time Traveller thus travels with Weena daily and sleeps beside her nightly without "lying" with her. He defends against the implications of such metonymic proximity by insisting that the Eloi are the "'little people,'" and Weena "'was exactly like a child'" (58). Like Marlow in Conrad's *Heart of Darkness* (1899), then, he eventually goes ashore but not "for a howl and a dance" (37). Here the Time Traveller practices restraint by focusing on work and on the subject of science fiction itself: "'the problems of the world had to be mastered,'" he remarks. "'I had not, I said to myself, come into the future to carry on a miniature flirtation'" (58). Readers can hardly blame him for such erotic reserve, since his account of the Eloi rests on tropes that position them as feminine infants, undersized things, or animals. Hence it would not do for our scientist/hero/narrator to divert himself from his important labors with cross-species copulation, no matter how ample the opportunities before him in the bucolic future.

Weena's sexual and psychological traits are of a piece and seem to have been influenced by late-Victorian biology textbooks like the one Wells published in 1893 while composing *The Time Machine*. As feminist scholars have shown at length, the biological sciences of that period construed female crania, brains, skeletons, torsos, muscles, height and so on as underdeveloped. At some point, every woman's progress up the phylogenetic tree apparently stopped. It followed that woman resembled children, other women, and savages more so than man. Using this model, scientists naturalized woman's physical status and, by illogical extension, women's social roles. Thus, while nineteenth-century European man evolved, rapidly recapitulating the history of the race and attaining higher elevations in the tree of life, "woman remained a child," Cynthia Eagle asserts, "weak-willed, impulsive, perceptive, markedly imitative rather than original, timid, and dependent" (54). Given the Eloi's physical weakness and timidity in the face of danger, the subspecies as a whole has de-evolved and hence become exaggeratedly feminine in the eyes of our muscular hero.

The Morlocks receive a contrasting, but no less invidious, set of comparisons. In his first encounter with one, the Time Traveller speaks of "'a queer little ape-like figure, its head held down in a peculiar manner,'" that flees before him (60). Reflecting on its escape down one of the wells that links the upper and lower worlds, he characterizes it as a "'human spider'" and "'little monster'" before realizing "'that this bleached, obscene, nocturnal Thing, which had flashed before me, was also heir to all the ages'" (61). So great is his revulsion that he compares the Morlocks's appearance to "'the half-bleached colour of the worms and things one sees preserved in spirit in a zoological museum.'" They are, in effect, "'filthily cold'" *specimens*, a degenerated life form amenable to a scientist's visual authority (64). Fixed in place by the mind and methods of science, the Morlocks's material bodies can thus be read — from a significant remove — for signs of exterior and interior decline. With this approach, the Time Traveller disavows the second subspecies — those of a masculine, brutish temperament — that he confronts. A proper masculinity must therefore reside between the gendered extremes defined by his scientific inquiry.

Reluctant to test his new hypotheses, the Time Traveller — over Weena's emotional objections — nevertheless pursues the Morlocks into a well that leads to the industrial Underworld. His downward passage poses several problems, which Wells signals by stating "descent" and its variants five times in one page (65). In *The Descent of Man* (1871), Darwin takes the term to mean both origin and development, insofar as "man is the modified descendent of some pre-existing [lower] form" (5). Aware that he will generate a firestorm by treating human variation as bound to the same laws of selection as those that led to the transmutation of other species, Darwin nevertheless asks if "the inherited effects of use and disuse" apply to man, adding, "Is man subject to similar malconformations, the result of arrested development, or reduplication of parts, &c, and does he display in any of his anomalies reversion to some former and ancient type of structure?" (5). More than one temporality is at work in these questions. Building on the competitiveness he borrows from Malthus and the gradualism he takes from Lyell, Darwin knows that species become more complex over time — unless, of course, an anomalous reversion occurs. Then the movement of descent is from higher to somewhat lower, not from lower to higher. Applied to human evolution, "descent" harbors within it an ethnocentric *scala naturae* whose contrasting types of development distort Darwin's confidence in the supremacy of European man. In response, moreover, to the semantic slippage inherent in his organizing metaphor, one might say — as Freud did of the term *heimlich* in "The Uncanny" — that descent "is a word the meaning of which develops towards an ambivalence, until it finally coincides with its opposite" (377). Uncannily, then, the Time Traveller descends in space and, once accosted by the impassioned Morlocks, in terms of his own development.

Exhausted by his climb, the Time Traveller swings into a "horizontal tunnel" that enables him to "lie down and rest"; shortly thereafter, "a soft hand touching [his] face" rouses him (65). Fascinated by his presence, the Morlocks approach him as a group, much as the Eloi first did — with glistening eyes, excited inter-group murmurings, and touch. Tentatively, the Lemur-like creatures fondle so as to appraise him in the dark. While the Time Traveller is blind to much of what is occurring, he has the presence of mind to know that the Morlocks have retrogressed, as a species, and yet their eyes have adapted to see in the absence of light. Thus their descent is in the direction of simplicity/decline and, in this one trait, complexity/evolution. Creatures of Necessity, they are as well more intelligent and dangerous than the Eloi. Not content to visually examine him — a methodological inversion the Time Traveller finds to be horrifying — the Morlocks take most of his matches and, as a small mob, "'clutched at me more boldly,'" running their hands over his clothes and body (67). Momentarily deterred when he strikes a match, the Morlocks then turn aggressive: "'In a moment I was clutched by several hands, and there was no mistaking that they were trying to haul me back'" into their cavern (67). First "clutched at" and then "clutched by several hands," the Time Traveller struggles to disengage "'from the clutches of the Morlocks'" when they pursue him to the edge of the well shaft and grasp his now supine body "'from behind'" (67).

At issue here is more than the threat of cross-species violence. Touch, as the Time Traveller well knows, is a more intimate sense than sight. Among the Eloi, he was first touched gently, to ascertain if he were real, and he remarks that "'[t]here was nothing in this at all alarming'" (45). In the Morlocks's lair, he is, in order, looked at, approached, touched softly on his face, fondled, examined, clutched, clutched at more aggressively, grabbed when lying down, and pulled so that he might be taken elsewhere and felt more intimately yet. In growing desperation, he lights his last match, which stuns the Morlocks before "'it incontinently went out'" (67). Earlier, when Wells first identifies the Time Traveller as an "'old-world savage animal,'" he speaks of the threat to him being "'incontinently slain.'" At the time, readers likely took "incontinently" to mean immediately. Yet the word refers first to unrestrained passions and sexual appetites. It follows that to be "incontinently slain" is to be brutally, passionately killed. If we are to believe our narrators' strategic foreshadowing, then, the Time Traveller has now been chased to the very edge of the shaft that brought him to the Underworld by unchaste primitives whose bodily fluids threaten to discharge. Prostrate before them, he is threatened with capture. As likely, the Morlocks wish to clutch him to their bodies in a kind of ecstatic grouping. Because Wells showed that an awareness of physical space must occur in relation to time, readers sense that the Time Traveller is threatened with the loss of clothes, flesh, blood, organs, sex, and thus life-vitality, should he be incorporated into the bodies of male Others. To be sure, rawer experiences might be imagined, but probably not in this moment by our hero. What he conceives as violence, then, readers may intuit as an impossible future-sex that he forestalls by answering the degenerates' primitive desire to consume him with primitive violence of his own. On this point, Wells sides with readers, since the Time Traveller no sooner "got over the well-mouth somehow" (67) and is kissed by Weena then he swoons. Her emotional attentiveness allies her with Victorian wives who sought to assuage the daily pain of their laboring husbands; his emotional failure aligns him with anxiety, women in general, and the feminized Eloi.

The Time Traveller escapes with his life but also with new knowledge. Even as the Morlocks examine him, he, in a chiasmatic reversal, is examining them. Despite being handicapped by darkness, he attends to what he smells and sees in the Morlocks's domain. Specifically, he notes that the cavern was "'very stuffy and oppressive, and the faint halitus of freshly shed blood was the air'" (66). The blood-smell can be traced to the Morlocks's breath as well as to a "'red joint'" of a "'large animal'" that he glimpses lying on a table (66). From this evidence, the Time Traveller concludes that, unlike the frugivorous Eloi, the beasts who seek to overwhelm him are carnivores. It takes, however, more than a day for him to see that the size of the joint suggests they were likely eating flesh from an Eloi's leg and hip, itself possibly torn from a living creature's pelvis. His partial epiphany is concussive:

> Ages ago, thousands of generations ago, man had thrust his brother man out of the ease and the sunshine. And now that brother was coming back — changed! Already the Eloi had begun to learn one old lesson anew. They were becoming reacquainted with Fear. And suddenly there came into my head the memory of the meat I had seen in the Underworld. It seemed odd how it floated into my mind: not stirred up as it were by the current of my meditations, but coming in almost like a question from outside. I tried to recall the form of it. I had a vague sense of something familiar, but I could not tell what it was at the time [68].

The security that Wells refers to in his letter to Huxley, and which his teacher held to be necessarily brief, must have ended at some point after the underclass leaves the earth for life in the dark (14). Repressed, pushed from sight, put to work in an industrial wasteland, its men compete for survival. Necessity reigns in such an Underworld, and thus it is where the distance between victimizer and victim is often smallest. Over generations, the most successful men become adept at violence. Specifically, they scour the countryside and kill the animals they catch at night until only birds — the creatures least amenable to capture — remain. By so doing they generate species extinction. As their supply of ready meat begins to run out, the Morlocks turn to cannibalizing their fellow humans, an adaptation that contributes to their becoming a degenerate subspecies.

The Time Traveller cannot be expected to account for the developmental trajectories of the Eloi and Morlocks easily. Trying to do so, we have seen, involves hypotheses that, once posed, are soon disproved. New hypotheses follow and they — as well as the plot — must be corrected as the data indicate. Not all realizations, moreover, derive from observation or a careful use of the hypothetico-deductive method in science fiction. Indeed, the more intimate the study, the more emotionally invested, the less likely that scientist/characters can treat phenomena dispassionately. Thus, following Brooks, does the "desire which is initiatory of narrative" now build and "animate[] the combinatory play of sense-making" (48). The Time Traveller, for his part, has most of the Eloi and Morlocks's story correct; yet when he confronts the image of the large animal's joint lying on the table (a castration-enactment if ever there was one), he does not link the absence of prey species aboveground to the incongruous size of the meal. Rather, he disavows what he sees. The "current of his meditations" changes from the kinds of thinking associated with science to the kinds of responses associated with emotion. Trying to remember how the flesh looks, he knows only that it offered "a vague sense of something familiar" that he cannot place. Thus, his failed memory is both hysterical, insofar as it proves deeply troubling to him, and worthy of repression.

The Time Traveller has lost himself in his thinking before. It occurred, early in his narration, as he first viewed the Sphinx, an uncanny figure from the human past that, like our hero, has inexplicably made its way to the degenerate future. Wells uses the figure of the diseased Sphinx to foreshadow this crucial plot point, for its inscrutable gaze and status as an impossible species remind readers that humans breach the bounds of repression when in thrall to violence or eros. Oedipus, we well know, kills several men at the crossroads near Delphi — despite having just been told by the Oracle that he would murder his father. Once at Thebes, he solves the riddle of the Sphinx — whose address likewise "com[es] in almost like a question from outside" (68). Despite having also been warned that he would lay with his actual mother and produce monsters, he gives in to his erotic desire, marries Jocasta, and fathers children with her. The Sphinx, in this expanded, associational sense, signals the mystery of human sexuality in its most basic, instinctual, even self-defeating forms. It calls as well to the twin imperatives to know and to reveal that Oedipus, our narrative forefather, pursues. Like Oedipus before him, then, the Time Traveller arrives at self-knowledge by solving a mystery posed by an Other in a place that is not his own. Such a process, Teresa de Lauretis observes, consolidates the authority of Oedipus and that of masculinity (111–112). To his credit, our future-hero practices restraint in the face of Others' erotic availability, perhaps because the lesson of the Sphinx and Oedipus has not been lost on him, or because he finds future-sex to be impossible, even unreal, since the forms it may take with the exaggeratedly feminine Eloi or, now, the brutish Morlocks, remain taboo. Unfortunately, sexual desire is no less enduring than the Sphinx. It, too, eludes repression only to recur, and so a hero's narrative restraint is likely to be tested anew.

Tomorrow's Men, Today

For much of its plot, *The Time Machine* treats the descent of man as late–Victorian science did. It, too, foregrounds evolution, alludes to the many victims that any competition for resources generates, and equates European man with civilization and Others with the vicissitudes of nature. That the Eloi and Morlocks have degenerated is beyond doubt, since the former are little more than cattle for the latter, who may, in an allusion to artificial selection, even see to their breeding. The Time Traveller is repulsed by this situation and especially by the Morlocks's role in it. Still, he "'trie[s] to look at the thing in a scientific spirit. After all, they were less human and more remote than our cannibal ancestors of three or four thousand years ago'" (71). As a narrator and man, he wants to believe that a wide interval separates his development from that of these retrograded and structurally interdependent subspecies. Once Necessity entraps him, however, and he realizes that Others have his time machine and he has de-evolved into a form of meat, such a separation is illusory. He goes in search of weapons and admits, upon procuring an iron lever, that he "'longed very much to kill a Morlock or so. Very inhuman, you may think, to want to go killing one's descendents!'" (74). Here the cathected language of sexuality, with its longing and wanting displaced into violence, announces his incipient atavism to an audience of friends and readers alike. Certainly, being under threat informs his speech, but so, too, does the intimacy he slowly acknowledges with Weena, the depth of which he admits to not understanding "'until it was too late'" (58).

The Time Traveller wounds his first Morlock with a muscular punch when Weena and he get stranded in the dark, far from shelter. Characteristically, she clings "'convulsively'" to him, and he carries her as the Morlocks, in waves, pursue them (77). While trying to light a fire and deter capture, he is "'caught by the neck, by the hair, by the arms, and pulled down'" (79). Cross-species touching that began as exploratory and tentative has now become incontinently invasive and violent. Fully "'overpowered'" by the Morlocks, whose teeth gnaw at his neck, he grabs his weapon "'and, holding the bar short, I thrust where I judged their faces might be. I could feel the succulent giving of flesh and bone under my blows, and for a moment I was free.'" A "'strange exultation'" comes over him, which the Time Traveller links to "'hard fighting'" (79). Readers see this impassioned violence as a "'savage survival'" that returns — as its own embodied desire — in response to physical intimacy of two kinds. The first relates to Weena and his sublimated desire for her as a woman-child — a desire that she tries repeatedly to excite through proximity, touch, multiple kissing scenes, and speech. Such excitation cannot overcome our hero's characteristic reserve because, in part, the frame narrative puts his experience at a remove from readers and before an audience of men who know and might judge him. The second, more immediate desire, turns on self-preservation. Touched in the moment, the Time Traveller vows "'to make the Morlocks pay for their meat'" (79). To survive, he must set aside femininity and its relational focus, now signaled by the loss of Weena to the Morlock mob and, alone, out-brutalize the brutes. There is no time, to his way of thinking, for future-sex here; masculine violence — with its insistent physicality — fully takes its place. The struggle for existence is thus not over shared residence on an entangled bank so much as between a predator species and its temporally unlikely prey. Depressed by the loss of his symbolic wife, blood spattered, and exhausted, the man from the past — in two senses of the phrase — recovers his time machine from another group of Morlocks and turns it on.

As the Time Traveller nears the lived present, he scans civilization for evidence of decline. Readers should not see his allusions to *fin-de-siècle* decadence as being in keeping with Max Nordau's *Degeneration*, which famously excoriates "the fashions in art and literature" as "manifestations of more or less pronounced moral insanity, imbecility, and dementia" (viii). Neither are we to see them as offering a return to an accepted and acceptable masculinity. After all, the Time Traveller now has first-hand evidence that degeneration spans the present and future. Like Morel, he cannot help but see that "deviations from the normal human type which are transmissible by heredity and which deteriorate progressively towards extinction" lurk, as a kind of potential, even in late–Victorian society and in persons like him (qtd. in Ackerknecht 55). Degeneration thus easily takes form in response to the right — which is to say, the wrong — social conditions and behavior. Professionals like the Psychologist and Medical Man know this best of all, since it is their job to grasp the etiology of illness by interpreting its visible signs. Despite having been mostly silenced by Wells's frame narrative, like Weena herself, they also may narrate from the vantage of the future using inherited theories and models of time. By diagnosing those who have retrogressed, they thus constitute their disciplinary authority and that of science. In this model of space/time, therefore, degeneration is itself a time machine — a means, that is to say, of hereditary transmission from past to future, from future to past. Hence understanding degeneration scientifically requires a kind of conceptual time travel all its own.

Once the Time Traveller again leaves the present on his machine, Hillyer is left to worry over masculinity and conclude the novella, since his friend never returns. In the epilogue, Hillyer proposes that theirs is an age when "men are still men," since excessive femininity presumably awaits in the future and brutality resides in the past (90). He admits, however, that the Time Traveller was less sanguine on the subject, thinking "but cheerlessly of the Advancement of Mankind, and [seeing] in the growing pile of civilization only a foolish heaping that must inevitably fall back upon and destroy its makers in the end" (90). To our intrepid voyager, masculinity and sex are impossible, sphinx-like conditions, at once impure, attenuated, and vulnerable to the predations of time. It follows that while sex plays a generative role in evolution, it may lack sufficient ruling force to stave off degeneration, much less the planetary entropy that Wells, following Huxley, imagines in the posthuman future. The art-rock group Devo once asked, "Are We Not Men?," and thus alluded both to devolution (from which the band derived its name) and to a key scene in *The Island of Doctor Moreau* (1895), a novella in which Wells dissolves the boundaries distinguishing species with more enthusiasm than he shows for the task in *The Time Machine*. The impetus for that scientific romance, Wells wrote, is traceable to his enduring belief that "humanity is but animal, rough-hewn to a reasonable shape and in perpetual internal conflict between instinct and injunction" ("Preface" ix). *The Time Machine*'s answer to the band's question almost has to be "no," because we, like the Eloi and Morlocks and the Time Traveller himself, possess a sexuality whose generative force may eventually compel us, too, to become "devo."

Works Cited

Ackerknecht, Erwin H. *A Short History of Psychiatry*. 2d ed. Trans. Sula Wolff. New York: Hafner, 1968. Print.

Brooks, Peter. *Reading for the Plot: Design and Intention in Narrative*. New York: Knopf, 1984. Print.

Conrad, Joseph. *Heart of Darkness*. 1899. Ed. Robert Kimbrough. New York: Norton, 1963. Print.
Darwin, Charles. *The Descent of Man and Selection in Relation to Sex*. 1871. 2d ed. Akron: Werner, 1874. Print.
———. *The Origin of Species by Means of Natural Selection or The Preservation of Favoured Races in the Struggle for Life*. 1859. New York: Avenel, 1979. Print.
De Lauretis, Teresa. *Alice Doesn't: Feminism, Semiotics, Cinema*. Bloomington: Indiana University Press, 1984. Print.
Devo. *Q: Are We Not Men? A: We Are Devo!* Warner, 1978. LP.
Eagle, Cynthia Russett. *Sexual Science: The Victorian Construction of Womanhood*. Cambridge: Harvard University Press, 1991. Print.
Freud, Sigmund. "The Uncanny." *Collected Papers*. Vol. 4. Trans. Joan Riviere. New York: Basic, 1959. 368–407. Print.
Geduld, Harry M. "Introduction." *The Definitive Time Machine: A Critical Edition of H. G. Wells's Scientific Romance*. Ed. Geduld. Bloomington: Indiana University Press, 1987. Print.
Huxley, Thomas H. "Evolution and Ethics. Prolegomena." *Evolution and Ethics and Other Essays*. New York: D. Appleton, 1903. 1–45. Print.
McConnell, Frank. *The Science Fiction of H. G. Wells*. New York: Oxford University Press, 1981. Print.
Miller, Karl. *Doubles: Studies in Literary History*. London: Oxford University Press, 1987. Print.
Morel, Bénédict Augustin. *Traité des Dégénérescences Physiques, Intellectuelles et Morales de L'espèce Humaine*. Paris: Jean-Baptiste Baillière, 1857. Print.
Nordau, Max. *Degeneration*. 1895. New York: Howard Fertig, 1968. Print.
Showalter, Elaine. *Sexual Anarchy: Gender and Culture at the Fin de Siecle*. New York: Penguin, 1990. Print.
Smith, David C. *H. G. Wells Desperately Mortal: A Biography*. New Haven: Yale University Press, 1986. Print.
Talbot, Eugene S. *Degeneracy: Its Causes, Signs, and Results*. London: Walter Scott, 1912. Print.
Torgovnick, Marianna. *Gone Primitive: Savage Intellects, Modern Lives*. Chicago: University of Chicago Press, 1990. Print.
Vernier, J. P. "Evolution as a Literary Theme in H. G. Wells's Science Fiction." *H. G. Wells and Modern Science Fiction*. Ed. Darko Suvin and Robert M. Philmus. Lewisburg: Bucknell University Press, 1977. Print.
Wells, H. G. *The Definitive Time Machine: A Critical Edition of H. G. Wells's Scientific Romance*. Ed. Harry M. Geduld. Bloomington: Indiana University Press, 1987. Print.
———. The Island of Dr. Moreau." *The Works of H. G. Wells*. Vol. 2. New York: Atlantic, 1924. Print.
———. "Preface to The Island of Dr. Moreau." *The Works of H. G. Wells*. Vol. 2. New York: Atlantic, 1924. Print.
———. *Text-Book of Biology*. London: W. B. Clive, 1893. Print.

Space Apes Want Our Women! Primate Lust in American Science Fiction

Matthew H. Hersch

For years, journalist Charles Siebert writes, people have held an "anthropocentric conception of humanlike apes as mythic beings, fearsome man-beasts, living cautionary tales against our own often beastly and rapacious tendencies" (49–50). Indeed, the strength and lack of reason possessed by King Kong and other fictional apes in American science fiction are intended to remind audiences of the boorish behavior humans have shed over the course of their multimillion-year evolution, and to which they might return if they are not vigilant. Apes crossing the threshold from beast to man — through education, breeding, or genetic manipulation — and then terrorizing humanity with their newfound powers have been a popular variant of the ape-man myth, serving to demonstrate that beneath the skin of every human male is a beast, barely removed from the jungle.

The recent 2011 movie *Rise of the Planet of the Apes* epitomizes the genre, while also suggesting that hyper-evolved apes appear in science fiction both as warnings and as forces of creative destruction, chastising "civilized" humans for their lingering barbarism to ape and human alike. The arrival of the Space Age provided science fiction writers with many new kinds of "man-beasts" modeled on the monkeys and chimpanzees that the United States launched into space from the late–1940s through the early–1960s. Whether launched from Earth by humans, encountered on distant planets, or created by scientists, fictional "space" apes in popular culture have often appeared less as cautionary tales than as ingenious and exuberant creatures rapidly evolving into a physically, intellectually, and morally superior form of life.

Yet however sophisticated they may become, these "space" apes have retained one odd atavism: an insatiable appetite for the companionship of human women. For centuries, Western writers have described semi-mythical apes drawn to the siren song of the human female and recounted in almost gleeful detail the products of their encounters. Throughout history, literature on human/ape mating has served a variety of scientific, moral, and even erotic functions, and its persistence in the twentieth century has injected modern science fiction texts with a healthy dollop of regressive sexual politics. Hyper-evolved ape males may dominate male humans through superior strength and reason; they may castigate humans for their immoralities, or condemn their greed and lust; yet they crave human women just as intensely as their less evolved brethren. For it is only by conquering human women that "space" apes strike the final blow against humanity's — and more specifically, the human male's — colossal ego. Attracted to human females but contemptuous of them, smug "space" apes and other hyper-evolved simians of American science fiction will stop at nothing to possess human women — as pets, lovers, and wives.

The Ape Menace

Modern zoology draws a distinction between monkeys and apes, the later of which constitute a taxonomic unit subdivided into two families: the lesser apes and the great apes, or *Hominidae*, which includes humans, chimpanzees, gorillas, and orangutans. Of these, chimpanzees are humanity's closest relatives, diverging at the level of genus but with substantial overlap in genetic material. Human fascination with apes appears to lie principally in their anatomical, intellectual, and emotional similarity to humans, which humans have exploited for centuries. Ambulatory and expressive yet accorded no rights under human law, apes have appeared throughout human culture as food sources, foils for human science, satirical stand-ins for despised populations, pets, and taboo mates.

With human dissection unlawful during much of recorded history, vivisection of monkeys provided Western medicine with some of its earliest descriptions of hominid viscera. Roman-era physician Galen notably wrote of his dissections of the famous "Barbary Ape" (which, in actuality, was a species of monkey). Five hundred years later, a monkey presumably spared from such a fate appears on the frontispiece of Andreas Vesalius's influential medical text *De Humani Corporis Fabrica Libri Septem*, which argued for the abandonment of medical knowledge gleaned from monkey vivisection in favor of that observed from autopsies of humans (Cormack and Ede 53, 139–40).

Though differing in certain key respects, humans and other primates bore enough similarity to intrigue ancient scholars about the potential for hybridization. Genetic analysis suggests that in the prehistoric era, sexual intercourse between proto-humans was likely routine, but no instance of more recent hybridization has ever been confirmed in a manner that would suit the standards of twenty-first century science (Dekkers 55). Such hybridization is most likely impossible: humans have twenty-three chromosomes, while chimpanzees have twenty-four, and even if humans and chimpanzees were close enough in the tree of life to hybridize, any viable offspring — a "humanzee" — would almost certainly be sterile (Rossiianov 310). Still, humans have obsessed about this odd form of miscegenation for centuries, filling various forms of media with representations of savage gorillas and other primate beasts carrying fair-skinned maidens off to some presumed despoilment. More recently, the existence of sexually transmitted diseases — such as HIV — believed to have jumped the species barrier from chimpanzees to humans has continued to trigger fears of human/ape sexual transgression.

Rumor and conjecture about human/nonhuman mating in the West predate the Classical era, and can be found in the spiritual texts of various populations. Hebrew scripture and Greek mythology speak on the subject of bestiality, while the work of Roman scholar Pliny the Elder describes a variety of women who, after intercourse with animals, produced hybrid offspring (especially human/bull and human/horse hybrids) which were either hidden, slain, or died shortly after birth. Aelian's second-century multi-volume, *On Animals*, similarly described a series of human/animal encounters (including some with baboons), most of which end poorly for the human partner (Salisbury 85).

Of all of the possible variations on the bestiality myth theme, stories of ape/human love have long been the most popular — a stock literary form serving a variety of social purposes (Dubois-Desaulle and Niemoeller 273). Medieval accounts in the West describe not merely illicit intimacies, but the conception and delivery of mysterious new beasts. In the eleventh-century, St. Peter Damian described an alleged case of human/ape copulation in his *De Bono Religiosi Status et Variorum Animatium Tropologia*, which introduced "Maimo," the supposed illegitimate offspring of an Italian countess and her husband's pet ape. No less noted a figure than Pope Alexander II claimed to have seen the creature, though no records of the supposed birth have survived (Salisbury 95). Indeed, historical records turn up no reliable first-hand witnesses to the creation of human/ape hybrids, let alone individuals willing to assume responsibility for their birth. The absence of direct evidence, though, did not make the existence of such creatures suspect to contemporary scholars. Medieval natural history tracts on beasts and monsters generally slighted direct observation in favor of legend and religious mythology (Stannard 443, 450).

In legends and myths of hybrid births, a human female invariably participates — often happily — in sexual congress with a male animal and suffers as a result, suggesting that these tales may have served a moral as well as an erotic or scientific function. Medieval natural philosophy categorized animate and inanimate matter according to a strict hierarchy of perfection, with humans nearly divine and all manner of beasts positioned below them. Interspecies sexual encounters said to produce dimwitted human/ape hybrids both reinforced the prevailing philosophical worldview and demonstrated the danger of usurping God's powers of creation. Churchmen like St. Augustine and St. Thomas Aquinas vigorously condemned zoophilia as an abomination, not surprising considering the ancient biblical proscriptions against sexual congress with animals. In a society in which sexuality itself was often viewed as animalistic, medieval texts described bestiality not only as a sin, but as a punishment that would await other sinners in the hereafter (Salisbury 84, 97). Read in this light, bestiality stories can easily be read as allegories about the hazards of wantonness, or of choosing one's human sexual partners unwisely. The woman who chooses to bed an animal is thoroughly debased in such encounters, and her monstrous offspring provides indelible proof of her transgression. In an era in which physical deformity was believed to reflect the immorality of the parents, bestiality myths also served to shield human fathers from blame for their monstrous offspring.

However deplorable the act, interspecies mating was said to engender curiosities that fascinated early-modern thinkers. The Renaissance in Europe produced explorations and discoveries that challenged medieval natural knowledge, including contacts with native peoples in the Americas and Asia that white Europeans refused to categorize as fully human but with whom they freely copulated. An increased fascination with the collection and classification of species brought inaccurate descriptions of odd beasts and hybrids, described in such works as Georges-Louis Leclerc, Comte de Buffon's *Histoire Naturelle* (Bowler and Morus 327) Meanwhile, interaction with North American natives often led seventeenth- and eighteenth-century scholars to romanticize nomadic hunter-gatherers as "noble savages" free of the decadence and corruption of civilized society.

It was the century that followed, though, that fundamentally altered the West's relationship with lower primates, especially apes. During the late 1800s, evolutionary theory and colonialism created new bonds of kinship between apes and humans and new forms of contact between the two. Whereas Charles Darwin elucidated the common ancestors of modern humans and other primates in his works on natural selection, pioneering neurologist Sigmund Freud replaced the delineations between animal and human with a new conception of man as beast, descended from baser creatures and consumed by clashing emotions (e.g., Bowler and Morus 157). Popular culture quickly absorbed these lessons: in Jack London's 1907 novel *Before Adam*, the author narrates the inner monologue of a proto-human. Tarzan, the British aristocrat-turned-ape man whose adventures were first chronicled in a 1912 magazine serial, is little more than an ape surrogate who, in the many later motion picture adaptations, seldom appears on screen without his adoptive chimpanzee brother, Cheetah. With Tarzan "aping" the behavioral norms of lower primates, a human woman, "Jane," must civilize him so that he may reclaim his birthright. Yet his sexual relationship with Jane complicates the story, providing a coupling that is morally sound yet oddly transgressive (Vernon 127).

Of course, Tarzan had found his way to Africa because of the increasing encroachment of Western society into the habitats of non-human primates. Propelled by steam and weapons technology, Europeans penetrated the furthest reaches of distant continents, often subduing local populations and harvesting resources for consumption back home. Among these were the rich flora and fauna of Africa, including apes, which European scientists both studied in the field and exploited as test subjects in laboratory experiments (Haraway 19–22). Indeed, surgical implantation of monkey testicles (by Russian-born French surgeon Serge Voronoff, among others) eventually attracted brief interest among elite Europeans who believed that the procedure would restore their youth and vigor. A similar fad involving the implantation of chimpanzee ovaries in human women not surprisingly triggered hybridization fears (McNeill D6).

Western colonialism in Africa and elsewhere is a frequent lens through which human/ape interaction appears in fiction, with apes serving as stand-ins for primitive peoples who either threaten Western explorers or are civilized by their exposure to them. Kidnapped from Africa as savage beasts, apes in these stories undergo geographical, temporal, and cognitive shifts as they are introduced to European society. Franz Kafka's short story "Ein Bericht für eine Akademie" (1917; translated as "A Report to an Academy," 2006), featured an ape captured in Africa and civilized by his contact with Europeans. In H. P. Lovecraft's 1920 short story "Facts Concerning the Late Arthur Jermyn and His Family," a British explorer learns some unpleasant facts about his "Portuguese" great-great-great grandmother. Two decades later, H. A. and Margaret Rey's 1941 *Curious George* and its sequels introduced a child-friendly ape imperfectly civilized under similar circumstances.

While occasional works joined a female ape with a male human, most perpetuated the ancient fantasy of the human female succumbing to the amorous advances of a male beast. By the early twentieth century, ape/human love had become the caricature of choice for polemicists (most of them white males) seeking to represent the savagery of other nations or of non-white peoples. If this propaganda is to be believed, male apes, while happy to mate with females of their own species, actually prefer human women, and will seek them out at every opportunity, often while wearing a Prussian Army helmet. Drawn from an earlier British propaganda piece, H. R. Hopps's "Destroy this Mad Brute" is among the more famous recruitment posters of World War I, depicting a deranged gorilla marching upon American shores with a semi-nude blonde woman draped over his hulking arm.[1] The ape's distinctive Pickelhaube helmet bears the word "militarism," and the ruins of Europe smolder in his wake (Gullace 68–69). Imagery of this type was frequently deployed in the era to lambaste any entity or institution — like large corporate monopolies in other editorial images — perceived as having its way with an innocent population.

The early decades of the twentieth century marked the high point of Western fascination with human/ape hybridization, in both the scientific community and in popular literature. While interest in hybridization often brought scandal, new research into plant and animal genetics, primatology, and artificial insemination encouraged breeding experiments in a variety of species, including apes. Unsubstantiated accounts suggest the existence of a successful fertilization and birth of a "humanzee" at the Yerkes National Primate Research Center in the 1920s, though the creature is said, like many semi-mythical beasts, to have been euthanized after birth. Confirmed as true, but less successful, were the 1927 efforts of Soviet biologist Ilya Ivanovich Ivanov to inseminate female chimpanzees with human sperm at a Pasteur Institute facility in French Guinea. Having heard from locals of encounters in the wild between male apes and female humans, and driven by a dedication bordering on obsession, Ivanov had, in consultation with French colonial leaders, later contemplated inseminating African women (without their knowledge) with ape sperm (Rossiianov 297, 299). A subsequent experiment in Soviet Georgia to inseminate a human female with orangutan sperm was never completed, despite Ivanov's successful recruitment of a despondent woman willing to be inseminated artificially and carry a human/ape hybrid to term (Rossiianov 306).

These macabre experiments were controversial enough to be conducted semi-secretly, but they received support from Soviet scientific authorities who saw in them a way to establish a true socialist biology, one that undermined traditional racial and class hierarchies. Despite the bioethical implications, the successful birth of a human/ape hybrid would provide strong evidence for the validity of evolutionary theory and, especially, for humanity's membership in the primate order. It might also discredit counter-revolutionary religious institutions that preached man's uniqueness and forbade crossbreeding experiments (Rossiianov 286). Caught up in a wave of anti-scientific political purges, though, Ivanov was arrested by the Soviet secret police in 1930 and died two years later, after a difficult incarceration.

Apes resisted Ivanov's hybridization experiments; in captivity, in fact, they rarely survived long enough to be of much use. Hybridization effort in contemporaneous science fiction proved similarly unsuccessful. The prehistoric King Kong, the star of feature motion pictures and novelizations produced by three different generations of Americans, is the best known of the human-loving apes. In each version, the core plot remains the same: a giant ape falls in love with a blond human woman and spends the rest of the movie seeking out her company before being killed for his transgressions. The gross disparity in size between King Kong and the object of his affection makes a physical relationship between the two impossible, and thus turns Kong's lust into an almost courtly affection. Kong is merely a stupid, sentimental animal consumed by his clueless affection for one semi-amused human, but without any real idea of how to express his affection physically besides cradling her in his giant hands.

This is evident in the various cinematic versions of the tale (1933, 1976, 2005) as Kong seeks only to gaze upon his prize and protect her from harm, in the form of human males who inevitably seek her rescue.[2] Yet, as Donna Haraway noted of the 1933 film, Kong is a more complex romantic partner than he may seem. His "admirable" and virile "sexuality" earns the audience's grudging respect. His "bestial over-reach" is tainted by "the unmistakable tone of racial crossing," but his tragic courage is undeniable, and his choice of paramour indicates an underlying "humanity." Fearless and vigorous, Kong could, Haraway suggests, be "the father of a new and better race" (161). Rather than conquering humanity, though, Kong succumbs to it: distracted and weakened by his love for his human bride, he is felled by machine gun fire from marauding airplanes. Terrifying as they may seem, though, in the pantheon of popular culture, giant "man-beasts" like Kong actually pose little threat to women. Far more dangerous, Hollywood has suggested, are "space" apes, beings who possess compatible reproductive anatomy as well as powers of reason and devious intentions far beyond those of normal apes.

Birth of the Space Ape

The utility of apes for medical experimentation has exposed them to successive dangers throughout history: dissection, drugs, even rapid acceleration and deceleration (Mackowski 153–54). In 1948, American rocket scientists under the direction of German missile engineer Wernher von Braun began a series of experiments aimed at employing surplus German V-2 rockets to launch monkeys into space. A flight the following year succeeded in launching a rhesus monkey to an altitude of eighty-three miles, but the "monkeynaut," Albert II, died on impact. Such flights would be a feature of the early years of what would be later known as the Space Age.

In 1959, two American monkeys, Able and Baker, became the first living creatures launched into space and recovered alive. Their flights, in the eyes of the physiological community, were an absolute necessity: early speculation on the space environment suggested that humans would be unable to function during protracted periods of weightlessness or be otherwise too overcome with stress to operate a space vehicle (Neufeld 341). The United States experimented with other animals: rats in smaller spacecraft, and pigs to test crew couches, since their spines simulated those of humans. The Soviet Union and France also launched monkeys into space, along with dogs and turtles, as well as a variety of invertebrates and smaller creatures. The National Aeronautics and Space Administration's (NASA) later launching of apes, though — the chimpanzees Ham in 1961 and Enos in 1962 — was a unique American achievement: strong and willful, chimps were closest to humans in intelligence, behavior, and physiognomy and could be trained to mimic the human pilots NASA would soon fly into space (Swenson, Grimwood, and Alexander 391–407).

One might have expected the amorous ape to disappear from movies in the Space Age, but with space monkeys already exploring the cosmos and gorilla suits plentiful in 1950s Hollywood, a woman carried off by a "space" ape was not an uncommon sight. Often, the prefix "space" was used to liven a movie genre that had become stale: westerns, road movies, horror films, and even teen films (like 1959's *Teenagers from Outer Space*) could be livened up with the addition of space aliens, spaceships, or space scientists. The 1951 film *The Day the Earth Stood Still* had nary an ape in the movie, but for reasons unknown, the hand of the unseen alien threatening human civilization in promotional materials produced for the movie was distinctly simian (McCurdy 73).[3] Similarly, the star of 1953's *Robot Monster* is neither a robot nor a monster, but a man in an ape suit with a television for a head and a fondness for the ladies.[4] Elsewhere, the fantastic nature of space travel itself was deployed to explain the existence of implausible plots and fantastic creatures. Apes imbued with super-intelligence as a result of contact with aliens or space-age science later appeared as comic book villains, such as DC Comics's Ultra-Humanite and Gorilla Grodd, often threatening the lives of human superheroes.

The end of ape flights in 1962 did not diminish the public's enthusiasm for this odd creation of twentieth-century technoscience. Vaguely realistic "space" apes appeared subsequently in science fiction in a variety of capacities, including crewmates for planetary explorers, as in 1964's *Robinson Crusoe on Mars*. More often, though, space apes served as human male surrogates or rivals. Later, semi-accurate portrayals of the early years of the Space Race like *The Right Stuff* (1983) and *Space Cowboys* (2000) featured plot points hinging upon the competition waged between America's human astronauts and their lower primate colleagues for seats in early space vehicles. The first humans who followed America's apes into space, one test pilot joked at the time, had little to be proud of, climbing into seats still littered with monkey droppings (Catchpole 160). More fanciful movies posited the training of intelligent monkey pilots (e.g., *Project X*, 1987; *Space Chimps*, 2008) able to replace humans in the cockpits of airplanes and space vehicles. In the animated television series *The Simpsons*, viewers learned that NASA's chimps came back from space superintelligent and now run the Space Shuttle program ("Deep Space Homer").

By 1967, "space" apes had not only become a cultural fixture, but also a threat to womanly virtue more dangerous than that posed by any previous fictional primate. In 1966, Desmond and Ramona Morris published *Men and Apes*, a book that simultaneously lampooned human/ape hybridization experiments and suggested their inevitability. The following year, Desmond Morris's influential sociobiological treatise *The Naked Ape* argued that the differences between humans and lower primates were fewer than previously thought. That year, an infatuated and verbose space gorilla landed on Earth to claim comic-book heroine Wonder Woman as his queen (*Wonder Woman* #170). In the comic, the ape possessed technology beyond human imagination and admired Wonder Woman for her strength and ferocity.[5]

The evolutionary parable, such as in 1968's *2001: A Space Odyssey*, which famously connected proto-humanity's mastery of weapons making to later innovations in human spaceflight, demonstrated both how far humans had come in their development and how simian they perhaps remained. Most notable among the popular culture products explicating the concept of the hyper-evolved "space" ape, though, are the seven *Planet of the Apes* movies 20th Century–Fox made between 1968 and 2011, inspired by a 1963 French novel about human astronauts who travel to a distant planet ruled by intelligent members of the taxonomic family of great apes. In the book, and even more so in the movies, the overgrown, verbal chimpanzees, gorillas, and orangutans who populate this world regard the fourth member of their taxonomic family—humans—with open contempt. As originally conceived in Pierre Boulle's novel, the apes the humans encounter are urban and industrialized. They are just beginning to experiment with space travel, having launched humans into space aboard rudimentary rockets. The motion picture adaptation made some changes to the original story but retained a romantic subplot between one of the human astronauts and an ape woman. Successful commercially and critically, the Apes franchise extended to television and comics while openly confronting issues of interspecies relations only suggested in other works.

The apes created by modern science fiction often instruct audiences by exaggerating human weaknesses: during Wonder Woman's encounter with the space gorilla, she remains unimpressed by his intellect and finds space ape males to be as selfish and violent as their Earth human counterparts. Sometimes, though, science fiction apes instruct from a position of moral superiority. This was the goal of the creators of the *Planet of the Apes* movies of the 1960s and 1970s. The humans who find themselves dominated by apes are supposed to both recognize the racism of human society and respect the ways in which apes live in harmony with nature. On the Ape Planet, evolved primates are vegetarians, and a social taboo against ape-icide tempers disputes and ensures a certain amount of civic calm.[6] Inhabitants of the Ape Planet interact peacefully, not only with each other, but with other animal species, respecting their ecosystems and practicing non-violence, at least with regard to non-humans. Indeed, the British accents of many of the actors playing the apes further signal to American audiences a certain degree of politesse (Greene and Slotkin 49–50).

In the Apes sequels of the 1970s, chimpanzees tackle a variety of human technologies before finally mastering spaceflight. These super-apes are unimpressed with their occasional human astronaut visitors; to them, humanity represents a degraded offshoot of the simian bloodline, one consumed by self-destructive urges that threaten the entire primate order. The original *Planet of the Apes* movie makes this point forcefully, citing the words of an ancient ape lawgiver who describes how humans, voracious and immoral, laid waste to every ecosystem they encountered:

> Beware the beast, man, for he is the Devil's pawn. Alone among God's primates, he kills for sport or lust or greed. Yea, he will murder his brother to possess his brother's land. Let him not breed in great numbers, for he will make a desert of his home and yours. Shun him! For he is the harbinger of death [*Planet of the Apes* 1968].

As any space ape will attest, humans are rapacious, violent, unprincipled, and best avoided. Left to their own devices, they will destroy themselves. Indeed, that was the fate which, in the 1968 *Plant of the Apes* movie, befell twentieth-century humans. When Taylor, at the conclusion of *Apes*, discovers remnants of the Statue of Liberty, he realizes that the Planet of the Apes is actually Earth, many centuries after humanity has all but extinguished itself in an unspecified orgy of violence. Extrapolating from the social and political unrest of the late 1960s and early 1970s, the Apes movies suggest that *homo sapiens* is destined to fall backward on the evolutionary ladder, losing their technology, and, ultimately, their capacity for complex thought and speech. While some hyper-evolved human mutants will likely survive the inevitable apocalypse, most will languish, surviving only by scavenging. The hyper-evolved apes around these wild humans will grow to despise them.

Apes in Charge and Women in Cages

Secretly knowing of humans' tendencies toward expansion and decay, Ape Planet leaders have condemned all humans to lives of servitude. In the greatest danger, though, are human females; because apes live in a society so sophisticated that they regard humans as animals, they are able to rationalize appalling exploitation of human women. The Women's Liberation movement trailed the Civil Rights movement by several years, and so even the progressive science fiction movies of the "Golden Age" of cinema reveal various unenlightened attitudes about gender. In Ape City, human females are clad in leather bathing suits, caged, enslaved, strapped to tables, and studied by scientists, all with obvious sexual overtones (*Planet of the Apes* 1968).

The producers of *Planet of the Apes* milked the possibility of human/ape mating, suggesting in promotional photographs that audience members might witness an act of bestiality if they waited patiently enough. Taylor's only female crewmate dies in the opening minutes of the 1968 movie, though, denying audiences the opportunity to see an ape transgress sexually with a blond woman (Greene and Slotkin 78). Actually depicting an ape experiencing intimacy with a woman would have been unconscionable in a mainstream movie, so the only romantic subplots *Apes* (and its 2001 remake) introduces are tepid consensual flirtations between human males and ape females. These mirror traditional social conventions that allowed white men, even in the most racist of eras, to take non-white mistresses, while denying white women the same privilege.

Taylor will eventually ride off into the sunset with a human woman, but before he goes, he cannot resist stealing a kiss from a female ape scientist, Zira, of whom he has grown fond. "Mr. Heston's glowering impatience injected undercurrents of interstellar/interspecies love that brought the movie to a boil," Elvis Mitchell recalled of the 1968 movie. "[H]e sized up Kim Hunter in her chimp makeup as if she was freshly grilled mutton" (E1). While Zira's husband, Cornelius, looks on, Taylor and Zira (at Taylor's request) enjoy a brief kiss, but only Taylor seems pleased by the experience. However much she respects Taylor, Zira is physically repulsed by the human male.

Mark Wahlberg's human astronaut, Davidson, the hero of the 2001 *Planet of the Apes* remake, finds himself in a similar predicament with the thoughtful chimpanzee daughter of an important ape leader. Unlike in the original movie, Helena Bonham Carter's ape, Ari, clearly desires the human astronaut, but Davidson does not reciprocate her affection. He is predestined instead to fall for the daughter of the chief of a local wild human tribe, despite Ari's assistance in facilitating his escape. Director Tim Burton, who appeared in one magazine photograph with his ape-costumed girlfriend (and their imaginary chimpanzee offspring) wanted to include in the movie a love scene between Davidson and Ari, but ultimately abandoned the plan (McMahan 180).[7]

Of course, human/animal sexuality violates Western norms and would likely render unmarketable any motion picture that depicted it. Taylor and Davidson, though they flirt with apes, must ultimately mate with wild humans: for Taylor, a mute named Nova, and for Davidson, the human Daena, played by Estella Warren. Despite the absence of interspecies sexuality in the movie, the producers still issued press photographs depicting Daena fondling the chins of two actors in gorilla suits.[8]

The suggestion of ape/human interaction proved so popular, however, that the original *Apes* movie spawned a number of motion picture, television, and print sequels, all building upon the theme of post-apocalyptic role-reversal between humans and apes (*Beneath the Planet of the Apes* 1970; *Escape from the Planet of the Apes* 1971; *Conquest of the Planet of the Apes* 1972; *Battle for the Planet of the Apes* 1973; *Planet of the Apes* [television series] 1974; *Return to the Planet of the Apes* [television series, animated] 1975). Meanwhile, popular pseudoscientific literature expounded on the concept of forbidden simian love. Max Flindt and Otto Binder's 1974 human origins treatise, *Mankind: Child of the Stars*, made an underwhelming and poorly-received case for prehistoric copulation between proto-humans and visiting space aliens. The product of these unions, they suggested, walk the Earth as modern humans.

Further eroding the boundaries between human and animal, the 1970s also saw a variety of extensive experiments on apes believed to have made the transition from animal to human. Celebrity chimpanzee "Nim Chimpsky" and gorilla "Koko" mastered an American Sign Language vocabulary of hundreds of words, though their achievements fell short of true language acquisition. At the same time, a partially hairless chimpanzee named "Oliver" achieved worldwide celebrity for certain oddly human-like behaviors, including bipedalism and apparent affection for human women. Though touted as a "missing link" between ape and man, Oliver's chromosomal analysis revealed him to be genetically identical to regular chimpanzees (Ely et al.).

Despite a decade-worth of comment and experimentation, no compelling evidence of radical ape evolution materialized in the 1970s, but literature about human-ape mating continued to appear. Nancy Friday's anthologies of female sexual fantasies, beginning with 1973's *My Secret Garden*, included a number with bestiality themes. Her 1991 sequel, *Women on Top*, featured a laboratory experiment in which a human woman volunteers to use her body as a semen collection vessel for a gorilla breeding experiment, an encounter that leaves the woman "sore" but "so satisfied" (111). Daniel Quinn's 1992 and 1997 novels *Ishmael* and *My Ishmael* posited the discover of a telepathic gorilla, while Peter Høeg's and Barbara Haveland's 1996 novel *The Woman and the Ape* describes a loving sexual relationship between a woman and a hitherto undiscovered ape man.

In a 1997 series of *Planet of the Apes*–inspired paintings, Spanish fantasy artist Luis Royo elaborated even more provocatively upon the subject of the movies. Just as humans now keep naked animals as pets, Royo suggests, hyper-evolved apes will take particular delight in restraining and displaying wild human women. Deprived of clothing, collared and leashed before their gorilla master, blonde and brunette human women abandon any pretense of concealing their genitalia, accepting their master's amusement. In another image, women are harnessed and broken, roped to the ceiling or forced to kneel, nude, before their keepers. Royo's escaping human female is also mesmerized by the broken Lady Liberty, but for different reasons. Nude and kneeling in deference, she worships the giant female face and marvels at an ancient past in which human women were once free. Manacles around her wrists, ankles, and thighs, replete with rings and other fittings, suggest that she has been restrained for unseemly purposes.[9] Images like these are a veritable encyclopedia of male fetishes: central to this form of erotic art is the male fantasy that human women, whose sexual instincts civilized society often represses, actually crave despoilment at the hands of these brutes.

In the newest addition of the literary fiction on ape/human mating, Benjamin Hale's *Evolution of Bruno Littlemore* (2011), a smug but brilliant chimpanzee raised on a steady diet of human culture beds a naïve primatologist resembling Jane Goodall. Educated by *Planet of Apes* and other human/ape science fiction tropes, chimp Bruno Littlemore imagines himself a "space" ape of sorts, "blasting away from the earth and into the cold vacuum of space at a velocity close to the speed of light, so that time dilates and millions of years go by, and one day I crash-land on an alien planet populated by a hostile race of talking hairless upright apes, only to discover to my horror that this is really earth" (475). Indeed, once talking Littlemore acquires enough language to organize his thoughts, he condemns, in his dictated memoir, "this animal, man, who had proven himself to be the enemy of all other things that are living" (290). About human women, though, Littlemore has mixed emotions: "My mother always knew I had a thing for human girls," Bruno later recalls, presaging an infatuation that soon escalates to bestiality and hybridization (29). The ape's indiscretion later proves devastating for all involved.

In its morality, *Bruno Littlemore* bears an uncanny resemblance to medieval texts, simultaneously offering lurid glimpses of forbidden sexuality and condemning the women who participate to a grisly fate. While a human male may kiss an ape and get away with it, human women who associate with lesser creatures undermine the bloodline and forfeit their humanity. Historical cartoons depicting African Americans as apes stoked white supremacist notions of race betrayal, suggesting that white women who consorted with Negroes would forfeit their whiteness and face criminal sanctions, exile from respectable society, and even a kind of racial death. This is the painful lesson that Wonder Woman learns during her 1967 encounter with the space ape. After the two battle each other, our human heroine is inexplicably transformed into a gorilla. Ironically, once he transforms her, the space ape no longer finds Wonder Woman attractive and turns her back into a human. Such punishments await other women who consent to ape/human love.

Conclusion

Long after NASA replaced lower primates with humans in its vehicles, "space" apes and other advanced simians have remained in the public consciousness.[10] The 2011 prequel *Rise of the Planet of the Apes* offered up yet another biomedically enhanced chimpanzee consumed by his disgust for humanity. Such creatures inform viewers not about the degraded condition of the ape, but of the degraded condition of the supposedly superior *homo sapiens*, whose everyday hypocrisies and cruelties crumble in the face of the honesty and cleverness of the jungle beast. Yet even science-fiction's "civilized" apes express their superiority through acts of unbridled lust virtually indistinguishable from those of their jungle cousins. Even in children's television, evil and intelligent apes and monkeys (like genius monkey "Mojo Jojo" of the animated series *The Powerpuff Girls*) spar with human heroines with whom they are often obsessed. Nintendo's *Donkey Kong*, created by Shigeru Miyamoto in 1981, spawned a series of arcade and console games in which an intrepid human plumber must climb a building's scaffolding to rescue a helpless princess from a vicious giant ape, who, as the hero approaches ever closer, grabs hold of his prey and spirits her away to a higher level.

The persistence of this trope signals many things—the prejudices of a particular era, the heterosexual male authorship of most science fiction, modern discomfort with the threat of women's liberation—but mostly, a lack of vision. As far as science fiction has come in critiquing human follies and imagining better worlds, it remains unwilling to confront the fundamental inequities of a gendered society, and is still startlingly naïve with regard to alternatives. Fortunately, Earth's present-day apes seem to pose little threat to human women except in fiction; nonetheless, it may be wise, for the time being, to remain vigilant, if only because our fears and fascination with human/ape miscegenation reflect more about our own selves than our ape brethren. As in much science fiction, we impose our darkest desires on the monsters we make, and then set them upon humanity to punish ourselves for our own wickedness.

Notes

The author wishes to thank Carmen Kroll, Kathy Matosich, Joanna Radin, and A. Bowdoin Van Riper. Early versions of this paper were presented in 2010 at the STS Graduate Students' Annual Conference and the Film & History Conference: Representations of Love in Film and Television. The organizers and attendees of these conferences provided many helpful suggestions, as did the editors of this anthology.

1. H. R. Hopps, "Destroy This Mad Brute," http://www.learnnc.org/lp/multimedia/10 612 (accessed March 7, 2012).

2. This dynamic renders their interaction safe for audiences, though that fact has not stopped Internet fan fiction artists from imagining the outcome of such a union. "Naomi Watts and Little Kong Pictures," http://www.freakingnews.com/Naomi-Watts-and-Little-Kong-Pictures-55651.asp (accessed March 7, 2012).

3. "The Day the Earth Stood Still," http://upload.wikimedia.org/wikipedia/en/3/3f/Day_the_Earth_Stood_Still_1951.jpg (accessed March 8, 2012).

4. "Robot Monster," http://upload.wikimedia.org/wikipedia/en/c/c5/Robotmonster.jpg (accessed March 8, 2012).

5. Allan Harvey, "Wonder Woman — Gorilla!!" http://thefifthbranch.com/gorilladaze/wonder-woman-gorilla/ (accessed March 8, 2012).

6. Ironically, this vision of ape society was inaccurate. Years later, primatologist Jane Goodall observed cannibalism and war among chimpanzee populations.

7. *The Sacred Scrolls*, http://planetoftheapes.wikia.com/wiki/File:Burtonscene20.jpg (accessed March 8, 2012).

8. *The Sacred Scrolls*, http://planetoftheapes.wikia.com/wiki/File:Burtonscene19.jpg (accessed March 8, 2012).

9. Luis Royo, *Millenium III*, http://www.luisroyofantasy.com/en/gallery/luis-royo-iii-millennium (accessed March 7, 2012).

10. For example, a 2002 episode of the WB television series *What's New, Scooby-Doo?*, entitled "Space Ape at the Cape," riffed on the cultural ubiquity of the interstellar primate, with evildoers disguising themselves as "space" apes in order to terrorize amateur detectives.

Works Cited

Boulle, Pierre. *Planet of the Apes*. New York: Gramercy Books, 2000. Print.
Bowler, Peter J., and Iwan Rhys Morus. *Making Modern Science: A Historical Survey*. Chicago: University of Chicago Press, 2005. Print.
Catchpole, John. *Project Mercury: NASA's First Manned Space Programme*. Chichester: Praxis, 2001. Print.

Cormack, Lesley B., and Andrew Ede. *A History of Science in Society: From Philosophy to Utility.* Toronto: University of Toronto Press, 2004. Print.
Dekkers, Midas. *Dearest Pet: On Bestiality.* New York: Verso, 1994. Print.
Dubois-Desaulle, Gaston, and Adolph Fredrick Niemoeller. *Bestiality: An Historical, Medical, Legal and Literary Study.* New York: privately printed, 1933. Print.
Ely, J. J., M. Leland, M. Martino, W. Swett, and C. M. Moore. "Technical Note: Chromosomal and MtDNA Analysis of Oliver." *American Journal of Physical Anthropology* 105.3 (1998): 395–403. Print.
Flindt, Max H., and Otto O. Binder. *Mankind: Child of the Stars.* Huntsville: Ozark Mountain Pub., 1999. Print.
Friday, Nancy. *My Secret Garden: Women's Sexual Fantasies.* New York: Trident Press, 1973. Print.
———. *Women on Top: How Real Life Has Changed Women's Sexual Fantasies.* New York: Simon & Schuster, 1991. Print.
Greene, Eric, and Richard Slotkin. *Planet of the Apes as American Myth: Race, Politics, and Popular Culture.* Hanover: Wesleyan University Press, 1998. Print.
Gullace, Nicoletta F. "Barbaric Anti-Modernism: Representations of the 'Hun' in Britain, North America, Australia, and Beyond," in *Picture This: World War I Posters and Visual Culture.* Edited by Pearl James. Lincoln: University of Nebraska Press, 2010. 61–78. Print.
Hale, Benjamin. *The Evolution of Bruno Littlemore.* New York: Twelve, 2011. Print.
Haraway, Donna Jeanne. *Primate Visions: Gender, Race, and Nature in the World of Modern Science.* New York: Routledge, 1989. Print.
Høeg, Peter, and Barbara Haveland. *The Woman and the Ape.* New York: Farrar, Straus and Giroux, 1996. Print.
Kafka, Franz. The *Metamorphosis and Other Stories.* Translated by Stanley Appelbaum. New York: Dover, 1996. Print.
London, Jack. *Before Adam.* New York: Macmillan, 1907. Print.
Lovecraft, H. P. *Dagon and Other Macabre Tales.* Sauk City: Arkham House, 1965. Print.
Mackowski, Maura Phillips. *Testing the Limits: Aviation Medicine and the Origins of Manned Space Flight.* College Station: Texas A&M University Press, 2005. Print.
McCurdy, Howard E. *Space and the American Imagination.* Washington, DC: Smithsonian Institution Press, 1997. Print.
McMahan, Alison. *The Films of Tim Burton: Animating Live Action in Contemporary Hollywood.* New York: Continuum, 2005. Print.
McNeill, Donald G., Jr. "Chimp to Human to History Books: The Path of AIDS." *New York Times* 18 Oct. 2011, D1. Print.
Mitchell, Elvis. "Get Your Hands Off, Ya Big Gorilla!" *New York Times* 27 Jul. 2001, E1. Print.
Morris, Desmond. *The Naked Ape: A Zoologist's Study of the Human Animal.* New York: McGraw-Hill, 1967. Print.
Morris, Ramona, and Desmond Morris. *Men and Apes.* London: Hutchinson, 1966. Print.
Neufeld, Michael. *Von Braun: Dreamer of Space, Engineer of War.* New York: Vintage Books, 2007. Print.
Quinn, Daniel. *Ishmael.* New York: Bantam/Turner Book, 1992. Print.
———. *My Ishmael.* New York: Bantam, 1997. Print.
Rey, H. A., and Margret Rey. *Curious George.* New York: Houghton Mifflin, 1941. Print.
Rossiianov, Kirill. "Beyond Species: Il'ya Ivanov and His Experiments on Cross-Breeding Humans with Anthropoid Apes." *Science in Context* 15 (2002): 277–316. Print.
Royo, Luis. *Millennium III.* New York: NBM, 1998. Print.
Salisbury, Joyce E. *The Beast Within: Animals in the Middle Ages.* New York: Routledge, 1994. Print.
Siebert, Charles. "Something Wild." *New York Times* 6 Mar. 2009, A27. Print.
Stannard, Jerry. "Natural History." *Science in the Middle Ages.* Ed. David C. Lindberg. Chicago: University of Chicago Press, 1980. 429–460. Print.
Swenson, Loyd S., Jr., James M. Grimwood, and Charles C. Alexander. *This New Ocean: A History of Project Mercury.* Washington, DC: NASA, 1966. Print.
Vernon, Alex. *On Tarzan.* Athens: University of Georgia Press, 2008. Print.

Movies and Television

Battle for the Planet of the Apes. Dir. J. Lee Thompson. Perf. Roddy McDowall, Claude Akins, Natalie Trundy. 20th Century–Fox, 1973.

Beneath the Planet of the Apes. Dir. Ted Post. Perf. James Franciscus, Kim Hunter, Maurice Evans. 20th Century–Fox, 1970.

Conquest of the Planet of the Apes. Dir. J. Lee Thompson. Perf. Roddy McDowall, Don Murray, Ricardo Montalban. 20th Century–Fox, 1972.

The Day the Earth Stood Still. Dir. Robert Wise. Perf. Michael Rennie, Patricia Neal, Billy Gray. 20th Century–Fox, 1951.

"Deep Space Homer." *The Simpsons.* FOX. 24 February 1994.

Escape from the Planet of the Apes. Dir. Don Taylor. Perf. Roddy McDowall, Kim Hunter, Bradford Dillman. 20th Century–Fox, 1971.

King Kong. Dir. John Guillermin. Perf. Jeff Bridges, Charles Grodin, Jessica Lange. Paramount Pictures, 1976.

King Kong. Dir. Merian C. Cooper and Ernest B. Schoedsack. Perf. Fay Wray, Bruce Cabot, Robert Armstrong. RKO Radio Pictures, 1933.

King Kong. Dir. Peter Jackson. Perf. Naomi Watts, Jack Black, Adrien Brody. Universal Pictures, 2005.

Planet of the Apes. Dir. Franklin J. Schaffner. Perf. Charlton Heston, Roddy McDowall, Kim Hunter. 20th Century–Fox, 1968.

Planet of the Apes. Dir. Tim Burton. Perf. Mark Wahlberg, Tim Roth, Helena Bonham Carter. 20th Century–Fox, 2001.

Planet of the Apes (Television). Dir. Arnold Laven, et al. Perf. Roddy McDowall, Ron Harper, James Naughton. 20th Century–Fox. 1974.

The Powerpuff Girls. Dir. Craig McCracken, et al. Perf. Cathy Cavadini, Elizabeth Daily, Tara Strong. Cartoon Network. 1998–2009.

Project X. Dir. Jonathan Kaplan. Perf. Matthew Broderick, Helen Hunt, William Sadler. 20th Century–Fox, 1987.

Return to the Planet of the Apes (Television). Dir. Doug Wildey. Perf. Austin Stoker, Philippa Harris, Henry Corden. 20th Century–Fox, 1975.

The Right Stuff. Dir. Philip Kaufman. Perf. Fred Ward, Dennis Quaid, Ed Harris. The Ladd Company, 1983.

Rise of the Planet of the Apes. Dir. Rupert Wyatt. Perf. James Franco, Freida Pinto, John Lithgow. 20th Century–Fox, 2011.

Robinson Crusoe on Mars. Dir. Byron Haskin. Perf. Paul Mantee, Victor Lundin, Adam West. Paramount Pictures, 1964.

Robot Monster. Dir. Phil Tucker. Perf. George Nader, Claudia Barrett, Selena Royle. Astor Pictures, 1953.

"Space Ape at the Cape." *What's New, Scooby-Doo?* WB. 11 October 2002.

Space Chimps. Dir. Kirk De Micco. Perf. Andy Samberg, Cheryl Hines, Jeff Daniels. 20th Century–Fox, 2008.

Space Cowboys. Dir. Clint Eastwood. Perf. Clint Eastwood, Tommy Lee Jones, Donald Sutherland. Warner Bros., 2000.

Teenagers from Outer Space. Dir. Tom Graeff. Perf. David Love, Dawn Bender, Bryan Grant. Warner Bros. Pictures, 1959.

2001: A Space Odyssey. Dir. Stanley Kubrick. Perf. Keir Dullea, Gary Lockwood, William Sylvester. MGM, 1968.

Technology as a Nexus for Homoerotic Desire in Boys' Series Books
Michael G. Cornelius

Ken straddled Sandy's legs, hanging over the edge of the bunk, and leaned forward until he could grasp Sandy's arms at the elbow.
  Bracing his feet he lifted the arms and then lowered them. Lifted them again and brought them down. Lifted them again— Over and over, finding each motion a desperate effort, Ken kept on...
  BRUCE CAMPBELL, *THE MYSTERY OF THE SHATTERED GLASS*, THE THIRTEENTH BOOK IN THE KEN HOLT SERIES, 134, 136

The movement behind him ceased. He squirmed around until he was face to face with Scotty. His friend smiled at him through swollen lips. "Turn back again," he whispered. "I was just resting."
  Rick obediently turned around again. It was an eternity before Scotty whispered, "Pull hard." Rick put all his strength into jerking his legs straight and then felt something give.
  "That's enough," Scotty whispered.
  JOHN BLAINE, *THE ROCKET'S SHADOW*, THE FIRST BOOK IN THE RICK BRANT SCIENCE-ADVENTURE SERIES,[1] 162

Geronimo hunkered down under the willows. "Something dry for you to put on."
  Chris unrolled the bundle, which included a white dinner jacket, black evening trousers, shirt, tie, and cummerbund. "For Pete's sake, where'd you get these?"
  ...Chris stripped off his sodden clothes and dressed hastily in the outfit which Geronimo had brought...
  As Chris transferred his waterproof emergency kit from his discarded wet cummerbund to the new one, he said, "Okay, now stop being so coy and tell me where all this came from."
  "Well, if you must know, I left Valaud's pal back in the bushes in his skivvies."
  Chris gave a low whistle. "Conscious?"
  "Let's say his eyes were closed."
  JACK LANCER, *X MARKS THE SPY*, THE FIRST BOOK IN THE CHRISTOPHER COOL/TEEN AGENT SERIES, 118–119

In her seminal study *Between Men: English Literature and Male Homosocial Desire*, Eve Kosofsky Sedgwick describes an erotic representation as a triangle, "useful as a figure by which the 'commonsense' of our intellectual tradition schematizes erotic relations," that imbues the two erotic rivals with a bond as powerful as the linkage between each rival and the object of their unioning, the beloved: "...in any erotic rivalry [triangle], the bond that links the rivals is as intense and potent as the bond that links either of the rivals to the beloved" (21). Thus Sedgwick argues that in such eternal triangles as Arthur, Lancelot, and Guinevere, the collocation of each individual is relevantly the same, one to the other, and that the two rivals are accoupled by the erotic and jealous passion of their rivalry as sure as each is joined to the beloved through their affection for the source of their union/disunion. As Tatiana Kuzmic writes of Sedgwick's triangle, "The appearance of a third party not only disrupts the original bond, but the male rivals complement each other to such a degree that the two of them begin to form a harmonious whole, thus rendering the woman unnecessary" (2). This whole represents the beginnings of a continuum that may ultimately lead to the exclusion of the female from the triadic union, rendering her superfluous, and directing the two men onto paths of homosocial, homoerotic, or indeed possibly even homosexual action or accord that the male pair would likely never achieve on their own.

Generally, though, the feminine point of the "eternal" polygon remains intact, as a reassurance to the audience of the heteronormativity of the rival males' identity configurations and as a deflection for the intense bond the rivalry itself generates in the first place. Thus any suggestion of non-heterosexualized activity or emotion from Arthur and Lancelot is dissipated by the passion over which they battle in regards to Guinevere, a passion that, in many versions of the popular narrative, ultimately results in the destruction of paradise (Camelot). In the end, it is the greedy nature of the eternal triangle, the unchecked passage of passion between all three individuals, that ensures both the triangle's eternalism and its destruction; doomed by the weight of its own emotions and yet generally unable to attain resolution as long as all three points of the triangle remain intact, the figure retains its constant state of anxious flux, neither consummating in happiness for one coupling or, conversely, none, until one side of the polygon is wholly and substantially obliterated.

What Sedgwick suggests in her study, however, is that the female becomes irrelevant, at least as far as the intense bonding of the male is concerned; in Sedgwick's reckoning, the female is merely a conduit for the expression of emotions that otherwise would remain unexpressed. Tension, then, in these texts is the best way to convey such worrisome feelings, emotions, and bonds that would otherwise be too suspect to be openly displayed. Homoeroticism, and perhaps homosexuality itself, is thus exhibited through antagonism and competition. Yet what of texts that create similar triangles with*out* the present female, or even male-focused, seemingly heteronormative works that nonetheless generally exclude the female altogether? How is such homoerotic desire expressed, if indeed it is at all? What happens to the "eternal triangle" when women are removed from its geometrics altogether?

One genre that acts to debar the feminine as a palpable presence is boys' series books. Early and mid–twentieth-century boys' series books are generally hallmarked by large groupings of males — homogenous in values, experiences, and class structure, but sometimes heterogeneous in ethnic background — who work to exclude females and create a male-dominated community whose main function is the perpetual functioning of the community itself, as an exercise of authority and power that reflected the role these boys would ascend to when they became adult men in the larger world. In these books, reflected in such series as the Hardy Boys, the Three Investigators, and the Rover Boys, relationships grow to be dependent upon the social matrix, as the individual is subsumed by the group, becoming an extension of a larger superego that functions mainly at the purposes of one or possibly two larger personalities that dominate the action of the group itself. Desire, need, and yearning take a backseat to "loftier" goals; dates occur usually within the matrix of the group itself, and function more as an end-product of mandated, privileged heterosexuality than any genuine expression for human (feminine) contact, connection, or longing.

However, in those boys' series that feature a male-male dyadic relationship as their cynosure — such as the Rick Brant series, the Ken Holt series, and the Christopher Cool series — the exclusion of all females for one *individual* male often results in a relationship that functions in ways beyond the standards of normative, hetero-expressive male behavior. These homoerotic underpinnings are not purposefully intended to be included in this relationship, but often result as a by-product of the closeness and intimacy that is constructed between the two main male characters. Thrust together, often in extraordinary circumstances, and generally eschewing the company of women in any meaningful way (even more so than their supergroup counterparts), the two boys, generally on the cusp of manhood and reaching the prime of their pubescence, conduct relationships that, intentionally or not, revel in homosocial/homoerotic underpinnings, creating levels of intimacy in scenes that, quite frankly, practically border on the sexual (such as those listed as epigraphs to this article). The two male youths become an extension of the other, often complementary and completing of the other, while relying solely on the other for fulfillment of all their emotional, social, and psychological needs. Interestingly, one of the most common ways that this relationship is cemented — and that this desire is expressed — is through technology, especially science-fiction technologies that far extend beyond the parameters of the talents of "normal" boys, thus excluding other males from the dyadic partnership. Technology becomes the glue that both binds them and a significant means through which they express their emotions and feelings toward the other. Employing Sedgwick's triangle of homoerotic desire, I plan to demonstrate in this essay how these books utilize technology to take the place of the woman who traditionally acts as the "beloved" nexus of male-male homoerotic desire in the eternal triangle. In these texts, admiring a powerful, "built-out" motorcycle or a stylish ray-gun allows for open admiration of symbols of the masculine/phallic, an admiration more blushingly felt — but rarely expressed — for the other male. Thus the larger purpose of technology in these books is to allow the central protagonist males to exclude the external world while at the same time express their own undercurrents of homoerotic desire and tension — their own feelings, one for the other. This essay looks to that purpose, to the role technology plays in the sexual lives of males in these dyadic relationships in boys' series books; focusing primarily on the three series noted above, this essay will demonstrate that for the dyadic male pair, technology is the best way to truly express what is going on in their hearts — and in their pants.

Some boys' series books of the early to mid–twentieth century featured a solitary central protagonist who acted largely as an individual, though often with a cadre of familial or companionable admirers and supporters. These series include Tom Swift, Tim Murphy, and Encyclopedia Brown, amongst others, where the main character has friends — sometimes even "best" friends — as well as family assistance in solving mysteries, but generally prefers to sleuth unaided and alone.[2] More commonly, boys' series books featured central characters who acted as the cynosure of a larger supergroup that functioned as an extension of the id of the chief protagonist(s). According to C. M. Gill, in boys' sleuth books, all-male social groups "underscore not only the power and importance of men, but also the primary way in which men both attain and retain this power," which is through the "male community" itself (40). Geoffrey L. Greif writes that while "[male] friendships vary in type and intensity," men generally reflect interconnections that Grief labels "shoulder-to-shoulder relationships"; they "do things together," achieving intimacy through activity and eschewing discourse in favor of camaraderie (4, 6). In these larger groups, the "emotional relationships (men have) with other men are weak and often absent" (Pleck qtd. in Tognoli 273). According to Jerome Tognoli, "men's inexpressive character is a cause of their truncated social relationships with one another" (273). Male social groups limit intimacy because they curtail or eschew open communication; in such groups, "men ... talk little about themselves, their feelings, or their relationships concerning significant others" (Tognoli 274). Tognoli continues: "non-intimacy among men ... stems from more subtle but ubiquitous role restrictions that specify that men remain more aloof from one another than is required of women" (275). These role restrictions, reflective of society as a whole, are a direct manifestation of the supergroup itself, who work to ensure the conformity of the male into the larger patriarchy around him. Such conformity is deemed necessary for the survival of both the individual male group member and the larger group itself. The group cannot fully function unless it both projects and practices social conventions and dicta; as Daniel Hruschka observes, any individual member espousing conduct that eschews the rules of the group is generally curtailed and reinstructed in patterns of behavior that reflect the group mentality, or is excised from the group altogether (209). The end result, according to Brant Burleson, is that "males use talking [primarily] to accomplish *things*" and not as a means of expressive communication within the confines of the group itself (5, emphasis original).

Dyadic pairs of males, however, work within a very different dynamic than the social supergroup or the autonomous, non-dependent male. As Joseph Epstein observes, "A best friend is ... a more sacred relation than any other, for it is freely chosen ... and the commitment, entered into voluntarily, is somehow felt to be deeper. Anyone who has had a best friend will know the exhilarating feeling of closeness and partnership it yields" (23–24). This delineation is reflected in the series books: Rick Brant describes his dyadic relationship with Don "Scotty" Scott as "closer than brothers ... because brothers fight with each other sometimes, and Scotty and he never did" (*Lost City* 2). This intimacy, however, has both positive and negative ramifications. Epstein adds, "A best friend is, as the philosopher George Santayana once put it, the person with whom you can be most human, which is another way of saying, be most yourself," suggesting that, unlike the autonomy and solitude of the non-dependent male or the performative conformity necessary for the functioning of the supergroup, the dyad works to reinforce the actual quiddities and identities of its representative coupling (23). Hruschka notes, however, that dyadic relationships can be especially limiting, because behavior is organized along a binaristic pattern of friendship that consistently insists one individual's needs on to the other, and vice versa (218). A group dynamic permits both a larger focus on communal ideals and a specific focus on the individual's desires and requirements, provided, of course, that those desires and requirements do not exceed the regulations and parameters of the group as a whole; the non-dependent male, naturally, works as a solitary agent and is ultimately answerable only to himself. The dyad, however, creates a dualism that, in order for the dyad to function as concinnously as possible, necessitates that each individual member of the dyad place the other member's desires and needs correspondent to his/her own. Georg Simmel, writing during the height of these series' popularity, speculated extensively about the differences between the dyadic relationship and a larger group:

> The difference between the dyad and the larger group consists in the fact that the dyad has a different relation to each of its two elements than have larger groups to their members. Although, for the outsider, the group consisting of two may function as an autonomous super-individual unit, it usually does not do so for its participants.... The social structure here rests immediately on the one and on the other of the two and the secession of either would destroy the whole. The dyad, therefore, does not attain that super-personal life which the individuals feel to be independent ... [qtd. in Pitcher and Schultz 125].

More proscriptive in behavior but more expressive in emotional need, the dyad thus presents a unique manifestation of male friendship: a relationship that finds an advantage in being exclusive of the larger world around it and wholly dependent on the other, allowing for a fuller manifestation of the individual selves who comprise the dyad; and yet, at the same time, one that is fraught with continuous peril, since the functioning of the relationship is persistently challenged by the tenuous nature of the duo itself. Male dyads face a continuing barrage of assaults on their own functionality: overtures from other males wishing to join the group; familial pressures; larger social pressures to conform to a more patriarchal standard of behavior; questions regarding the intimate nature of the friendship itself; and, most significantly, the constant threat of the female, since the presence and blossoming of romance indicates a dyadic shift from the homogendered relationship to the more socially common and acceptable (for males, anyway) heterogendered one.

Because of all this, dyadic representations of male friendship in series books are rare. However, in each of the three series listed here, a dyadic male pair is continually placed at the cynosure of narrative events. All of these relationships are brought together in extraordinary ways: Christopher Cool and his dyadic pal, Geronimo Johnson, are recruited as partners for TEEN (Top-secret Educational Espionage Network), a branch of the Central Intelligence Agency (CIA) featuring college students as secret agents. Ken Holt and his dyadic partner, Sandy Allen, are brought together when Ken, escaping from a pair of would-be kidnappers, stumbles into the offices of the Allen family newspaper asking for aid. Similarly, Rick and Scotty meet when Scotty saves Rick from a vicious attack perpetrated by villains meant to dissuade Rick from his current course of action.[3] In each instance the extraordinary circumstances under which these friendships are generated is designed to excuse both their intensity and their immediacy, demonstrating that even the creators of these series recognize the unusual nature of the friendships showcased within.

Yet despite their differentiated status, dyadic male friendships are still governed by the same set of principles that preside over all male friendships. Or are they? Greif notes that, as a rule, male friendships are less verbally communicative (than female friendships or male/female dyadic pairings); are less physically demonstrative; proffer fewer compliments for the other males in group; and are more competitive as a whole. In fact, Grief records that competition is actually a prominent form of communication in male friendships, falling in with the notion that communal activities are important to male friendships, especially pre-marriage and early adult males, and Burleson's observation, previously noted, that male communication is action-directed, and used mainly within the confines of the group to accomplish collective objectives and ambitions (163).

Dyadic boys' series pairings, however, tend to act in ways that are seemingly contradictory to several of Greif's rules. Boys' series protagonists are often quite complimentary of their friends, offering praise and frank admiration for the various abilities that are demonstrated and feats that are accomplished. Of course, these are young men thrown into extraordinary circumstances involving high-tech mysteries, technological conflict, and international espionage, so in this case, the praise hardly seems unwarranted. Perhaps more interesting is just how physically demonstrative, and downright affectionate, the two boys can be. Physical contact and intimate proximity are two hallmarks of these male dyadic relationships. At the conclusion of his first meeting with Ken Holt, for example, Sandy Allen initiates physical contact between the two: "Sandy stopped on his way to the door and dropped his hand on Ken's shoulder encouragingly" (*Skeleton Island* 33). Despite the presence of other men in the room, Sandy is the only one to actually touch Ken. Later, they have a more intimate exchange: "Weakly he [Ken] let his head rest against Sandy's hand" (*Skeleton Island* 77). The other dyads are often as demonstrative. Rick Brant is often finding excuses to touch Scotty, such as when playing a practical joke on him: "He took the length of wire in his hand and placed the hand on Scotty's shoulder" (*Rocket's Shadow* 119). These exchanges create a sense of intimacy between the two boys, intimacy that can also be reflected in their speech and patterns of behavior with one another. At one point in the first book in the series, Scotty, talking about himself and Rick, says, "We won't say a word. We're mad at each other anyway!" (*Rocket's Shadow* 161). In another book, Rick is eager to show Scotty his new invention, a type of walkie-talkie designed for short-range communication between the two. Scotty marvels at Rick's ingenuity (as he usually does, complimenting him,) but he also asks, "But why should we send messages back and forth? We're together all the time" (*Lost City* 23). Such a seemingly careless remark belies the connectivity of the two boys; sounding more akin to a married couple than two male friends, this sense of intimacy permeates the relationship between the dyadic pair. Each, for example, shares a living space: Chris and Geronimo share a dormitory room at Kingston University; Ken and Sandy share Sandy's room at his house after Ken moves in with the Allen family at the conclusion of the first adventure in the series; and Scotty and Rick have adjoining (and connected) rooms in the Brant family compound on Spindrift Island, though Scotty spends so much time in Rick's room that he more often is depicted falling asleep on Rick's bed than on his own.

Masculine physicality is very important to these works; depicting, describing, and admiring the male form is a standard part of these texts. In the second Rick Brant adventure, Rick begins the text by looking around the dining room table and describing the individuals he sees. All of the males are described by their specific physical parameters: Julius Weiss is "a meek-looking little man with just a fringe of hair on his head"; Hobart Zircon "was a huge barrel of a man, over six feet tall, with a bushy shock of hair and a voice that shook the walls"; Scotty himself is described as a "tall, husky boy with black hair and a merry face" (*Lost City* 2). "Husky" is a telling word here; though today it is commonly seen as an undesirable descriptor with a negative connotation leaning toward descriptions of fatness, in mid-century texts "husky" was generally a complimentary word, reflecting a construct of a healthy, athletic male form (it is no accident that Rick himself as well as Sandy Allen are also consistently labeled "husky.") Lawrence R. Schehr suggests that appreciation for the masculine form is ultimately less objective than demonstrative:

> The attributes of masculine beauty, whatever they may be, are invariably translated into the world of the manly, into what is impressive. Again, the English language gets it right: a man is handsome just as a sum of money can be handsome: bigger *is* better. These attributes become cathected onto the body of power so that masculine beauty, instead of being part of an aesthetic, becomes the index of a reinforced ideology of power and phallocentrism [79].

It is evident what Rick values in his descriptions of the masculine. In comparing Professor Weiss to Professor Zircon, he notes, "He [Weiss] seemed frail compared with the good-natured Hobart Zircon, who sat next to him" (*Lost City* 2). The two women at the table, Rick's mother and sister, receive a distinctly different treatment in noting their physicality. Rick's sister Barby is merely described as "pretty," with no specifics about her physicality depicted; Rick's mother lacks any somatic description at all (3). This works to further emphasize the male and the ways in which maleness captures Rick's perspective and incarnates in his own masculine gaze.

The other series also reflect this admiration for the male form. In an extended scene in the first Christopher Cool adventure, *X Marks the Spy*, Chris stumbles into a hotel room only to find it is occupied:

> A huge, bull-like man was lying asleep on the bed in his underwear....
> Holding his breath, Chris tiptoed across the room. He had nearly made it to the window when —*crash!*
> The snores ended with an explosive snort as the sleeper in the bed stirred. Chris barely had time to [hide] behind an armchair, then the bedsprings creaked as the man sat upright.
> "How do I get out of this one?" Chris thought nervously.
> Presently the man got up, stalked over to the windows, and drew the curtains aside.... The fellow was much bigger than he had appeared while horizontal — at least six-feet-six — and was muscled like Mr. America....
> Chris began to perspire freely.
> Chris estimated his chest as somewhere around forty-nine or fifty inches exhaled, and his collar size as eighteen or nineteen at the smallest.
> The TEEN agent literally stopped breathing in fear that the man might glance behind the chair at any moment. Instead, he turned away, and began rummaging on the floor of the closet.
> "Now what?" Chris wondered.
> The answer came as the man straightened up, clutching a pair of enormous dumbbells. For the next five minutes he went through a vigorous exercise routine....
> Cold sweat trickled down Chris's skin. He caught several fleeting glimpses of the fellow's biceps bulging like pumpkins.
> Chris was numb with cramp and prolonged anxiety when the [man] finally put away the dumbbells. He walked to the bathroom.... Soon after came the hissing noise of the shower [*X Marks the Spy* 76–77].

This extended scene revels in the world of the fleshy, developed male; the scene is in no way related to the plot of the narrative, and, indeed, serves no other purpose than to demonstrate Chris's unmitigated admiration and anxiety of the form presented before him.

Unlike other male characters in boys' series books, the dyadic pair do not shy away from physical intimacy, and, indeed, are often placed into situations where such intimacy is forced upon them. All of the pairings endure numerous and repeated instances of captivity wherein the boys are restrained and confined by the books' varying villains. Indeed, the Ken Holt series is infamous among its fans for its many scenes of extended bondage, wherein Ken and Sandy are tied together in a physically close and often intimate manner:

> "Force your knees apart and bring your legs down over my head...."
> Sandy ducked his head and brought it up between Ken's legs, so that Ken's crossed ankles thrust themselves out before his chin....
> They sprawled in a tangle, Ken's legs still fastened around Sandy's neck, their chests heaving, their bodies aching. Ken tugged and Sandy squirmed and wriggled. Finally Ken was free [*Iron Box* 168–169].

Such scenes can last chapters and while (likely) unintentionally homoerotic, they *are* intentionally physical. The result is a type of "affective energy" that reflects the intense bonds created in these pairings (Mieszkowski 3). Ken and Sandy, Rick and Scotty, and Chris and Geronimo may not be romantic or sexual pairings, but they are decidedly intimate.

Despite this proximal physicality, however, these dyadic pairings demonstrate difficulty in being verbally communicative with one another. This is the one "rule" Greif establishes for male friendship that seems to remain intact in these relationships. When Rick first meets Scotty, for example, he longs to tell him more than he feels he is able: "He [Rick] wanted to say more, to tell Scotty how much fun it was and what good times the family had together, but it was hard to talk about anything so personal and important" (*Rocket's Shadow* 33). In the first Ken Holt adventure, during a scene where Ken and Sandy are hiding onboard a ship, Ken says to Sandy, "And now tell me the story of your life," a gesture meant not only to pass the time but also to increase the intensity of the growing bond between the two of them (*Skeleton Island* 117). The narrative, however, perhaps too reticent to demonstrate such obvious verbal intimacy between the two boys, shows very little of what Sandy recounts, and none of it firsthand; instead, all the reader is made privy to is that Sandy "talked of the Allen family and the *Advance*," the Allen family newspaper (117).

What more directly absorbs both the reader's attention in that same scene, as well as Rick and Sandy's, is a lengthy, pages-long discussion about the operation of the ship itself. Sandy, who worked on a similar vessel the previous summer, schools Rick in the functions of the various objects and areas of the ship and the wide range of procedures the ship must go through in order to get underway. Intense, detailed discussion of the ship's operations comprises several chapters, and the boys' verbal exchanges are dominated by the topic of maritime technology and procedure. Thus it is clear that whereas the personal details of Sandy's life are a subject matter too delicate for the series to project, the technical aspects and details of their adventure are the stuff series boys' dreams are made of.

Technological discussion abounds in each of these series. Statements such as "Pyrogallol ... is a developing agent — it turns the silver bromide on a film to metallic silver" and "He ransacked the spare-parts kit and finally rigged up a workable rectifier that would transform power from the big generator to the proper direct-current voltage" are commonplace in the texts (Campbell *Black Thumb* 90, Blaine *Lost City* 207). In the books, technology is depicted as being firmly within the subject realm of the masculine: "technology accentuates and emphasizes a particular male subjectivity" (Burrill 2). Derek A. Burrill, quoting Claudia Springer, notes that this is especially true of the

"...industrial technologies [that] represent the 'dry solidarity' and 'hard physical strength' of the male" (3). According to Fred Erisman, the function of technology in boys' series literature is to proffer "the picture of American youth as mechanically competent" (14). Erisman notes that technology and a technical education was a way to become "universally acknowledged and respected" (15). Russell B. Nye, writing about the Tom Swift, Boy Inventor series, suggests that what made the series so popular was that "Tom Swift grasped the technology of the machine age and brought it under control" (83). Erisman echoes this when he suggests that in these books, "technology is something that *can* be, and *must* be, mastered" (24). This construct is reflected by the books themselves: "Ken snorted. 'My brains against your brawn — you don't have a chance'" (Campbell *Black Thumb* 12).

Mastering technology, though, can reflect more meaning than simply understanding the ins and outs of mechanical procedures and complex devices. After all, Martin Heidegger once famously wrote, "Technology is a human activity" (288). Steven Zani, elucidating Heidegger, suggests that technology "describes man's relationship to the world" (175). He continues: "The work of technology is not just humanity recognizing the world, but rather a process of shaping and framing that changes the very nature of what it works upon ... technology doesn't just help humanity; on some fundamental level it *is* humanity; it's the way humanity reveals and becomes itself" (175–176). Thus "mastering" technology is a means through which the subject male can become master over larger aspects of his own quiddity, his own identity, and represents a socially acceptable — indeed, a socially admired — methodology of expressing male subjectivity. William J. McKinney writes, "While our most commonly used connotation of 'technology' is that of devices or tools, an expanded notion defines 'technology' as also referring to techniques and skills. Finally, 'technology' is expanded to include any means to an end" (187). As a "technique" in expressing maleness — as a "means to an end" in male communication — technology becomes a representation of a particular type of maleness — educated, modern, superior, cool — that aids in constructing a methodology for male patterns of communication in these texts. McKinney observes, "An important facet of technology is that it is designed with a purpose" (188). For these texts, that purpose reflects less technical mastery than mastery over the male range of emotions and wide spectrum of possible masculine sensations.

In boys' series books, the central protagonists remain highly constrained by the genre of the texts. As Glenna Andrade notes, "genre is both a literary focus and a social construction" (164). She continues: "Even though many stories incorporate elements of other genres, such as when a romance includes detective elements or when historical fiction integrates adventure hero qualities, each hero remains central within the formula of his or her own genre"

(164). As central protagonists within the rigid confines of boys' series literature, the characters under examination in this essay are proscribed by a formulaic system that had been in place for decades before each series' genesis. The formula — which had many variants but remained consistent through mid-century series texts — was codified in 1899 by Edward Stratemeyer with the inception of the Rover Boys series, and has been simply described as "good mystery and lots of action, with some educational material" (Herz 8).[4] While the "educational material" could be information about the places the characters visited or the objects encountered during the story, the "action" was always to be "tension without violence" (Herz 12). In the series, "tension is created through the *possibility* that something catastrophic may happen" (Herz 12). It was considered vital that "the books contained nothing prurient or off-color, and even the sanitized 'violence' involved no blood. It is true that the boys and the villains repeatedly got tied up, hit on the head, or nearly drowned, and that they tumbled down cliffs or fell through trapdoors, but they never died brutal deaths ... by the standards of the late twentieth century, the series books were remarkably tame and included no tobacco and not the slightest hint of sex, even on the part of the villains" (Greenwald 36). Ultimately, the books were intended to reflect "good, wholesome adventure and suspense" (Herz 13).

In an earlier work on boy detective books, I noted the importance of genre to series books in general:

> Boys' and girls' sleuthing stories, in general, are designed to uphold the status quo and confirm patriarchal American values. Boy sleuth books create characters that reflect the best in boys of their time; hard-working, socially conscious, justice-oriented young men who work to right wrongs, restore order, and maintain civil peace in their hometowns and abroad.... Any other aspect of the series not designed to further the interests of justice or to aid in solving the mystery are generally dismissed. Thus dates always lead to clues, and family vacation destinations become the coincidental hideout of a nefarious gang of rogues or thieves. In a boy sleuth book, the mystery is cynosure. As such, these texts are robustly self-conscious of their genres; genre is both the means through which the boy sleuths interact with their world and their reason for said interaction ["Introduction" 7–8].

The broad and distinctive absence of sexuality, violence, personal (internalized) conflict, and other such hallmarks of masculinized adventure tales stringently inhibits the means through which the central protagonists can express themselves and understand and navigate their worlds. The inclusion of the male dyadic relationship in these texts — so different from other, more community-oriented series books — works to further negate the possibilities for male expression, since camaraderie, group activity, and heteronormative expressions of dating (visiting the malt shop with female "chums") are all abandoned in favor of the dyadic relationship. These series thus create conditions under which these protagonist figures become wholly dependent on the other chief male peer in their lives without the methodologies through which other boys in series books articulate and communicate the various aspects of their identities that are permitted to be revealed by both generic and masculine convention. Thus technology becomes not only a means of expressing the self but also a chief way of underscoring the emotional bond present in the dyadic pair. Indeed, for each of these three pairings, technology is a common mode of expressing any sense of emotion at all. One such example is admiration. In these series, descriptions of technologies — such as vehicles — are often presented in rapturous, glowing, almost pornographic detail, as in this example from a Christopher Cool book: "[Chris] headed for a bulletlike Jaguar on the parking lot near the dormitory. The 4/2 liter engine purred like a well-fed pussycat, then broke into a full-throated jungle roar as the gleaming black Jag shot down the driveway into Madison Circle.... A leather-jacketed motorcyclist stared enviously at the sleek car" (Lancer *X Marks the Spy* 1–2, 4). Both Chris and the motorcyclist can admire technology, since it is a "guy" thing to do.

In relying so heavily upon technology as a basis for their own communication and relationship, however, these male dyadic pairings create a version of Sedgwick's triangle that both enables and transforms their duality in intriguing ways. Sedgwick argues that "an erotic triangle is likely to be experienced in terms of an explicit or implicit assertion of symmetry between genders and between homo- and hetero-social or sexual bonds" (47). "Symmetry," or commonality, according to Greif, is the basis for friendship amongst males, especially pre-marriage, young adult males who, since they are also generally post-familial, "rely a great deal on their friends," more so than at any other time during masculine psychosocial development (163). Kuzmic suggests that the main mode of communication between the rival males in any triangle reflects another of Greif's significant aspects that comprise male friendship; according to her, the "active aspect" of the triangle is based on "rivalry" or competition: "To acquire and maintain their hold on power, men are compelled to privilege their relationships with each other; but at the same time, to prove their (hetero)sexual prowess, they must engage in relationships with women" (2). In boys' series books, competition abounds, and the boys, in a very jocular manner, often spar and compete with one another. They do not do so, however, either for the benefit of or over an attendant female. Rather, competition becomes another means of communication and way of expressing affection and emotion that otherwise would go unexpressed.

As the "beloved" object of the triangle in relationship with the dyadic male pair, technology allows each boy to maintain his own sense of authority and demonstrate a mastery that is often lacking when the third fixed point of the triangle is a female. Sedgwick write that the triangle represents a desire "to consolidate partnership with authoritative males in and through the body of females" (38). Here, though, the body is cool steel, the veins wires, and the blood electricity; since the spectrum of technology is diffuse and variable, each boy is allowed mastery over his own realms. Sandy, for example, is an expert on photography and maritime technology, while Ken knows geography (especially in navigating New York City) and vehicles. Rick is a genius with electronics, while Scotty, who has spent time in the Marines, is an expert with firearms. Chris and Geronimo are both often given technological "gadgets" to use in their spy activities, though, just as often, they are given different gadgets that require their own specific expertise (Chris, for example, is fluent in over a dozen languages, while Geronimo is more competent with weaponry).

Technology, then, elevates and sustains each member of the dyad, promoting their relationship with and dependency upon one another as well as each individual member through continued demonstrations of expertise and skill. Again, this facilitates communication and admiration, one to the other, through a socially preferable means. Sedgwick writes that "men promoting the interests of men" and "men loving men" are not distinct and disconnected objectives but, rather, two loosely fixed points on a broad axis describing and encompassing male social behavior and intimacy (15). In these books, technology provides a way for each boy to do both: to promote and, yes, to love the other.

Open expressions of "love" are not common in series books, whether for other members of the group, members of heterosexual relationships, or even for the families of the series protagonists. Indeed, the most expressive characters in boys' series books are the members of these dyadic pairings. Geronimo often refers to Chris with his special nickname, *choonday*, the Apache word for "friend" (Chris's "pet name" for Geronimo is, unfortunately, "redskin," a horrible epithet that is designed to demonstrate the two boys' affection but mostly works to demarcate Geronimo as Other compared to Chris and seems appallingly out of date, even for 1967, when the first book in the series was published). At one point, Rick, facing the prospect of an extended expedition away from his family, thinks to himself: "I wouldn't want to go if Scotty weren't going along" (*Lost City* 2). Upon meeting Sandy, Ken longs to be accepted into the Allen family, and the two become such fast friends so rapidly that, at one point during their first adventure, they are amazed that they have only known each other for one day. In each series the "special" nature of the dyadic relationship is always mentioned, a type of sentimental expression not found in any other series book, boy's or girl's.

Sylvia Mieszkowski, analyzing and quoting Sedgwick, relates, "There is no fixed boundary between the accepted 'social bonds between persons of the same sex' and the repressed, denied and condemned erotic or sexual relations between men. Patriarchy's ideology ... insists on the categorical as well as essential differentiation of non-sexualised homosocial bonds on one hand and homosexual bonds on the other. In contrast to this, Sedgwick stresses 'the potential unbrokenness of a continuum'" (Sedgwick 12, 14; Mieszkowski 3). In other words, while the bonds between each dyadic pair may not reflect a repressed homosexual desire for the other, they do allow for the *possibility* of the existence of such bonds, whereas in other boys' series books, reflecting either the group sociality or the solitary individuation of a lone protagonist, the entelechy of any emotional attachments are restricted by generic and social/patriarchal conventions. The existence of such all-encompassing friendships, then, relationships that do not shy away from physical contact or emotional rejoinders (at least those couched in euphemism or related only in the individual's mind) allows for the possibility of even further emotional, psychological, or sexual bondage. It can be no coincidence that these books feature extended scenes of physical bondage between the two youths; such connectivity is only reflective of the further connections at work between the two represented males (in one notorious Ken Holt book, Ken and Sandy spend three chapters tied together; in another, Sandy uses his teeth to unzip Ken from some of his outer garments in order to free the two boys. Indeed, it is a rare edition of any of these series wherein the two members of the dyad are not somehow restrained or confined together in close, intimate quarters).

Greif writes that post-family, pre-marriage men define themselves largely through their friendships (164). If this is indeed the case, the dyadic pairings in these texts all use technology as the language of their own definition. Perhaps Heidegger was right when he noted, as Zani paraphrased it, "technology *is* us" (174). For these three pairs of male duos, technology certainly provides a more expressive mode of communication — including communication about their selves, their ambitions, and their emotions — than any other such similar characters had throughout boys' series book. Burrill writes that technology creates a space "where the digital boy can ... *prove* his manhood (and therefore his place within the patriarchy, the world of capital, and the Law) (2, emphasis original). This is certainly true. Yet in these examples, technology also creates a space where the boy can explore aspects of his manhood that the patriarchy and such other masculine institutions would normally insist be suppressed, repressed, or altogether denied existence. By creating a triangle with technology taking on the role of the beloved, Rick and Scotty, Ken and Sandy, and Chris and Geronimo have all crafted a methodology that allows them to not only enter into an unusually intense dyadic pairing with another like youth but also to express themselves — both physically and emotionally — in ways that their counterparts in other boys' series books never do. Ultimately, McKinney may have put it best when he noted that one definition of technology is anything which can provide a "means to an end" (187). In this case, the means is a triangle of emotional, psychological, and even erotic potentiality, and the end, rather than being represented by a fixed conclusion or point in the triangle, may best be seen as a beginning — the beginning of a long continuum whose road could lead just about anywhere.

Notes

1. Rick Brant books are alternately labeled "Science-Adventure Stories," "Electronic Adventures," and, ultimately, "SCIENCE Adventures." All three monikers reflect the technological focus of the series.

2. The culminating figure of the "solitary" sleuth is, of course, James Bond, who rejects socialization with other males as a general rule. (Many of Bond's male colleagues, outside of Q and M, often turned traitor, which may explain his predilection for solitude from other males.) This reinforces the notion of the solitary sleuth as anti-social and differentiated from the other representative males in their series. This remains true in boys' series books; Tom Swift engages largely with older males, while Encyclopedia Brown's "best friend" is female; his relationships with the other peer-aged males in his series are general functional or, more compellingly, antagonistic. For more on the socialization in boys' series books, see Michael G. Cornelius, "(No) Sex and (No) Violence in the Christopher Cool, TEEN Agent Series" in *The Boy Detectives: Essays on the Hardy Boys and Others*, ed. Michael G. Cornelius (Jefferson, NC: McFarland, 2010), 143–168). Specifically, see 145–148; 156–157.

3. The Ken Holt series ran for eighteen volumes from 1949 to 1963. It was created and authored by the husband and wife team of Sam and Beryl Epstein, who published the books under the pseudonym Bruce Campbell. The Rick Brant series included twenty-four volumes and was published between 1947 and 1968 (the last volume, *The Magic Talisman*, was released as a limited edition volume in 1990). The series was authored by Harold L. Goodwin and published under the name John Blaine; Peter J. Harkins co-authored the first three volumes in the series. The Christopher Cool, TEEN Agent series ran for six volumes from 1967–1969, all published under the Stratemeyer Syndicate pseudonym Jack Lancer. According to John Axe, the first three volumes were actually penned by James "Jim" Duncan Lawrence, a prolific Syndicate ghostwriter who also wrote volumes in the Hardy Boys, Tom Swift, and Nancy Drew series and who would later pen the newspaper comic strip adventures of master spy James Bond himself. Jerry Mundis wrote the next two volumes, and Richard Deming the last. For more, see John Axe, "Christopher Cool TEEN Agent: The Series and Its Cover Art" in *Susabella Passengers and Friends*, Jul 2005: 36–43.

4. Edward Stratemeyer (1862–1930) was a prolific American author of children's literature who has often been credited for ushering in the "modern" era of children's serial fiction, especially with his first well-known series, The Rover Boys (started 1899). Stratemeyer wrote and/or created some of the most famous juvenile series of all time, including The Bobbsey Twins (started 1904), Tom Swift (started 1910), The Hardy Boys (started 1927), and Nancy Drew (started 1930), among may others. Stratemeyer also founded the famous Stratemeyer Syndicate, a book packager through which he oversaw the continuance of these series and dozens more.

Works Cited

Andrade, Glenna. "Hermione Granger as Girl Sleuth." *Nancy Drew and Her Sister Sleuths: Essays on the Fiction of Girl Detectives*. Eds. Michael G. Cornelius and Melanie E. Gregg. Jefferson, NC: McFarland, 2008. 164–178. Print.

Blaine, John. *The Lost City.* New York: Grosset & Dunlap, 1947. Print.
_____. *The Rocket's Shadow.* New York: Grosset & Dunlap, 1947. Print.
Burleson, Brant. "The Experiences and Effects of Emotional Support: What the Study of Cultural and Gender Differences Can Tell Us About the Close Relationships, Emotions, and Interpersonal Communications." *Personal Relationships* 10 (2003): 1–23. Print.
Burrill, Derek A. *Die Tryin': Videogames, Masculinity, and Culture.* New York: Peter Lang, 2008. Print.
Campbell, Bruce. *The Black Thumb Mystery.* New York: Grosset & Dunlap, 1950. Print.
_____. *The Mystery of the Iron Box.* New York: Grosset & Dunlap, 1952. Print.
_____. *The Mystery of the Shattered Glass.* New York: Grosset & Dunlap, 1958. Print.
_____. *The Secret of Skeleton Island.* New York: Grosset & Dunlap, 1949. Print.
Cornelius, Michael G. "Introduction: The Nomenclature of Boy Sleuths." Ed. Michael G. Cornelius. *The Boy Detectives: Essays on the Hardy Boys and Others.* Jefferson, NC: McFarland, 2010. 1–18. Print.
Epstein, Joseph. *Friendship: An Exposé.* Boston: Houghton Mifflin, 2006. Print.
Erisman, Fred. *Boys' Books, Boys Dreams, and the Mystique of Flight.* Fort Worth: Texas Christian University Press, 2006. Print.
Gill, C. M. "Hardy Camaraderie: Boy Sleuthing and Male Community in the Hardy Boys Mysteries." Ed. Michael G. Cornelius. *The Boy Detectives: Essays on the Hardy Boys and Others.* Jefferson, NC: McFarland, 2010. 35–50. Print.
Greenwald, Marilyn S. *Secret of the Hardy Boys: Leslie McFarlane and the Stratemeyer Syndicate.* Athens: Ohio University Press, 2004. Print.
Greif, Geoffrey L. *Buddy System: Understanding Male Friendships.* Oxford: Oxford University Press, 2009. Print.
Heidegger, Martin. "The Question Concerning Technology." In *Basic Writings.* New York: Harper & Row, 1977. Print.
Herz, Peggy. *Nancy Drew and the Hardy Boys.* New York: Scholastic Books, 1977. Print.
Hruschka, Daniel. "Defining Cultural Competence in Context: Dyadic Norms of Friendship Among U.S. High School Students." *ETHOS* 37.2 (2009): 205–224. Print.
Kuzmic, Tatiana. "The Mind, the Body, and the Love Triangle in *Anna Karenina.*" *Tolstoy Studies Journal* 19 (2007): 1–14. Print.
Lancer, Jack. *X Marks the Spy.* New York: Grosset & Dunlap, 1967. Print.
McKinney, William J. "James Bond and the Philosophy of Technology: It's More Than Just the Gadgets of Q Branch." *James Bond and Philosophy: Questions Are Forever.* Eds. Jacob M. Held and James B. South. Chicago: Open Court, 2006. 187–197. Print.
Mieszkowski, Sylvia. "Impossible Passions—Shakespeare and Parker." *Deutsche Shakespeare-Gesellschaft* 1 (2003): n pag. Web. 11 Jun 2011.
Nye, Russell B. *The Unembarrassed Muse: The Popular Arts in America.* New York: Dial Press, 1970. Print.
Pitcher, Evelyn Goodenough, and Lynn Hickey Schultz. *Boys and Girls at Play: The Development of Sex Roles.* New York: Praeger, 1983. Print.
Schehr, Lawrence R. *Parts of an Andrology: On Representations of Men's Bodies.* Stanford, CA: Stanford University Press, 1997. Print.
Sedgwick, Eve Kosofsky. *Between Men: English Literature and Male Homosocial Desire.* New York: Columbia University Press, 1985. Print.
Tognoli, Jerome. "Male Friendship and Intimacy across the Life Span." *Family Relations* 29.3 (Jul 1980): 273–279. Print.
Zani, Steven. "James Bond and Q: Heidegger's Technology, or 'You're Not a Sportsman, Mr. Bond.'" *James Bond and Philosophy: Questions Are Forever.* Eds. Jacob M. Held and James B. South. Chicago: Open Court, 2006. 173–186. Print.

(Inter)Mediated Sexuality in the Science Fiction of J. G. Ballard
Clare Parody

"The great twin leitmotifs of the 20th century," argued J. G. Ballard in his introduction to *Crash!*, "are sex and paranoia" which, unsurprisingly, emerge as the central themes of his science fiction (i). Across Ballard's novels and short stories, sexually explicit content plays an important role in communicating his neurotic, entropic future visions. Anatomies of the sexualized and fetishized body, reconfigurations of sexual acts, and remappings of sexual desire define the futures his science fiction posits; at the same time, they act as prisms through which he refracts his diagnoses of the present's social and psychological pathologies. In its exploration of literal auto-eroticism, for example, Ballard's 1973 novel *Crash!* was, for Ballard, "an extreme metaphor for an extreme situation," and its presentation of characters aroused by car accidents an expression of the interrelation between technology and "our own psychopathologies" (ii, iii). This weight of meaning that the sexual explicitness of Ballard's novels carries speaks to the fact that he saw pornography as "in a sense ... the most political form of fiction, dealing with how we use and exploit each other, in the most urgent and ruthless way" (iii).

Ballard's engagement with human sexuality, meanwhile, is often bound up in science fictional dialogues with the media landscape of Britain and America in the twentieth century, in particular the pervasiveness of visual or compositely visual media (cinema, newspapers, photography, television, the internet) as a means of representing and transmitting information, to the point where the screen or the image, rather than direct experience, is our primary interface with reality. Ballard's science fiction is broadly concerned with the effects of media saturation on the individual and collective psyche. Its fictional "realms" are not only "brutal" and "erotic" (and brutally erotic), but also "over-lit"; that is, they are cultures of surveillance, of endlessly mediated experience, shaped and pervaded by technologies of spectacle, voyeurism, and exhibition

(*Crash!* iii). Ballard's morbid, affectless narrators and protagonists, who process violence and tragedy as "stylization" and "theatre," and obsessively assemble and pore over collections of photographs at the expense of real relationships, illustrate how the overexposure such societies produce makes the "real" banal, while the deferred and the reconstructed grows ever more "vivid" (*Crash!* 14, 13; "The Spectre at the Feast" 61). Ballard's characters illustrate how, in such a visual culture, the relationship between individuals and the world around them increasingly becomes conceptualized as that of the spectator to the spectacle, confusing the boundary between the private and the public, and reframing reality as performance, such that generations are conditioned into socially sanctioned voyeurism, and the acts of individuals are shaped by the assumption that someone, somewhere, is watching. Ballard's engagement with hypermediated culture, however, is often focused on and through sexual psychology and behavior. The implications of the dominance of mediation over experience are played out in paraphilic characters. Vaughan, James, and Catherine in *Crash!* and the splintered personalities populating 1970's *The Atrocity Exhibition* are voyeurs and exhibitionists. They are aroused by the spectacle of violence, and masturbate over glossy images of celebrities; their sexual desires and encounters are displaced onto and through technology.

Ballard described *Crash!* as at once a diagnosis of contemporary perversions and "the first pornographic novel based on technology," suggesting that he saw pornography as both a symptom of individual and social pathology and a powerful artistic language through which to illustrate and communicate this pathology (iii). Likewise, he seems to have seen the forms and conventions of visual media as valuable means of articulating and exploring the social diseases they cause. This idea frequently comes through in his essays. When talking of his interest as a science fiction writer in "the landscape of technology and the communications industry," Ballard emphasizes that, in his eyes, the clearest "reflections of this landscape" are to be found in photography and the cinema, and argues that *because* of how heavily it has become implicated in the filtering, distortion, and "*creation* of reality," television is paradoxically a medium that structures a true representation of the state of present reality ("Some Words" 53, 53; quoted in Bukatman 42). More significantly, however, the "brutal, erotic and overlit realms" of his science fiction are conveyed through a style that is characteristically *intermedial* (*Crash!* iii).

The term "intermedial" has been coined to refer to forms of relation between media or between texts in different media that may be characterized as dynamics of synthesis, hybridization, and cross-pollination, of one medium being made present in and through another, as distinct from the "merely additive" and combinatory relation implied by the term "multimedia" (Swalwell 47). Intermediality may take the form of a literal synthesis between two or more media forms, as when the representational technology of videogames is used to produce digital films. It may comprise play with "structural homologies" between media, such as bringing out the aural and visual dimensions of a line of text (Higgins 61). It may also take the form of the attempted replication by a work in one medium of the representational mechanisms of others, for example, an attempt to imitate visual perspective or the gaze of a camera in a text-based medium.

Ballard's science fiction is often described in critical discourse as having visual qualities. Colin Greenland suggests that when reading Ballard's novels and short stories, "pictorial comparisons are the first that come to mind," while Lynne Fox argues that "Ballard's imagination is primarily visual ... his writing expresses ideas first 'seen' in terms of shape, light, color and line rather than in the language of narrative" (92, 132). I invoke the term "intermedial" here to connect these observations to a more formal theoretical framework, and to frame Ballard's style not only as visual in a general sense, but more specifically as borrowing from and making present in his writing the forms, conventions, and representational strategies of visual media, from the collage to the photograph to the film camera.

This essay takes as its subject how Ballard uses an intermedial language to articulate, critique, and embody how media saturation rewires sexual desire and behavior. It examines the complex and necessarily often ironic relation between Ballard's formal experimentation with the structures, syntaxes, and vocabularies of visual media in his science fiction and his probing of hyper-mediated, hyper-sexualized individuals and societies, focusing in particular on two novels. Firstly, it considers sexuality in the alienating and alienated world of *The Atrocity Exhibition*, analyzing the novel's presentation of sex as spectacle, its exploration of celebrity iconography as object of desire, and how it draws on techniques of collage and photography to abstract, distort, and geometrize the eroticized body. It then turns to *Crash!* and its picture of aberrant, fetishistic sexual psychology in a society characterized by violence, nymphomania, and technophilia. This essay reads the novel as structured by the gaze, and considers how this ironizes and complicates its pathologizing of voyeurism; it also examines where photographs and films appear intradiegetically as loci of sexual acts and encounters. Finally, it approaches the novel as Ballard labeled it in his introduction—as pornography—and discusses the particular visual rhetoric of the erotic it employs as such.

The Atrocity Exhibition: *Bodies on Display*

Upon its publication in 1970, *The Atrocity Exhibition* was met with much disgust, confusion, condemnation, and even attempted censorship (Walls 75).

It is, in many ways, an alienating novel. It is filled with violent imagery (car crashes; deconstructed, dissected, mutilated bodies; bombings and bonfires) and fetishistic sexuality, and is clinically graphic in its descriptions of both. It holds nothing sacred, and undermines and perverts political ideologies and their figureheads indiscriminately, recasting them as objects of ambivalent desire and unarticulated resonance in Ballard's view of society as disintegrating, over-stimulated, and consequently affectless. The novel's moral and emotional compass is deviant, unresponsive to tragedy, and fixated upon triviality. It marks, furthermore, the zenith of Ballard's formal experimentation. Its narrative is a collection of what Ballard called "condensed novels," paragraphs elaborating single images, actions, or ideas, or sometimes just listing a set of related thoughts; these paragraphs are readable in any order and connected by the principle of association, rather than a linear thrust of plot. They cluster around and iterate key ideas, rather than representing a series of events: apocalypse; psychological breakdowns; sterile sexual encounters; celebrity culture; the perfect death; the underlying logics and geometries of the universe. The novel's approach to character, meanwhile, is "prismatic" rather than novelistic (Walls 76). That is, its notional "protagonist" is refracted into a spectrum of identities, different from chapter to chapter, loosely associated by variations on a common surname (Traven); each of "Traven's" personalities then has its own wife, all called Margaret and only trivially different, and one of a selection of mistresses, and no single character or aspect of character has any real identity beyond the symbolic.[1] Stylistically, the novel is dominated by extravagant and oblique juxtapositions and comparisons, and is made even more obscure today by its abundance of context-bound references (as Ballard acknowledged in supplying glosses and supplementary annotation in more recent editions). It is never clear what actually happens to its characters, and what is hallucination or surreal flight of fancy on their parts.

Yet the world of *The Atrocity Exhibition* is no distant and nightmarish future. Indeed, its backdrops are the mundane vistas of urban space in the second half of the twentieth century: concrete overpasses, car parks, shabby apartment blocks, streets lined with billboards. More importantly, however, the social and economic landscape of the novel is a familiar one, of capitalism and consumer culture, dominated by advertising, obsessed with technological advance and the new opportunities for gratification it brings. Moreover, it is saturated with media, subject to "an onslaught of news, advertisements, paid political announcements, fashion, living room wars, celebrity and urban sprawl" (Bukatman 35–36). Really, at heart, the world of *The Atrocity Exhibition* is barely removed from that of its readers, then and now. The novel simply exposes this normalized everyday reality as bizarre and extreme, and brings out that this reality produces fractured, compulsive psychologies and a culture at once anxious and lethargic, aggressive and detached, over-sexed and yet passionless. As Adrian Pocobelli argues, *The Atrocity Exhibition* is thus a typical disaster novel, "portray[ing] the human psyche in extreme situations" — except "the extreme situation is our everyday lives: our consciousness, the postures of our bodies, the media" (18).

As William Burroughs notes in his introduction to *The Atrocity Exhibition*, sexual psychology in particular is one of the novel's thematic cruces. The novel prods, Burroughs suggests, at the "roots of sexuality," particularly the non-sexual ones (*The Atrocity Exhibition* vii). It displays and dissects its characters' masturbatory habits, and examines their fetishistic attachments to inappropriate objects; it challenges the eroticism of spread thighs, exposed genitalia, and other such "diorama[s] of flesh" by describing them with clinical explicitness, instead sexualizing broken bodies and open wounds (*The Atrocity Exhibition* 59). Traven "eroticiz[es]" the "punctured bronchus" of Elizabeth Taylor in a fantasy of her death, but thinks of the naked body of his mistress as a "bizarre exhibit," a "sterile" collection of anatomical terms: "mons," "areola" (12, 20). The novel presents picture after picture of sexuality pushed to extremes by the deadening of response produced by overstimulation, of desire with little sense of boundary between the public and the private, the moral and the immoral, the consensual and the non-consensual. The way its characters look at and respond to each other's bodies has been rerouted by the elision of sexual desire into a hunger for and fascination with violence and technology, affected by the culture of spectacle and consumerism in which they live. Traven begins to desire the mysterious Karen Novotny when he thinks of her in terms of technology and pictures "the coil hanging in her womb like a steel foetus"; he sees his naked mistress as an inferior copy of a sex doll, comparing her body to "the texture of a rubber mannequin fitted with explicit vents," rather than the other way around (22, 20). In one of the many scenes where Traven and his mistress have sex, she looks around at the mathematical models of "interlocking cubes and cones" littering Traven's apartment, which he explains are "fusing sequences ... for a doomsday weapon"; the language of mathematics then bleeds into the novel's description of their intercourse, their bodies likewise figured as interlocking geometries (7). Climax and apocalypse are thus confused and conflated, and the locus of desire is unclear.

Intermediality, meanwhile, is one of the novel's formal cruces. Specifically, as Fox observes, and as interviews with Ballard himself bear out, "collage is the form, subject and method of enquiry" of *The Atrocity Exhibition* (72). Ballard aligns his practice in *The Atrocity Exhibition* with the "cut-up" style of Burroughs, an approach to textual heterogeneity which, as Scott Bukatman notes, draws upon the history of collage art in the early part of the twentieth century (39). Certainly, a principle of decontextualization, reconfiguration, and juxtaposition can be understood as informing the accretive, associative, episodic structure of the novel's narrative, as well as its "prismatic" rendering of character. Furthermore, the picture at the center of each "condensed novel" often has a collaged quality to its composition, incorporating disparate, incongruous, and loosely connected images juxtaposed without explanation or overlaid onto a background landscape: a "wheel-less Pontiac," a "smashed neurosurgical unit," and a Coke bottle all lying on an expanse of sand (*The Atrocity Exhibition* 45). This intermediality, I would argue, extends and enriches *The Atrocity Exhibition*'s presentation of the effect of a culture of spectacle on individuals' sexual psychology.

The primary consequence of Ballard's collage technique is to produce a text that, reflexively, functions like an exhibition. The novel arrays and displays images, moments, and people as a collection, replicating in its own structure the literal exhibitionism of its characters, who organize exhibitions both private and public: Traven's colleague Dr. Nathan displays for shadowy C.I.A. figure Captain Webster his documentation of Traven's psychological decline; the novel begins with an "annual exhibition" of paintings by patients in some unnamed asylum (1). *The Atrocity Exhibition* thus stages in its own form the transformation of the intimate and the private into spectacle and entertainment that it critiques and pathologizes in its world and characters. The novel's collage structure "exhibits" bodies, desires, and sexual acts, just as its characters display severe psychological and physical trauma as art, producing and showing "cine-films of induced psychoses" (1), "elaborate" sculptures of "conceptual car crash[es]," and "expressed brain tissue" carefully rendered in "white acrylic smears" (29).

Through this formal principle, *The Atrocity Exhibition* thus works to implicate the reader in its analysis and critique. Its collage structure repeatedly positions the reader as spectator on an exhibition of what should be private; moreover, it additionally ensures that this spectatorship is active, not passive. As Ballard himself emphasizes in the introduction to later editions of the novel, because of its associative, non-linear organization, readers may pick up the text and "simply turn the pages until a paragraph catches [their] eye"; reading is a case of browsing Ballard's collection of images as one might browse through the paintings at a gallery (vi). Not only, therefore, does Ballard's collage technique position readers as voyeuristically complicit in the erosion of privacy and relentless exposure of sexuality that preoccupy the novel, it also confers upon them a degree of moral agency and responsibility for it. *The Atrocity Exhibition* thus engages the issue that fault and perversity in the cultures of spectacle it critiques lie not only with the media for producing invasive, salacious material, but also with readers and viewers for consuming it.

Collage, however, also produces a particular *kind* of spectatorial gaze. As Bukatman puts it, collage is a language of the "blip culture" produced by media-saturated capitalist societies, in which experience is kaleidoscopic and reality mediated and remediated in bite-sized chunks from an array of different sources (39). It speaks to mediascapes dominated by "an aesthetics of the glance," characterized by exposure to a constant and multicursal flow of quantified segments or fragments of information (Hansen 135). Collage is both a way of representing the mental landscapes of individuals in such a culture, a means by which artists may, as Max Ernst observes, "fix on paper or canvas the stupefying photograph of their thoughts and desires," and a way of replicating them in the viewer, or, in this case, the reader (cited in Gee 46). Collage structures a spectatorial gaze that is wandering, distracted and distractible, tangential and shallow. Through Ballard's use of the form in *The Atrocity Exhibition*, therefore, not only are readers made voyeurs, but their voyeurism is structured as casual, glancing, disinterested and desensitized, akin to flicking through the pages of a magazine. The novel thus communicates that media-saturated societies not only produce sexual pathologies like voyeurism, they pathologize them still further, stripping voyeurism of even the passion and depth of fixation — at least an intense and genuinely felt emotion, however aberrant.

The Atrocity Exhibition also, however, engages intermedially with photography. The medium of photography is made present in the novel in two ways. Firstly, the text is full of descriptions of photographs of various types and in various contexts, from advertisements, to reproductions of paintings, to crime and accident scene documentation, to medical imaging (including X-rays). Many of the "condensed novels," meanwhile, that make up *The Atrocity Exhibition*'s collaged narrative can themselves be understood as conceived and designed as verbalized photographs. They have some of the qualities of the photographic image: minimal narrative content; an arrested temporality; significance located in the composition of lines, angles, and objects; and the emotional content and development of character non-explicit and for the most part secondary.

The Atrocity Exhibition is particularly fascinated, however, with the different ways in which a camera can transform an image, particularly of the human body. Ballard describes a picture of Elizabeth Taylor, for example, magnified such that "the wall on his [Traven's] right, the size of a tennis court, contained little more than the right eye and cheekbone," and a later a composite image of "the optimum auto-crash victim," constructed from "unidentified bodies of accident victims ... Cadillac exhaust assemblies ... [and] the mouth-parts of Jacqueline Kennedy" (13, 154). Many of the photos described in the novel, however, isolate and highlight "angles and postures," abstracting and estranging the human form (32). As verbalized photographs, meanwhile, Ballard's "condensed novels" themselves repeatedly geometrize the human body in similar ways. Both his narration and the novel's characters describe bodies in terms of planes, arcs, and diagrams, and particularly in sexual contexts, as when Traven's mistress Catherine Austin finds herself in an awkward clinch with one of his students: "The planes of his cheekbones and temples intersected with the slabs of rain-washed cement, together forming a strange sexual modulus" (33).

The imagined and verbalized photographs in *The Atrocity Exhibition* stand as a study in the distortion and deformation of the body, one that radically defamiliarizes what should seem natural, and more importantly, that deliberately plays with the line between attraction and revulsion. In the elegance of their compositional geometries, the images challenge and encourage the reader to find beauty in bone and musculature laid bare, either by the scalpel, through the violence of an explosion or car crash, or through the techniques of medical imaging; the novel asks the reader to look at Karen, for example, through "a lateral section through [her] left axillary fossa, the elbow raised in a gesture of pique," to see a fetching coquettishness in the stark lines of an X-ray (68). The compositions take the lingering *fixation* of the erotic gaze, meanwhile, to and beyond its limits. They exaggerate nudity into obscene and grotesque expanses of blown-up skin; they escalate explicitness to the point of isolating and magnifying exposed genitalia and amplify the penetrative nature of the gaze *ad absurdum*, giving it access all the way to internal organs. The text's series of described photographs thus reconfigures the human body as erotic site/sight, reframing and estranging the normalized conditions of desire, rendering grotesque socially acceptable softcore conceptualizations of the erotic, and displacing attraction and arousal onto extremity, abnormality, and brutality.

One of the primary fissures in the human sexual psyche *The Atrocity Experiment* explores, however, is a desire for celebrities. The novel is full of references to and representations of contemporary media sex symbols, from Jackie Kennedy to Marilyn Monroe to Ronald Reagan. Throughout, Ballard positions the orientation of sexuality towards public figures as a disease of media saturation and a pathological form of desire, perhaps most clearly in the "condensed novel" "Why I Want to Fuck Ronald Reagan," a fictional scientific study of sexual responses to the then Presidential candidate. Erotic fantasies of Reagan are presented in the language and framing of psychiatric diagnosis, and thus constructed as paraphilic; it is repeatedly implied, however, that it is specifically the fact that this desire is mediated desire — produced by the media and always deferred by the media — that makes it aberrant. Arousal is presented as defined by the rhythms, forms, and images of the media landscape, and exposed in this as abnormal and surreal: the study describes masturbation to composites of "imaginary genitalia" that have been "constructed using (a) the mouth parts of Jacqueline Kennedy, (b) a Cadillac, (c) the assembly kit prepuce of President Johnson"; that is, to a jumbled collection of oversexualized and inappropriately sexualized images, with some consumerist pornography mixed in, entirely dislocated from anything resembling an actual person (167). It describes Reagan's face "superimposed" onto participants' usual sexual partners, intervening and creating distance in actual, *im*-mediate sexual relations while providing only an illusory, insubstantial substitute. The section also discusses fantasies of Reagan as "husband, doctor, insurance salesman, marriage counselor," unimaginatively echoing the tired formulae of pornography, and comprised only of "cinetized postures," empty of meaning (167). Throughout *The Atrocity Exhibition*, however, Traven and his associates think about and describe celebrities in explicit and often violently sexual terms, with particular fixation on the genitals, further emphasizing the exploitative and violative aspects of how celebrity culture makes bodies available for public scrutiny and consumption.

A further level of intermediality, however, comes into play in *The Atrocity Exhibition*'s invocations and evocations of public figures that amplifies and augments this discourse. *The Atrocity Exhibition* frequently speaks in the media language of celebrity culture; for the most part, celebrities appear in the novel simply as names and faces, staring down from billboards and up from magazine photographs, referenced often, casually, and with an assumption of familiarity in both narration and dialogue. This visual and verbal language of shorthand, name-dropping, posturing, and faux-candidness encapsulates the paradoxes and fault lines in the media construction that is the modern celebrity: ubiquitous yet remote, overexposed yet fundamentally unknowable, repeated yet never really articulated, intense and multifaceted personal and cultural significance ascribed to and projected onto it, yet in itself ultimately somewhat depthless and meaningless. In *The Atrocity Exhibition*, this discourse is woven into the casual violence and obscenity of the novel's narration and descriptions, their hallucinatory drifting between the real and the unreal, and their distracted, desensitized gaze. The sexual fixation with celebrities the novel critiques is thus further brought out as shallow, simulacral, invasive, unrequited and unrequitable, founded on illusion and voids of meaning.

Thus *The Atrocity Exhibition* uses an intermedial style, borrowing the representational techniques of collage and photography and the discourses of celebrity culture to articulate a layered, reflexive exploration of the fissures in human sexuality produced by a hyper-mediated culture. This exploration is only one part, however, of a novel preoccupied with social and psychological apocalypse more broadly. In *Crash!*, written five years later, Ballard's engagement with the impact of technology on society and the individual is almost entirely focused through sex.

Crash! *The Voyeur's Gaze*

Crash! develops *The Atrocity Exhibition*'s embryonic discourse on literal auto-eroticism into an extended exploration of sexuality oriented entirely towards the car and the car crash. It centers around the character of Vaughan, a television scientist whose life is propelled by the desire to die in a car collision with Elizabeth Taylor, and a group of auto-eroticists drawn together by their fascination with him, particularly the novel's narrator, "James Ballard," his wife Catherine, and Dr. Helen Remington, who is involved in a car crash with "James Ballard" early in the novel; she survives, though her husband does not. The novel traces the development of various permutations of sexual relations between these four characters and the role of technology in them.

As Ballard put it, the novel expresses a "nightmare marriage between sex and technology," a vision of how modern technology allows us to express and "harness" our "innate perversity" (*Crash!* iii). The technology in question, however, is not only the car, so symbolically rich and polyvalent, but also media technologies. Alongside *Crash!*'s exploration of how the car and the car crash can structure and metaphorize sexual desire is an exploration of how cameras, photographs, movies, and closed-circuit television become technologies of sexual intercourse and paradigms of desire that is more detailed and focused than *The Atrocity Exhibition*'s similar thematic discourses.

Central to the novel's engagement with this theme is an examination of the impact on sexual psychology of a mediascape in which mediated sexual content is so omnipresent that viewed representations of sexual acts are a central part of individual sexual experience, a mediascape that provides consumers with what Anne Friedberg calls a "*mobilized and virtual* gaze," through which these consumers may become voyeur and vicarious participant in an array of idealized, abstracted, and fantastic sexual acts (65). At the heart of *Crash!*'s future vision is the idea of a shift in the emphasis of individual and collective sexualities away from direct physical, emotional, and sensory stimulation towards vicarious and voyeuristic desire. Sexuality within the novel is structured as much, if not more, by eroticized acts of watching and looking as by the immediate experience of intercourse, from narrator "James Ballard's" fantasies, later enacted, of watching his wife have sex with Vaughan, to Vaughan's collection of photographs of crashes and victims for the purposes of sexual gratification.

Key to the novel's engagement with this idea is the reflection and amplification of this narrative content in the formal structures of the text. The determining formal principle of *Crash!* is the gaze, in the sense that its narration and descriptions become at times as close an equivalent as is possible of the film image, an "expression of experience by experience ... an act of seeing that makes itself seen" that structures Friedberg's "mobilized and virtual gaze" (Sobchack 45). As in *The Atrocity Exhibition*, then, Ballard discusses and dissects his subject through co-opting the forms and techniques that have produced it.

Carol Clover offers two conceptualizations of the narrative gaze, the "assaultive" gaze (that which is directly and immediately perceptually present before the enacted event, simulated in the reader or viewer, that is, the gaze of the camera or the narrator) and the "reactive" or "pluperfect" gaze (that which watches an event after the fact, that is, the actual modality of the reader or viewer's gaze) (188). It is the assaultive gaze, or a verbal equivalent thereof, that constitutes the basic structural principle of *Crash!*—the first-person narrative of "James Ballard," who is at once participant in and voyeur of the events described in the novel. Ballard uses first-person not only to give readers an insight into his narrator's head, but also to provide, as the camera does, a perceptual avatar for them, an "I"/eye through which they can see the world of the text. The intermediality of Ballard's text — its textual-visual pseudo-hybridity — therefore allows him to represent simultaneously both the act of looking and the psychology of this act. This psychology is notably dominated by pure, unreconstructed and unprocessed perception. "Ballard's" narration is distinctly unreactive, functioning for the most part as a transcription of what he sees or imagines seeing, with little added commentary on or emotional response to it, occasionally filtered through extravagant similes or metaphors that hint at depths of latent, unarticulated significance, but that more often than not appear as simple observations of superficial visual similarity or congruity. "James Ballard" is a hyperbolic, caricatured avatar in many ways, but not least as an exaggeration of the author's self-confessed visual sensibilities.

This mode of narration, then, serves to illustrate Ballard's theory that cognition becomes subordinated to perception in an image-oriented culture, film and television producing "a kind of brain-bypass" ("Courting the Cobra" 23). It also allows Ballard to present what he saw as some of the consequences of this. For example, "Ballard's" narration expresses that media saturation both produces and reflects a world that, morally speaking, is "almost infantile," a world "where any demand, any possibility, whether for life-styles, travel, sexual roles and identities, can be satisfied instantly" (*Crash!* i). Structuring the novel through the concept of the gaze produces a narrative with no internal moral compass; Ballard the author is indiscernible behind (or even, at points, indistinguishable from) "Ballard" the narrator, and "James Ballard" is characteristically amoral, unconcerned with rationalizing his actions within any framework other than the geometric. "James Ballard's" perception-led narrative, therefore, is constructed as both product and cause of a world motivated by stimulation and gratification, which goes largely unprocessed and unexamined by its inhabitants, and in which most moral categories are inoperable. As Jean Baudrillard notes, for example, the concept of the taboo or the "perverse" has little meaning in the world of the novel, with every desire permissible and acceptable. Everything is viewed indiscriminately with "clinical detachment" (Ballard, quoted in Goddard 54). Over the course of the novel, "James Ballard's" relentlessly, even monotonously explicit narration of unusual and extreme sexual acts even begins to have a similar effect on the reader; personal disgust or revulsion is gradually eroded by the desensitizing effect of constant exposure to an impressive spectrum of perversions.

Equally, however, and relatedly, this narrative style can be understood as modeling the psychology of voyeurism as Ballard, for whom this sexual pathology holds much interest, understood and theorized it. In his non-fiction, Ballard conceptualizes the voyeur's eye as "bereft of emotion, [a gaze] in which all action is suspended, all drama subordinate to the endless moment of the stare" ("In the Voyeur's Gaze" 67). "James Ballard's" narration in *Crash!* can thus be read as another study in how the excesses of a media-saturated culture drive this already arguably abnormal sexual psychology to the point of pathology. The hyperbolic visuality of "Ballard's" narrative entails an obsessive focus on detail that distracts from and even arrests narrative momentum, where minute gestures are the most significant events ever registered; all feeling and response is then secondary to this (if present at all), to the point that the psyche of "James Ballard" appears wholly dominated by the endless moment of the stare. This is the future of the individual unconscious as Ballard imagines it, a "demise of feeling and emotion [that] has paved the way for all our most real and tender pleasures," and a gradual restructuring of the psyche such that "elements from the margins of one's mind — the gestures of minor domestic traffic, movements through doors, a glance across a balcony — become transformed into the materials of an eerie and overlit drama" ("The Innocent as Paranoid" 91, 93).

The greatest extent of Ballard's pathologizing of voyeurism, furthermore, is the intimation that within the sort of media-saturated culture that sustains, normalizes, and even relies upon it (that is, the world of *Crash!*), the concept of voyeurism is in fact no longer really applicable, because the conceptual opposition of the private and the public on which the idea of voyeurism is necessarily predicated is only ambivalently perceived. The indiscriminate chronicling and dissemination of information from all spheres of experience in print and other news media work to erode this boundary while superficially sustaining it, where journalists emphasize the "private" nature of their "scoops" as a primary point of interest. Film and other visual media, meanwhile, structure a deferred voyeuristic experience that, by dint of being socially sanctioned, can only ambivalently be called such. As Vivian Sobchack notes, the nature of the film image itself confuses the distinction between the private and the public, insofar as it "transposes what would otherwise be the invisible, individual, and intrasubjective privacy of direct experience as it is embodied into the visible, public, and intersubjective sociality of a language of direct embodied experience" (42). Certainly, in the world of *Crash!*, the concept of privacy seems inoperable. As Baudrillard puts it, it is a "world without secrets," in which nothing is hidden, all is accessible and on display, from the mind to the body, and "James Ballard's" narrative is, I would argue, crucial to illustrating this (190, translation mine). The lack of moral or intellectual rationalizations of what "Ballard" sees suggests that he has no self- or culturally-imposed restraints on what he is willing to watch, and similarly that there is nothing he would hide from the reader (the fact that the novel's subject sits far outside the margins of socially acceptable sexual content suggests the same). Furthermore, the first-person narrative form in itself contributes to the impression of a "world without secrets," in that it dismantles perhaps the only boundary preserved in such a culture of display: the privacy of the inner self. This is only reinforced by the extreme visual bias (and hence alignment with the film camera, as Sobchack conceptualizes it) of the narration, in that, as Bukatman observes, it suggests "Ballard" to have no real ego to speak of, no inaccessible consciousness, just a perceptual apparatus that may be freely reproduced and co-opted (41).

Embedded within this basic narrative structure, however, is also a range of instances of Clover's "pluperfect" gaze, constant diegetic references to and descriptions of, in particular, photographs and short films. "Ballard" tells us that Vaughan has, for example, "compiled an elaborate photographic dossier" of certain car crash victims, outlining for us an inventory of images of wreckages, wounds, reconstructive surgery, and prosthetic limbs (*Crash!* 78). In his job as a "TV scientist," meanwhile, Vaughan re-enacts and films actual, theoretical, and idealized collisions, meticulously constructing and recording the perfect crash, right down the pattern of the blood-splatter on the victim's forehead (87). This is a form of intermediality common in literature since the advent of optical recreations, where intra-textual references to other media and works within them are used to metaphoric or metonymic effect (usually, either to analogize cognitive or perceptual processes, or to connote experiences or cultural and aesthetic discourses associated with them). Specifically, I would argue that the significance of these films and photographs within the text lies in their explicit association with sexual desire — in particular, in the fact that not only is their content sexualized (if not always obviously or traditionally sexual), but the acts of looking at and recording them are framed as erotic experiences.² "Ballard" perceives, for example, a homoerotic dimension to viewing them alongside Vaughan, thus implying that viewing them constitutes a quasi-sexual act. Furthermore, he experiences the sexual content of the images vicariously, noting, for example, how the nipple of a woman "seemed to extrude itself into [his] mouth," to the point that the fictions and representations created by Vaughan come to "overlay" "Ballard's" sexual response to his wife Catherine, more powerful than immediately felt sexual contact (81, 89). This functions for Ballard as an extension of *Crash!*'s exploration of how, in a world in which a significant proportion of any individual's sexual contact is mediated, sexuality increasingly becomes simulacral, oriented toward the sexual image rather than direct sexual experience. It forms part of and reinforces the same discourse structured by the creation of a narrator who is both a compulsive fantasist (and who shows no signs of distinguishing between fantasy and reality; certainly, the narrative barely differentiates them, switching between the two levels with minimal framing devices) and obsessed with cataloguing the geometries and composition of every body and conjunction of bodies he sees or in which he participates, and a protagonist fixated upon the idea of achieving a sexualized car crash with Elizabeth Taylor (perhaps the clearest expression within the novel of sexual desire entirely deferred onto the image).

Peter Nicholls argues, however, that "Ballard's triumph in *Crash!* ... is to have correctly analysed the disease from within, while simultaneously being its most obvious symptom" (31). Indeed, perhaps what is ultimately most striking about the intermediality of Ballard's text is that it stands as an example of such representations of sex, the consumption of which it analyzes. *Crash!* is not only a novel "about" pornography, it is a novel that its author has explicitly designated as pornographic; as I already noted in the introduction to this essay, Ballard argues that *Crash!* is "the first pornographic novel ... based on technology" (*Crash!* iii). Sexual content within the narrative is overwhelmingly dominant, while the quasi-visual, perception-led mode of representation, and the corresponding banality and transparent referentiality of Ballard's language, help construct this content as nothing more than literal representations of sex for the sake of representing sex.³

Immediately, this generic classification has the effect of implicating the reader in the novel's presentation of image-oriented sexualities, in that it necessarily constructs the reader as a consumer of pornography just as much as "James Ballard." Any critical analysis of "Ballard's" actions is thereby compromised, although by no means precluded. The heavy visual bias of *Crash!*'s narrative only reinforces and enables this, in imitating the camera's "expression of experience by experience" and correspondingly inducing in the reader the film viewer's more immediately, unreconstructedly perceptual processing of this expression. This is central to the novel's articulation of Ballard's insistence that the violent, degenerate, hypersexualized world of *Crash!* is not "an imaginary disaster, however imminent, but ... a pandemic cataclysm" affecting us all, right now (*Crash!* ii). However, recognizing Ballard's belief, noted above, that pornography is "the most political form of fiction," Ballard's decision to write a "pornographic novel" may also be understood as a means of exploring and representing such social and psychological constructions of sexuality as feed into and are influenced by the paradigms and traditions of pornographic fiction.

This negotiation of form and theme principally takes place on the level of the text's visual imagination. Pornography can be said to have a generic identity in that associated with the term is a particular visual rhetoric, a repertory of images assumed to be arousing: particular colors of skin or hair, facial expressions or sexual positions, physical proportions and bodily modifications. As Patrick Hudson notes, however, the visual rhetoric of *Crash!*'s sexual content deviates from contemporary generic norms, "contrast[ing] 'normal' sexual signals — lingerie, nudity, arousal — with signs that seem grossly inappropriate — cars, violence, evidence of violence" (57). This is a key aspect of *Crash!*'s depiction of the reconstruction of collective and individual sexuality. The precise make-up of pornography's generic syntaxes is heavily culturally dependent, and as such indexes and reflects socially acceptable paradigms of sexual desire and sexual behavior, and the cultural mores and contexts that have produced them. In choosing to write within this genre, therefore, and produce his own visual rhetoric of the erotic, Ballard is able to articulate changes in these contexts and paradigms by illustrating their effects on the culture's visual semiotics of arousal.

The clearest example of this is, of course, the eroticized inscription on the bodies of the novel's characters of the confusion within the world of *Crash!* between sex and violence, and the increasing displacement of sexual desire from the flesh onto the machine (a more efficient, elegant, and extreme way of achieving the desired gratification and stimulation). Mid-coitus, for example, "James Ballard's" thoughts are constantly occupied with finding formal congruities between the bodies of his partners and the bodies of the cars they fuck in, "slender membranes ... reflected in the glass dials of the instrument panel ... plastic laminates ... the same tones as [Helen's] pubic hairs," to the point that it becomes unclear whether his partners' bodies are arousing in their resemblance to cars, or vice versa, or even if the car is arousing in itself (63). As Baudrillard notes, meanwhile, throughout *Crash!* familiar erogenous zones are replaced with "symbolic wounds" on a body "confused with technology in its violent and violating aspects": wounds; scars; deformed, amputated, or prosthetic limbs; or any other evidence of literal and conceptual collisions between the body and technology are refigured as erotic (184, translation mine). This is epitomized in "Ballard's" fixation with the mutilated body of Gabrielle, the "deep buckle groove [and] corrugated skin" of her scars "more exciting [to him] than the membrane of a vagina" (146).

Conclusions

In *The Atrocity Exhibition* and *Crash!* Ballard explores how human sexuality is configured and reconfigured by technology and by media saturation. The novels present a picture of how technophilia and a culture of spectacle influence how people desire each other's bodies, the acts and objects they take pleasure in, and the ways in which they touch and look at each other (or not, as the case may be). Both novels do so in a language that borrows heavily from the representational techniques and conventions of visual media, finding verbal equivalents for the eye of the film camera, the associative, conductive logic of the collage, and the freeze-frame of the photograph. This formal intermediality occasionally augments and extends the novel's thematic discourses, sometimes adding a layer of irony and hypocrisy, but most importantly, repeatedly works to make the reader complicit in the social and cultural diseases the novels diagnose. This is significant in science fiction novels that are less extrapolations from the present and more slight exaggerations, keenly aware that the pathologies and fissures they represent are present realities as much as future possibilities.

Notes

1. For convenience, this essay will consistently use the name Traven to refer to the protagonist of the novel, rather than switching between the multiple names he is given throughout the novel.
2. This runs contrary to Baudrillard's assertion that "the position of Vaughan [as a photographer] is never that of the voyeur or the pervert" and insistence that the primary function of Vaughan's dossiers is to reinforce the novel's presentation of a "world without secrets"; however, I would argue that this assessment misunderstands how far the novel's dismantling of the concept of privacy is related to its sexual themes (190, translation mine).
3. In 1996, David Cronenberg scripted and directed a film adaptation of *Crash!* to critical acclaim. The movie is in many respects an insightful interpretation of the novel's themes and methods, and offers an expert expression of the novel's visual symbolism, constructed around an elegant and precise play of reflections and color correspondences between the gleaming cars and the actors' bodies. Notably, however, it is significantly less sexually explicit than Ballard's novel. Its most profound resonance with its source is thus inadvertent — the act of cross-media translation standing as an illustration that the prurient, morbid, invasive gaze of the film, television, or closed-circuit television camera has the further sin of hypocrisy, filtered and censored by pretences of prudery. In this, furthermore, the adaptation brings out that *Crash!*, and to a

lesser extent *The Atrocity Exhibition*, demonstrate that the hybridity of Ballard's intermedial language is in itself a powerful tool for unpacking and exposing our hyper-mediated, hyper-sexualized culture, rather than simply a means of borrowing the tools of visual media. It is only through finding verbal equivalents for these visual tools that Ballard is able to deal in a degree of sexual explicitness that allows him to critique this hypocrisy in the modern media gaze and expose the violence and salaciousness it dissembles. The fact that this makes him somewhat complicit in this hypocrisy is, perhaps, a fittingly Ballardian irony.

WORKS CITED

Ballard, J. G. *The Atrocity Exhibition*. 1970. London: HarperCollins, 1993. Print.
———. *Crash!* 1973. London: Vintage, 1995. Print.
———. "Courting the Cobra." *A User's Guide to the Millennium: Essays and Reviews*. Ed. J. G. Ballard. London: HarperCollins, 1998: 23–24. Print.
———. "In the Voyeur's Gaze." *A User's Guide to the Millennium: Essays and Reviews*. Ed. J. G. Ballard. London: HarperCollins, 1998: 65–9. Print.
———. "The Innocent as Paranoid." *A User's Guide to the Millennium: Essays and Reviews*. Ed. J. G. Ballard. London: HarperCollins, 1998: 91–98. Print.
———. "Some Words about *Crash!*" *Foundation* 9 (1975): 44–54. Print.
———. "The Spectre at the Feast." *A User's Guide to the Millennium: Essays and Reviews*. Ed. J. G. Ballard. London: HarperCollins, 1998: 59–61. Print.
Baudrillard, Jean. "*Crash!*" *Science Fiction* 1 (1984): 184–192. Print.
Bukatman, Scott. *Terminal Identity: The Virtual Subject in Postmodern Science Fiction*. Durham: Duke University Press, 2005. Print.
Burroughs, William. Preface. *The Atrocity Exhibition*. By J. G. Ballard. London: HarperCollins, 1993. Print.
Clover, Carol J. "The Eye of Horror." *Viewing Positions: Ways of Seeing Film*. Ed. Linda Williams. New Brunswick: Rutgers University Press, 1994: 184–230. Print.
Friedberg, Anne. "Cinema and the Postmodern Condition." *Viewing Positions: Ways of Seeing Film*. Ed. Linda Williams. New Brunswick: Rutgers University Press, 1994: 59–83. Print.
Fox, Lynne. "The Influence of Surrealist Art in the Novels of J. G. Ballard." Diss., University of Kent, 1992.
Gee, Malcolm. "Max Ernst and Surrealism." *Surrealism: Surrealist Visuality*. Ed. Silvano Levy. Edinburgh: Keele University Press, 1997: 45–56. Print.
Goddard, James. "Ballard on *Crash!* Answers to Some Questions." *Cypher* 10 (1973): 53–4. Print.
Greenland, Colin. *The Entropy Exhibition: Michael Moorcock and the British "New Wave" in Science Fiction*. London: Routledge, 1983. Print.
Hansen, Miriam. "Early Cinema, Late Cinema: Transformations of the Public Sphere." *Viewing Positions: Ways of Seeing Film*. Ed. Linda Williams. New Brunswick: Rutgers University Press, 1994: 134–52. Print.
Higgins, Hannah. "Intermedial Perception or Fluxing Across the Sensory." *Convergence: The International Journal of Research into New Media Technologies* 8 (2002): 59–76. Print.
Hudson, Patrick. "Stress Deformations: A Review of *Crash!*" *The Zone* 6 (1997/8): 56–7. Print.
Nicholls, Peter. "Jerry Cornelius at the Atrocity Exhibition: Anarchy and Entropy in *New Worlds* Science Fiction 1964–1974." *Foundation* 9 (1975): 22–44. Print.
Pocobelli, Adrian. "'Pre-Uterine Claims': Cultural Contexts and Iconographic Parallels in Ballard's *The Atrocity Exhibition*." *New York Review of Science Fiction* 194 (2004): 18–21. Print.
Sobchack, Vivian. "Phenomenology and the Film Experience." *Viewing Positions: Ways of Seeing Film*. Ed. Linda Williams. New Brunswick: Rutgers University Press, 1994: 36–58. Print.
Swalwell, Melanie. "New/Inter/Media." *Convergence: The International Journal of Research into New Media Technologies* 8 (2002): 46–56. Print.
Walls, Richard. "Animated Artifacts: On *The Atrocity Exhibition*." *Science Fiction Eye* 8 (1991): 75–77. Print.

Human, Alien, Techno — What Next? Evolutionary Psychology, Science Fiction and Sex
Sherry Ginn

To reiterate what my collaborator Michael G. Cornelius notes in his introduction to this collection, "the construct of 'science fiction' itself is something of a paradox" (13). The word "fiction" signifies fantasy, the imaginary, the invented, that which is divorced from "reality." Fiction has always spoken to and explored what is considered to be "reality," but in its very construction one sees the seeds for a departure from the tangible into realms that exist beyond this real world. On the other hand, "science" concerns knowledge grounded in actuality. Science is the systematic study of the material world; this knowledge is gained through observation, experimentation, and the judicious recording and interpretation of reality and fact. Taken together, then, these two words create that aforementioned oxymoron: "science fiction," which, for all intents and purposes, as Cornelius points out, could be translated into "real unreality," or less literally, "unreal reality." Unlike fantasy, which creates entirely new realms of possibility, science fiction constructs its possibilities from what is real or from what is possible. As Cornelius observes:

> The fact that science fiction and its most common manifestations — space flight, technology, alien realms — are so connected to the future, and to our visions and re-visions of the future, suggests that the genre is concerned not with what is *un*real, but rather with what *may* be real, or may soon be real. The flights of fancy that govern science fiction are grounded in the tangible, in the realm of what is possible, real, hoped for, and feared [13–14].

As this study has demonstrated, one aspect of human behavior that must be included "in the realm of what is possible, real, hoped for, and feared" is sex. Many critics have noted that science fiction, far from being concerned with lofty visions of the future, is truly about the time and place in which it is constructed, and thus one could artfully trace the history of human sexuality through an exploration of the literature of science fiction. Such a thoroughgoing examination is beyond the scope of this essay; however, I will attempt to set in motion one means of such an exploration by examining the ways in which sexuality is described and portrayed in several twentieth and twenty-first century print and visual examples. In order to do so, I will endeavor to follow in the footsteps of Cornelius's introduction, by generically focusing on the "real unreality" that science fiction itself both posits and promises; however, unlike my collaborator, whose work concentrates a bit on the more fictive elements in reading science fiction, this essay will use a more scientifically-derived tool — the lens of evolutionary psychology — as a methodology to scrutinize not only the ways in which corporeal sexuality manifests itself in the genre of science fiction but also as a means to elucidate the ways in which "reality" — or perceptions of such — generically intercede with unreality in these works as well.

A Short Lesson on Sex and Evolutionary Psychology

Psychology is defined as the scientific study of behavior and mental processes. Explanations for these behaviors and mental processes arise from a number of perspectives, and one such perspective emphasizes evolution. Evolutionary psychology indicates that behaviors and mental processes that increase the probability of an organism's survival will be selected, meaning that the organism will survive to reproduce and the traits that aided in that survival will be transmitted to the next generation. One of the behaviors which evolutionary psychologists study centers on reproduction, attempting to explain the differing sexual behaviors displayed by men and women in terms of evolution (Peplau).

According to evolutionary psychologists, men and women have different mating strategies. For example, some men and women display jealousy toward their partners, yet men and women display differences in the types of jealousy they exhibit. Men are more likely to be jealous of *sexual* infidelity in their partners, whereas women are more likely to be jealous of *emotional* infidelity. In other words, men are more likely to be jealous if their lovers engage in sexual activity with another person, and women are more likely to be jealous if their lovers develop an emotional attachment to another person. Evolutionary psychologists, such as David Buss and his associates, propose that this jealousy stems from evolutionary forces that dictate mating strategies (Buss, Larsen, Westen and Semmelroth; Buunk, Angleitner, Oubaid, and Buss).

Evolutionary psychologists also suggest that men and women have different strategies with respect to reproduction (Myers). Because men produce millions of sperm cells in each ejaculate, but only one is necessary for fertilization, it is in a man's evolutionary interests to impregnate as many females as possible. This ensures that some of his offspring will reach the age of maturity and his genes will be transmitted to future generations. Men thus have little "energy" invested in their offspring. Women, on the other hand, only carry one offspring (normally) at a time, and it is in her best interest to ensure that that one offspring survives to maturity so that it can transmit her genes to future generations. Because women invest more "energy" in their offspring's survival, women are motivated in different ways than men in relation to reproductive behavior. Men want to mate with as many women as possible to increase the odds that one offspring will survive to maturity. Women, on the other hand, want to mate with one man who will help them raise and protect their offspring so that the offspring can reach maturity. Although any given woman might not know who the father of her child is, she will always know that her offspring is her own. Until recently, men could not reliably know that a woman's children are his; hence different reasons for jealousy. If she is sexually unfaithful, then her offspring might not be his, and he is raising a child not his own. If he is emotionally unfaithful, he might leave her, which would leave her and her child undefended, rendering them unsafe in an unsafe environment. She will also lose her mate's resources and his paternal investment (Buss).

However, it must be noted that this process occurs at an unconscious level. Our natural desires are simply our genes' way of making more genes, ensuring that humans and those genes survive into the future (Dawkins). Such a theory might posit that genes will do *anything* in order to survive, including coding for sexual preferences and emotional expression. Thus, men generally prefer to mate with women whose physical attributes, such as youthful faces, suggest fertility, whereas women prefer to mate with men who have the resources, such as wealth and power, necessary to provide for offspring. These behaviors were coded into human genes and passed through myriad generations, ensuring not only human survival, but genetic survival as well. Because humans are coded for survival and our genes will do anything to survive, science fiction provides a means by which we can speculate about the ways in which our genes will ensure this. Thus science fiction can posit how human beings will survive as a species; what human beings will be willing to do to survive as a species; who we will be willing to do it with; whether we actually have a choice; and what the results will be.

Sex of the Biological Variety

Although this is a very brief description of evolutionary psychology and its tenets on human mate selection and reproduction, the theory can be used to delve into many of the sexual relations depicted in science fiction, both literary and cinematic. This is especially true of post-apocalyptic science fiction that envisions a dystopian future. In these nightmarish visions, the strongest people, usually men, control valuable resources, such as food, water, territory, and weapons. The strongest often also control sexual access to both male and female slaves and subordinates. Sexual access may be consensual (if one can consider the powerless as able to give consent), or it may not, with women and children being victimized by sexual predators. Men are also victimized; however, rape of men by men could more readily be explained in terms of domination, feminizing the victims and making them more easily controlled. Reading or viewing this type of science fiction can be disturbing, as sexual violence occurs as a means of control in addition to a means of reproduction. Thus, these stories provide support for evolutionary psychology's suppositions that men can, and will, mate with multiple sexual partners.[1]

One powerful example of such a post-apocalyptic narrative can be found in Harlan Ellison's novella *A Boy and His Dog* (1969). Set in the 2020s, the text follows the adventures of a young boy named Vic and his telepathic dog, Blood, survivors of the Third World War. Vic relies on Blood's keen sense of smell to locate females with whom he can copulate, often doing so against their will. There are very few women left, and they are difficult to find, hence Vic's use of Blood. Vic must also use Blood's keen sense of smell to escape from the rover gangs who rape young boys when they can find them. Vic never says in the novella whether he has been raped, although he does say that he has not been averse to engaging in homosexual activity in the past. These statements indicate that Vic wants to engage in sexual activity, and while he prefers female partners, he will take what he can get. The film based on this novella is more explicit about Vic's sexual activities. When he discovers a young woman raped by a roverpak, his only comment is, "Why did they have to cut her? She could've been used two or three more times" (*A Boy and His Dog*). In both the film and the novel, Vic tells Quilla June that she might as well not fight because he is going to do it regardless. As a matter of fact, he threatens to shoot her leg, telling her she'll still "get screwed just the same" (34).

Other examples exploring sexuality in a post-apocalyptic future include novels such as Margaret Atwood's *The Handmaid's Tale* and Octavia Butler's *Lilith's Brood* (the Xenogenesis Trilogy), as well as television series such as *Terra Nova*, *Falling Skies*, and *The Walking Dead*. In *The Handmaid's Tale* (1986), set in the post–United States Republic of Gilead, women have four roles: wife, handmaid, servant, or prostitute. Handmaids are assigned to a married couple and serve as sexual surrogates for the wives: they have sexual relations with the husband while the wife's participation in the process is passively holding the handmaid's hands as she reclines in the wife's lap. Atwood's Gilead reflects a conservative religious culture in which women are not allowed to read or write and are expected to fulfill their religiously sanctioned role of reproduction. Although men in this society are also only supposed to copulate for procreative purposes, the novel exposes the hypocrisy of the men in Gilead by showing them frequenting prostitutes and even engaging in sexual relations with their handmaids outside of the Ceremony, sometimes clandestinely and sometimes with their wives' consent. The handmaids also have sexual relations with the husbands outside of Ceremony and with other men.

This novel can be read as an example of the sexual strategies employed by men and women in terms of sexual selection. According to Darwin, sexual selection has two forms. The first involves competition for a mate: as members of the same sex compete with each other, the competition's outcome means that the victor has greater access to females. The second form involves preference for a mate: members of one sex choose a mate based on their preferences for particular qualities in that mate. The men in the novel wish to copulate with a variety of women. Indeed, one character states that nature made men that way, hence the need for prostitutes who are readily available for sexual congress whenever the male wishes it (270). The women also wish to copulate with a variety of men, albeit without the knowledge of their partners. Such behavior is perfectly natural, according to evolutionary psychologists. Because women invest a tremendous amount of energy in pregnancy, lactation, and nurturance, they are motivated to select a male who will commit to a long-term relationship with them, as that is the best way for the woman to ensure that her offspring survive to maturity. However, women also want to mate with the best *possible* male, and that might not be the one with whom she is partnered. Hence, as Atwood demonstrates, a woman's optimal strategy might be to marry one man who will provide her children with food and security until their maturity, but continue to engage in sexual relations with other, more (genetically) desirable men, to ensure that her children are best able to adapt to their environment. In *The Handmaid's Tale*, the novel's protagonist, Offred, either has sex with, or is offered sex with, several men. Her fertility is not in question, as she had a child prior to events in the story. Knowing that she is fertile prompts these offers; Serena Joy, the wife in the story, seems perfectly willing to have Offred impregnated by any man as long as the child can be passed off as her husband's. Such a strategy would serve Offred's reproductive future, whereas it would undermine the Commander's, as he would be nurturing a child who is probably not his biological child.

In the TNT television series *Falling Skies* (2011–present), humanity has been invaded and virtually exterminated by a race of beings whose identity and agenda are unknown. Human children are kidnapped by the aliens and implanted with a device that allows them to be controlled by a group of aliens the surviving humans refer to as "Skitters," spider-like, biological entities. Certain scenes within Season One hint that these "Skitters" might have once been human or another subjugated species of the "Mechs," the giant, mechanical aliens, but indicate that the "Skitters" view their human captives as children. As in most post-apocalyptic fiction, adversity brings out the worst in some humans, and *Falling Skies* is no exception. The first season episode "The Armory" finds the human protagonists chancing upon a group of marauders, led by a miscreant named Pope. At the end of the episode a young woman named Maggie, who is supposedly a member of Pope's gang, kills two of the gang and intimates that they had kidnapped and raped her for some time prior to the events occurring in this episode. Believing her to be reconciled to her fate, the gang had begun to trust her with weapons, much to their ultimate regret. In *Falling Skies* the alien invaders serve as a catalyst for black-and-white delineations of "good" and "bad," with any given survivor having to choose on which side he or she will fall, attempting to save humanity by grouping together for mutual support and defense, or preying upon their fellow beings in any way possible in a bid to survive.

Octavia Butler's *Xenogenesis Trilogy* may also be used as an example of post-apocalyptic fiction and a proposal of how humankind will respond to a threat of extermination. In this case, however, the extermination of humankind came at the hands of humankind, and the alien protagonists, the Oankali, have taken the surviving humans onto their space ships. The Oankali's *raison d'être* is to sample the genetic material of other species, but to do so in a way that is beneficial to themselves as well as their partners in "trade." The Oankali are able to extract the genetic material of those species with whom they "trade" and in the process repair and refine the genetic material. For example, they are able to cure humans of various diseases to which they are susceptible, such as sickle cell anemia, cancer, neurofibromatosis, and heart disease. Such manipulations make the humans better as a species, and yet many humans are frightened of and spurn the advances of the Oankali. For their part the Oankali wish to mate with humans, whom they consider to be extremely attractive — so attractive, in fact, they consider themselves to be under the humans' spell. In actuality the Oankali do not physically mate with the humans, not in the sense of having sexual intercourse (at least not as we understand it). Yet they do have sensory appendages that are capable of interacting with their human mates, and the resultant experience is extremely pleasurable. A specific type of Oankali, an ooloi, is actually required for the experience to occur, particularly if a child is desired. The child then possesses a combination of human and Oankali traits and is considered to be a "construct." One consequence of mating with an Oankali, however, is that humans no longer have any desire for contact — physical contact — with another human. Thus, the Oankali allow humans to survive and to breed; however, not all humans wish to breed with the aliens. As a matter of fact, they are so adamant about not breeding with the Oankali that they become "Resistors" and make war on those who accept the Oankali. Many of the Resistors depicted in the three books of the trilogy are extremely violent, willing to kill any humans that associate with the aliens. Some of the Resistors will also rape human women when they find them alone and unprotected, a testament to the biological imperative to mate and the psychological imperative to hurt and harm others.

Evolutionary psychology is not just for the apocalypse; it can also be used to analyze the sexual activity of characters in other forms of science fiction. Indeed, using evolutionary psychology as a methodology to read the changing sexual mores of science fiction enhances the astounding social and cultural changes that science fiction so capably reflects, especially over the last fifty years. For instance, the three-part *Farscape* (1999–2003) episode "Look at the Princess" is one such example. In this episode the living space ship Moya inadvertently enters space around a Royal Planet at the time of the Princess' ascension to the throne ("Look at the Princess, Part 1: A Kiss is but a Kiss"). The crew travels to the planet to trade for goods and arrive in time for the many celebrations in honor of Princess Katralla's birthday and ascension. Scientists on this planet have created an elixir which can identify a genetically compatible match for reproduction. The elixir is placed on the tip of the tongue, and the two interested parties kiss. If they are genetically compatible, their elixir tastes sweet. Thus, the elixir completely eliminates the guess work involved in choosing a mate with whom to procreate. Unfortunately for the Princess, her DNA has been ruined. There are no compatible males on her planet with whom she can procreate, and in order to inherit the throne she must be able to bear children. If she is unable to find a compatible male by the time of her birthday, then her brother, Prince Clavor, who is responsible for her condition, will inherit the throne and rule as Regent (in this society the throne can only be held by a woman, with her consort serving as Regent). Katralla decides to test John Crichton, a human man stranded in this part of the universe. Much to her delight, and his surprise, they are genetically compatible. Crichton is then forced to marry the Princess in order to save his life (Simpson and Thomas).

Several interesting notions can be observed in this episode with respect to sexual selection and mating. As noted, sexual reproduction is not left to chance. When any individual on the planet wishes to reproduce, s/he simply tests another's saliva for a genetic match. This does not mean that people do not enjoy sexual congress with each other, as evidenced by Dregon's obvious infatuation with Aeryn Sun. In addition, Councilor Tyno is in love with the

Princess, and she with him. She wants to marry him, but as all the men on their planet, he is genetically incompatible with her. She is willing to marry him, even though she might lose her throne. Yet he is unwilling to allow her to make the sacrifice, especially since he knows that a 2000-year-old peace would be destroyed once her brother became Regent. Thus, Tyno's love for Katralla and his love of his planet lead him to do the noble thing: he realizes that Katralla must marry Crichton in order to ensure the continuity of their way of life. Katralla must bear a female child, who can inherit the throne and continue the Royal line. The male with whom she chooses to breed is unimportant to her Dynastic imperative. Although Crichton and Aeryn are in love with each other, she is unwilling to admit her feelings for him, even though he is willing and able to declare his for her ("Look at the Princess, Part 2: I Do, I Think"). Nevertheless Crichton's love for Aeryn does not stop him from sharing a night of sex and passion with Jena, Prince Clavor's fiancée (who is actually a spy), when she rescues him from those who are plotting to prevent his marriage to the Princess ("Look at the Princess, Part 3: The Maltese Crichton"). This episode ends with Aeryn challenging Crichton to take the test, revealing that they are genetically compatible.

Scattered throughout this trilogy of episodes are the continual visual images of Chiana and D'Argo, two members of Moya's crew, having passionate and intensely vigorous sex. Later in the series, D'Argo will increasingly fall in love with Chiana and begin to envision a life with her. He is disheartened to learn that they are not a genetic match, although Chiana tells him that their parts, the parts that give them pleasure, do match.

Aeryn Sun, on the other hand, finds the idea of developing an emotional attachment to another person, especially one who is not a Peacekeeper, to be beyond her upbringing. Aeryn was born in space. Peacekeeper soldiers are bred to fill the ranks, but we never learn if soldiers are chosen to bear children or if their pregnancies happen naturally. Aeryn does mention breeding rosters, but never explains what those actually are. Aeryn learns that she is pregnant during Season Three, but does not tell Crichton because she does not know who the father of the child is. When she finally discusses her pregnancy with him, she explains Peacekeeper reproduction briefly, telling him that a female soldier can carry a fetus in stasis for up to seven cycles (years) before the child leaves stasis, develops and is born. In *Farscape: The Peacekeeper Wars* (2004) we learn that Peacekeepers are actually human in species, but that their evolution was enhanced by a race of beings called the Idalons. One way in which their evolution was enhanced was that gestation took a matter of days rather than months once the fetus was released from stasis. These two "improvements" ensured that female soldiers were not pregnant during a military campaign and that, once in gestation, they were not out of action for very long, which could be detrimental to their unit. If Aeryn is any example, female soldiers are capable of giving birth and returning to duty immediately following the birth with no ill effects, which is exactly what Aeryn does in *Farscape: The Peacekeeper Wars*. As Crichton anxiously hovers over Aeryn during the pregnancy and tries to control her actions, she reminds him that she is only pregnant, not incapacitated.

The vision of sexuality and childbirth in the Peacekeeper universe is both repellant and attractive. Peacekeepers are freely sexual and engage in intercourse regularly. The female soldiers may or may not become pregnant. If they do, they give birth to their children, male or female, when convenient for their unit. Those Peacekeepers whose job it is to raise such children do so. Gestation is quick and childbirth is apparently painless. However, if Aeryn is an example, then she found such a life unsatisfying and unfulfilling, vowing never to bear a child or allowing it to be raised in such a way (Ginn *Our Space*). Sexuality as depicted in this trilogy of episodes illustrates ways in which a species can ensure its survival. The Sebaceans on the Royal Planet have developed a method whereby genetic compatibility is not left to chance encounters. Any given person on the planet will always know with whom they can procreate; science has thus found a way to separate reproduction from recreation. Sexual relations are engaged in for pleasure; however, males and females ultimately know exactly with whom their genes are compatible. The process of reproduction is likewise controlled within the Peacekeeper command structure. Peacekeeper soldiers may "recreate" with whomever they choose, but are generally not allowed to mate unless placed on a roster for breeding. The process is extremely efficient, designed to keep female soldiers pregnant for as short a time as possible with minimal downtime for birth. Offspring are raised in communal care and do not know their mothers or fathers.

Non-Biological Sex and Reproduction

Humans are social creatures and require companionship, even if the companion is only used for sexual gratification. This is perhaps one reason why science fiction examines human/machine sex. This topic has been explored in numerous books and films, from Ira Levin's *The Stepford Wives* (1975, 2004) to *Cherry 2000* (1987) to Joss Whedon's *Serenity* (2005). Relationships depicted in these books and films are predicated upon men's need for a subservient partner, one who does not demand attention, conversation, equality, or even an orgasm. I should point out that a woman might also appreciate a "mechanical man" who does his share of the housework, does not strike, belittle or endanger her, and provides personal companionship along with sexual gratification — all without a word of complaint.

Numerous examples of these human/machine encounters can be found in contemporary science fiction television. For instance, Security Chief Tasha Yar propositions the android Lt. Commander Data after contracting a virus that makes the *Enterprise*'s crew act "drunk" in the *Star Trek: The Next Generation* (1987–1994) episode "The Naked Now." He replies that he is programmed with more than two thousand ways of providing pleasure, and the two spend the evening together, although she later makes him swear never to mention it again. Ensign Harry Kim almost panics when the reclaimed Borg Seven of Nine says that she will copulate with him — and will not hurt him in the process — in the episode "Revulsion" from the series *Star Trek: Voyager* (1995–2001). Mr. Universe in the film *Serenity* (2005) not only has a "lovebot," but marries her in an obviously traditional Jewish ceremony. *Battlestar Galactica* (2004–2009) is replete with both male and female humans mating with male and female Cylons. Despite the "man and machine" aspect of these couplings, these matings are nonetheless heterosexual in nature and reinforce evolutionary psychology's tenet about the drive to procreate. This is especially true of the Cylon Six, whose desire to bear a child is almost pathological throughout the series.

Cross-species sexuality is generally not discussed or presented, unless both species are humanoid. The series *Babylon 5* (1994–1998) attempted to redress any potential problems related to such activity by issuing an ordinance against such behavior, recognizing that there are human beings who will be attracted to non-humanoid creatures for a variety of reasons, not the least of which might be curiosity or the threat of danger. The same might be true of "aliens" and quite a number of stories, novels, and films have explored this issue. Certainly one example of this was on *Babylon 5*, where the Narn G'Kar was sexually attracted to human women, and the human women on the station were apparently quite willing to accommodate his desire. However, in many cases, cross-species matings have deadly consequences for the human involved in the process. Examples here include any of the humans mating with the alien in the various *Species* films, and Ilia's required documentation of sexual abstinence when serving with humans in *Star Trek: The Motion Picture* (1979). One example from television occurred on *The X-Files* (1993–2002) episode "Genderbender," when a member of a mysterious group called the Kindred leaves the group to "become one of [us]" because humans can "enjoy pleasures [that the Kindred] can't" ("Genderbender"). This being can not only mate with humans, but change its sex at will to accomplish the task, thereby mating with both male and female humans. The problem is that the sexual act causes massive coronaries in the human partner. It is possible that these examples serve as evolutionary psychology cautionary tales: the exotic may be sexually alluring, but the exotic can also be deadly. Such encounters might serve the immediate purpose of sexual gratification, but not the process of sexual reproduction.

The issue of cross-species sexuality, even among humanoids, can complicate matters of reproduction. Although many sexual encounters described or depicted in science fiction occur in the pursuit of pleasure, some of these couplings lead to deeper feelings as the partners fall in love and desire children. Not every possible sexual mating, however, can result in children, since each species may have a different number of chromosomes, different base pair sequences on their DNA, or different reproductive physiology. Problems such as these have been explored in several science fiction media, such as Cylon Eight/Sharon's pregnancy on *Battlestar Galactica*.

Couples who found it easy to fall in love with one another, marry, or otherwise pair-bond often found it difficult to produce children. One example occurred on *Babylon 5*, when Delenn conceived Captain Sheridan's child. She was only able to do so after her transformation into a Human/Menbari hybrid, although the pregnancy was very difficult for her and she only bore one son during their twenty-year marriage. Another depiction of this difficulty occurred when the Trill Jadzia Dax married the Klingon Worf on *Star Trek: Deep Space Nine*. Jadzia needed to undergo genetic manipulation in order to become pregnant.

Regardless of whether these cross-species matings will result in desired children, people do get pregnant and have children in science fiction. Traditional and alternative forms of reproduction and gestation have long been explored in science fiction novels, stories, and films. Some of these depictions and descriptions are liberating, while some are enslaving. On science fiction television, reproduction is generally accomplished in the traditional fashion — the female carrying the child to term — although exceptions can be found. On *The X-Files*, Dana Scully undergoes *in vitro* fertilization, using sperm donated by her partner Fox Mulder, in an attempt to bear a child. First she is told that the attempt was unsuccessful, but later learns that she is indeed pregnant. Having been told that all of her ova were harvested for experimentation, we can only conclude that the embryo fertilized *in vitro* did, in actuality, embed in her uterus. Scully eventually delivered a son.

Voyager was the first *Star Trek* series to allow major characters to fall in love with one another, marry, and reproduce through the relationship of Tom Paris and B'Elanna Torres, although minor characters had been doing it all along. Yet it was *Star Trek: Enterprise* that more completely explored alternative forms of reproduction. Chief Engineer Charles "Trip" Tucker is impregnated in the episode "Unexpected" after an away mission to help a group of aliens known as Xyrillians repair their ship. Trip playfully flirts with his Xyrillian counterpart and they share a moment of exquisite intimacy during a work break. Upon learning that he has inadvertently become pregnant, the humans search for the Xyrillians in an attempt to learn more about the species' physiology, since Trip desperately wants to have the embryo removed. The Xyrillians express surprise that cross-species mating occurred. They remove the embryo from Trip's body and all returns to normal, although Trip is chagrined to know that he will go down in history as the first human male to become pregnant. Trip is also involved in the later episode, "Cogenitor," when the *Enterprise* encounters an alien race known as the Vissians. This species consists of three genders: male, female, and cogenitor. The cogenitors make pregnancy possible among the Vissians and are apparently passed among the Vissians whenever a male and female wish to procreate. Trip believes that the cogenitor is being exploited by its people, especially when he realizes that it has the same intellectual ability as the other members of its species. He tries to help "liberate" it from its lowly status, but only succeeds in giving it awareness with no hope. In the end the cogenitor kills itself rather than continue the existence it now believes is meaningless.

Sex of the Virtual Variety

Sexual relations have also become less and less physical as science fiction explores the possibility of engaging in sexual relations in the virtual world. The word "virtual" refers to something that is not real, though it may display qualities of the real. Virtual also means existing or "resulting in essence or effect though not in actual fact, form, or name" or existing "in the mind, especially as a product of the imagination" ("virtual"). In the field of computer science, virtual means "created, simulated, or carried on by means of a computer or computer network" ("virtual"). A computer models the physical equivalent of a real world, for example, and increasingly these worlds are interactive, allowing a user or users to engage with the simulations created in the computer space. Indeed, according to Steven Shaviro and Donna J. Haraway, these representations allow one to become beyond human, or posthuman, extending beyond one's bodies, beyond the flesh. Nevertheless, it is interesting that human beings still wish to experience the pleasures of the flesh, even when and if they do not have flesh themselves (Salter 1121).

The virtual world as we understand and use it today was conceived with the development of the first computing machines created decades ago. From the beginning, scientists and engineers proposed the theoretical possibility of creating a being that combined the physical with the cyber world. Robots, cyborgs, and androids were the result of such theorizing, and various science fiction and fantasy media, ranging from Karel Capek's *R.U.R.* (*Rossum's Universal Robots*, 1921) to Fritz Lang's *Metropolis* (1927) to Isaac Asimov's "Three Laws of Robotics" (1940, 1985) to Philip K. Dick's *Do Androids Dream of Electric Sheep?* (1968) explored the ramifications of the development of such creatures and how human beings sh/would interact with, use, and abuse them. Certainly the idea that these creatures could be used sexually was explored, along with the idea that these creatures could also use and abuse humans. Karen Blair wrote that *Star Trek: The Original Series* illustrated problems inherent with the creation of humanoid robots: "in the tradition of mermaids and other half-human, half-alien females ... [artificial life forms] are so appealing to men in fantasy because, while being clearly female, they can't be confused with a fully human other" (293). She also notes that when Gene Roddenberry proposed a new show featuring a male android, network executives balked at the idea that a male android would have sex with a human female. Such an android, Blair noted, "could be programmed for superhuman excellence and mere men would look puny and stupid by comparison" (293). Roddenberry eventually created that male android, named Data in *Star Trek: The Next Generation*, and Data, as previously noted, was fully functional.

Nevertheless, the most interesting aspect of the three sequel *Star Trek* series — *The Next Generation, Deep Space Nine,* and *Voyager* — involved the development and usage of the "holodecks." Created for recreational use by the crew, holodecks can simulate any environment desired by the user. The user can also create beings with which to interact. *The Next Generation* generally did not explore the issue of sexual relations between holodeck figures and crew members. However, this issue was broached in *Deep Space Nine*; the Ferengi Quark owned and operated a brothel, in which the sex workers were holograms, that was apparently well frequented by patrons to his bar. This aspect of Quark's was increasingly downplayed as the show's seven-year run continued. Despite the fact that holodecks require an enormous expenditure of energy, Captain Janeway authorized the establishment and maintenance of a holodeck aboard *Voyager* as a means of fostering crew morale when the starship was lost in the Delta Quadrant. Indeed, the crew eventually created an entire village where they could visit; Captain Janeway fell in love with one of the men living in the village, a side-effect to be expected when one can create one's "ideal" partner.[2]

The recent *Battlestar Galactica* spin-off *Caprica* (2009–2010) also explored the idea of virtual reality and, especially, virtual sex. Computer simulations were so advanced on *Caprica* that people could plug into a virtual world of their own or someone else's creation. Caprican society was portrayed as highly sophisticated but also decadent, and the youth were very detached and jaded — so jaded, in fact, that they spent most of their time living as their avatars in a virtual world where they could explore any type of experience, the more dangerous, decadent, and perverse the better. They might have sexual relations with anyone or anything imaginable and could explore the "reality" of death and dying in the virtual world, pushing themselves and their comrades to the limits of endurance. *Caprica* was the prequel to *Battlestar Galactica* (2004–2009), presenting the story of the origin of the Centurion Cylons and their eventual development of the humanoid Cylons — made in the image of their creator, a Caprican man named Daniel Graystone. The genesis of the Cylons' anger at their Creators lies with a teenage girl, angry at her parents and desiring revenge, named Zoe Graystone. Nevertheless, however determined the Cylons are to exterminate their makers, they are unable to do the one thing that their makers can do, and that is reproduce biologically. Wanting to become their makers, they eventually (re)create the ability to bear living children.

Conclusions

This essay has admittedly surveyed only a handful of the many science fiction works that could be analyzed using evolutionary psychology as a theoretical framework. It must be noted that each of the examples presented herein could also be analyzed using other frameworks, such as feminist theory. Furthermore, this essay is not meant to provide an argument one way or the other as to the merit of evolutionary psychology as a means of explaining human behavior. Instead, I posit that both writers and consumers of science fiction have been exposed to the tenets of evolutionary psychology over the past thirty or forty years. The fact that the stories examined in this paper can be readily analyzed using the tenets of evolutionary psychology attests to the ease with which it has entered into the popular culture.

Each of the examples used in this essay yields evidence of the use of sexual selection as a force guiding the characters' behavior. The behavior of many male characters in science fiction, such as G'Kar (*Babylon 5*), the Commander (*The Handmaid's Tale*), and Vic ("A Boy and His Dog") supports the contention that men are motivated to engage in sexual behavior with a variety of partners, regardless of whether they have emotional attachments with them. The behavior of female characters, such as Aeryn Sun on *Farscape*, supports the contention that women are *not* motivated to engage in such sexual behavior per se, but rather are motivated to form emotional attachments with partners. The examples used herein, however, just as easily yield evidence of how sexual selection does not always guide a character's behavior. Some male characters in science fiction are monogamous, such as Wash on *Firefly* and Sheridan on *Babylon 5*, or rarely engaged in sexual activity at all, such as Mal on *Firefly*. Some females are promiscuous, having sexual relations with a variety of men for a variety of reasons: in the case of Chiana on *Farscape* and Gwen Cooper on *Torchwood*, such activity was simply a choice of pleasure; for Inara Serra on *Firefly* and Echo in *Dollhouse*, promiscuous sexual activity reflected her social role; a desire for pregnancy prompted Number Six's sexual behavior on *Battlestar Galactica*; and necessity of survival did the same for Offred in *The Handmaid's Tale*. What each of the examples contained herein can tell us is that human sexual behavior is quite complicated, and that the reasons why people engage in sexual behavior are as varied as the beings who are doing the engaging. Ultimately, as science fiction tells us, sex may be depicted in ways that stretch the bonds of credulity and the fabric of imagination itself— but always, in the end, both scientifically and fictively speaking, sex remains, essentially, very, very real.

Notes

Portions of this essay were originally published in *Foundation: The International Review of Science Fiction* as "For Women It's Love, for Men It's Sex: Evolutionary Psychology Meets Science Fiction" 39.105 (Spring 2010) and in Ginn, *Power and Control in the Television Worlds of Joss Whedon* (Chapter 2), McFarland, 2012.

1. This description of evolutionary psychology refers only to heterosexual people. Although Buss and other evolutionary psychologists examine the theory with respect to homosexuality, I have left that discussion for another time.

2. Not all "perfect" mates are satisfying, as presented on *Buffy the Vampire Slayer* (1997–2003). Warren Mears created his perfect android woman, but quickly grew bored with a woman who fulfilled his every whim and ultimately abandoned her ("I Was Made to Love You").

Works Cited

A Boy and His Dog. Dir. L. Q. Jones, Harlan Ellison (Story), and L. Q. Jones (Screenplay). First Run Features, 1975, 2003. DVD.
Atwood, Margaret. *The Handmaid's Tale*. New York: Everyman's Library (Alfred A. Knopf), 2006. Print.
Battlestar Galactica: The Complete Series. Universal Studios, 2010. DVD.
Blair, Karen. "Sex and *Star Trek*." *Science Fiction Studies* 10 (1983): 292–297. Print.
Buss, David M. *The Evolution of Desire: Strategies of Human Mating*. New York: Basic Books, 1994. Print.
_____, Randy J. Larsen, Drew Westen, & Jennifer Semmelroth. "Sex Differences in Jealousy: Evolution, Physiology, and Psychology." *Psychological Science* 3 (1992): 251–255. Print.
Butler, Octavia E. *Lilith's Brood*. New York: Grand Central, 2000.
Buunk, Bram P., Alois Angleitner, Viktor Oubaid, & David M. Buss. "Sex Differences in Jealousy in Evolutionary and Cultural Perspective: Tests from the Netherlands, Germany, and the United States." *Psychological Science* 7 (1996): 359–363. Print.
Caprica: Season 1.0. Universal Studios, 2010. DVD.

Caprica: Season 1.5. Universal Studios, 2010. DVD.
"Cogenitor." Writer J. P. Farrell. *Star Trek: Enterprise the Complete Second Season*. Paramount, 2005. Broadcast 30 April 2003. DVD.
"Cyberwoman." Writer Chris Chibnall. *Torchwood: The Complete First Season*. BBC Video, BBC Worldwide Ltd., 2008. Broadcast 5 November 2006. DVD.
Darwin, Charles. *The Descent of Man and Selection in Relation to Sex*. London: Murray, 1871. Print.
_____. *The Origin of Species by the Means of Natural Selection, or Preservation of Favoured Races in the Struggle for Life*. London: Murray, 1859. Print.
Dawkins, Richard. *The Selfish Gene*. Oxford: Oxford University Press, 1976. Print.
Ellison, Harlan. *A Boy and His Dog*. New York: E-Reads, 2008. Print.
Falling Skies: Season One. TNT Productions and DreamWorks Television, 2011. Originally aired 19 June–7 August 2011.
Farscape: The Peacekeeper Wars. Writers Rockne S. O'Bannon and David Kemper. The Jim Henson Company and Hallmark Entertainment, 2004. DVD.
"Genderbender." Writers Paul Barber and Larry Barber. *The X-Files Season One*. 20th Century–Fox Home Entertainment, 2006. Broadcast 21 January 1994. DVD.
Ginn, Sherry. "For Women's It's Love, For Men It's Sex: Evolutionary Psychology meets Science Fiction." *Foundation: the International Review of Science Fiction* 39 (2010): 28–38. Print.
_____. *Our Space, Our Place: Women in the Worlds of Science Fiction Television*. Lanaham, MD: University Press of America, 2005. Print.
_____. *Power and Control in the Television Worlds of Joss Whedon*. Jefferson, NC: McFarland, 2012. Print
_____. "Sexual Relations and Sexual Identity Issues: Brave New Worlds or More of the Old One?" *Illuminating Torchwood: Essays on Narrative, Character and Sexuality in the BBC Series*. Ed. Andrew Ireland. Jefferson, NC: McFarland, 2010. Print.
Haraway, Donna J. *Simians, Cyborgs, and Women: The Reinvention of Nature*. London: Free Association, 1991. Print.
"I Was Made to Love You." Writer Jane Espenson. *Buffy the Vampire Slayer The Complete Fifth Season on DVD*. Beverly Hills: 20th Century–Fox Home Entertainment, 2003. Broadcast 20 February 2001.
"Look at the Princess, Part 1: A Kiss Is but a Kiss." Writer David Kemper. *Farscape Season 2 on DVD*. The Jim Henson Company. Distributed by ADV Films, 2002. Broadcast 21 July 2000.
"Look at the Princess, Part 2: I Do, I Think." *Farscape Season 2 on DVD*. The Jim Henson Company. Distributed by ADV Films, 2002. Broadcast 28 July 2000.
"Look at the Princess, Part 3: The Maltese Crichton." *Farscape Season 2 on DVD*. The Jim Henson Company. Distributed by ADV Films, 2002. Broadcast 4 August 2000.
Myers, David G. *Exploring Social Psychology*. 6th ed. New York: McGraw-Hill, 2012. Print.
"The Naked Now." *Star Trek The Next Generation Season One*. Paramount, 2002. Broadcast 3 October 1987. DVD.
Peplau, Letitia Anne. "Human Sexuality: How Do Men and Women Differ?" *Current Directions in Psychological Science* 12 (2010): 37–40. Print.
"Revulsion." Writer Lisa Klink. *Star Trek Voyager Season Four*. Paramount, 2004. Broadcast 1 October 1997. DVD.
Salter, Anastasia. "Virtually Yours: Desire and Fulfillment in Virtual Worlds." *The Journal of Popular Culture* 44 (2011): 1120–1137. Print.
Serenity. Director/Writer Joss Whedon. Universal Studios, 2005. DVD.
Shaviro, Steven. "The Erotic Life of Machines." *Parallax* 8 (2002): 21–31. Print.
Simpson, Paul, and Ruth Thomas. *Farscape: The Illustrated Season 2 Companion*. London: Titan Books, 2001. Print.
Star Trek: The Motion Picture. Director Robert Wise. Paramount Studios, 1979. Film.
"Suns and Lovers." Writer Justin Monjo. *Farscape The Complete Third Season on DVD*. The Jim Henson Company. Distributed by ADV Films, 2003. Broadcast 23 March 2001.

Torchwood: Children of Earth. BBC Video. Writers Russell T. Davies, J. Fay, and J. Moran. BBC Worldwide Ltd, 2009. DVD.

Torchwood: Miracle Day. Starz Originals, BBC Wales, BBC Worldwide Productions, 2011. Originally aired 8 July–9 September 2011.

"virtual." The Free Dictionary by Farlex, 2012. Web. 28 March 2012.

"Unexpected." Writers Rick Berman and Brannon Braga. *Star Trek: Enterprise the Complete First Season.* Paramount, 2005. Broadcast 17 October 2001. DVD.

Conclusion: Sexing Science Fiction, Take Two
Sherry Ginn

Although a number of books have been written exploring issues related to gender in science fiction (including one by me), few, in recent years, have examined sex in science fiction. The science fiction editor of McFarland's Critical Explorations in Science Fiction and Fantasy series, Donald Palumbo, published two books on the subject of sex in science fiction and fantasy in 1986, one exploring visual and one exploring literary media. Those monographs or edited collections that have proposed to explore the issue in recent years generally do so by investigating one particular franchise, such as *Star Trek*, or one particular aspect of manifested sexuality in science fiction, such as queer sexualities. Thus, Michael G. Cornelius and I proposed that, in compiling this collection, we would strive to create conditions that would allow for a broader examination of the issue and act of sexuality in science fiction, an examination that has been sorely lacking since Palumbo's earlier works. Here we have presented a collection that explores issues ranging from the aesthetic to the virtual as they relate to sexual activity, attitudes, and behavior.

Several essays in this collection detailed quite subtle indications of sex and sexuality, notably Cornelius' own investigation of homoeroticism in boy's series fiction, and both Thomas G. Cole II's and Larry T. Shillock's examinations of works by H. G. Wells. Cornelius' look at the friendship patterns established between dyadic young male protagonists of boys' series fiction noted that these patterns were couched in suggestive language which reinforced an intensively physical — albeit platonic — relationship between the boys. Indeed, Cornelius proposed that the homosocial and homoerotic bonds between the male protagonists in these stories were supported, if not actually perpetuated, by some type of technological innovation, whereby the boys displaced their sexual desire for each other onto some type of object. Thus the "object of desire" in these stories was truly an *object* rather than a *subject*, i.e., a "real" person.

This notion of an "object of desire" was also discussed by Clare Parody in her examination of the fiction of J. G. Ballard, especially with respect to his novel *Crash!* Ballard's description of this novel as the first pornographic novel based on technology is repeatedly reinforced by the explicit descriptions of sexualized body parts juxtaposed with wrecked cars and other images of damaged technology. Ballard suggests that humankind's desire for technology has transcended desire as "yearning" and replaced it with its sexualized synonym, "lust."

The desire for technology can also be examined with respect to reproduction as well as sexuality. Erin Grayson Sapp's essay explored three twentieth-century novels — one each by Katherine Burdekin, Theodore Sturgeon, and Marge Piercy — for their depictions of future societies that had removed the very idea of fatherhood from human consciousness. Such attempts were made with the hope that eliminating patriarchy, the primary factor that these works posit contributes to inequality, would eliminate said inequalities, especially those related to sex and gender. Yet attempts to devalue the concept of fatherhood, exclude fathers from rearing children, rename all parents "mothers," or change the actual biology of humans were ultimately unsuccessful, at least in the fictional accounts discussed by Sapp.

If the role of fathers is difficult to eliminate from human consciousness, the role of mother is likewise the same. Although mothers have been vilified throughout history, it was Sigmund Freud whose theories placed the blame for all adult psychological traumas squarely on the shoulders of mothers. Freud's conception of the all-powerful mother, whose actions during the first five years of life can have devastating consequences on the psyche of both male and female children, has retained a significant place in both popular culture and psychology throughout the twentieth and into the twenty-first centuries.[1]

Robert C. Pirro examined the science fiction short stories of Italian writer Primo Levi via the lens of a preœdipal period of development, noting that many of Levi's stories featured Freud's devouring mother. Pirro also argued that even when Levi's stories did not contain an actual mother, some mother-like figure often assumed a central role in the story. In addition, male scientists or physicians sought to usurp the female role of reproduction, as if dominating the mother-figure would allow these males to vanquish that all-encompassing figure.

Cole and Shillock provided insight into Wellsian speculations about science and the ways in which science addressed the contentious issues of gender and sexuality in the nineteenth century. Each of those essays can be read as an extrapolation of Darwinian proposals with respect to evolution. Cole's examination of *The Island of Dr. Moreau* illustrated Wells' speculation about science and its quest to supplant the natural course of evolution. What would happen to beings ranked lower than humans on the evolutionary scale if their evolution could be accelerated, Cole speculates, and how would such lesser beings, including women, react to attempts to render them more civilized, i.e., more "man"-like? *The Time Machine* carried that theme even further by speculating upon Wells' vision of mankind's future evolution. In this view, women had not evolved to be the equivalent of men; rather, both women and men devolved to the level of children or savages.

Further discussions of how evolution factors into sexual behavior was proposed in my essay examining the strategies employed by each sex with respect to sexuality and reproduction. Evolutionary psychology proposes that women wish to mate with one man who will provide for their offspring; however, men wish to mate with multiple partners in order to maximize their reproductive potential. A number of science fiction novels, stories, and films illustrate how men may choose to exercise this desire by engaging in sexual behavior with women against their will. Others illustrate how men may copulate with a variety of women using a less repugnant and more practical manner, i.e., by paying for it. Martin A. Monto notes that

> men are attracted to paid sex because they desire sexual acts they cannot receive from their partners; they are able to have sex with larger number of partners; they are attracted to specific physical characteristics; they like the limited emotional involvement; and they are excited by the illicit nature of the act [77].

Each of these reasons for engaging a prostitute was illustrated in Joss Whedon's *Firefly* and *Dollhouse*, and Heather M. Porter dissected sex and sex workers in her essay on these particular Whedon series. Porter's essay likewise addressed the issue of status for sex workers, noting that *Firefly* presents a view of such a man or woman enjoying not only a life of some eminence, but one of independence as well. That "enlightened" view was not presented in *Dollhouse*, where the Actives were programmed to engage and even enjoy their sexual encounters, but were unable to actually consent to them. Although not specifically discussed with respect to prostitution, evolutionary psychology's hypotheses with respect to male sexual behavior would support Monto's contention that men wish to have sex with a large number of partners. Prostitution would also provide men with the opportunity to engage in sexual activity for the sake of the sex without risking emotional involvement with the sex worker or the sex worker's impregnation.

The biological imperative to reproduce was also examined in essays written by Echo E. Savage and Anca Rosu. Savage's exploration of Octavia Butler's Xenogenesis trilogy illustrates one way in which humanity attempts to save itself from extermination — with the help of a group of aliens, the Oankali.

These aliens find humans intensely attractive and combine their own DNA with humans' in order to perpetuate both species. Rosu also examined Butler's fiction — in her case the Patternist series — likewise exploring the way in which one man controlled the breeding patterns of whole groups of people in order to create a lineage of his own making. Both Savage and Rosu's essays reinforced the essential heterosexual aspects of Butler's fiction with respect to reproduction, although Rosu does note that the Patternist series is decidedly more perverse than the Xenogenesis trilogy with respect to sexuality. Indeed, the protagonist of the former series is not averse to copulating with his daughter if that will further his genetic plans.

The biological imperative to reproduce can also explain why space aliens and similar Others desire human women. Matthew H. Hersch discussed this issue with respect to primates in his essay on "space" apes. A number of science fiction and fantasy franchises, such as the Planet of the Apes series, hint at the possibility of inter-primate sexual interactions. Non-human primates may covet sexual intercourse with human women for a variety of reasons, including a desire to debase the women in revenge for the centuries of degradation which primates have suffered at the hands of mankind. In addition, human/nonhuman primate couplings would perhaps enhance the genetic potential of the nonhuman primate and eventually affect the species' evolution.

Nevertheless, such fictional treatments can also be read as a metaphor for the concept of miscegenation. Cynthia J. Miller and A. Bowdoin Van Riper explore this issue in their essay, discussing science fiction's exploration of the alien Other and its attempts to be/come human, often while deceiving the humans with whom it interacts. Certainly a number of genre writers have proposed that various racial and ethnic groups are instantiated as the alien Other, most prominently blacks. Allison Whitney's essay continues with this discussion by noting the ways in which, even in the supposedly enlightened United Federation of Planets in the Star Trek universe, blacks may serve as the alien Other and be excluded from complete representation.

If there is perhaps one lesson this collection truly espouses, it is that sex makes for both interesting science and interesting fiction. Nothing remains more generally important — or more generally verboten — in both the real and reading lives of people everywhere than sex. This collection reflects what, we hope, is only the beginning of a newly-emerging conversation around the ways in which genre fiction represents, re-conceptualizes, and re-imagines sex for continuing generations of fans and the larger culture in which such texts are inscribed and discharged.

There is more to say on this subject, as there is always more to say on sex. Perhaps the works contained herein will inspire others to boldly go where these writers have so far gone.

NOTES

1. Sigmund Freud (1856–1939) proposed a theory of psychosexual development that has generated enormous controversy. The first three stages span the first five years of life. Stage one is referred to as the "oral stage," and proposes that the mouth is the site of pleasure for a child during the first year of life. Stage two is referred to as the "anal stage," and proposes that the anus is the site of pleasure for a child during the second year of life. Stage three is referred to as the "phallic stage," and proposes that the genitals are the site of pleasure for a child from the ages of roughly three through five or six. Boy children during this stage experience the Oedipal complex, in which they desire to possess their mothers and eliminate their fathers. Boys eventually realize that they cannot compete with their fathers for their mother's affection and begin the process of socialization, internalizing the father's values into their own psyche. It is during this stage that the conscience is formed. Freud proposes a similar pattern for female children, but suggested that it was not nearly as traumatic for girls as for boys, and that is why girls do not have a very high standard of morality. For obvious reasons, Freud is not popular with many feminist theorists (or even non-feminist ones, for that matter).

WORKS CITED

Freud, Sigmund. *The Freud Reader*. Ed. Peter Gay. New York: W. W. Norton, 1995. Print.

Monto, Martin A. "Why Men Seek Out Prostitutes." *Sex for Sale: Prostitution, Pornography, and the Porn Industry*. Ed. Ronald Weitzer. New York: Routledge, 2000. 67–84. Print.

Palumbo, Donald, ed. *Eros in the Mind's Eye: Sexuality and the Fantastic in Art and Film*. Santa Barbara: ABC-CIIO/Greenwood, 1986. Print.

———, ed. *Erotic Universe: Sexuality and Fantastic Literature*. Santa Barbara: ABC-CLIO/Greenwood, 1986. Print.

About the Contributors

Thomas G. **Cole** II is pursuing a Ph.D. in the Department of English at the University of Florida, where his dissertation explores the ways in which women and bodies at the end of the 19th century call attention to the limits — epistemological and ethical — of science, technology and modernity. His research primarily focuses on women's and gender studies issues in Gothic and science fiction literature as well as popular culture. His essay "(The) Bikini: EmBodying the Bomb" appeared in *Genders*.

Michael G. **Cornelius** is the author or editor of 14 books, including *Nancy Drew and Her Sister Sleuths: Essays on the Fiction of Girl Detectives* (co-edited with Melanie E. Gregg; McFarland, 2008) and the companion, *The Boy Detectives: Essays on the Hardy Boys and Others* (McFarland, 2010). *Of Muscles and Men: Essays on the Sword and Sandal Film* was released in 2011 (McFarland). He has published in numerous journals and book anthologies, and he is also an award-winning novelist. He is the chair of the Department of English and Mass Communications at Wilson College in Chambersburg, Pennsylvania.

Sherry **Ginn** earned both her M.A. (1984) and Ph.D. (1988) in general-experimental psychology from the University of South Carolina and teaches psychology at Rowan-Cabarrus Community College. She has published numerous articles in the fields of neuroscience and psychology, but focuses her extracurricular work on the intersection of popular culture with psychology and neuroscience. She wrote *Our Space, Our Place: Women in the Worlds of Science Fiction Television* (2005) and *Power and Control in the Television Worlds of Joss Whedon* (McFarland, 2012).

Matthew H. **Hersch** is a lecturer in science, technology and society in the Department of History and Sociology of Science at the University of Pennsylvania, where he received his Ph.D. He held the 2009–2010 HSS-NASA Fellowship in the History of Space Science and a 2007–2008 Guggenheim Fellowship at the Smithsonian Institution. He received a political science degree from MIT and a J.D. from the NYU School of Law and specializes in 20th-century American technology and its relationship to popular culture. His book *Inventing the American Astronaut* is forthcoming (Palgrave Macmillan).

Cynthia J. **Miller** is a cultural anthropologist, specializing in popular culture and visual media. She has written for a wide range of journals and essay collections: *Télévision: Le moment experimental* (in French, INA/Apogee, 2011); *Learning from Mickey, Donald and Walt: Essays on Disney's Edutainment Films* (McFarland, 2011); *Science Fic-*

tion Film, Television, and Adaptation: Across the Screens (Routledge, 2011); *Race, Oppression, and the Zombie: Cross-Cultural Appropriations of the Caribbean Tradition* (McFarland, 2011); and *The Gothic Imagination: Conversations on Fantasy, Science Fiction, and Horror* (Palgrave, 2011).

Clare **Parody** completed her Ph.D. at the University of Liverpool on the subject of media convergence and transmedia storytelling in early 2012, having obtained her B.A. in English from the University of Oxford and an M.A. in science fiction studies from the University of Liverpool. Her research interests lie in theories of cross-media influence and adaptation and speculative fiction. She has published essays on character in the 21st century revival of *Doctor Who*, and on adaptation as part of the franchising of fictional properties.

Robert C. **Pirro** is a professor of political science at Georgia Southern University and specializes in political theory. He is writing a book tentatively titled "Motherhood and Fatherland: Primo Levi's Virtuous Republic Under the Shadow of Auschwit" and published *The Politics of Tragedy and Democratic Citizenship* (Continuum, 2011). He contributed an essay, "Homer's Lies, Brad Pitt's Thighs," on Wolfgang Petersen's blockbuster film *Troy* to the edited volume *Of Muscles and Men: Essays on the Sword and Sandal Film* (McFarland, 2011).

Heather M. **Porter** is a line producer and coordinating producer in reality television. A member of the Producers Guild and the Academy of Television Arts and Sciences, she has worked on five seasons of *Hell's Kitchen* and recently finished her third season of *RuPaul's Drag Race*. She has presented at all four Slayage Conferences and is co-producing a documentary on the academic study of Joss Whedon's works. Her interests lie in quantitative analyses of images of violence, intelligence, and sex in the science fiction and fantasy genres.

Anca **Rosu** (Ph.D., Rutgers) is a professor at DeVry University in the College of Liberal Arts & Sciences. Her specialties are literature, writing, composition and cultural studies, and she teaches a variety of courses. She has written articles and presented research on the Romanian poets and on composition, postcolonial literature, and science fiction at the MLA, NEMLA, and the Popular Culture Association conferences. She wrote *The Metaphysics of Sound in Wallace Stevens* (University of Alabama Press, 1995).

Erin Grayson **Sapp** is a doctoral candidate at Tulane University completing an interdisciplinary liberal arts Ph.D. Her degree program focuses on gender and sexuality studies, and her dissertation work explores the intersection of science/technology with sex/gender and identifies works of visual and literary art that exemplify these crossroads. Her art history M.A. thesis examined contemporary body art through the lens of postmodern gender theory.

Echo E. **Savage** lives and works in beautiful Boise, Idaho. Her research interests primarily include postcolonial and multicultural literature, specifically representations of the socially and culturally transgressive body and its subversive agency within rigidly defined power structures. She is currently working on projects that explore questions related to these concerns in works by Arundhati Roy, Harriet Jacobs, and Louise Erdrich.

About the Contributors

Larry T. **Shillock** is a professor of English and an assistant academic dean at Wilson College. His research interests include critical theory, the history of affect, the modern novel, and classical Hollywood cinema. His scholarship has appeared in *Social Epistemology* and *Philological Papers* and in two books edited by Michael G. Cornelius and published by McFarland: *The Boy Detectives* (2010) and *Of Muscles and Men* (2011). He is writing a book on the transgressions — narrative and otherwise — associated with the femme fatale in American film noir.

A. Bowdoin **Van Riper** is an independent scholar whose work focuses on the history of modern science and technology, sci-tech images in popular culture, and historical memory on film. His work has appeared in *Film & History*, *New Scientist*, *Journal of Popular Film and Television*, and collections such as *Icons of Evolution* (ed. Brian Regal, 2008), *Sounds of the Future* (ed. Mathew J. Bartowiak, McFarland, 2009), and *Too Bold for the Box Office* (ed. Cynthia J. Miller, 2012). He is the author of *A Biographical Encyclopedia of Scientists and Inventors in American Film and TV Since 1930* and *Undead in the West* (Scarecrow, 2011 and 2012).

Alison **Whitney** is an assistant professor of film and media studies in the Department of English at Texas Tech University. She holds a Ph.D. in cinema and media studies from the University of Chicago. Among her research interests are film genres including science fiction, horror, and melodrama, film technologies including large-format and 3D, and representations of space exploration in cinema.

Index

Actives 86, 89, 90, 95, 97, 98, 99, 240
Aldiss, Brian 137
aliens 1, 3, 4, 5, 6, 7, 8, 9, 10, 12, 13, 13n2, 14n3, 14n5, 18, 20, 21, 23, 24, 25, 27, 29, 30, 34, 41, 42, 43, 44, 47, 50, 51, 53, 54, 55, 56, 57, 58, 61n7, 62, 64, 65, 71, 78, 79, 84n2, 221, 225, 226, 227, 230, 231, 232, 233, 240, 241
android 17, 21, 22, 65, 72, 82, 177, 181, 182, 230, 233, 235n2
Angier, Carole 104, 105, 107, 111, 114n2
Auschwitz 102, 103, 109, 110, 114, 115n3
auto-eroticism 204, 213

Babylon 5 23, 25, 230, 231, 234, 235
Ballard, J.G. 12, 239
Battlestar Galactica 27, 29, 230, 231, 233, 234, 235
Baudrillard, Jean 38, 215, 216, 218, 219n2
bestiality 172, 173, 180, 182
bisexuality 127
Blaine, John 187, 202n3
Burgoyne (172) 1, 2, 3, 5, 6, 7
Butler, Octavia 9, 224, 226, 240, 241

Caird, Mona 144, 146, 149n14
Campbell, Bruce 187, 202n3
capitalism 36, 41, 42, 45, 126, 207, 210
captivity narrative (Indian, Barbary) 43, 64, 67, 68, 69, 70, 73, 74, 81, 83, 84n2
Chodorow, Nancy 10, 107
clone 17, 21, 25, 31n5
Cobbe, Frances Power 143
colonialism 9, 11, 13, 17, 62, 64, 66, 67, 68, 69, 71, 72, 74, 79, 81, 83, 84, 136, 138, 140, 173, 174, 175
colonization 43, 64
communism 124
Companion 86, 88, 89, 90, 97, 98, 99
construct (Butler) 45, 51, 59, 226
Cornelius, Michael G. 198, 202n8, 221, 238

cyborg 11, 28, 29, 62, 72, 73, 84n3, 126, 233
Cylon 26, 27, 29, 230, 231, 234

Darwin, Charles 47n2, 135, 139, 140, 143, 148, 152, 153, 155, 160, 162, 163, 173, 225, 239
Data, Lt. Commander 21, 22, 65, 66, 67, 70, 71, 72, 73, 74, 76, 77, 78, 82, 84n1, 84n5, 230, 233
degeneration 11, 152, 153, 157, 158, 159, 164, 165, 167, 168
devolution 168
Dollhouse 10, 86, 87, 89, 90, 91, 92, 95, 96, 97, 98, 99, 100, 235, 240
dystopia 22, 43, 54, 65, 67, 120, 224

Earth 9, 17, 18, 20, 21, 22, 24, 25, 26, 30, 31, 51, 53, 59, 63, 65, 66, 67, 70, 75, 83, 84n1, 129, 157, 160, 164, 170, 177, 178, 179, 181, 182, 184
Echo (character) 86, 96, 99, 100, 235
Eloi 12, 153, 157, 158, 159, 160, 161, 162, 163, 164, 165, 166, 168
U.S.S. *Enterprise* 13n2, 14n4, 63, 64, 66, 67, 68, 70, 72, 73, 75, 76, 77, 79, 80, 81, 82, 83, 230, 232
ethnocentrism 156
evolution 11, 12, 35, 41, 69, 72, 73, 126, 143, 152, 153, 155, 156, 157, 160, 162, 163, 166, 168, 170, 173, 175, 178, 179, 181, 182, 222, 223, 224, 225, 226, 227, 228, 230, 231, 234, 235, 235n1, 239, 240, 241
U.S.S. *Excalibur* 1, 2, 3, 5
extraterrestrials 8, 24, 41, 42, 51, 53, 54, 55, 77, 79

Farscape 27, 28, 227, 228, 229, 234, 235
femininity 136, 137, 140, 141, 142, 143, 145, 146, 147, 148, 149n11, 156, 161, 162, 166, 188, 189
feminism 52, 76, 103, 117, 119, 120, 121, 122,

123, 128, 131, 136, 137, 138, 140, 143, 148, 148n7, 149n15, 161, 234, 242n1
Fin-de-siècle 135, 137, 153, 161, 167
Firefly 10, 86, 87, 88, 89, 90, 91, 92, 95, 96, 97, 98, 99, 100, 235, 240
Foucault, Michel 34, 35, 36, 41, 45, 46, 47
Frankenstein 10, 135, 136, 137, 148n8
Freud, Sigmund 39, 41, 65, 128, 163, 173, 239, 242n1
Future-sex 11, 152, 153, 164, 166, 167

gender 1, 3, 5, 7, 13, 13n2, 19, 25, 26, 28, 30, 34, 38, 45, 50, 51, 52, 54, 56, 58, 59, 61n3, 61n6, 68, 71, 74, 75, 78, 79, 82, 92, 95, 103, 104, 117, 118, 121, 122, 123, 124, 125, 127, 131, 132, 134, 145, 156, 180, 199, 232, 238, 239
genitalia 4, 6, 23, 182, 208, 211, 212
Golem 103, 111, 112, 113, 115n4
Grand, Sarah 134, 146, 147, 149n14

Haraway, Donna J. 28, 41, 47n3, 126, 176, 232
hermaphrodite 1, 3, 5
Hermat 1, 2, 3, 5, 6, 13n2
heterocentricity 51, 58
heteronormativity 9, 18, 30, 51, 52, 53, 54, 57, 58, 59, 60, 188, 189, 198
heterosexuality 9, 14n2, 14n5, 34, 50, 52, 54, 55, 57, 58, 59, 60, 60n2, 61n3, 61n4, 65, 91, 183, 188, 199, 200, 230, 235n1, 241
Homo sapiens 124, 126, 159, 179, 183
homoerotica 12, 187, 188, 189, 190, 196, 217, 238
homophobia 55, 56, 57
homosexuality 14n2, 34, 51, 52, 53, 57, 61n3, 188, 189, 199, 201, 224, 235n1
homosocial 140, 188, 189, 199, 201, 238
humanism 58
humanity 21, 22, 23, 28, 29, 35, 42, 43, 47, 51, 56, 58, 63, 89, 119, 144, 148, 155, 156, 168, 170, 171, 175, 176, 178, 179, 183, 184, 197, 225, 226, 240
humankind 29, 124, 153, 226, 239
humanoid 8, 18, 23, 26, 29, 140, 230, 231, 233, 234
Huxley, Thomas H. 143, 152, 153, 160, 164, 168
hybrid 20, 25, 26, 27, 28, 29, 31, 111, 140, 172, 173, 175, 220, 231
hybridization 28, 172, 174, 175, 176, 178, 182, 205

imperialism 64, 67, 71, 74, 83, 140
Inara (character) 86, 88, 89, 96, 98, 99, 100, 235

incest 37, 39, 46
Ivanov, Ilya Ivanovich 175, 176

Jameson, Fredric 138, 139, 140

King Kong (character) 170, 176

Lancer, Jack 187, 202n3
Levi, Primo 10, 239

man-beast 170, 176
masculinity 40, 45, 55, 56, 74, 77, 114, 128, 129, 135, 136, 144, 145, 148, 153, 155, 156, 157, 160, 162, 167, 166, 168, 190, 194, 196, 197, 198, 199, 201
masturbation 4, 205, 208, 212
maternal powers 106, 110, 114
miscegenation 9, 17, 18, 19, 20, 21, 22, 23, 24, 25, 26, 27, 28, 29, 30, 31, 172, 184, 241
Morlocks 12, 153, 159, 162, 163, 164, 165, 166, 167, 168

natural selection 155, 156, 173
New Woman 11, 134, 135, 136, 137, 141, 144, 146, 148, 149n14, 160

Oankali 42, 43, 44, 45, 46, 47, 51, 52, 53, 54, 55, 56, 57, 59, 226, 227, 240
Oedipus 165, 242n1, 166
Ooloi 42, 43, 44, 45, 46, 54, 55, 56, 57, 59, 60, 61n3, 61n4, 226
orientation, sexual 7, 19, 30
origin story 64, 66
other 1, 2, 3, 4, 6, 7, 8, 9, 10, 12, 14n3, 14n4, 14n5, 17, 20, 21, 22, 23, 24, 29, 50, 51, 53, 54, 55, 56, 58, 60, 61n3, 68, 72, 78, 84, 164, 166, 200, 241

Palumbo, Donald 238
paternity 11, 117, 118, 123, 126, 128, 129, 130, 131, 132
patriarchy 11, 14n2, 58, 65, 73, 117, 118, 123, 125, 126, 128, 130, 131, 132, 134, 142, 143, 145, 191, 192, 198, 201, 239
Patternist/patternist 35, 36, 37, 39, 42, 47n2, 241
penis 4, 6
phallic 77, 190, 242n1
phallocentrism 194
Planet of the Apes (film series) 170, 178, 179, 180, 181, 182, 183, 241
Pocahontas 64, 74, 75
pornography 4, 19, 199, 204, 205, 206, 212, 217, 218, 239
power 20, 35, 36, 38, 39, 40, 42, 43, 44, 45, 46, 47, 50, 51, 52, 54, 57, 58, 60,

61n5, 64, 65, 68, 73, 86, 87, 90, 94, 97, 98, 99, 103, 106, 107, 108, 110, 114, 118, 119, 120, 122, 123, 125, 128, 129, 130, 131, 144, 145, 146, 170, 173, 176, 189, 190, 194, 196, 199, 223
preœdipal 102, 103, 104, 105, 106, 107, 108, 109, 110, 112, 113, 114, 239
primal scene 65, 66, 67, 71, 73, 83
primitive mother 111
promiscuity, sexual 37, 39, 128
prostitution 10, 21, 25, 37, 86, 87, 88, 89, 90, 92, 95, 97, 98, 99, 119, 224, 225, 240

queer 14n3, 51, 55, 60, 238

race (racism) 7, 9, 13n2, 17, 18, 19, 20, 22, 25, 26, 28, 30, 31n2, 34, 36, 37, 50, 51, 52, 54, 55, 62, 68, 74, 78, 79, 80, 124, 126, 128, 129, 16, 176, 182, 183, 225, 228, 232
rape 19, 37, 86, 90, 94, 97, 98, 99, 103, 121, 145, 149n12, 224, 227
reproduction 118, 119
robot 21, 25, 26, 72, 115, 115n5, 177, 232, 233
Rousseau, Jean-Jacques 39
Royo, Luis 182
Russ, Joanna 7

Sedgwick, Eve Kosofsky 188, 190, 199, 200, 201
Seed, David 135, 138, 139, 148n3
Serenity 88, 95, 96, 98, 99, 229, 230
sexual activity 12, 44, 96, 97, 120, 222, 224, 227, 235, 238, 240
sexual congress 6, 8, 9, 10, 11, 14n2, 14n5, 55, 61n4, 90, 93, 98, 173, 225, 227
sexual incident 92, 95, 96, 98, 99
sexuality 3, 4, 5, 7, 8, 9, 10, 13, 17, 18, 19, 34, 35, 36, 37, 38, 39, 41, 42, 43, 44, 45, 46, 47, 47n2, 53, 54, 56, 61n7, 65, 71, 82, 87, 88, 89, 90, 91, 98, 103, 104, 135, 166, 168, 173, 176, 181, 183, 198, 204, 206, 207, 208, 209, 211, 212, 213, 217, 218, 219, 222, 224, 229, 230, 231, 238, 239, 240, 241
sexualization 10

shape shifter 17, 21
Shelley, Mary 10, 135
Showalter, Elaine 136, 137, 140, 148n6
Simmel, Georg 192
sociobiology 41, 47n3, 52
space apes 11, 241
speculative fiction 4, 5, 53, 128, 132
Star Trek 1, 2, 3, 5, 9, 13n1, 13n2, 14n2, 14n4, 14n5, 23, 25, 26, 29, 62, 63, 65, 71, 74, 75, 78, 79, 82, 231, 233, 238, 241
Star Trek: Deep Space Nine (TV series) 21, 23, 26, 27, 31n3, 231, 233
Star Trek: Enterprise 25, 231
Star Trek: First Contact 9, 62, 63, 64, 65, 66, 67, 68, 69, 74, 79, 81, 83, 84n3, 84n4
Star Trek Generations 63, 72
Star Trek: New Frontier 1, 2, 3, 13n1
Star Trek: The Next Generation (TV series) 1, 13n1, 13n2, 14n4, 21, 26, 29, 62, 63, 71, 78, 79, 80, 84n2, 84n5, 230, 233
Star Trek: Voyager (TV series) 14n5, 23, 26, 29, 84n3, 84n4, 230, 231, 233
Starfleet 2, 3, 4, 5, 62, 67, 69, 70, 81
Suvin, Darko 135

utopia 25, 43, 50, 52, 54, 58, 63, 64, 65, 66, 74, 81, 82, 83, 117, 118, 119, 120, 121, 122, 124, 127, 131, 132, 159

Victorian 149n12, 153, 156, 160, 161, 164, 166, 167
vivisection 137, 138, 143, 144, 147, 148, 148n5, 149n12, 149n15, 171
voyeurism 204, 205, 206, 209, 210, 213, 214, 215, 216, 219n2
Vulcans 3, 5, 25, 26, 31n5, 31n6, 65, 75, 82

Wells, H. G. 11, 238, 239, 240
wet nurse 10, 102, 106
Whedon, Joss 10, 86, 87, 88, 90, 95, 97, 98, 99, 100, 229, 235, 240
whore 21, 86, 89, 98
woman question 134, 135, 136, 140, 144, 146

xenophobia 9, 17, 25, 43

Milton Keynes UK
Ingram Content Group UK Ltd.
UKHW020331150824
446933UK00003B/43